Sir George Biddell Airy, Royal Greenwich Observatory

Reduction of Twenty Years' Photographic Records
of the barometer and dry-bulb and wet-bulb thermometers, and twenty-seven years'
observations of the earth thermometers, made at the Royal Observatory

ISBN/EAN: 9783337381301

Printed in Europe, USA, Canada, Australia, Japan

Cover: Foto ©Andreas Hilbeck / pixelio.de

More available books at **www.hansebooks.com**

Sir George Biddell Airy, Royal Greenwich Observatory

Reduction of Twenty Years' Photographic Records

of the barometer and dry-bulb and wet-bulb thermometers, and twenty-seven

years' observations of the earth thermometers, made at the Royal Observatory

REDUCTION

OF

TWENTY YEARS' PHOTOGRAPHIC RECORDS OF THE BAROMETER AND DRY-BULB AND WET-BULB THERMOMETERS,

AND

TWENTY-SEVEN YEARS' OBSERVATIONS OF THE EARTH THERMOMETERS,

MADE AT

THE ROYAL OBSERVATORY, GREENWICH:

UNDER THE DIRECTION OF

SIR GEORGE BIDDELL AIRY, K.C.B. M.A. LL.D. D.C.L.,

ASTRONOMER ROYAL.

PUBLISHED BY ORDER OF THE BOARD OF ADMIRALTY,

IN OBEDIENCE TO HER MAJESTY'S COMMAND.

LONDON:
PRINTED BY GEORGE EDWARD EYRE AND WILLIAM SPOTTISWOODE,
PRINTERS TO THE QUEEN'S MOST EXCELLENT MAJESTY.
FOR HER MAJESTY'S STATIONERY OFFICE.

1878.

GENERAL INDEX.

C 897.   Wt. 14856.

ROYAL OBSERVATORY, GREENWICH.

REDUCTION of the PHOTOGRAPHIC RECORDS of the BAROMETER, and of the DRY-BULB and WET-BULB THERMOMETERS, each during TWENTY YEARS; and of the EYE-OBSERVATIONS of the EARTH-THERMOMETERS during TWENTY-SEVEN YEARS.

§ 1. *Preliminary.*

The present volume contains three separate series of results, deduced from the discussion of three corresponding series of observations. These are: (I.), the photographic records of the barometer registered during the period 1854 to 1873; (II.), the photographic records of the dry-bulb and wet-bulb thermometers registered during the period 1849 to 1868; and (III.), the eye-observations of the thermometers whose bulbs are sunk to different depths in the ground, made during the period 1847 to 1873. These subjects will be treated in the order mentioned. The apparatus, by means of which the photographic records were made, will be first described, referring for the details of instruments and their mounting, &c., principally to the several Introductions to the Magnetical and Meteorological Observations; which are included in the annual volumes of Greenwich Observations, and are also published separately. The reduction of the photographs to numbers, and the manner of forming the various tables, will next be explained. Afterwards the Earth-Thermometers, the observations made with them, and the tables deduced therefrom, will be described.

§ 2. *Photographic self-registering Apparatus for continuous Record of the Readings of the Barometer.*

The arrangement of the apparatus employed for obtaining photographic record of the indications of the Barometer is as follows:—

Near to the north wall of the Magnetic Basement there is fixed a syphon-barometer; the bore of the tube at its extremities, both upper and lower, is about 1·1 inch. A glass float, partly immersed in the mercury in the lower extremity of the tube, is partially supported by a counterpoise acting on a light lever, leaving a definite part of the weight of the float to be supported by the mercury. This lever is lengthened to carry a vertical plate of mica (made opaque by being blackened), in which is a small aperture whose distance from the fulcrum was, until 1864, June, eight times that of the distance of the point of attachment of the float wire, and whose vertical movement was therefore four times that of the barometric column. In 1864, June, the lever carrying the plate of mica was slightly shortened, and the amount of vertical motion of the mica thereby proportionately reduced in magnitude. Through the small aperture (a horizontal slit) in the plate of mica, the light from the illuminating lamp (a gas flame), condensed by a vertically placed cylindrical lens, falls upon the exposed surface of the photographic paper on the revolving cylinder (to be immediately described). This barometer was brought into use in the year 1848, but its indications were not satisfactory until the mercury was boiled in the tube by Messrs. Negretti and Zambra, in the year 1853, since which time they have appeared to be unexceptionable. The present reductions commence with the year 1854.

The cylinder on which the record was originally made is of glass, 11½ inches high in its cylindrical part, and 14½ inches in circumference, having hemispherical end (similar to those used as shades or protectors to clocks, works of art, &c.). The cylinder is covered internally with a black pigment, and stopped at the open end by insertion in a metallic cap. The cap has no pivot, but there is a perforation through its center, which, when the cylinder is mounted, is fitted upon a vertical spindle projecting upward from the center of a horizontal circular brass plate, which sustains the weight of the vertical cylinder and turns horizontally, being supported by three antifriction wheels (each in a vertical plane) carried by the fixed frame.

The glass cylinder was covered when in use by another cylinder slightly larger and having similar hemispherical end; its open end was fixed, by friction, on the rim of the metallic cap to which the inner cylinder was attached, a collar of tape being inserted between; a second collar was also placed between the cylinders near their hemispherical ends.

In the month of April 1868 an accurately turned cylinder of ebonite, 11½ inches high and 14½ inches in circumference, was substituted for the glass cylinder used until that time. To the ends of the cylinder are fixed circular brass plates; the lower plate has a diameter somewhat greater than that of the cylinder, and is perforated at its center, to allow the cylinder to be fitted upon the vertical spindle projecting upward from the center of the horizontal circular brass plate resting on antifriction wheels before mentioned.

The ebonite cylinder is covered when in use by slipping over it a tube of glass, kept in position at its lower end by a narrow projecting collar of ebonite, and at its upper end by being fixed to a flat plate of brass having a central aperture, which is fitted to a small projection on the flat top of the ebonite cylinder.

Uniform rotatory motion is given to the horizontal brass plate resting on anti-friction wheels and supporting the cylinder, as before described, by means of a strong chronometer movement. The center of the chronometer is vertically below the axis of the rotating cylinder. An arm revolves on the face of the chronometer in the same manner as the ordinary hour hand, and a fork at the end of the arm takes hold of a winch fixed to the horizontal brass plate that sustains the cylinder.

To prepare the cylinder for register of indications, it is covered with a sheet of sensitised paper, the moisture on which usually causes the overlapping ends to adhere with sufficient firmness; the glass cover is then slipped over it, and the whole is placed in position by fitting the central perforation of the lower brass plate of the cylinder upon the central vertical spindle of the rotating brass plate which is moved by the clock-work.

The cylinder originally revolved in 12 hours, and thus made two revolutions in the course of one day. But on account of the occasional intermingling of the earlier and later portions of a daily record, the time of revolution was, in the month of November 1857, altered. The cylinder was then made to revolve in 24 hours instead of 12 hours as before.

The cylinder is further covered when in use by a circular zinc casing having two vertical apertures on opposite sides. Through one of these apertures the light from the fixed lamp, after passing through the cylindrical lens and the slit in the strip of mica before mentioned, falls on the paper wrapped round the cylinder. The other aperture is that through which the light is received which produces the register of Magnetic Vertical Force, this register and that of the Barometer being both made on the same cylinder. To avoid however any intermingling of the two registers, that of the Vertical Force Magnet is made on the lower part of the cylinder, and that of the Barometer on the upper part.

The light used for producing the photographic trace is that of ordinary coal-gas, usually charged with the vapour of coal-naphtha.

The whole of the barometric self-registering apparatus here described was originally mounted in the Upper Magnet Room; in the month of June 1864 it was moved to a nearly corresponding position in the then newly excavated Magnetic Basement.

To form on the paper a base-line for the proper measure of curve ordinates, the light from the gas flame that produces the register is, by means of a fixed prism and lens, made to form a spot of light on the paper in a definite position, so that, as the cylinder turns horizontally, a line is traced on the paper, which becomes the instrumental base-line.

The following is the method of determining when certain parts of the photographic trace are actually made. A moveable plate or shutter is provided, by means of which the light which falls upon the slit in the plate of mica can be cut

a 2

off or let on at pleasure. An assistant occasionally cuts off the light (registering in a book the clock-time of doing so); after a few minutes he again lets in the light (again registering the time). The effect of the two operations is to make a visible interruption in the trace, corresponding to a registered period, and such interruption is usually made three times on each day. Then, after the sheet is removed from the cylinder, perpendiculars are dropped from the points of interruption of the trace on to a line drawn, in a convenient position, parallel to the instrumental base-line. The several places at which the perpendiculars meet this line define points on the sheet corresponding to the registered times. The whole length of the exposed part of the photographic sheet (confining our attention to the period since 1857, November,) corresponds to the known time of rotation of the cylinder, 24 hours, and the circumference of the cylinder is 14½ inches. A scale of this length, properly divided into hours and fractions of hours, being applied to the line of abscissæ (drawn as described), so that its reading for the points of interruption of the trace shall agree with the registered times of interruption of the light, the divisions of hours are at once transferred from the scale to the line of abscissæ. In practice it is found that, after removal from the cylinder, the length of the exposed part of the paper is not always the same. It became convenient, therefore, to use a scale which would admit of small expansion and contraction, and, during great part of the period, scales of vulcanized caoutchouc, mounted in brass frames, were used, one end of the scale being fixed to the brass frame, whilst the other end could be acted upon by a screw; thus the length of the scale was slightly varied at pleasure. Afterwards, however, cardboard scales of slightly different lengths were used, adapted to various lengths of the exposed part of the sheet.

The scale of barometric measure on the sheet is readily established by occasional comparison of the changes in the photographed record with the corresponding changes of reading given by the eye-observations of the Standard Barometer.

The photographic barometer is, as has been mentioned, a syphon barometer, supported at its lower end. The height of the column of mercury in its lower tube (on which the record depends) is, therefore, very slightly influenced by any change of temperature that may usually occur during the course of a single day. The value of corrected barometer-reading, corresponding to the instrumental base-line on each sheet, is consequently found very approximately by combining the curve ordinates (measured by a cardboard scale), for the times at which eye-observations of the Standard Barometer are made, with the corresponding readings of the Standard Barometer reduced to 32° (Fahrenheit). The mean of the separate values thus obtained on each day is adopted as a working value of the base-line for the day. It is an instrumental value, sufficiently accurate for ordinary purposes, but when great exactness is required (as in the present inquiry) it becomes necessary to make further special reference to the eye-observations, in a way that will be hereafter described.

Finally, another line is drawn on the sheet parallel to the instrumental base-line, such that its ordinate is some precise tenth of an inch of barometer-reading. Each sheet thus carries its own scale of barometric measure. And in this state the sheets are preserved for further use.

A copy of one of the photographed barometer sheets is placed at the end of the Tables, Plate I.

§ 3. *Photographic self-registering Apparatus for continuous Record of the Readings of the Dry-Bulb and Wet-Bulb Thermometers.*

The apparatus used for photographic registration of the indications of the dry-bulb and wet-bulb thermometers is placed under a shed, situated about 28 feet south (magnetic) of the south-east angle of the south arm of the Magnetic Observatory, and about 25 feet east (magnetic) of the present position of the stand carrying the thermometers for eye-observations. The shed is 10 ft. 6 in. square, and rests upon posts 8 feet high. On a braced stand, under its center, is fixed a rectangular zinc casing, inclosing the vertically-placed cylinder on which the records are made, and the two photographic thermometers, the dry-bulb thermometer towards the east, and the wet-bulb thermometer towards the west.

It should be stated that previous to 1862, September, the position of the shed with the apparatus was a little different from that above described ; it then stood about 15 feet further to the south (magnetic), and rather more than 20 feet further west (magnetic). The stand carrying the thermometers for eye-observations has also been moved ; previous to the year 1863 it occupied a position about 23 feet south (astronomical) of the south-west angle of the south arm of the Magnetic Observatory ; in the year mentioned it was moved about 12 feet further south, to the position which it still occupies.

The shed is open at the sides, excepting that moveable boards are provided, to be attached in different positions (regulated by the annual course of the seasons), so as to prevent the direct rays of the sun from falling on the thermometer-bulbs, which project below the rectangular casing before mentioned, for proper exposure to the external air. The bulbs are 8 inches in length and 0·4 inch internal bore, and their centers are about 4 feet above the ground. The bulb of the thermometer employed as wet-bulb is covered throughout its whole length with muslin, which is kept moist by means of the capillary passage of water along cotton wicks leading from a vessel filled with rain-water. And there are small adjustments, permitting the raising or dropping of the thermometers, so that the register of their readings in different parts of the year may be made on a convenient part of the paper which is carried by the revolving cylinder.

The thermometer-frames are covered by plates having vertical apertures, which are so narrow that any light which may pass through them is completely or almost completely intercepted by the broad flat column of mercury in the thermometer-tube. Across these plates is placed a fine wire at every degree (Fahrenheit); those at the decades of degrees, and also those at 32°, 52°, 72°, and 92° being thicker than the others. About 9 inches from each thermometer, to the east of the dry-bulb, and to the west of the wet-bulb, the illuminating light (a flame of naphthalized gas) is placed. In each case the light, condensed by a cylindrical lens whose axis is vertical, shines through the thermometer tube above the surface of the mercury, and forms a well-defined line of light upon the photographic paper which is wrapped round the cylinder. As the cylinder revolves horizontally under the light which passes through the thermometer tube, the paper receives a broad sheet of photographic trace, whose breadth (in the direction of the axis of the cylinder) varies with the varying height of the mercury in the thermometer-tube. The light in its passage through the vertical aperture is partially intercepted by the wires placed across the tube at every degree, and there are, therefore, left upon the paper corresponding lines in which there is no photogenic action, and which serve as points of reference for interpretation of the thermometric indication. The thicker lines (produced by the thicker wires placed at certain degrees as before described) permit of easy identification of particular divisions of the thermometric scale.

The cylinder on which the records were made throughout the whole of the period now under discussion (as regards the thermometric registers) was one of glass, 13½ inches high in its cylindrical part, and 19 inches in circumference, generally similar to, and generally mounted in the same way as that at first used for the barometer (described at page 2). Its axis, when mounted, is vertical, and it turns horizontally, motion being given to a horizontal brass plate on which the cylinder rests by a chronometer-movement placed below, exactly in the same way as described for the barometer. [In the year 1869 a cylinder of ebonite was substituted for the glass cylinder, which had been used until that time.]

The cylinder during the period here treated revolved in 48 hours, and the daily photographic traces of the two thermometers were simultaneously registered on opposite sides of the cylinder, each 24-hourly trace occupying one half of the circumference. [The time of revolution was afterwards changed to 50 hours, and subsequently again to 52 hours, in order to avoid the intermingling of the two records that would occur during a movement of the cylinder sometimes slightly exceeding 24 hours.]

The cylinder, having a sheet of prepared paper wrapped upon it, and being covered by its outer glass cover in the same way as is described for the barometer, is similarly mounted upon the brass plate which is in connexion with the chronometer-movement. The cylinder is further covered by a fixed circular zinc casing, having vertical apertures on opposite sides, through which the light producing the traces falls on the paper on the cylinder. Each aperture can be at any time closed by a sliding plate or shutter at pleasure.

The whole apparatus, including the stems of the two thermometers and their respective lights, is contained in the rectangular zinc casing before spoken of, for exclusion of daylight.

To establish the scale of time, occasional interruptions of the light are made at registered times, by means of the sliding shutters above described. The appearance of the interruption on the sheet is that of a white line parallel to the axis of the cylinder, interrupting the broad sheet of photographic trace. One of the white lines traced on the sheet by some one of the degree-wires of the thermometer-plate being taken for a line of abscissæ, the interruptions define the points corresponding to the registered times. The exposed part of the photographic sheet corresponds to 18 hours; the circumference of the cylinder is 19 inches. The 24 hours scale for each register should therefore be 9·5 inches long. But on account of small variations in the length of the exposed part of the paper on different sheets, scales of vulcanized caoutchouc, capable of slight expansion and contraction (as described in the barometric section), were at first used for laying down the divisions of hours on the adopted line of abscissæ; afterwards, scales of cardboard, of slightly different lengths, were used.

It is usual, finally, to rule from each of the points indicating hours on the line of abscissæ, an ordinate to meet or cut the outline of the broad photographic trace. These lines, by reference to the lines which are formed by the interruptions produced by the degree wires, define the instrumental record of temperature at each hour. In this state the sheets are preserved for further use.

A copy of one of the photographed dry-bulb and wet-bulb thermometer sheets is placed at the end of the tables, Plate II.

The photographic thermometers were brought into use in the year 1848; the present reductions commence with the year 1849.

§ 4. *Extraction of numbers from the Photographs of the Barometer and of the Dry-Bulb and Wet-Bulb Thermometers, and correction of the numbers for Instrumental Error.*

The Photographic records have been treated in the following manner.

For the barometer, a cardboard scale, graduated according to the known value of the barometric scale on the sheet, being provided; by means of this scale and the adopted value of the instrumental base line, the instrumental record at each hour was translated into figures by one person holding the photographic sheet, and entered by another into the skeleton form prepared to receive it.

In the thermometer records, the point of intersection of each hour line with the photographic trace defines, by reference to the photographed degree lines, the instrumental record of temperature; and its value for each hour, for both the dry-bulb and wet-bulb thermometers, was similarly read by one person from the photographic sheet, and entered by another into the proper form (a separate form for each thermometer).

The numbers were afterwards again read from the photographic sheets for examination, and the photographic values of the different elements for the hours at which eye observations were made were compared with the eye observations of the standard instruments. The succession of numbers, as entered on the sheets, was also examined for the detection of clerical error.

No further reference is made to the photographic sheets; they are, however, bound in volumes, and are carefully preserved in the Record Room of the Observatory.

The instruments and apparatus were occasionally dismounted for alterations and repairs during the periods of observation here treated; occasionally, also, there were imperfect photographs. Had these causes not operated, the number of separate entries for each element would have been, in round numbers, about 175,000. The entries really amount, for the barometer, to about 166,000, and for each of the two thermometers, to about 161,000; or, in all, nearly half a million of separate measures were made from the photographic sheets.

The form into which the readings were first entered is one having a double argument, the horizontal argument ranging through the 24 hours of the civil day, and the vertical argument through the days of a calendar month. The means of the numbers standing in the vertical columns being then taken, we obtain the mean monthly photographic values of the particular element at each hour of the day.

It becomes necessary now to explain the manner of correcting the photographic readings, for instrumental error. The standard barometer and the standard dry-bulb and wet-bulb thermometers of the Observatory are read by eye at 9^h a.m., noon, 3^h p.m., and 9^h p.m. of every civil day, except on Sundays and a few other days. The comparison of these readings, corrected for temperature in the case of the barometer, with the corresponding readings from the photographs, gives the correction applicable to the photographic readings at those hours. As the individual readings are not used in further investigations, it is not necessary to apply corrections individually to the separate photographic readings, but they are applied to the means of groups.

For each of the hours above mentioned, the mean correction is taken through all the days of a month. Between these hours the corrections are interpolated for the intermediate hours, so that we have the mean corrections for the month at the separate hours of the day. The means of the photographic readings for each separate hour having been taken through the month (as already mentioned); by applying to these means the corrections found as described, we have the mean barometer or thermometer reading through the month for each hour of the day, and, consequently, the mean diurnal inequality for the month, with the utmost accuracy.

In addition to the grouping by calendar months, other combinations of the days were also made, in order to determine the modification produced in the ordinary diurnal curve (under all atmospheric circumstances) by the action of special atmospheric conditions, such as a particular direction of wind, the existence of a high or low mean temperature, or of a high or low mean atmospheric pressure, or of a clear or overcast state of the sky. Days of similar character, as defined by some one of these circumstances, being grouped together, and the means of the hourly values through a group being taken; these means are corrected for instrumental error, by finding the mean correction through all the days of the group, applicable to the photographic value, for each of the hours at which corresponding eye observations were made; and interpolating corrections for the intermediate hours, exactly in the same way as has been described for calendar months. The special groupings made will be mentioned in following sections, when speaking of the Tables in which the different results are to be found.

Referring again to the sheets for calendar months, into which the photographic values were first entered; by taking the means, in the horizontal direction, of the twenty-four values standing in each line, we obtain the mean daily photographic value of either element. To correct these daily means for instrumental error we ought, in strictness, to apply on each day a correction derived from the four comparisons with the eye-observations of the day. But it was found that the fluctuations of these corrections through a month were usually small. For the barometer it was sufficient to apply in each month the mean of all the daily corrections to the mean photographic reading for each day; for the thermometer the mean correction was more frequently determined. Mean daily values, corrected for instrumental error, thus found, are used for determining the mean reading of the barometer, and that of the thermometer, for each day of the year through the whole range of the twenty years in each case employed.

It was considered desirable to employ the long series of hourly barometric values obtained from the photographic records, in a discussion of the question of lunar influence on the atmosphere. In an inquiry of this kind, new time scales (dividing the interval between two successive upper meridian passages of the moon into 24 hours) should, in strictness, be laid down on the photographic sheets. But considering the excessive additional labour involved in doing this, and the probable

b

small magnitude of the lunar effect, it was decided to make use, in the investigation, of the values already obtained for solar hours. The following is a description of the method employed.

On the large sheets, containing each the hourly values for one calendar month, a mark in red ink is made on each day between the two hourly values which respectively precede and follow the time of moon's transit at Greenwich. Now one lunar day usually includes twenty-five of these solar hours. Beginning then with New Moon, the values are transferred to other sheets (ruled with twenty-five vertical columns) in such way that the barometer reading for the first solar hour following the moon's meridian passage shall, on successive days, throughout the lunar month, stand in the first vertical column; that the reading for the second solar hour following the moon's meridian passage shall occupy, on successive days, the second vertical column; and so on. Occasionally, when the 25th value is wanting, that at the next succeeding solar hour is taken. Each of the sheets into which the values are transferred contains one lunar month. The means of the values in each vertical column through the lunar month being taken, we obtain twenty-five mean photographic values, the interval between each two of which is about the $\frac{1}{25}$th part of a lunar day, the first value corresponding to an epoch following lunar noon by about the $\frac{1}{50}$th part of a lunar day.

No correction for instrumental error has been applied to the photographic means in the lunar arrangement; it will be seen that this is not necessary. Referring to the solar arrangement, it may be mentioned that the corrections to the individual photographic values are small, and fluctuate little from day to day, though they indicate the existence of a slight inequality whose period is diurnal. But in the lunar arrangement, it is to be remarked, that the lunar day, in the course of a lunar month, commences successively at every part of the solar day. Therefore, in the lunar arrangement, the small inequality in the march of the correction through the solar day becomes eliminated in the means of lunar months, and especially in the means of many lunar months; and the values remain affected (as regards instrumental error) with simply a small constant error, which, as the object of the arrangement is entirely to ascertain differences, is of no importance whatever. Consequently no correction for instrumental error is required.

§ 5. *Explanation of the Tables containing Results deduced from the Observations of the Barometer.*

All absolute barometric values contained in the tables now to be described are corrected for temperature, by reduction to 32° Fahrenheit, but no reduction to sea-level is made. The values refer to a position which is considered to be 150 feet above the mean level of the sea.

The formation of Tables I. to XII. requires no special remark. Table XIII. (the numbers in which are collected from the preceding tables) gives the mean reading of the barometer at every hour of the day in each month through the whole range of years. Table XIV. is formed from Table XIII. by subtracting, in Table XIII., the mean value in each month from all the separate hourly values in the month. The numbers in Table XIV. are graphically represented in Plate III. The mean monthly values of barometer reading inserted on this diagram are those of Table XXI.

On Table XIV. a few remarks may be offered. It will be seen that there are in each month the double maxima and minima, indicating semidiurnal period. There is the morning minimum, the forenoon maximum, the afternoon minimum, and the evening maximum. There is also, in most months, evident indication of diurnal period, shown by the greater depression of the afternoon minimum as compared with the morning minimum, and a tendency to depression of the evening maximum as compared with the forenoon maximum. These peculiarities are best seen in the graphical representation. The magnitude of the co-efficient of the diurnal term, it is seen, will be usually small, as compared with that of the semidiurnal term. In fact, as regards the general average, if x represents the interval elapsed since midnight (reckoned in arc, 15° to each hour), it appears that the numbers given "For the Year" in Table XIV. may be approximately represented by the expression $+0^{in} \cdot 0029 \cdot \sin (25° + x) +0^{in} \cdot 0090 \cdot \sin (142° + 2 x)$. The diurnal term has a real existence, and is not the result of accidental circumstances, for it receives confirmation from what is observed at other places. For instance, the variations of the barometer have been photographically registered at the Oxford Observatory for a number of years. Collecting the yearly results[*] from the annual volumes of observations from 1858 to 1874, the numbers found by subtracting the mean reading for the whole period, from the mean reading at each even hour, are as follows :—

	in.		in.		in.
Midnight +	· 006	8 a.m. +	· 006	4 p.m. —	· 013
2 a.m. —	· 001	10 ,, +	· 010	6 ,, —	· 005
4 ,, —	· 007	Noon +	· 001	8 ,, +	· 006
6 ,, —	· 002	2 p.m. —	· 010	10 ,, +	· 010

and these numbers are nearly represented by the expression $+0^{in} \cdot 0034 \cdot \sin (51° + x) +0^{in} \cdot 0098 \cdot \sin (156° + 2 x)$. The co-efficients are nearly similar in magnitude at the two places, although the angles, indicating nodal points, are somewhat different. The difference is equivalent to about half an hour in time in the semi-diurnal term, and $1\frac{3}{4}$ hour in the diurnal term, the nodal points being passed earlier at Oxford than at Greenwich.

---

[*] Astronomical and Meteorological Observations made at the Radcliffe Observatory, Oxford.

The co-efficient of the diurnal portion of the inequality does not appear to have at all places such comparatively small magnitude. For, according to observations made on the American continent (at Washington * and at Albany † for instance), it approaches or even exceeds in magnitude that of the semidiurnal term, the values of both being very much larger than at Greenwich.

Table XV. gives the maxima and minima in each month, with the times of their occurrence, simply as inferred from the numbers in Table XIV. Comparing together the different months of the year, it will be seen that the morning minimum and forenoon maximum are most early in summer, and become later again towards winter. The afternoon minimum and the evening maximum, on the contrary, are most late in summer, and become earlier again towards the end of the year. The two former appear to follow nearly the change in the time of sunrise; the two latter follow the change in the time of sunset. As a consequence of this, the interval between the forenoon maximum and afternoon minimum is much shorter in winter than in summer, whilst that between the evening maximum and morning minimum is much longer in winter than in summer. See also Plate III., in which the times of sunrise and sunset at Greenwich are noted by short lines crossing the curves.

Table XVI. gives the approximate times of the day in each month at which the mean barometer reading coincides with the mean for the month, as found by simple interpolation between the numbers given in Table XIV.

Table XVII. contains mean monthly readings for each separate month through the whole period, extracted from Tables I. to XII. Table XVIII. gives the extremes of these monthly readings. (The slight difference between the concluded monthly means for April, June, and November, in Tables XIII. and XVII., is due to the insertion in Table XVII. of values deduced from the eye-observations.)

Tables XIX. and XX. give the results of a different grouping of the numbers contained in Tables I. to XII. In those tables different years are grouped together, in order to obtain the mean diurnal inequality for each month through the range of years, as exhibited in Table XIV. But to form Table XIX. the twelve months of each year are grouped together, to obtain the diurnal inequality for each year separately, in order to show what variation exists from year to year. Table XX. is formed from Table XIX. (The numbers at the foot in Tables XIX. and XX. represent identically the same results as those found in the last columns of Tables XIII. and XIV. respectively, excepting that in Tables XIII. and XIV. the values have been carried one decimal place further. The difference between the mean

---

* Astronomical and Meteorological Observations made at the United States Naval Observatory during the year 1866, Appendix I.
† Annals of the Dudley Observatory, Vol. II.

yearly value for 1857 in Tables XVII. and XIX. is due to the insertion in Table XVII. of the eye-observation value in the month of November 1857.)

Table XXI. gives the mean reading of the barometer for every day of the year through the whole range of years, as deduced from the twenty-four hourly values on each day. On single days in the series on which there is no available photographic value, that given by the eye-observations is used, in order that the concluded mean daily values shall properly represent the whole period. The mean monthly values in consequence differ slightly, in some months, from those contained in Tables XIII. and XVII. The depression about November 23, following a great elevation, is remarkable. Table XXII., formed from Table XXI., requires no explanation.

The tables which next follow, XXIII. to XXXV., refer to the arrangement of the observations according to the special atmospheric condition of direction of wind. The days on which the wind continued, throughout the day, on some one of the eight points of azimuth are, in this arrangement, grouped together, as explained at page 9. A list of days fulfilling the necessary conditions for the years 1869 to 1873 is given in Table XXIII.; those for the years 1854 to 1868, completing the information for the twenty years, will be found (as explained in the heading to Table XXIII.) in Table LXXXVIII. in the Thermometric Section. The days omitted (for reasons given on page 8), in forming the succeeding tables, are indicated as explained at the commencement of Table XXIII.

An inspection of Tables XXIV. to XXXI. will show the effect produced on the pressure in twenty-four hours by the action of each wind, in every month of the year. The double maxima and minima are shown, but the diurnal curve is in each case usually thrown also up or down, sometimes considerably. Comparing together the first and last numbers in each column, we find as follows :—

The N. wind increases the pressure, much in winter, but not so much in summer.

The N.E. wind increases the pressure in winter, but has little effect in summer.

The E. wind diminishes the pressure in summer, but not so much in winter.

The S.E. wind diminishes the pressure throughout.

The S. wind diminishes the pressure throughout, but apparently most in summer.

The S.W. wind diminishes the pressure in winter, but has little effect in summer.

The W. wind increases the pressure throughout, but rather more in summer.

The N.W. wind increases the pressure throughout, but very much in winter.

In regard to the change made in the pressure by the action of the wind during twenty-four hours, it is to be observed that the various groups, on which the numbers in Tables XXIV. to XXXI. depend, include isolated days, and also smaller and larger groups of days. With the N., E., S.E., S., and N.W. winds, isolated days or smaller groups predominate, but with the N.E., S.W., and W. winds the larger groups prevail. The magnitude of what may be called the initial effect of each wind is, therefore, probably more nearly indicated in the results for the winds first mentioned than in those for the other winds.

Tables XXXII. and XXXIII. contain results derived from Tables XXIV. to XXXI. The numbers in Table XXXIII. are represented graphically in Plate IV. The mean values of barometer reading inserted on this diagram are those of Table XXXII.

Table XXXIV. gives the mean barometer reading in each month under all circumstances, and also under each wind, as taken from Table XXI., and Tables XXIV. to XXXI. respectively. Table XXXV. gives the deviation of the mean for each wind in each month, from the mean for the month under all circumstances. These numbers must not by any means be taken as indicating the actual change of pressure usually produced, inasmuch as the anterior condition, as regards pressure, is not, in any case, necessarily an average condition. Each wind may succeed some one particular wind more often than any other, and thus begin its action in a state of atmosphere which varies from the average state more often in one particular way. As illustrating this, it is interesting to study Tables XXXIV. and XXXV. in connexion with Tables XXIV. to XXXI. Thus, it is seen that the effect of the N. and N.W. winds in the month of January (Tables XXIV. and XXXI. respectively) is greatly to increase the previous pressure. But according to Table XXXV. the mean pressure with N. and N.W. winds is lower in January than the mean pressure under all circumstances. And the explanation is (as Tables XXIV. and XXXI. show) that in these cases the wind has usually begun to act when the barometer reading was low. Again (Table XXVI.) the E. wind diminishes the previously existing pressure generally throughout the year. But (Table XXXV.) the mean reading with E. wind is generally higher than the mean under all circumstances. Or, as Table XXVI. shows, the E. wind usually begins to act with high barometer. The relation between the change produced in twenty-four hours by any wind, and the average pressure under the same wind, on the mean of all months, may be studied in Plate IV. On the average of all months the barometer is most depressed with the S. wind, and most elevated with the N.E. wind. The order of winds, beginning with that under which the barometer is most depressed, is S., S.W., W., N.W., S.E., N., E., and N.E.

Table XXXVI. contains the result of the arrangement of the readings of the barometer for the whole twenty years, for solar hours, according to the time of the moon's meridian passage. The manner in which mean hourly values, through each lunar month, for the twenty-five solar hours occurring in the lunar day, were obtained, is explained at page 10. It is only necessary to further mention that all the lunar months commencing in January are grouped together and the hourly means taken; and these means appear under January in Table XXXVI. Similarly for February and other months. The results are affected with a very small constant error, the value of which is not necessarily the same in different months (see page 10).

Table XXXVII. is formed from Table XXXVI., and gives in each month the deviation of the barometric reading, at each hour through the lunar day, from the mean reading for the month. Examination of the numbers contained in this table does not show any certain trace of either semidiurnal or diurnal period. See note at the foot of the table.

As a general remark applying to the investigation of barometric inequality in this latitude, it may be pointed out that the periodical variations are small in magnitude, whilst the accidental fluctuations are comparatively very large. A long series of observations is therefore required, in order to determine accurately the small periodic variations. In tropical climates, on the contrary, the periodical variations are greater in magnitude, whilst the accidental fluctuations are smaller; these conditions are favourable to the good determination of periodical variations in comparatively short periods of time. The annual barometric curve, for instance, appears at some places to be perceptible in the observations of a single year. But in this latitude many year's observations are, for the same purpose, necessary, on account apparently of the very different conditions which frequently prevail in the same season in different years.

§ 6. *Explanation of the Tables containing Results deduced from the observations of the Dry-Bulb and Wet-Bulb Thermometers.*

The formation of Tables XXXVIII. to LXVII. requires no special remark. Dry-Bulb thermometer readings (giving the Temperature of the Air) and Wet-Bulb thermometer readings (giving the Temperature of Evaporation) are treated in the same way. Tables LI. and LXVI. are formed respectively from Tables L. and LXV. In Tables LXVIII. and LXX. the Dew Points have been formed by combination of each Air Temperature in Tables L. and LII. with its corresponding Evaporation Temperature in Tables LXV. and LXVII. respectively, by use of the table of factors given in Glaisher's "Hygrometrical Tables," 5th Edition, page iv. Table LXIX. is formed from Table LXVIII.

For diagrams of the mean diurnal curves of Air Temperature, Evaporation Temperature, and Dew Point, see Plate V.

Tables LXXI. to LXXIII. give mean hourly values, through the whole range of years, of the Temperature of the Air, Temperature of Evaporation, and the Dew Point, for periods of three months. They are formed from Tables L., LXV., and LXVIII. These numbers are graphically represented in Plate VI.

Tables LXXIV. to LXXVI. give the Mean Temperatures of the Air, Evaporation, and Dew Point, for periods of three months for every year, deduced from Tables LII., LXVII., and LXX. These numbers are graphically represented in Plate VII.

Table LXXVII. gives the Mean Temperature of the Air, for every day of the year through the whole range of years, as deduced from the twenty-four hourly values on each day. As in the corresponding Table XXI., referring to the Barometer, here also, on single days in the series on which there is no available photographic value, that given by the eye observations is used, in order properly to represent the period. On this account the monthly means slightly differ from those contained in Tables L. and LII. A remarkable elevation of temperature is shown about December 6.

The tables which next follow refer to the arrangements of the observations of the Temperature of the Air and of Evaporation according to special atmospheric circumstances, in order to exhibit the change thereby produced in the ordinary diurnal curves. Days of similar character are grouped together as explained at page 9. In these arrangements, the temperature of the air and the temperature of evaporation are, in all cases, both treated.

Tables LXXVIII. to LXXXII. refer to the grouping of the observations according to days of High Mean Temperature and of Low Mean Temperature. The distinction of these may appear somewhat vague, but it has been customary at the Royal Observatory to make a comparison of the mean temperature of every day with the average of mean temperatures on the same nominal day for a long series of years, by which means we have been able to discriminate the two classes of days with very little uncertainty.

The actual lengths of the Warm and the Cold Waves, and the days omitted in forming the succeeding tables, are given in Table LXXVIII. If in any wave, in consequence of omissions, the observations are available on one day only, the day is set down as an omitted day, and the wave is rejected in forming the tables that follow; sometimes waves containing two available days are thus rejected. The end of a year is not considered as dividing a wave, and the last wave of any year (as will be seen in Table LXXVIII.) usually includes some days, more or less, of the following year. In taking annual means, the simple means of the means of separate waves are taken; no respect is given to the lengths of waves.

The following is a list of waves of unusual length :—

1849, January 8 to March 8	-	- high temperature,	60 days.
1852, December 2 to 1853, January 31		- high ,,	61 ,,
1853, November 9 to 1854, January 6		- low ,,	59 ,,
1859, January 10 to March 20	-	- high ,,	70 ,,
1860, May 27 to October 4	-	- low ,,	131 ,,
1862, June 9 to September 6	-	- low ,,	90 ,,
1862, December 3 to 1863, March 7		- high ,,	95 ,,
1865, August 20 to October 17	-	- high ,,	59 ,,

The effect of the long cold wave of 1860 will be seen hereafter in the Earth Temperatures. See Plate X.

For diagrams of the mean diurnal curves of Air Temperature, in Waves of High and Low Mean Temperature, see Plate V.

Tables LXXXIII. to LXXXVII. refer to the grouping of the observations according to days of High and Low Mean Atmospheric Pressure. The distinction of days is determined by reference to a mean value deduced from the observations of a series of years, in the same way as described for temperature. The actual lengths of the Waves, and the days omitted in forming the succeeding tables, are given in Table LXXXIII. The waves are further treated in exactly the same way as those of High and Low Temperature.

The following is a list of waves of unusual length :—

1854, February 21 to April 19,	-	- high atmospheric pressure,	58 days.
1855, January 29 to March 27,	-	- low ,,	58 ,,
1857, November 28 to 1858, January 31, high		,,	65 ,,
1863, December 4 to 1864, February 6, high		,,	65 ,,

For diagrams of the mean diurnal curves of Air Temperature, in Waves of High and Low Mean Atmospheric Pressure, see Plate V.

Tables LXXXVIII. to CVIII. refer to the grouping of the observations according to days distinguished by the continuance of the wind throughout the day on some one of the eight points of azimuth. Table LXXXVIII. gives a list of such days; those omitted in forming the succeeding tables being indicated as explained at the commencement of the table. And Tables LXXXIX. to CVIII. contain the results of the grouping.

An inspection of these tables will show the effect produced on the temperature in twenty-four hours by the action of each wind, in every month of the year. Comparing the Air Temperature at midnight (Tables LXXXIX. to XCVI.) with the temperature at the following midnight (which can be closely estimated by remarking the change in the numbers just previously to 11h. p.m.) in each particular case, we find as follows :—

The N. wind sensibly lowers the temperature in all months except April and
September.

The N.E. wind lowers the temperature generally, but least in the summer months.

The E. wind lowers the temperature in January and December, and raises it
generally in other months.

The S.E. wind raises the temperature in nearly every month.

The S. wind raises the temperature in nearly every month, in some months
considerably.

The S.W. wind somewhat raises the temperature in nearly every month.

The W. wind somewhat raises the temperature in summer, and lowers it generally
in other months, considerably in some months.

The N.W. wind lowers the temperature throughout, very considerably in January,
February, and December.

The remarks on page 13, in reference to analogous barometric changes, apply
also here. It is however to be observed, that changes of pressure are in a greater
degree progressive than those of temperature. A large change of temperature
will occasionally directly follow change of wind, and especially a sudden change
of wind. And as the condition of selection of days is the continuance of the wind
in the same direction through the twenty-four hours, such changes escape recog-
nition in the above-mentioned statement of the effects produced by different winds.
Otherwise, as in the Barometric section, the initial effect of each wind is probably
more nearly indicated in the results for the N., E., S.E., S., and N.W. winds than in
those for the N.E., S.W., and W. winds.

The change shown between the beginning and ending of the day when the N.W.
wind blows (Table XCVI.) may, for illustration, be taken as practically representing
in magnitude the initial effect of this wind. Selecting the month of December, the
following diagram gives the mean air temperature curve for this month (Table L.),
with the curve for the same month when the N.W. wind blows (Table XCVI.), and
affords a good idea of the effect of wind.

MEAN TEMPERATURE OF THE AIR IN THE MONTH OF DECEMBER.

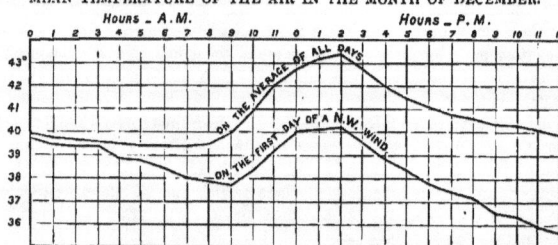

It will be observed in the above example that the position of the curve is changed gradually without much change of its form. In other instances, as may be seen by comparing the numbers contained in Tables LXXXIX. to XCVI. with those in Table L., the form of the curve is also changed. This signifies that the diurnal ranges for the same month under different winds are different, and it will be found interesting to compare together in this respect the numbers contained in the several Tables LXXXIX. to XCVI.

Tables CV. to CVIII. contain results derived from Tables LXXXIX. to CIV. The numbers in Table CV. are represented graphically in Plate VIII.

Tables CIX. to CXVIII. refer to the grouping of the observations according to cloudless and overcast days. Tables CIX. and CX. give respectively lists of days sensibly cloudless and completely overcast; days omitted in forming the succeeding tables being indicated as explained at the beginning of each table. And Tables CXI. to CXVIII. contain the results of the grouping.

For diagrams of the mean diurnal curves of Air Temperature on cloudless and overcast days, see Plate VIII. The curve of temperature under all circumstances is also added for the purpose of comparison.

Comparing (Table CXI.) the air temperature at midnight with that at the following midnight (estimated in the same way as described for winds) it appears that a clear sky lowers the temperature considerably in the months of November, December, and January, and raises it generally in other months. An overcast sky (Table CXV.) scarcely disturbs the temperature. The diurnal ranges are much increased in clear weather and diminished in cloudy weather. This will be seen also in Plate VIII.

Table CXIX. gives a collection of some of the mean results in regard to Temperature of the Air under different atmospheric circumstances, extracted from the preceding tables, for the purpose of comparison. · The order in which the means appear is as follows : 1, mean under all circumstances of weather ; 2 to 9, means for the days of prevalence of wind from each of the eight principal points ; 10 and 11, means for cloudless days and for overcast days. By subtracting in each month the mean temperature under all circumstances from the mean temperature under each atmospheric condition, the deviation in each case, as referred to the general average, is found. Numbers so obtained are given in Table CXX.

The remarks on Table XXXV. in the Barometric section, as respects effect of wind, apply in some degree also here. The numbers in Table CXX. must not be taken as indicating the exact effect which each wind usually produces, because the anterior condition as regards temperature is not in any case necessarily an average condition, and may deviate from the average more often in one particular way. But the numbers do strictly indicate the amount by which the mean temperature

c 2

under each wind deviates from the average temperature under all circumstances. The effects may be briefly stated as follows :—

The N. wind depresses the temperature throughout the year.

The N.E. wind does the same, except in summer, when its effect is small.

The E. wind lowers the temperature very much in winter, raises it generally in summer.

The S.E. wind nearly the same, but less markedly in winter.

The S. wind raises the temperature much in winter, but scarcely affects it in summer.

The S.W. wind nearly the same.

The W. wind decidedly raises the temperature in winter and lowers it in summer.

The N.W. wind lowers the temperature generally, but most in summer.

The effects of the thermometric influences of the wind are seen most strikingly in contrasts of opposite winds. Thus :—

In January, change of wind from N. to S. raises the temperature by 8°·2; in June by 0°·7 only.

Again in January, change from N.E. to S.W. raises the temperature 11°·0; in June only 0°·3.

The difference between the mean of the numbers for E. and S.E. winds, and that for the S. and S.W. winds, as contrasted between the summer months and the winter months, is remarkable. Thus in June, July, and August the excesses of the mean deviation for E. and S.E. winds above the mean deviation for S. and S.W. winds are 2°·9, 1°·2, and 4°·7 respectively. But in November, December, January, and February, the means for S. and S.W. exceed those for E. and S.E. by 5°·4, 9°·4, 0°·2, and 7°·6 respectively.

On the average of all months the N. wind is absolutely the coldest wind, the warmest is S.W. The order of winds as regards temperature, beginning with the coldest, is N., N.E., N.W., E., S.E., W., S., S.W. But this order is different in different months, as will have been seen by what precedes.

As regards the effect of clouds, the temperature with cloudless sky is much lower than the mean in winter, and much higher in summer. With overcast sky, the temperature is lower in summer, but differs little from the mean in winter. The latter circumstance is principally due to the greater preponderance of cloudy weather in winter, during which season the cloudy state becomes nearly the mean state.

This completes the discussion of the influence of special atmospheric circumstances on the diurnal changes of Temperature.

The Tables which follow contain simply extracts from preceding tables intended to show merely the extremes in maximum and minimum of different series of indications, with the times at which they occur.

The mean temperature of the air at every hour of the day in each month through the whole range of years having been found (Table L.), the lowest and highest of these hourly values are set down in Table CXXI. for each month. And similarly for the Temperature of Evaporation, using Table LXV.

The mean temperature of the air in each month in every year having been found by combining all the hourly values in each month (Table LII.), the lowest and highest of these monthly values through the whole range of years are set down in Table CXXII. for each month. And similarly for the Temperature of Evaporation, using Table LXVII.

The mean temperature of the Dew Point at every hour of the day in each month through the whole range of years having been found (Table LXVIII.), by combination of the corresponding Air and Evaporation Temperatures, the lowest and highest of these hourly values of Dew Point are set down in Table CXXIII. for each month.

Table CXXIV. gives extremes of temperature in the means of the aggregates of groups defined by physical circumstances. The lowest and highest hourly values in waves of high and low temperature and high and low atmospheric pressure, both for temperature of the air and temperature of evaporation, are extracted from the lowest lines of Tables LXXIX., LXXX., LXXXI., LXXXII., LXXXIV., LXXXV., LXXXVI., and LXXXVII. The lowest and highest hourly values in regard to the eight directions of the wind, are extracted from the numbers contained in the last column of Tables LXXXIX. to CIV., and the lowest and highest hourly values for cloudless and overcast days from those given in the several columns of Tables CXI., CXIII., CXV., and CXVII.

§ 7. *Thermometers whose Bulbs are sunk to different depths below the surface of the Ground for Observations on Earth-Temperature.*

These thermometers were made by Messrs. Adie, of Edinburgh, under the immediate superintendence of the late Professor J. D. Forbes, the graduation being made by Professor Forbes himself. They are four in number, and are all placed in one hole in the ground, the diameter of which in its upper half is 1 foot and in its lower half about 6 inches. The place of the hole is 20 feet south (magnetic) of the extremity of the south arm of the Magnetic Observatory, and opposite the center of its south front. Each thermometer is attached in its whole length to a slender piece of wood, which is planted in the hole with it. The vacant space remaining after each thermometer was placed in position, was filled up with dry sand.

The bulbs of the thermometers are cylindrical, 10 or 12 inches long and 2 or 3 inches in diameter. The bore of that part of the tube which extends from the bulb to the graduated scale is very small. In that part of the tube to which the scale is attached the bore is much larger.

The centers of the bulbs of these thermometers are sunk into the ground to the depths respectively of 3·2 feet (3 French feet); 6·4 feet (6 French feet); 12·8 feet (12 French feet); and 25·6 feet (24 French feet).

The fluid in the thermometers is alcohol, tinged with a red colour.

The parts of the tubes which project above the surface of the ground (in each case about 30 inches, a little more or less) are protected by a wooden case or box fixed to the ground; the sides of the box are perforated with numerous holes, and it has a double roof. In the front of the box, which faces the north, is a large plate of glass, through which the thermometers are read. Within the box are two smaller thermometers; one whose bulb is sunk one inch in the ground, and one whose bulb is in the free air, nearly in the center of the box.

The ranges of the scales at first provided were found to be in all cases insufficient, and a little of the fluid has, in consequence, been at different times removed from each of the four thermometers. It was afterwards found that too great a quantity had been taken from the 3·2 feet thermometer, and a small amount was, at a later time, again added. These changes were always accompanied by proper corresponding alteration of the engraved scales. The ranges of the scales now are, for the 3·2 feet thermometer, 37°·0 to 68°·0; for the 6·4 feet thermometer, 44°·0 to 62°·0; for the 12·8 feet thermometer, 43°·0 to 58°·0; and for the 25·6 feet thermometer, 46°·0 to 55°·5. The lengths of 1° on their scales are respectively 0·5 inch, 0·9 inch, 1·1 inch, and 1·9 inch.

§ 8. *Explanation of the Tables referring to Earth-Temperature.*

These tables contain results for the twenty-seven years from 1847 to 1873, derived from the eye-observations of the thermometers described in the last section, including also for comparison those of the standard dry-bulb thermometer.

Table CXXV. contains the mean monthly temperatures of the air derived from the standard dry-bulb. The values for 1847 are the simple means of two-hourly observations; those for 1848 are the means of usually six observations daily, corrected for diurnal inequality by application of corrections derived from Mr. Glaisher's paper "On the corrections to be applied to Meteorological Observations" in the *Philosophical Transactions* for 1848, Part 1. The means for 1849 and all succeeding years are found by combining eye-observations, taken usually four times on each day, and corrected for diurnal inequality, with observations of the maximum and minimum corrected by a quantity (taken from

Mr. Glaisher's paper) peculiar to the period of the year. These temperatures may be regarded as accurate mean temperatures. The means for quarterly periods have also been added. [The series of mean temperatures deduced from eye-observations is here employed for reference, since the photographic records have not yet been reduced later than the year 1868.]

Table CXXVI. contains monthly means of readings, made at noon, of the thermometer which is enclosed within the case covering the upper ends of the deep sunk thermometers; Table CXXVII., monthly and quarterly means for the thermometer whose bulb is placed one inch below the surface of the ground; and Tables CXXVIII. to CXXXI., monthly means for the thermometers whose bulbs are sunk below the surface of the ground to the depths of 3·2, 6·4, 12·8, and 25·6 feet respectively.

The quarterly means, and yearly means commencing with October, given in Tables CXXV. and CXXVII., were really prepared for a special purpose, but, as giving a certain information, they have been allowed here to remain.

The results contained in Tables CXXVI. to CXXXI. are throughout the means of readings taken at noon. Between 1846, April, and 1847, December, however, observations were made every two hours, at the end of which period it was found that the daily mean, as regards the 3·2, 6·4, 12·8, and 25·6 feet thermometers, agreed so nearly with the reading at noon that, commencing with the year 1848, observations were made at noon only. The following table contains the corrections, found from the observations made in 1846 and 1847, which should be subtracted from the values given in the Tables, in order to obtain mean values. It will be seen that the corrections for the four deep thermometers are extremely small.

Month.	Thermometer within Case.	Thermometer whose Bulb is sunk to the Depth of				
		1 inch.	3·2 feet.	6·4 feet.	12·8 feet.	25·6 feet.
	o	o	o	o	o	o
January	1·0	0·0	0·03	0·01	0·01	0·01
February	1·9	0·0	0·03	0·01	0·01	0·01
March	4·3	0·6	0·03	0·01	0·01	0·01
April	4·5	0·8	0·07	0·03	0·01	0·01
May	5·0	1·3	0·07	0·03	0·01	0·01
June	5·6	1·6	0·11	0·05	0·03	0·01
July	5·1	1·4	0·11	0·05	0·03	0·01
August	4·5	1·0	0·11	0·05	0·03	0·01
September	4·8	1·0	0·11	0·05	0·03	0·01
October	3·3	0·8	0·04	0·03	0·03	0·01
November	1·9	0·3	0·04	0·01	0·01	0·01
December	1·5	0·3	0·03	0·01	0·01	0·01

The corrections contained in this table are not in any case applied.

Table CXXXII. gives the mean monthly results through the whole range of years, collected from the previous tables (CXXV. to CXXXI.) The numbers are graphically represented in Plate IX. Excepting the Mean Temperature of Air, the curves, relatively to mean values, are in each month too high by the amounts given in the table on page 23. These are, however, sensible only for the thermometers " within case " and " 1 inch deep."

The observations of these thermometers, as far as the end of 1859, have been elaborately reduced by Professor J. D. Everett; his memoir on the subject is printed as an Appendix ,to the Greenwich Observations, 1860. The tables now presented include the results discussed by Professor Everett, with addition of those for the years 1860 to 1873.

Table CXXXIII. gives for each thermometer the mean of the monthly means in each year, the limits of the years being defined by the following considerations. The examination of preceding tables has sufficiently shown that the wave of heat travels downward from the highest thermometer to the lowest, in such a manner that, whereas the highest temperature in the upper thermometers occurs near the end of July, that in the lowest thermometer occurs near the end of November. In order, therefore, to exhibit the downward path of a wave of heat spread over the entire year, it is necessary in the successive steps downwards to adopt as commencement of the year later and later times. It appeared that this might be done with sufficient accuracy by adopting for the surface-thermometers and for the depth of $3 \cdot 2$ feet, the beginning of January; for the depth of $6 \cdot 4$ feet, the beginning of February; for the depth of $12 \cdot 8$ feet, the beginning of March; and for the depth of $25 \cdot 6$ feet, the beginning of May. The numbers in Table CXXXIII. have been computed in conformity with these considerations, and show the temperatures, at different depths, on the mean of different years. The numbers in each vertical column of Table CXXXIV. are formed by comparing in Table CXXXIII. each number with the mean of all the numbers, for every thermometer. The interpretation of the results contained in Tables CXXXIII. and CXXXIV. will be seen more clearly in Plate X. The remark made on Plate IX. applies also to Plate X., but with this difference, that the curves for the " within case " and " 1 inch deep " thermometers are, relatively to mean values, each too high by a constant amount, which amount is, in each instance, the mean of the numbers given in the table on page 23. But as the object of Plate X. is to show variations from year to year, the slight relative displacement of the two curves is of no importance whatever. The propagation of the waves of temperature downwards is interestingly shown in Plate X. And the variations of temperature from year to year, as regards the four deep sunk thermometers, appear to agree closely, so far as we have been able to make comparison, with those found by Professor Smyth from observations of similar thermometers at the Edinburgh Observatory. See *Edinburgh Observations*, Vol. 14.

The numbers in Tables CXXXV., CXXXVI., CXXXVII., CXXXVIII., CXXXIX., CXL., and CXLI., showing extremes of temperature, are simply extracted from Tables CXXV., CXXVI., CXXVII., CXXVIII., CXXIX., CXXX., and CXXXI.

§ 9. *Description of the Illustrative Plates.*

Following the Tables are ten Plates. Plates I. and II. give copies of the photographic traces made by the Barometer and by the Dry-Bulb and Wet-Bulb Thermometers respectively; for the Barometer from 1869, February 25^d. 0^h. to February 26^d. 0^h., astronomical reckoning, or from February 25 at noon to February 26 at noon, civil reckoning; for the Dry-Bulb and Wet-Bulb Thermometers, from 1865, August 1^d. 1^h. to August 2^d. 1^h., astronomical reckoning, or from August 1, 1^h p.m. to August 2, 1^h p.m., civil reckoning. The photographs for these days may be taken as fair specimens of the ordinary photographs, after they have been furnished with the various hand-ruled lines, to make them immediately available for extract of the reading of the barometer or of either of the thermometers at every hour, or oftener if required.

In the Barometer sheet the record commences near the middle of the sheet, and proceeds towards the right hand, is continued from the left side, and terminates near the middle of the sheet. The times marked against the trace show the places of interruption of the trace by the attendant, who shuts off the light at convenient times for the purpose of establishing the time scale. The small variations of the barometer are very well shown. The line against which 29^{in}·630 is written is the instrumental base line, traced photographically as described at page 3, and the value thus written against this line is that determined by combination of the ordinates, measured for the times of the eye-observations, with the eye-readings of the Standard Barometer. Another line, having in this case value 29^{in}·5, is ruled, so that the sheet may show on the face of it the instrumental barometric scale.

In the Thermometer sheet the white space below corresponds to that part of the thermometer-tube through which the passage of light is interrupted by the mercury in the thermometer tube. The left-hand traces are those of the wet-bulb thermometer, the right-hand traces those of the dry-bulb thermometer. Through the dark part of the photographic trace will be seen the horizontal lines formed by the fine wires indicating the scale of degrees on each thermometer. The vertical broad white lines show the interruptions in the photographic traces made by shutting off the light, the times of interruption and re-admission of the light being entered immediately below. A little lower on the sheet the eye-readings of the Standard

Wet-Bulb and Dry-Bulb Thermometers are entered, the hours to which they refer being indicated by dotted lines. The vertical lines ruled in ink, for every hour, are ruled through points determined by applying a scale of hours to the sheet, in the manner explained at page 7. Among the various irregularities of the outlines of the photographic traces, two depressions will be remarked as more conspicuous than others, at 4h. 0m. and 23h. 20m. These correspond to showers of rain, which are registered as occurring about 3h. 50m. and 23h. 0m., the latter being the heavier. [The edge of the dry thermometer trace is not quite correctly represented between 10h. and 16h., and in some copies, in both registers, the figures 50, 60, and 70, indicating degrees, are not placed, as they should be, on the thicker white lines. See page 6.]

The diagrams on Plates III. to X. simply exhibit, in a graphical form, numbers given in the Tables. Proper references to or explanations of these plates will be found at the places where the corresponding tables are described. It is proper to remark that, in some of these diagrams, the ordinate of the last point of the curve at the terminating midnight does not correspond with that of the first point at the initial midnight. The reason is, that the collection of a complete group of observations under a special circumstance, as for instance, with the wind blowing in a definite direction, implies that the first of these observations has started from a different anterior special circumstance, and the atmospheric state does not instantly change from that which is peculiar to the anterior circumstance, to that which is peculiar to the following circumstance; and therefore, the very first observations are influenced thereby. It may happen also that the very last observations are influenced by the approach of the next coming circumstance.

§ 10. Concluding Remarks.

In a subject so complicated as Meteorology, where indications of one class (as temperature) are undoubtedly affected by those of several other classes (as season, force and direction of wind, barometric pressure, rain, &c.), and each of these is affected by all the others; and not only by the existence of others, but also by the circumstances of the beginning and ending of their action; it is impossible to say what series of reductions may be considered as fairly exhaustive. All that has been attempted here, is to make those reductions of the barometrical and thermometrical observations which in the first instance are most obviously necessary. The meteorological stores, however, of the Royal Observatory are very rich, and may well be trusted for the supply of materials for giving answer to almost any question, as regards the phenomena at a particular place, that can arise in Meteorology.

In the work now brought to a close, the extraction, from the Photographs, of all the fundamental numbers on which the printed tables depend, the severe examination for errors, the divisions of the tables required for the different groupings, the formation and verification of the means, and in fact the whole of the heavier work, as regards the Thermometric Reductions, was performed by or under the immediate superintendence of James Glaisher, Esq., F.R.S., late Superintendent of the Magnetical and Meteorological Department of the Royal Observatory. Other parts, of a somewhat lighter character, have been added by William Ellis, Esq., Mr. Glaisher's successor in office. The Barometric Reductions were commenced in the last few months of Mr. Glaisher's term of office, and have been continued and brought to a conclusion by Mr. Ellis. Valuable assistance has been given throughout by William C. Nash, Esq., Assistant in the Magnetical and Meteorological Department, who also made the drawings of the curves for the engraver. I trust that the whole work may be considered as a model of accuracy on a very large scale.

ADDENDUM.

Note on the Exposure of the Standard Dry-Bulb and Wet-Bulb Thermometers.

It seems proper to describe briefly the manner of exposure of the standard dry-bulb and wet-bulb thermometers used for eye observations, referred to at page 5, and further spoken of at pages 8 and 22; since the process of correction of the indications of the photographic dry-bulb and wet-bulb thermometers, described at page 8, is equivalent to giving their indications in terms of the standard dry-bulb and wet-bulb.

On a post, firmly fixed in the ground, a frame revolves, consisting of a horizontal board as base, of a vertical board projecting upwards from it, connected with one edge of the horizontal board, and of two parallel inclined boards (separated about three inches), connected at the top with the vertical board and at the bottom with the other edge of the horizontal board, the outer inclined board being covered with zinc. The air passes freely between all these boards. The standard dry-bulb and wet-bulb thermometers are attached to the outside and near the center of the vertical board; their bulbs are about four feet above the ground, and project about three inches below the horizontal board. Above the thermometers is a small projecting roof to protect them from rain. The frame is always turned so as to present its inclined side towards the sun. It is presumed that the thermometers are thus sufficiently shielded, without interrupting the free circulation of air around their bulbs. The position of the stand was slightly shifted in the year 1863, as mentioned on page 5.

INDEX TO TABLES AND PLATES.

C

(D.) List of Plates.

ROYAL OBSERVATORY, GREENWICH.

RESULTS

OF THE

OBSERVATIONS OF THE BAROMETER,

1854 TO 1873.

(All absolute barometric values contained in these Tables are corrected for temperature by reduction to 32° Fahrenheit. The values refer to a position which is considered to be 159 feet above the Mean Level of the Sea.)

TABLE I.—MEAN READING of the BAROMETER at every HOUR of the DAY

Year.	Number of Days employed in forming the Means.	Midnight.	1h. a.m.	2h. a.m.	3h. a.m.	4h. a.m.	5h. a.m.	6h. a.m.	7h. a.m.	8h. a.m.	9h. a.m.	10h. a.m.	11h. a.m.
		in.	in.	in.	in.	in.	in.	in.	in.	in.	in.	in.	in.
1854	28	29·664	29·660	29·664	29·663	29·660	29·659	29·659	29·666	29·679	29·687	29·693	29·690
1855	31	30·025	30·022	30·019	30·014	30·007	30·002	29·996	29·998	30·004	30·011	30·017	30·021
1856	26	29·386	29·387	29·392	29·397	29·400	29·399	29·402	29·414	29·423	29·433	29·441	29·445
1857	31	29·638	29·631	29·628	29·626	29·624	29·619	29·617	29·620	29·625	29·637	29·645	29·647
1858	31	30·193	30·188	30·184	30·181	30·178	30·176	30·172	30·172	30·175	30·177	30·179	30·181
1859	31	30·051	30·049	30·051	30·051	30·049	30·045	30·044	30·047	30·056	30·060	30·059	30·060
1860	30	29·506	29·504	29·509	29·512	29·517	29·519	29·522	29·528	29·533	29·540	29·542	29·540
1861	31	30·007	30·003	30·001	29·998	29·996	29·994	29·995	29·997	29·999	30·007	30·011	30·016
1862	31	29·735	29·733	29·731	29·729	29·723	29·717	29·714	29·709	29·707	29·712	29·715	29·713
1863	28	29·648	29·644	29·637	29·628	29·618	29·608	29·601	29·596	29·597	29·601	29·607	29·610
1864	26	30·034	30·026	30·023	30·020	30·015	30·011	30·009	30·008	30·013	30·022	30·029	30·030
1865	31	29·415	29·407	29·408	29·405	29·400	29·398	29·397	29·399	29·408	29·415	29·420	29·421
1866	31	29·723	29·712	29·707	29·700	29·692	29·684	29·680	29·685	29·690	29·697	29·706	29·705
1867	31	29·493	29·480	29·480	29·493	29·487	29·483	29·484	29·490	29·501	29·510	29·520	29·525
1868	31	29·761	29·757	29·761	29·760	29·759	29·755	29·752	29·751	29·755	29·763	29·773	29·767
1869	31	29·869	29·857	29·853	29·848	29·846	29·844	29·846	29·852	29·860	29·869	29·876	29·879
1870	31	29·820	29·811	29·811	29·809	29·801	29·798	29·798	29·804	29·813	29·821	29·832	29·830
1871	31	29·653	29·651	29·653	29·652	29·647	29·642	29·640	29·642	29·651	29·660	29·663	29·659
1872	31	29·465	29·457	29·434	29·447	29·441	29·439	29·442	29·447	29·459	29·470	29·480	29·482
1873	31	29·560	29·556	29·556	29·557	29·555	29·552	29·558	29·565	29·575	29·583	29·589	29·591
Means	..	29·7323	29·7272	29·7266	29·7245	29·7207	29·7172	29·7164	29·7195	29·7262	29·7338	29·7398	29·7406

TABLE II.—MEAN READING of the BAROMETER at every HOUR of the DAY

Year.	Number of Days employed in forming the Means.	Midnight.	1h. p.m.	2h. p.m.	3h. p.m.	4h. p.m.	5h. p.m.	6h. p.m.	7h. p.m.	8h. p.m.	9h. p.m.	10h. p.m.	11h. p.m.
		in.	in.	in.	in.	in.	in.	in.	in.	in.	in.	in.	in.
1854	28	30·030	30·027	30·021	30·016	30·012	30·011	30·015	30·023	30·036	30·047	30·053	30·056
1855	28	29·595	29·592	29·588	29·587	29·581	29·581	29·577	29·584	29·597	29·608	29·609	29·614
1856	18	29·923	29·922	29·925	29·925	29·927	29·927	29·927	29·935	29·946	29·951	29·957	29·962
1857	26	29·931	29·935	29·935	29·928	29·924	29·928	29·930	29·938	29·947	29·956	29·959	29·962
1858	28	29·854	29·848	29·847	29·842	29·842	29·842	29·841	29·845	29·849	29·851	29·849	29·852
1859	28	29·803	29·801	29·803	29·804	29·804	29·806	29·808	29·813	29·823	29·831	29·837	29·840
1860	29	29·865	29·861	29·859	29·855	29·852	29·850	29·850	29·850	29·855	29·861	29·863	29·865
1861	28	29·699	29·694	29·694	29·688	29·686	29·687	29·687	29·690	29·694	29·700	29·704	29·706
1862	28	29·914	29·914	29·911	29·905	29·901	29·900	29·899	29·900	29·907	29·910	29·912	29·914
1863	26	30·169	30·170	30·172	30·165	30·165	30·167	30·169	30·175	30·184	30·189	30·194	30·197
1864	25	29·817	29·819	29·815	29·814	29·811	29·806	29·802	29·796	29·789	29·784	29·782	29·780
1865	27	29·730	29·731	29·729	29·726	29·724	29·726	29·729	29·736	29·745	29·751	29·735	29·757
1866	28	29·559	29·560	29·561	29·557	29·536	29·534	29·550	29·547	29·546	29·545	29·542	29·542
1867	28	29·902	29·897	29·896	29·889	29·890	29·894	29·896	29·903	29·914	29·923	29·931	29·933
1868	29	29·982	29·976	29·973	29·968	29·963	29·963	29·963	29·967	29·976	29·981	29·986	29·985
1869	28	29·807	29·801	29·796	29·790	29·784	29·786	29·787	29·793	29·805	29·813	29·818	29·815
1870	19	29·686	29·684	29·680	29·675	29·668	29·667	29·666	29·668	29·672	29·675	29·677	29·672
1871	28	29·801	29·817	29·832	29·843	29·840	29·838	29·833	29·843	29·849	29·854	29·859	29·862
1872	29	29·654	29·651	29·645	29·637	29·631	29·629	29·630	29·637	29·642	29·649	29·656	29·660
1873	28	29·914	29·911	29·907	29·900	29·898	29·896	29·900	29·907	29·916	29·917	29·921	29·919
Means	..	29·8348	29·8325	29·8302	29·8256	29·8230	29·8229	29·8232	29·8275	29·8347	29·8398	29·8431	29·8452

in each YEAR from 1854 to 1873, for the MONTH of JANUARY.

Noon.	1ʰ. p.m.	2ʰ. p.m.	3ʰ. p.m.	4ʰ. p.m.	5ʰ. p.m.	6ʰ. p.m.	7ʰ. p.m.	8ʰ. p.m.	9ʰ. p.m.	10ʰ. p.m.	11ʰ. p.m.	Mean.	Year.
in.	in.	in.	in.	in.	in.	in.	in.	in.	in.	in.	in.	in.	
29·679	29·671	29·667	29·670	29·673	29·676	29·684	29·690	29·695	29·694	29·695	29·698	29·676	1854
30·012	30·005	30·001	29·999	29·998	29·999	29·998	30·001	30·004	30·006	30·009	30·009	30·008	1855
29·435	29·430	29·432	29·440	29·448	29·451	29·455	29·459	29·456	29·452	29·448	29·449	29·428	1856
29·641	29·632	29·627	29·630	29·635	29·641	29·643	29·645	29·644	29·643	29·640	29·639	29·634	1857
30·175	30·167	30·162	30·162	30·166	30·171	30·176	30·181	30·183	30·180	30·179	30·176	30·177	1858
30·045	30·035	30·025	30·023	30·016	30·030	30·033	30·038	30·039	30·038	30·037	30·035	30·043	1859
29·533	29·522	29·520	29·526	29·531	29·536	29·538	29·537	29·537	29·534	29·535	29·535	29·527	1860
30·013	30·008	30·006	30·012	30·018	30·021	30·025	30·029	30·031	30·028	30·031	30·031	30·011	1861
29·706	29·696	29·694	29·698	29·703	29·710	29·714	29·717	29·719	29·719	29·719	29·718	29·715	1862
29·609	29·603	29·602	29·609	29·614	29·620	29·629	29·637	29·639	29·642	29·641	29·638	29·620	1863
30·023	30·011	30·008	30·008	30·009	30·011	30·011	30·014	30·015	30·015	30·016	30·016		1864
29·411	29·405	29·407	29·409	29·412	29·412	29·410	29·406	29·400	29·397	29·395	29·393	29·406	1865
29·695	29·687	29·688	29·700	29·705	29·713	29·720	29·725	29·731	29·733	29·732	29·730	29·706	1866
29·518	29·513	29·513	29·517	29·518	29·518	29·519	29·521	29·523	29·527	29·527	29·524	29·508	1867
29·730	29·735	29·726	29·727	29·726	29·726	29·729	29·733	29·738	29·743	29·745	29·746	29·747	1868
29·869	29·861	29·856	29·862	29·866	29·868	29·870	29·868	29·867	29·863	29·858	29·851	29·860	1869
29·823	29·816	29·818	29·822	29·826	29·828	29·834	29·839	29·839	29·841	29·842	29·842	29·822	1870
29·647	29·638	29·636	29·636	29·637	29·640	29·644	29·650	29·653	29·657	29·655	29·654	29·648	1871
29·472	29·468	29·462	29·464	29·468	29·471	29·470	29·470	29·466	29·463	29·460	29·456	29·461	1872
29·579	29·568	29·564	29·570	29·577	29·582	29·584	29·585	29·587	29·585	29·584	29·584	29·573	1873
29·7318	29·7234	29·7207	29·7243	29·7278	29·7312	29·7343	29·7373	29·7382	29·7380	29·7374	29·7362	29·7294	..

in each YEAR from 1854 to 1873, for the MONTH of FEBRUARY.

Noon.	1ʰ. p.m.	2ʰ. p.m.	3ʰ. p.m.	4ʰ. p.m.	5ʰ. p.m.	6ʰ. p.m.	7ʰ. p.m.	8ʰ. p.m.	9ʰ. p.m.	10ʰ. p.m.	11ʰ. p.m.	Mean.	Year.
in.	in.	in.	in.	in.	in.	in.	in.	in.	in.	in.	in.	in.	
30·053	30·046	30·041	30·038	30·036	30·035	30·046	30·050	30·049	30·052	30·054	30·053	30·038	1854
29·608	29·600	29·595	29·590	29·590	29·590	29·589	29·588	29·600	29·604	29·606	29·608	29·596	1855
29·955	29·947	29·941	29·939	29·942	29·941	29·946	29·954	29·961	29·970	29·974	29·974	29·945	1856
29·938	29·938	29·935	29·935	29·935	29·932	29·938	29·944	29·950	29·958	29·958	29·959	29·943	1857
29·852	29·842	29·836	29·832	29·833	29·837	29·841	29·848	29·847	29·849	29·851	29·851	29·845	1858
29·832	29·821	29·813	29·811	29·811	29·813	29·824	29·831	29·832	29·832	29·829	29·827	29·819	1859
29·864	29·857	29·851	29·848	29·848	29·851	29·861	29·867	29·870	29·877	29·882	29·882	29·860	1860
29·702	29·690	29·690	29·679	29·674	29·676	29·676	29·683	29·689	29·688	29·691	29·693	29·689	1861
29·912	29·906	29·901	29·902	29·906	29·909	29·914	29·917	29·919	29·918	29·918	29·918	29·909	1862
30·190	30·177	30·170	30·169	30·168	30·167	30·170	30·172	30·172	30·177	30·177	30·177	30·168	1863
29·774	29·763	29·755	29·755	29·757	29·764	29·771	29·775	29·781	29·784	29·784	29·788	29·786	1864
29·757	29·752	29·743	29·740	29·737	29·740	29·743	29·744	29·743	29·742	29·742	29·742	29·740	1865
29·534	29·521	29·514	29·512	29·512	29·518	29·524	29·537	29·546	29·548	29·553	29·553	29·543	1866
29·918	29·917	29·913	29·907	29·903	29·907	29·913	29·916	29·919	29·921	29·919	29·915	29·910	1867
29·981	29·974	29·966	29·965	29·967	29·971	29·976	29·979	29·977	29·978	29·976	29·974	29·974	1868
29·817	29·807	29·798	29·796	29·794	29·803	29·823	29·830	29·832	29·831	29·828	29·827	29·808	1869
29·664	29·653	29·644	29·636	29·636	29·636	29·639	29·641	29·640	29·643	29·642	29·644	29·639	1870
29·855	29·849	29·839	29·836	29·836	29·841	29·850	29·855	29·859	29·863	29·868	29·868	29·850	1871
29·654	29·649	29·645	29·643	29·646	29·652	29·657	29·659	29·658	29·658	29·655	29·653	29·647	1872
29·910	29·898	29·893	29·891	29·888	29·893	29·899	29·903	29·904	29·905	29·905	29·902	29·904	1873
29·8402	29·8305	29·8238	29·8209	29·8210	29·8239	29·8302	29·8353	29·8373	29·8400	29·8405	29·8404	29·8319	..

TABLE III.—MEAN READING of the Barom

Year.	Number of Days employed in forming the Means.	Midnight.	1ʰ. a.m.	2ʰ. a.m.	3ʰ. a.m.	4ʰ. a.m.	5ʰ. a.m.	6ʰ. a.m.	7ʰ. a.m.	8ʰ. a.[
		in.	in.	in.	in.	in.	in.	in.	in.	in.
1854	31	30·205	30·203	30·198	30·190	30·185	30·183	30·184	30·192	30·19
1855	31	29·559	29·557	29·552	29·543	29·534	29·527	29·526	29·536	29·54
1856	29	30·050	30·051	30·047	30·043	30·041	30·041	30·042	30·043	30·04
1857	29	29·755	29·750	29·743	29·735	29·727	29·726	29·723	29·728	29·72
1858	31	29·775	29·774	29·771	29·766	29·766	29·766	29·769	29·773	29·78
1859	27	29·817	29·807	29·797	29·786	29·780	29·776	29·774	29·772	29·77
1860	31	29·691	29·690	29·683	29·676	29·672	29·671	29·673	29·675	29·67
1861	31	29·634	29·631	29·626	29·621	29·616	29·613	29·617	29·621	29·62
1862	22	29·555	29·552	29·550	29·548	29·543	29·544	29·546	29·547	29·55
1863	27	29·707	29·709	29·708	29·704	29·703	29·706	29·705	29·708	29·70
1864	29	29·527	29·528	29·524	29·517	29·514	29·512	29·513	29·511	29·51
1865	31	29·717	29·718	29·716	29·715	29·714	29·713	29·717	29·719	29·72
1866	31	29·526	29·524	29·523	29·519	29·517	29·520	29·516	29·534	29·54
1867	31	29·627	29·623	29·623	29·618	29·616	29·619	29·621	29·629	29·63
1868	31	29·805	29·806	29·803	29·796	29·795	29·798	29·804	29·817	29·82
1869	31	29·644	29·643	29·638	29·629	29·625	29·627	29·633	29·638	29·64
1870	31	29·870	29·865	29·861	29·852	29·849	29·846	29·848	29·853	29·86
1871	31	29·803	29·889	29·880	29·870	29·865	29·864	29·860	29·877	29·88
1872	31	29·635	29·635	29·631	29·627	29·625	29·627	29·635	29·642	29·64
1873	31	29·641	29·639	29·634	29·628	29·625	29·626	29·629	29·636	29·63
Means	..	29·7317	29·7298	29·7254	29·7191	29·7157	29·7153	29·7177	29·7226	29·72

TABLE IV.—MEAN READING of the Barom

Year.	Number of Days employed in forming the Means.	Midnight.	1ʰ. a.m.	2ʰ. a.m.	3ʰ. a.m.	4ʰ. a.m.	5ʰ. a.m.	6ʰ. a.m.	7ʰ. a.m.	8ʰ. a.[
		in.	in.	in.	in.	in.	in.	in.	in.	in.
1854	30	30·022	30·016	30·009	30·000	29·995	29·991	29·993	29·996	30·00
1855	30	29·948	29·944	29·940	29·935	29·933	29·927	29·930	29·940	29·94
1856	30	29·625	29·619	29·613	29·606	29·599	29·598	29·599	29·603	29·60
1857	30	29·620	29·618	29·616	29·614	29·612	29·614	29·619	29·623	29·62
1858	30	29·777	29·771	29·756	29·764	29·763	29·763	29·771	29·777	29·78
1859	30	29·611	29·615	29·610	29·606	29·604	29·605	29·609	29·612	29·61
1860	26	29·723	29·722	29·719	29·718	29·719	29·724	29·729	29·739	29·74
1861	30	29·993	29·993	29·990	29·991	29·991	29·991	29·994	29·999	30·00
1862	25	29·858	29·857	29·857	29·856	29·856	29·856	29·861	29·865	29·86
1863	29	29·832	29·833	29·832	29·829	29·828	29·826	29·828	29·829	29·83
1864	30	29·908	29·910	29·910	29·908	29·908	29·909	29·913	29·916	29·92
1865	30	29·972	29·969	29·966	29·962	29·960	29·939	29·964	29·967	29·97
1866	30	29·746	29·745	29·740	29·740	29·739	29·741	29·748	29·752	29·75
1867	30	29·643	29·643	29·640	29·637	29·633	29·633	29·641	29·650	29·64
1868	..	..	..	..	..	..	..	..	..	..
1869	30	29·828	29·826	29·824	29·821	29·820	29·823	29·831	29·840	29·84
1870	29	30·027	30·022	30·016	30·013	30·010	30·010	30·016	30·021	30·02
1871	30	29·638	29·652	29·645	29·635	29·631	29·631	29·638	29·645	29·64
1872	30	29·737	29·734	29·731	29·731	29·728	29·730	29·737	29·741	29·74
1873	30	29·831	29·826	29·822	29·820	29·819	29·821	29·823	29·827	29·82
Means	..	29·8089	29·8061	29·8023	29·7993	29·7973	29·7975	29·8024	29·8075	29·81

In the month of

in each YEAR from 1854 to 1873, for the MONTH of MARCH.

Noon.	1h. p.m.	2h. p.m.	3h. p.m.	4h. p.m.	5h. p.m.	6h. p.m.	7h. p.m.	8h. p.m.	9h. p.m.	10h. p.m.	11h. p.m.	Mean.	Year.
in.	in.	in.	in.	in.	in.	in.	in.	in.	in.	in.	in.	in.	
30·200	30·193	30·183	30·176	30·171	30·167	30·172	30·179	30·183	30·193	30·197	30·198	30·190	1854
29·557	29·551	29·544	29·539	29·537	29·531	29·537	29·545	29·558	29·568	29·574	29·578	29·549	1855
30·039	30·033	30·027	30·022	30·019	30·018	30·017	30·023	30·027	30·032	30·032	30·030	30·036	1856
29·726	29·714	29·707	29·702	29·699	29·702	29·708	29·711	29·710	29·721	29·720	29·720	29·724	1857
29·783	29·775	29·767	29·761	29·758	29·758	29·759	29·762	29·762	29·762	29·760	29·757	29·769	1858
29·772	29·765	29·759	29·753	29·750	29·750	29·754	29·751	29·754	29·764	29·764	29·762	29·771	1859
29·673	29·662	29·653	29·649	29·646	29·647	29·649	29·654	29·656	29·653	29·654	29·633	29·666	1860
29·624	29·616	29·610	29·605	29·602	29·602	29·606	29·614	29·624	29·629	29·633	29·633	29·620	1861
29·557	29·552	29·541	29·537	29·534	29·531	29·531	29·533	29·536	29·539	29·541	29·542	29·515	1862
29·704	29·690	29·682	29·677	29·674	29·677	29·684	29·688	29·695	29·704	29·706	29·708	29·699	1863
29·515	29·511	29·508	29·508	29·507	29·511	29·514	29·516	29·520	29·524	29·528	29·533	29·517	1864
29·731	29·726	29·719	29·715	29·716	29·715	29·720	29·727	29·731	29·738	29·739	29·741	29·724	1865
29·540	29·534	29·527	29·525	29·521	29·521	29·526	29·533	29·534	29·536	29·536	29·535	29·531	1866
29·636	29·629	29·624	29·620	29·617	29·616	29·617	29·625	29·627	29·637	29·635	29·631	29·627	1867
29·837	29·831	29·825	29·821	29·820	29·822	29·828	29·833	29·835	29·837	29·837	29·837	29·822	1868
29·639	29·634	29·630	29·624	29·623	29·627	29·636	29·643	29·648	29·652	29·651	29·650	29·638	1869
29·874	29·871	29·862	29·858	29·859	29·863	29·873	29·879	29·884	29·892	29·893	29·893	29·867	1870
29·891	29·886	29·877	29·866	29·858	29·859	29·874	29·881	29·884	29·884	29·878	29·878	29·878	1871
29·639	29·633	29·623	29·615	29·611	29·614	29·622	29·629	29·633	29·635	29·634	29·635	29·632	1872
29·633	29·623	29·618	29·613	29·613	29·614	29·620	29·631	29·635	29·641	29·641	29·641	29·631	1873
29·7286	29·7213	29·7144	29·7093	29·7067	29·7073	29·7119	29·7175	29·7222	29·7270	29·7280	29·7280	29·7217	..

in each YEAR from 1854 to 1873, for the MONTH of APRIL.

Noon.	1h. p.m.	2h. p.m.	3h. p.m.	4h. p.m.	5h. p.m.	6h. p.m.	7h. p.m.	8h. p.m.	9h. p.m.	10h. p.m.	11h. p.m.	Mean.	Year.
in.	in.	in.	in.	in.	in.	in.	in.	in.	in.	in.	in.	in.	
29·988	29·982	29·976	29·967	29·964	29·958	29·962	29·971	29·978	29·983	29·988	29·989	29·989	1854
29·944	29·936	29·929	29·919	29·916	29·915	29·915	29·923	29·935	29·939	29·944	29·944	29·936	1855
29·611	29·605	29·599	29·595	29·592	29·595	29·596	29·600	29·608	29·614	29·618	29·615	29·606	1856
29·637	29·634	29·631	29·625	29·624	29·626	29·628	29·634	29·641	29·642	29·643	29·643	29·628	1857
29·798	29·794	29·790	29·787	29·783	29·780	29·779	29·781	29·781	29·780	29·782	29·786	29·781	1858
29·624	29·619	29·618	29·613	29·611	29·606	29·605	29·607	29·610	29·616	29·617	29·614	29·613	1859
29·759	29·758	29·755	29·754	29·753	29·756	29·763	29·773	29·782	29·791	29·795	29·795	29·752	1860
30·007	30·006	29·998	29·992	29·991	29·990	29·990	29·994	30·000	30·008	30·012	30·013	29·999	1861
29·863	29·861	29·857	29·852	29·847	29·847	29·845	29·850	29·859	29·863	29·861	29·862	29·858	1862
29·819	29·811	29·808	29·805	29·803	29·803	29·805	29·809	29·816	29·824	29·827	29·830	29·814	1863
29·925	29·920	29·914	29·906	29·903	29·903	29·903	29·908	29·914	29·920	29·924	29·925	29·915	1864
29·963	29·954	29·944	29·935	29·932	29·930	29·933	29·938	29·948	29·964	29·968	29·968	29·938	1865
29·752	29·747	29·741	29·735	29·730	29·729	29·730	29·735	29·742	29·747	29·748	29·747	29·744	1866
29·641	29·635	29·629	29·620	29·617	29·615	29·614	29·613	29·619	29·625	29·627	29·627	29·634	1867
..	..	..	..	..	..	..	..	..	..	..	..	..	1868
29·837	29·833	29·828	29·820	29·817	29·817	29·820	29·824	29·833	29·837	29·837	29·837	29·831	1869
30·007	30·000	29·991	29·979	29·974	29·971	29·971	29·975	29·983	29·987	29·989	29·989	30·001	1870
29·652	29·649	29·645	29·640	29·639	29·643	29·647	29·656	29·666	29·666	29·666	29·669	29·649	1871
29·737	29·734	29·729	29·724	29·722	29·723	29·729	29·739	29·751	29·757	29·760	29·766	29·737	1872
29·825	29·820	29·814	29·807	29·807	29·808	29·812	29·822	29·832	29·840	29·840	29·842	29·825	1873
29·8099	29·8052	29·7998	29·7934	29·7909	29·7903	29·7919	29·7975	29·8052	29·8107	29·8129	29·8134	29·8041	..

were not sufficiently complete to be used.

TABLE V.—MEAN READING of the BAROMETER at every HOUR of the DAY

Year	Number of Days employed in forming the Means	Midnight.	1ʰ. a.m.	2ʰ. a.m.	3ʰ. a.m.	4ʰ. a.m.	5ʰ. a.m.	6ʰ. a.m.	7ʰ. a.m.	8ʰ. a.m.	9ʰ. a.m.	10ʰ. a.m.	11ʰ. a.m.
		in.	in.	in.	in.	in.	in.	in.	in.	in.	in.	in.	in.
1854	31	29·675	29·671	29·667	29·661	29·657	29·655	29·659	29·666	29·673	29·676	29·676	29·675
1855	27	29·727	29·720	29·713	29·710	29·707	29·702	29·703	29·707	29·710	29·712	29·707	29·702
1856	31	29·662	29·655	29·653	29·646	29·643	29·643	29·644	29·645	29·648	29·649	29·649	29·648
1857	27	29·808	29·805	29·806	29·802	29·798	29·801	29·803	29·806	29·811	29·814	29·813	29·811
1858	30	29·753	29·750	29·748	29·749	29·751	29·756	29·762	29·767	29·770	29·773	29·772	29·770
1859	31	29·809	29·807	29·805	29·801	29·798	29·797	29·797	29·797	29·795	29·795	29·793	29·794
1860	22	29·770	29·767	29·764	29·760	29·760	29·761	29·764	29·766	29·768	29·768	29·763	29·761
1861	31	29·933	29·931	29·929	29·927	29·925	29·928	29·929	29·930	29·935	29·936	29·933	29·933
1862	21	29·792	29·788	29·785	29·783	29·781	29·780	29·782	29·775	29·775	29·778	29·776	29·775
1863	31	29·866	29·864	29·863	29·862	29·860	29·862	29·864	29·866	29·868	29·871	29·868	29·865
1864	12	29·740	29·735	29·728	29·726	29·722	29·721	29·719	29·709	29·707	29·708	29·708	29·704
1865	31	29·775	29·769	29·767	29·762	29·760	29·762	29·767	29·773	29·776	29·778	29·781	29·779
1866	31	29·823	29·820	29·816	29·811	29·808	29·810	29·814	29·815	29·818	29·819	29·818	29·817
1867	31	29·736	29·732	29·731	29·726	29·726	29·730	29·732	29·739	29·741	29·742	29·743	29·745
1868	29	29·862	29·861	29·856	29·853	29·851	29·854	29·860	29·864	29·868	29·865	29·863	29·861
1869	31	29·663	29·658	29·655	29·650	29·648	29·652	29·653	29·656	29·661	29·659	29·659	29·656
1870	31	29·902	29·900	29·898	29·895	29·894	29·898	29·903	29·910	29·912	29·911	29·910	29·907
1871	30	29·914	29·910	29·907	29·903	29·903	29·908	29·914	29·917	29·919	29·920	29·919	29·915
1872	29	29·736	29·729	29·725	29·721	29·719	29·721	29·722	29·723	29·725	29·722	29·717	29·711
1873	31	29·814	29·809	29·808	29·805	29·802	29·803	29·806	29·808	29·809	29·808	29·807	29·805
Means	..	29·7980	29·7841	29·7813	29·7777	29·7757	29·7773	29·7800	29·7810	29·7844	29·7852	29·7859	29·7817

TABLE VI.—MEAN READING of the BAROMETER at every HOUR of the DAY

Year	Number of Days employed in forming the Means	Midnight.	1ʰ. a.m.	2ʰ. a.m.	3ʰ. a.m.	4ʰ. p.m.	5ʰ. a.m.	6ʰ. a.m.	7ʰ. a.m.	8ʰ. a.m.	9ʰ. a.m.	10ʰ. a.m.	11ʰ. a.m.
		in.	in.	in.	in.	in.	in.	in.	in.	in.	in.	in.	in.
1854	30	29·751	29·744	29·740	29·736	29·731	29·729	29·728	29·730	29·734	29·736	29·735	29·729
1855	30	29·855	29·851	29·849	29·846	29·844	29·842	29·845	29·853	29·862	29·867	29·871	29·868
1856	30	29·877	29·874	29·870	29·868	29·868	29·871	29·873	29·877	29·881	29·883	29·884	29·884
1857	28	29·887	29·886	29·878	29·872	29·872	29·876	29·878	29·883	29·886	29·888	29·885	29·883
1858	28	29·931	29·930	29·927	29·924	29·922	29·923	29·928	29·934	29·937	29·935	29·932	29·933
1859	30	29·765	29·764	29·762	29·762	29·760	29·761	29·761	29·764	29·767	29·770	29·770	29·769
1860	25	29·601	29·599	29·594	29·591	29·589	29·592	29·599	29·606	29·610	29·614	29·613	29·617
1861	30	29·782	29·780	29·778	29·776	29·776	29·777	29·779	29·783	29·787	29·785	29·785	29·783
1862	27	29·750	29·747	29·745	29·743	29·740	29·741	29·742	29·743	29·744	29·743	29·736	29·733
1863	30	29·733	29·730	29·729	29·727	29·728	29·728	29·731	29·731	29·733	29·733	29·732	29·733
1864	..	..	..	..	..	..	..	..	..	..	..	..	..
1865	30	30·042	30·040	30·037	30·034	30·033	30·035	30·030	30·042	30·045	30·046	30·047	30·045
1866	30	29·774	29·769	29·764	29·760	29·766	29·766	29·772	29·777	29·784	29·784	29·784	29·784
1867	30	29·951	29·947	29·945	29·939	29·939	29·942	29·945	29·946	29·949	29·948	29·948	29·944
1868	30	29·978	29·977	29·974	29·974	29·974	29·979	29·984	29·990	29·995	29·996	29·994	29·988
1869	30	29·927	29·924	29·920	29·917	29·915	29·919	29·919	29·922	29·923	29·923	29·922	29·925
1870	30	29·952	29·949	29·945	29·942	29·943	29·950	29·954	29·959	29·961	29·950	29·950	29·955
1871	29	29·787	29·781	29·774	29·768	29·766	29·764	29·764	29·766	29·767	29·768	29·765	29·763
1872	30	29·744	29·740	29·739	29·734	29·735	29·740	29·743	29·747	29·750	29·749	29·747	29·744
1873	30	29·803	29·797	29·795	29·790	29·789	29·791	29·796	29·801	29·804	29·803	29·802	29·801
Means	..	29·8363	29·8333	29·8295	29·8265	29·8257	29·8275	29·8304	29·8344	29·8379	29·8386	29·8378	29·8361

In the month of June 1864 the photographic records

in each YEAR from 1854 to 1873, for the MONTH of MAY.

Noon.	1ʰ. p.m.	2ʰ. p.m.	3ʰ. p.m.	4ʰ. p.m.	5ʰ. p.m.	6ʰ. p.m.	7ʰ. p.m.	8ʰ. p.m.	9ʰ. p.m.	10ʰ. p.m.	11ʰ. p.m.	Mean.	Year.
in.	in.	in.	in.	in.	in.	in.	in.	in.	in.	in.	in.	in.	
29·677	29·673	29·673	29·668	29·666	29·664	29·667	29·673	29·680	29·691	29·696	29·699	29·672	1854
29·702	29·699	29·693	29·688	29·682	29·675	29·675	29·681	29·684	29·696	29·699	29·699	29·700	1855
29·646	29·644	29·642	29·640	29·639	29·643	29·645	29·651	29·658	29·666	29·669	29·667	29·650	1856
29·806	29·802	29·795	29·792	29·788	29·786	29·785	29·785	29·794	29·807	29·811	29·814	29·802	1857
29·769	29·763	29·760	29·757	29·760	29·761	29·763	29·765	29·775	29·783	29·784	29·786	29·764	1858
29·790	29·785	29·781	29·775	29·775	29·776	29·777	29·781	29·789	29·800	29·806	29·808	29·793	1859
29·757	29·752	29·747	29·743	29·741	29·740	29·742	29·748	29·749	29·752	29·751	29·748	29·756	1860
29·929	29·925	29·918	29·913	29·909	29·905	29·906	29·911	29·915	29·920	29·922	29·922	29·924	1861
29·769	29·765	29·761	29·758	29·760	29·759	29·760	29·761	29·765	29·775	29·778	29·779	29·773	1862
29·860	29·852	29·847	29·843	29·841	29·842	29·840	29·841	29·851	29·859	29·863	29·866	29·858	1863
29·709	29·709	29·713	29·713	29·716	29·716	29·714	29·715	29·716	29·720	29·719	29·720	29·717	1864
29·775	29·769	29·763	29·758	29·752	29·747	29·746	29·749	29·736	29·771	29·772	29·774	29·766	1865
29·814	29·808	29·806	29·804	29·804	29·801	29·803	29·810	29·818	29·824	29·826	29·827	29·814	1866
29·741	29·736	29·733	29·730	29·728	29·725	29·727	29·731	29·740	29·747	29·747	29·747	29·736	1867
29·855	29·849	29·844	29·837	29·834	29·834	29·836	29·841	29·850	29·859	29·865	29·868	29·854	1868
29·652	29·649	29·646	29·641	29·639	29·636	29·639	29·643	29·651	29·661	29·665	29·666	29·652	1869
29·900	29·893	29·884	29·877	29·874	29·871	29·874	29·881	29·891	29·901	29·905	29·909	29·896	1870
29·910	29·907	29·899	29·891	29·888	29·884	29·884	29·887	29·898	29·906	29·911	29·914	29·905	1871
29·700	29·703	29·701	29·695	29·694	29·691	29·695	29·700	29·710	29·717	29·721	29·719	29·714	1872
29·797	29·793	29·790	29·781	29·775	29·775	29·777	29·782	29·792	29·802	29·805	29·807	29·798	1873
29·7784	29·7738	29·7699	29·7652	29·7632	29·7616	29·7627	29·7668	29·7741	29·7829	29·7857	29·7870	29·7772	··

in each YEAR from 1854 to 1873, for the MONTH of JUNE.

Noon.	1ʰ. p.m.	2ʰ. p.m.	3ʰ. p.m.	4ʰ. p.m.	5ʰ. p.m.	6ʰ. p.m.	7ʰ. p.m.	8ʰ. p.m.	9ʰ. p.m.	10ʰ. p.m.	11ʰ. p.m.	Mean.	Year.
in.	in.	in.	in.	in.	in.	in.	in.	in.	in.	in.	in.	in.	
29·729	29·726	29·726	29·726	29·723	29·720	29·721	29·728	29·734	29·747	29·749	29·750	29·734	1854
29·868	29·867	29·861	29·855	29·850	29·844	29·843	29·850	29·855	29·870	29·873	29·875	29·857	1855
29·880	29·876	29·871	29·868	29·865	29·864	29·864	29·871	29·877	29·885	29·891	29·893	29·873	1856
29·878	29·874	29·870	29·866	29·865	29·864	29·864	29·866	29·870	29·878	29·880	29·881	29·876	1857
29·930	29·926	29·920	29·914	29·910	29·908	29·910	29·910	29·912	29·922	29·929	29·928	29·924	1858
29·768	29·761	29·758	29·754	29·754	29·755	29·754	29·757	29·764	29·773	29·776	29·778	29·764	1859
29·613	29·613	29·613	29·611	29·612	29·611	29·611	29·617	29·624	29·636	29·642	29·646	29·611	1860
29·782	29·777	29·774	29·775	29·770	29·770	29·771	29·771	29·779	29·790	29·793	29·793	29·780	1861
29·732	29·727	29·724	29·718	29·716	29·714	29·710	29·711	29·712	29·718	29·719	29·722	29·730	1862
29·731	29·727	29·725	29·722	29·721	29·718	29·715	29·717	29·720	29·732	29·733	29·734	29·728	1863
30·039	30·030	30·026	30·020	30·014	30·009	30·009	30·009	30·013	30·024	30·014	30·026	30·030	1864
													1865
29·778	29·769	29·767	29·763	29·760	29·756	29·758	29·762	29·769	29·779	29·779	29·780	29·771	1866
29·938	29·931	29·927	29·921	29·916	29·916	29·918	29·921	29·929	29·939	29·938	29·942	29·937	1867
29·985	29·980	29·976	29·969	29·963	29·958	29·959	29·962	29·967	29·979	29·984	29·987	29·978	1868
29·923	29·921	29·918	29·914	29·910	29·905	29·907	29·910	29·918	29·928	29·930	29·930	29·920	1869
29·950	29·943	29·939	29·933	29·927	29·923	29·924	29·929	29·939	29·957	29·958	29·946	29·924	1870
29·762	29·758	29·757	29·754	29·735	29·734	29·735	29·760	29·765	29·776	29·777	29·777	29·767	1871
29·738	29·734	29·727	29·721	29·716	29·713	29·715	29·717	29·729	29·739	29·742	29·736	29·730	1872
29·797	29·794	29·792	29·786	29·783	29·780	29·780	29·783	29·789	29·797	29·801	29·802	29·794	1873
29·8327	29·8282	29·8248	29·8204	29·8174	29·8148	29·8151	29·8188	29·8245	29·8351	29·8378	29·8392	29·8293	··

were not sufficiently complete to be used.

RESULTS OF THE OBSERVATIONS OF THE BAROMETER

TABLE VII.—MEAN READING of the BAROMETER at every Hour of the Day

Year.	Number of Days employed in forming the Means.	Midnight.	1ʰ. a.m.	2ʰ. a.m.	3ʰ. a.m.	4ʰ. a.m.	5ʰ. a.m.	6ʰ. a.m.	7ʰ. a.m.	8ʰ. a.m.	9ʰ. a.m.	10ʰ. a.m.	11ʰ. a.m.
		in.	in.	in.	in.	in.	in.	in.	in.	in.	in.	in.	in.
1854	31	29·823	29·821	29·817	29·812	29·808	29·804	29·803	29·807	29·814	29·816	29·815	29·815
1855	29	29·754	29·751	29·746	29·741	29·738	29·731	29·728	29·732	29·737	29·738	29·739	29·736
1856	29	29·817	29·815	29·815	29·812	29·813	29·815	29·817	29·819	29·819	29·824	29·826	29·825
1857	29	29·824	29·819	29·815	29·808	29·808	29·810	29·814	29·821	29·825	29·829	29·832	29·831
1858	27	29·796	29·789	29·787	29·785	29·784	29·786	29·788	29·791	29·797	29·797	29·795	29·791
1859	31	29·955	29·954	29·951	29·947	29·945	29·944	29·944	29·945	29·948	29·950	29·949	29·949
1860	31	29·861	29·857	29·854	29·852	29·851	29·850	29·851	29·853	29·856	29·855	29·854	29·854
1861	20	29·632	29·627	29·625	29·622	29·622	29·621	29·621	29·625	29·628	29·628	29·626	29·628
1862	?8	29·799	29·800	29·799	29·798	29·794	29·792	29·789	29·788	29·788	29·790	29·788	29·785
1863	28	29·947	29·948	29·946	29·945	29·946	29·948	29·949	29·951	29·934	29·951	29·950	29·944
1864	29	29·866	29·866	29·864	29·863	29·863	29·865	29·868	29·873	29·877	29·877	29·875	29·875
1865	29	29·808	29·805	29·802	29·798	29·799	29·800	29·804	29·808	29·812	29·813	29·811	29·812
1866	31	29·779	29·773	29·764	29·762	29·762	29·764	29·768	29·774	29·777	29·778	29·778	29·776
1867	29	29·753	29·747	29·742	29·739	29·741	29·743	29·746	29·750	29·754	29·755	29·756	29·754
1868	31	29·907	29·902	29·896	29·891	29·892	29·893	29·898	29·903	29·908	29·907	29·905	29·904
1869	31	29·931	29·928	29·926	29·922	29·923	29·928	29·934	29·939	29·943	29·943	29·943	29·940
1870	31	29·832	29·836	29·823	29·817	29·814	29·818	29·823	29·827	29·830	29·831	29·830	29·829
1871	31	29·603	29·687	29·682	29·677	29·676	29·680	29·684	29·689	29·692	29·693	29·694	29·695
1872	31	29·766	29·759	29·754	29·748	29·747	29·749	29·750	29·756	29·760	29·764	29·768	29·768
1873	31	29·799	29·796	29·792	29·789	29·790	29·793	29·799	29·803	29·807	29·807	29·803	29·802
Means	..	29·8171	29·8135	29·8099	29·8064	29·8059	29·8067	29·8089	29·8128	29·8163	29·8173	29·8169	29·8156

TABLE VIII.—MEAN READING of the BAROMETER at every Hour of the Day

Year.	Number of Days employed in forming the Means.	Midnight.	1ʰ. a.m.	2ʰ. a.m.	3ʰ. a.m.	4ʰ. a.m.	5ʰ. a.m.	6ʰ. a.m.	7ʰ. a.m.	8ʰ. a.m.	9ʰ. a.m.	10ʰ. a.m.	11ʰ. a.m.
		in.	in.	in.	in.	in.	in.	in.	in.	in.	in.	in.	in.
1854	29	29·885	29·882	29·878	29·872	29·869	29·866	29·871	29·878	29·884	29·894	29·894	29·893
1855	29	29·856	29·853	29·849	29·846	29·842	29·841	29·847	29·851	29·858	29·864	29·867	29·866
1856	29	29·734	29·731	29·724	29·722	29·720	29·720	29·724	29·730	29·737	29·742	29·743	29·736
1857	31	29·846	29·843	29·838	29·835	29·831	29·833	29·837	29·838	29·843	29·848	29·847	29·844
1858	31	29·842	29·836	29·832	29·830	29·828	29·831	29·834	29·839	29·843	29·844	29·841	29·836
1859	31	29·829	29·829	29·825	29·820	29·815	29·815	29·818	29·820	29·824	29·828	29·827	29·828
1860	31	29·577	29·572	29·565	29·558	29·555	29·553	29·554	29·559	29·563	29·566	29·569	29·565
1861	25	29·870	29·867	29·866	29·863	29·863	29·863	29·878	29·875	29·878	29·882	29·880	29·879
1862	31	29·795	29·791	29·787	29·783	29·782	29·780	29·781	29·784	29·788	29·793	29·791	29·790
1863	27	29·770	29·770	29·765	29·759	29·754	29·754	29·754	29·753	29·756	29·757	29·757	29·758
1864	30	29·932	29·932	29·932	29·931	29·931	29·932	29·936	29·940	29·943	29·946	29·944	29·939
1865	31	29·709	29·708	29·704	29·702	29·600	29·703	29·708	29·711	29·718	29·722	29·723	29·720
1866	31	29·641	29·634	29·628	29·625	29·623	29·627	29·632	29·641	29·645	29·649	29·649	29·647
1867	31	29·837	29·835	29·831	29·825	29·824	29·825	29·827	29·833	29·838	29·848	29·842	29·840
1868	29	29·767	29·764	29·760	29·754	29·751	29·751	29·755	29·760	29·762	29·762	29·763	29·762
1869	31	29·073	29·069	29·066	29·062	29·958	29·961	29·966	29·973	29·979	29·982	29·981	29·978
1870	31	29·811	29·805	29·801	29·796	29·794	29·797	29·801	29·806	29·810	29·812	29·816	29·815
1871	31	29·868	29·862	29·858	29·856	29·834	29·837	29·852	29·864	29·868	29·871	29·874	29·873
1872	29	29·768	29·794	29·791	29·790	29·786	29·787	29·791	29·797	29·804	29·811	29·810	29·809
1873	31	29·778	29·775	29·771	29·766	29·762	29·765	29·770	29·775	29·778	29·779	29·780	29·774
Means	..	29·8059	29·8025	29·7985	29·7946	29·7921	29·7933	29·7977	29·8020	29·8065	29·8058	29·8099	29·8074

In each YEAR from 1854 to 1873, for the MONTH of JULY.

Noon.	1ʰ. p.m.	2ʰ. p.m.	3ʰ. p.m.	4ʰ. p.m.	5ʰ. p.m.	6ʰ. p.m.	7ʰ. p.m.	8ʰ. p.m.	9ʰ. p.m.	10ʰ. p.m.	11ʰ. p.m.	Mean.	Year.
in.	in.	in.	in.	in.	in.	in.	in.	in.	in.	in.	in.	in.	
29·813	29·812	29·808	29·803	29·798	29·791	29·788	29·794	29·801	29·811	29·815	29·818	29·808	1854
29·736	29·736	29·732	29·728	29·723	29·717	29·717	29·722	29·729	29·739	29·746	29·745	29·735	1855
29·820	29·817	29·814	29·811	29·811	29·812	29·809	29·810	29·810	29·817	29·819	29·819	29·816	1856
29·828	29·825	29·824	29·824	29·820	29·818	29·816	29·821	29·830	29·840	29·844	29·846	29·824	1857
29·787	29·788	29·788	29·787	29·785	29·781	29·779	29·780	29·787	29·793	29·797	29·798	29·789	1858
29·944	29·939	29·935	29·930	29·929	29·928	29·927	29·927	29·930	29·937	29·942	29·944	29·942	1859
29·851	29·843	29·842	29·838	29·834	29·834	29·834	29·835	29·840	29·848	29·850	29·852	29·848	1860
29·625	29·622	29·619	29·617	29·614	29·609	29·610	29·612	29·615	29·620	29·620	29·617	29·622	1861
29·785	29·779	29·778	29·774	29·774	29·771	29·770	29·773	29·777	29·787	29·790	29·790	29·786	1862
29·942	29·937	29·935	29·930	29·925	29·921	29·919	29·919	29·924	29·933	29·936	29·938	29·939	1863
29·871	29·864	29·862	29·860	29·855	29·851	29·850	29·853	29·855	29·865	29·868	29·870	29·865	1864
29·809	29·804	29·801	29·799	29·794	29·791	29·791	29·795	29·800	29·811	29·814	29·815	29·804	1865
29·773	29·766	29·764	29·761	29·758	29·758	29·760	29·763	29·773	29·780	29·785	29·786	29·770	1866
29·757	29·755	29·754	29·751	29·748	29·745	29·745	29·751	29·757	29·764	29·764	29·765	29·752	1867
29·899	29·892	29·883	29·876	29·869	29·865	29·869	29·876	29·887	29·896	29·903	29·906	29·893	1868
29·933	29·926	29·918	29·913	29·905	29·909	29·899	29·899	29·903	29·920	29·923	29·924	29·924	1869
29·834	29·819	29·816	29·808	29·802	29·799	29·798	29·803	29·811	29·822	29·824	29·823	29·818	1870
29·692	29·691	29·689	29·686	29·684	29·686	29·686	29·688	29·694	29·703	29·702	29·700	29·689	1871
29·766	29·762	29·759	29·754	29·750	29·746	29·747	29·752	29·760	29·766	29·771	29·772	29·758	1872
29·797	29·793	29·788	29·783	29·779	29·775	29·776	29·779	29·786	29·797	29·802	29·804	29·793	1873
29·8126	29·8085	29·8055	29·8016	29·7980	29·7947	29·7945	29·7979	29·8038	29·8123	29·8158	29·8166	29·8087	..

In each YEAR from 1854 to 1873, for the MONTH of AUGUST.

Noon.	1ʰ. p.m.	2ʰ. p.m.	3ʰ. p.m.	4ʰ. p.m.	5ʰ. p.m.	6ʰ. p.m.	7ʰ. p.m.	8ʰ. p.m.	9ʰ. p.m.	10ʰ. p.m.	11ʰ. p.m.	Mean.	Year.
in.	in.	in.	in.	in.	in.	in.	in.	in.	in.	in.	in.	in.	
29·892	29·891	29·887	29·883	29·881	29·875	29·876	29·882	29·892	29·901	29·905	29·912	29·885	1854
29·862	29·857	29·857	29·851	29·851	29·850	29·846	29·849	29·857	29·863	29·866	29·868	29·855	1855
29·731	29·728	29·728	29·722	29·716	29·714	29·710	29·714	29·720	29·722	29·724	29·724	29·725	1856
29·841	29·837	29·833	29·830	29·830	29·828	29·829	29·830	29·835	29·840	29·843	29·843	29·837	1857
29·831	29·827	29·822	29·814	29·812	29·810	29·808	29·811	29·818	29·826	29·829	29·829	29·828	1858
29·825	29·823	29·817	29·812	29·811	29·808	29·807	29·806	29·810	29·822	29·824	29·826	29·820	1859
29·559	29·554	29·551	29·549	29·547	29·547	29·549	29·555	29·562	29·567	29·569	29·569	29·559	1860
29·876	29·869	29·866	29·862	29·859	29·858	29·857	29·859	29·866	29·870	29·870	29·867	29·868	1861
29·797	29·785	29·782	29·779	29·779	29·777	29·778	29·781	29·790	29·798	29·802	29·800	29·787	1862
29·755	29·752	29·751	29·747	29·746	29·743	29·742	29·745	29·756	29·759	29·761	29·761	29·755	1863
29·931	29·924	29·919	29·914	29·910	29·905	29·904	29·907	29·915	29·924	29·927	29·931	29·928	1864
29·716	29·711	29·710	29·704	29·700	29·698	29·699	29·705	29·712	29·723	29·725	29·728	29·711	1865
29·642	29·637	29·637	29·632	29·632	29·632	29·629	29·629	29·648	29·649	29·647	29·658	29·638	1866
29·833	29·830	29·826	29·822	29·819	29·815	29·817	29·822	29·830	29·836	29·834	29·834	29·830	1867
29·756	29·752	29·750	29·745	29·740	29·740	29·742	29·745	29·756	29·772	29·772	29·761	29·755	1868
29·973	29·967	29·959	29·953	29·948	29·947	29·948	29·955	29·970	29·979	29·984	29·986	29·969	1869
29·808	29·807	29·802	29·797	29·794	29·792	29·796	29·804	29·817	29·825	29·827	29·827	29·806	1870
29·862	29·854	29·846	29·841	29·836	29·833	29·834	29·842	29·850	29·855	29·856	29·858	29·848	1871
29·802	29·801	29·796	29·794	29·790	29·789	29·789	29·797	29·806	29·810	29·811	29·811	29·800	1872
29·770	29·766	29·761	29·755	29·751	29·750	29·752	29·758	29·768	29·772	29·773	29·774	29·768	1873
29·8027	29·7986	29·7950	29·7903	29·7877	29·7853	29·7856	29·7905	29·7989	29·8054	29·8080	29·8089	29·7990	..

B

TABLE IX.—MEAN READING of the BAROMETER at every HOUR of the DAY

Year	Number of Days employed in forming the Means	Midnight	1h. a.m.	2h. a.m.	3h. a.m.	4h. a.m.	5h. a.m.	6h. a.m.	7h. a.m.	8h. a.m.	9h. a.m.	10h. a.m.	11h. a.m.
		in.	in.	in.	in.	in.	in.	in.	in.	in.	in.	in.	in.
1854	30	30.048	30.048	30.044	30.040	30.036	30.031	30.032	30.038	30.047	30.054	30.056	30.053
1855	28	30.004	29.999	29.993	29.988	29.984	29.979	29.981	29.986	29.990	29.993	29.990	29.984
1856	30	29.657	29.657	29.653	29.650	29.646	29.649	29.653	29.657	29.660	29.663	29.660	29.661
1857	30	29.794	29.789	29.785	29.782	29.778	29.778	29.780	29.781	29.786	29.794	29.795	29.793
1858	16	29.825	29.819	29.809	29.803	29.799	29.800	29.804	29.809	29.812	29.820	29.821	29.816
1859	28	29.699	29.696	29.690	29.686	29.682	29.681	29.684	29.691	29.700	29.708	29.708	29.708
1860	30	29.741	29.734	29.732	29.730	29.728	29.728	29.734	29.744	29.755	29.764	29.768	29.767
1861	26	29.708	29.702	29.697	29.693	29.689	29.692	29.696	29.701	29.707	29.710	29.710	29.706
1862	27	29.891	29.885	29.881	29.877	29.873	29.872	29.875	29.876	29.883	29.889	29.887	29.885
1863	29	29.714	29.712	29.706	29.700	29.696	29.694	29.693	29.695	29.698	29.701	29.699	29.700
1864	30	29.769	29.766	29.761	29.760	29.758	29.761	29.767	29.778	29.784	29.791	29.792	29.789
1865	30	30.073	30.071	30.067	30.063	30.060	30.060	30.065	30.074	30.081	30.089	30.090	30.087
1866	30	29.578	29.574	29.570	29.566	29.565	29.564	29.569	29.573	29.575	29.576	29.576	29.575
1867	28	29.900	29.896	29.893	29.889	29.884	29.883	29.889	29.894	29.902	29.910	29.912	29.910
1868	30	29.720	29.714	29.709	29.705	29.700	29.697	29.700	29.707	29.709	29.712	29.710	29.704
1869	30	29.655	29.651	29.644	29.639	29.630	29.623	29.628	29.637	29.646	29.653	29.658	29.655
1870	30	29.909	29.904	29.900	29.894	29.894	29.893	29.901	29.908	29.912	29.915	29.916	29.909
1871	30	29.718	29.713	29.706	29.698	29.695	29.696	29.702	29.711	29.718	29.728	29.733	29.732
1872	30	29.686	29.684	29.681	29.672	29.672	29.672	29.678	29.684	29.691	29.696	29.696	29.692
1873	30	29.799	29.796	29.790	29.785	29.781	29.781	29.787	29.795	29.802	29.804	29.806	29.800
Means	..	29.7944	29.7905	29.7837	29.7811	29.7775	29.7767	29.7810	29.7870	29.7929	29.7986	29.7991	29.7963

TABLE X.—MEAN READING of the BAROMETER at every HOUR of the DAY

Year	Number of Days employed in forming the Means	Midnight	1h. p.m.	2h. p.m.	3h. p.m.	4h. p.m.	5h. p.m.	6h. p.m.	7h. p.m.	8h. p.m.	9h. p.m.	10h. p.m.	11h. p.m.
		in.	in.	in.	in.	in.	in.	in.	in.	in.	in.	in.	in.
1854	29	29.717	29.714	29.707	29.699	29.691	29.684	29.679	29.681	29.692	29.700	29.704	29.703
1855	30	29.525	29.526	29.526	29.521	29.517	29.514	29.514	29.523	29.533	29.540	29.540	29.541
1856	31	29.991	29.987	29.984	29.981	29.979	29.981	29.983	29.988	29.998	30.005	30.005	30.003
1857	31	29.714	29.712	29.708	29.703	29.701	29.699	29.700	29.705	29.711	29.714	29.711	29.707
1858	31	29.834	29.832	29.829	29.827	29.826	29.826	29.829	29.837	29.846	29.849	29.850	29.845
1859	28	29.537	29.535	29.530	29.528	29.525	29.525	29.525	29.520	29.535	29.536	29.536	29.535
1860	31	29.871	29.868	29.864	29.857	29.854	29.851	29.850	29.856	29.856	29.868	29.868	29.867
1861	26	29.874	29.872	29.871	29.864	29.864	29.865	29.869	29.872	29.884	29.889	29.886	29.883
1862	17	29.688	29.686	29.686	29.670	29.671	29.665	29.658	29.655	29.659	29.667	29.660	29.658
1863	31	29.657	29.656	29.650	29.645	29.642	29.642	29.643	29.642	29.649	29.655	29.655	29.656
1864	29	29.681	29.679	29.673	29.669	29.668	29.668	29.671	29.675	29.682	29.684	29.688	29.687
1865	31	29.476	29.473	29.466	29.455	29.451	29.444	29.446	29.448	29.451	29.453	29.451	29.451
1866	30	29.941	29.937	29.932	29.927	29.925	29.925	29.927	29.933	29.941	29.943	29.943	29.943
1867	27	29.738	29.734	29.729	29.721	29.718	29.720	29.720	29.728	29.736	29.739	29.746	29.744
1868	31	29.785	29.786	29.777	29.777	29.779	29.779	29.783	29.787	29.796	29.806	29.800	29.811
1869	31	29.867	29.862	29.858	29.851	29.849	29.849	29.852	29.861	29.870	29.874	29.875	29.874
1870	31	29.600	29.598	29.593	29.584	29.579	29.578	29.576	29.576	29.578	29.580	29.581	29.575
1871	31	29.796	29.790	29.784	29.778	29.773	29.771	29.773	29.782	29.789	29.794	29.799	29.798
1872	31	29.545	29.541	29.537	29.532	29.530	29.531	29.533	29.539	29.548	29.551	29.551	29.551
1873	30	29.739	29.738	29.730	29.725	29.721	29.717	29.718	29.723	29.728	29.727	29.727	29.724
Means	..	29.7288	29.7263	29.7216	29.7158	29.7128	29.7118	29.7126	29.7176	29.7253	29.7287	29.7295	29.7278

In each YEAR from 1854 to 1873, for the MONTH of SEPTEMBER.

Noon.	1ʰ. p.m.	2ʰ. p.m.	3ʰ. p.m.	4ʰ. p.m.	5ʰ. p.m.	6ʰ. p.m.	7ʰ. p.m.	8ʰ. p.m.	9ʰ. p.m.	10ʰ. p.m.	11ʰ. p.m.	Mean.	Year.
in.	in.	in.	in.	in.	in.	in.	in.	in.	in.	in.	in.	in.	
30·047	30·041	30·033	30·027	30·021	30·017	30·014	30·020	30·027	30·036	30·041	30·044	30·037	1854
29·977	29·969	29·966	29·959	29·955	29·948	29·946	29·952	29·958	29·962	29·966	29·965	29·975	1855
29·659	29·655	29·651	29·645	29·641	29·642	29·644	29·652	29·657	29·658	29·659	29·657	29·633	1856
29·789	29·786	29·782	29·778	29·777	29·778	29·780	29·784	29·793	29·796	29·798	29·798	29·786	1857
29·813	29·810	29·803	29·802	29·800	29·798	29·803	29·811	29·819	29·820	29·820	29·821	29·811	1858
29·708	29·706	29·704	29·701	29·699	29·702	29·706	29·713	29·721	29·725	29·725	29·722	29·703	1859
29·766	29·762	29·762	29·759	29·757	29·758	29·764	29·771	29·774	29·775	29·774	29·770	29·755	1860
29·703	29·698	29·695	29·689	29·687	29·685	29·685	29·687	29·690	29·695	29·698	29·696	29·697	1861
29·880	29·870	29·863	29·859	29·857	29·855	29·858	29·863	29·866	29·874	29·874	29·874	29·874	1862
29·698	29·695	29·692	29·688	29·690	29·692	29·691	29·697	29·699	29·699	29·700	29·698	29·698	1863
29·783	29·778	29·774	29·767	29·766	29·764	29·766	29·772	29·778	29·780	29·779	29·779	29·773	1864
30·079	30·071	30·063	30·059	30·051	30·050	30·053	30·060	30·067	30·073	30·072	30·072	30·068	1865
29·577	29·575	29·574	29·570	29·570	29·573	29·580	29·586	29·588	29·591	29·589	29·589	29·576	1866
29·909	29·906	29·901	29·896	29·895	29·900	29·906	29·914	29·920	29·920	29·921	29·919	29·903	1867
29·700	29·693	29·686	29·676	29·671	29·673	29·679	29·689	29·697	29·702	29·703	29·702	29·699	1868
29·650	29·643	29·639	29·636	29·633	29·631	29·636	29·642	29·647	29·646	29·645	29·637	29·642	1869
29·908	29·904	29·899	29·895	29·894	29·895	29·901	29·907	29·918	29·923	29·925	29·927	29·906	1870
29·730	29·726	29·721	29·714	29·711	29·706	29·708	29·715	29·720	29·722	29·718	29·713	29·715	1871
29·686	29·680	29·677	29·671	29·666	29·667	29·669	29·677	29·685	29·687	29·686	29·687	29·681	1872
29·796	29·790	29·785	29·779	29·778	29·781	29·785	29·793	29·801	29·806	29·808	29·807	29·793	1873
29·7930	29·7879	29·7837	29·7785	29·7760	29·7757	29·7787	29·7853	29·7912	29·7945	29·7951	29·7938	29·7873	..

In each YEAR from 1854 to 1873, for the MONTH of OCTOBER.

Noon.	1ʰ. p.m.	2ʰ. p.m.	3ʰ. p.m.	4ʰ. p.m.	5ʰ. p.m.	6ʰ. p.m.	7ʰ. p.m.	8ʰ. p.m.	9ʰ. p.m.	10ʰ. p.m.	11ʰ. p.m.	Mean.	Year.
in.	in.	in.	in.	in.	in.	in.	in.	in.	in.	in.	in.	in.	
29·694	29·687	29·684	29·681	29·681	29·684	29·687	29·697	29·704	29·711	29·712	29·712	29·696	1854
29·534	29·523	29·520	29·519	29·518	29·517	29·517	29·526	29·531	29·533	29·541	29·542	29·527	1855
29·997	29·988	29·985	29·984	29·983	29·985	29·990	29·996	29·998	30·007	30·008	30·005	29·992	1856
29·700	29·691	29·689	29·685	29·684	29·690	29·694	29·698	29·706	29·712	29·714	29·716	29·703	1857
29·838	29·827	29·823	29·824	29·823	29·829	29·837	29·845	29·850	29·856	29·857	29·856	29·837	1858
29·531	29·520	29·514	29·510	29·507	29·506	29·506	29·507	29·505	29·509	29·509	29·508	29·522	1859
29·864	29·857	29·851	29·848	29·849	29·850	29·858	29·863	29·867	29·868	29·869	29·871	29·861	1860
29·878	29·871	29·864	29·864	29·865	29·867	29·871	29·874	29·877	29·881	29·881	29·881	29·873	1861
29·650	29·641	29·644	29·641	29·642	29·655	29·660	29·670	29·675	29·682	29·683	29·682	29·665	1862
29·643	29·630	29·627	29·622	29·625	29·634	29·644	29·652	29·656	29·662	29·664	29·667	29·647	1863
29·680	29·670	29·665	29·661	29·660	29·660	29·663	29·669	29·670	29·673	29·673	29·671	29·672	1864
29·443	29·437	29·427	29·428	29·431	29·438	29·450	29·458	29·461	29·465	29·466	29·462	29·442	1865
29·936	29·928	29·923	29·921	29·921	29·927	29·934	29·939	29·942	29·946	29·945	29·943	29·934	1866
29·738	29·728	29·728	29·730	29·730	29·737	29·744	29·746	29·745	29·743	29·741	29·736	29·734	1867
29·800	29·794	29·787	29·783	29·783	29·788	29·796	29·800	29·803	29·806	29·807	29·806	29·794	1868
29·868	29·863	29·861	29·861	29·863	29·870	29·879	29·883	29·887	29·891	29·891	29·889	29·869	1869
29·574	29·571	29·568	29·566	29·569	29·573	29·580	29·586	29·591	29·591	29·589	29·589	29·581	1870
29·772	29·786	29·784	29·779	29·781	29·790	29·794	29·797	29·803	29·803	29·802	29·788		1871
29·542	29·533	29·526	29·521	29·520	29·525	29·533	29·538	29·541	29·544	29·546	29·545	29·537	1872
29·714	29·702	29·696	29·687	29·684	29·690	29·698	29·702	29·708	29·712	29·709	29·710	29·713	1873
29·7208	29·7121	29·7083	29·7056	29·7062	29·7103	29·7168	29·7222	29·7257	29·7300	29·7304	29·7299	29·7199	..

TABLE XI.—MEAN READING of the BAROMETER at every Hour of the Day

Year.	Number of Days employed in forming the Means.	Midnight.	1ʰ. a.m.	2ʰ. a.m.	3ʰ. a.m.	4ʰ. a.m.	5ʰ. a.m.	6ʰ. a.m.	7ʰ. a.m.	8ʰ. a.m.	9ʰ. a.m.	10ʰ. a.m.	11ʰ. a.m.
		in.	in.	in.	in.	in.	in.	in.	in.	in.	in.	in.	in.
1854	30	29·714	29·708	29·703	29·696	29·690	29·686	29·682	29·690	29·700	29·706	29·710	29·711
1855	30	29·861	29·860	29·859	29·856	29·854	29·851	29·850	29·856	29·863	29·868	29·871	29·874
1856	30	29·914	29·912	29·907	29·905	29·903	29·902	29·901	29·904	29·905	29·912	29·914	29·911
1857	..	..	..	..	..	..	..	..	..	..	..	..	..
1858	30	29·783	29·779	29·774	29·770	29·763	29·759	29·753	29·755	29·759	29·761	29·765	29·763
1859	29	29·828	29·823	29·820	29·817	29·815	29·815	29·816	29·819	29·824	29·832	29·835	29·837
1860	30	29·706	29·702	29·700	29·699	29·695	29·696	29·696	29·700	29·704	29·709	29·710	29·708
1861	29	29·573	29·569	29·569	29·567	29·567	29·568	29·569	29·573	29·576	29·580	29·579	29·576
1862	30	29·806	29·801	29·798	29·795	29·789	29·787	29·786	29·788	29·796	29·797	29·799	29·796
1863	30	29·876	29·874	29·873	29·871	29·869	29·869	29·869	29·873	29·872	29·879	29·886	29·881
1864	25	29·696	29·688	29·681	29·675	29·671	29·664	29·661	29·660	29·663	29·663	29·659	29·655
1865	30	29·721	29·716	29·714	29·709	29·706	29·705	29·705	29·709	29·716	29·713	29·728	29·725
1866	30	29·798	29·793	29·791	29·783	29·777	29·777	29·775	29·778	29·788	29·793	29·798	29·798
1867	28	30·119	30·115	30·113	30·108	30·104	30·104	30·104	30·108	30·115	30·120	30·123	30·122
1868	30	29·849	29·844	29·841	29·834	29·831	29·828	29·827	29·832	29·841	29·843	29·847	29·849
1869	30	29·771	29·761	29·760	29·754	29·748	29·748	29·751	29·759	29·767	29·773	29·781	29·778
1870	30	29·632	29·628	29·625	29·620	29·618	29·619	29·619	29·627	29·634	29·641	29·648	29·646
1871	30	29·818	29·814	29·811	29·805	29·803	29·803	29·806	29·813	29·821	29·824	29·828	29·825
1872	25	29·512	29·511	29·513	29·513	29·514	29·516	29·519	29·524	29·536	29·539	29·543	29·540
1873	27	29·680	29·676	29·675	29·667	29·667	29·665	29·666	29·670	29·678	29·685	29·692	29·690
Means	..	29·7714	29·7672	29·7647	29·7603	29·7571	29·7560	29·7558	29·7598	29·7667	29·7714	29·7745	29·7729

In the month of November 1857 the photographic records

TABLE XII.—MEAN READING of the BAROMETER at every Hour of the Day

Year.	Number of Days employed in fortnine the Means.	Midnight.	1ʰ. a.m.	2ʰ. a.m.	3ʰ. a.m.	4ʰ. a.m.	5ʰ. a.m.	6ʰ. a.m.	7ʰ. a.m.	8ʰ. a.m.	9ʰ. a.m.	10ʰ. a.m.	11ʰ. a.m.
		in.	in.	in.	in.	in.	in.	in.	in.	in.	in.	in.	in.
1854	31	29·751	29·746	29·748	29·747	29·742	29·735	29·734	29·741	29·753	29·767	29·778	29·780
1855	28	29·767	29·767	29·773	29·774	29·772	29·769	29·766	29·774	29·784	29·790	29·795	29·793
1856	31	29·637	29·634	29·634	29·637	29·634	29·636	29·639	29·648	29·654	29·660	29·665	29·662
1857	27	30·218	30·217	30·218	30·218	30·216	30·214	30·213	30·214	30·221	30·226	30·232	30·230
1858	31	29·759	29·761	29·768	29·772	29·773	29·776	29·779	29·781	29·786	29·790	29·794	29·788
1859	30	29·639	29·636	29·637	29·637	29·635	29·635	29·637	29·637	29·643	29·650	29·651	29·649
1860	31	29·502	29·498	29·497	29·497	29·496	29·493	29·493	29·497	29·501	29·503	29·505	29·505
1861	31	29·968	29·969	29·967	29·964	29·962	29·961	29·961	29·963	29·968	29·976	29·985	29·986
1862	25	29·846	29·846	29·845	29·842	29·839	29·839	29·840	29·844	29·851	29·853	29·861	29·862
1863	31	29·980	29·974	29·970	29·962	29·953	29·946	29·937	29·933	29·935	29·944	29·953	29·951
1864	31	29·883	29·880	29·879	29·877	29·872	29·866	29·865	29·867	29·871	29·877	29·881	29·876
1865	31	30·069	30·067	30·067	30·067	30·066	30·061	30·062	30·063	30·068	30·076	30·081	30·075
1866	31	29·795	29·795	29·796	29·793	29·793	29·790	29·791	29·795	29·800	29·810	29·818	29·814
1867	26	29·833	29·829	29·830	29·827	29·825	29·820	29·820	29·811	29·822	29·835	29·842	29·841
1868	31	29·386	29·382	29·390	29·393	29·392	29·389	29·389	29·389	29·398	29·402	29·409	29·400
1869	31	29·638	29·634	29·634	29·630	29·614	29·618	29·617	29·619	29·626	29·634	29·639	29·636
1870	31	29·744	29·741	29·742	29·741	29·737	29·734	29·732	29·732	29·737	29·743	29·749	29·749
1871	31	29·926	29·924	29·924	29·926	29·922	29·918	29·907	29·924	29·928	29·935	29·942	29·944
1872	31	29·384	29·380	29·384	29·385	29·385	29·385	29·380	29·396	29·409	29·419	29·431	29·430
1873	31	30·119	30·114	30·113	30·109	30·105	30·101	30·100	30·104	30·111	30·119	30·125	30·123
Means	..	29·7922	29·7897	29·7909	29·7899	29·7870	29·7843	29·7846	29·7872	29·7936	29·8010	29·8076	29·8048

in each YEAR from 1854 to 1873, for the Month of NOVEMBER.

Noon.	1ʰ. p.m.	2ʰ. p.m.	3ʰ. p.m.	4ʰ. p.m.	5ʰ. p.m.	6ʰ. p.m.	7ʰ. p.m.	8ʰ. p.m.	9ʰ. p.m.	10ʰ. p.m.	11ʰ. p.m.	Mean.	Year.
in.	in.	in.	in.	in.	in.	in.	in.	in.	in.	in.	in.	in.	
29·702	29·693	29·686	29·682	29·683	29·686	29·684	29·687	29·687	29·687	29·684	29·684	29·693	1854
29·866	29·859	29·835	29·835	29·836	29·860	29·864	29·869	29·872	29·878	29·879	29·877	29·863	1855
29·904	29·896	29·893	29·893	29·895	29·899	29·900	29·903	29·906	29·910	29·911	29·908	29·904	1856
..	..	..	..	..	..	..	..	..	..	..	..	..	1857
29·755	29·746	29·740	29·739	29·742	29·743	29·747	29·747	29·751	29·750	29·751	29·749	29·756	1858
29·832	29·826	29·823	29·822	29·823	29·827	29·833	29·835	29·839	29·840	29·839	29·837	29·827	1859
29·701	29·694	29·690	29·688	29·690	29·694	29·700	29·700	29·702	29·700	29·699	29·699	29·699	1860
29·568	29·561	29·553	29·553	29·555	29·561	29·567	29·569	29·568	29·573	29·572	29·573	29·568	1861
29·791	29·780	29·779	29·784	29·786	29·792	29·796	29·800	29·801	29·803	29·804	29·803	29·794	1862
29·871	29·859	29·854	29·855	29·856	29·859	29·865	29·870	29·876	29·885	29·888	29·891	29·872	1863
29·641	29·626	29·620	29·617	29·617	29·619	29·621	29·622	29·623	29·620	29·619	29·617	29·646	1864
29·720	29·711	29·708	29·709	29·714	29·721	29·727	29·730	29·731	29·738	29·737	29·737	29·720	1865
29·786	29·778	29·773	29·775	29·777	29·784	29·791	29·792	29·795	29·800	29·798	29·797	29·787	1866
30·109	30·100	30·091	30·091	30·093	30·097	30·102	30·103	30·102	30·103	30·104	30·104	30·106	1867
29·838	29·833	29·829	29·829	29·829	29·833	29·835	29·838	29·839	29·842	29·841	29·839	29·837	1868
29·770	29·768	29·764	29·762	29·763	29·768	29·771	29·775	29·773	29·772	29·765	29·763	29·765	1869
29·640	29·633	29·628	29·627	29·629	29·636	29·642	29·646	29·647	29·650	29·651	29·650	29·633	1870
29·816	29·810	29·808	29·807	29·810	29·813	29·818	29·822	29·824	29·827	29·822	29·821	29·815	1871
29·528	29·518	29·507	29·503	29·498	29·496	29·495	29·491	29·486	29·483	29·484	29·482	29·511	1872
29·687	29·685	29·681	29·684	29·687	29·694	29·701	29·708	29·711	29·718	29·723	29·726	29·689	1873
29·7645	29·7567	29·7517	29·7513	29·7528	29·7569	29·7610	29·7636	29·7649	29·7673	29·7669	29·7663	29·7626	..

were not sufficiently complete to be used.

in each YEAR from 1854 to 1873, for the Month of DECEMBER.

Noon.	1ʰ. p.m.	2ʰ. p.m.	3ʰ. p.m.	4ʰ. p.m.	5ʰ. p.m.	6ʰ. p.m.	7ʰ. p.m.	8ʰ. p.m.	9ʰ. p.m.	10ʰ. p.m.	11ʰ. p.m.	Mean.	Year.
in.	in.	in.	in.	in.	in.	in.	in.	in.	in.	in.	in.	in.	
29·774	29·769	29·768	29·774	29·779	29·779	29·776	29·780	29·783	29·784	29·787	29·783	29·765	1854
29·788	29·778	29·773	29·770	29·772	29·769	29·771	29·774	29·775	29·773	29·775	29·776	29·776	1855
29·650	29·640	29·638	29·639	29·641	29·641	29·644	29·646	29·646	29·646	29·646	29·645	29·643	1856
30·216	30·202	30·199	30·202	30·203	30·206	30·210	30·214	30·219	30·226	30·230	30·233	30·217	1857
29·774	29·763	29·760	29·763	29·765	29·771	29·774	29·779	29·779	29·782	29·783	29·788	29·775	1858
29·641	29·631	29·629	29·633	29·639	29·643	29·646	29·648	29·652	29·654	29·655	29·652	29·642	1859
29·498	29·492	29·489	29·492	29·496	29·496	29·498	29·499	29·498	29·495	29·495	29·493	29·497	1860
29·982	29·976	29·972	29·973	29·979	29·979	29·980	29·983	29·984	29·986	29·987	29·987	29·975	1861
29·852	29·840	29·840	29·846	29·850	29·854	29·857	29·859	29·861	29·863	29·865	29·865	29·851	1862
29·942	29·930	29·925	29·931	29·937	29·946	29·953	29·959	29·965	29·966	29·969	29·972	29·931	1863
29·862	29·854	29·851	29·853	29·854	29·858	29·863	29·869	29·874	29·876	29·875	29·875	29·869	1864
30·062	30·051	30·046	30·048	30·049	30·050	30·052	30·053	30·053	30·053	30·053	30·054	30·060	1865
29·798	29·782	29·774	29·771	29·769	29·769	29·771	29·774	29·774	29·777	29·775	29·777	29·787	1866
29·827	29·818	29·810	29·812	29·810	29·815	29·815	29·816	29·821	29·828	29·832	29·837	29·824	1867
29·384	29·366	29·358	29·361	29·366	29·371	29·378	29·381	29·380	29·384	29·385	29·394	29·385	1868
29·625	29·617	29·617	29·619	29·618	29·617	29·619	29·618	29·617	29·615	29·616	29·624	1869
29·738	29·733	29·730	29·730	29·731	29·733	29·732	29·734	29·735	29·736	29·738	29·738	29·736	1870
29·929	29·919	29·913	29·911	29·912	29·916	29·920	29·924	29·931	29·935	29·938	29·942	29·928	1871
29·413	29·415	29·413	29·416	29·417	29·416	29·414	29·416	29·417	29·414	29·411	29·410	29·407	1872
30·115	30·109	30·102	30·099	30·102	30·103	30·106	30·110	30·109	30·110	30·108	30·108	30·109	1873
29·7940	29·7843	29·7803	29·7822	29·7844	29·7866	29·7889	29·7918	29·7937	29·7953	29·7961	29·7973	29·7912	..

TABLE XIII.—MONTHLY MEAN READING of the BAROMETER at every HOUR of the DAY through the RANGE of YEARS 1854 to 1873.

Hour, Greenwich Mean Solar Time (Civil reckoning).	January.	February.	March.	April.	May.	June.	July.	August.	September.	October.	November.	December.	Yearly Means.
	in.	in.	in.	in.	in.	in.	in.	in.	in.	in.	in.	in.	in.
Midnight	29.7323	29.8348	29.7317	29.8089	29.7880	29.8363	29.8171	29.8059	29.7944	29.7288	29.7714	29.7922	29.7868
1ʰ. a.m.	29.7272	29.8325	29.7298	29.8061	29.7841	29.8333	29.8135	29.8025	29.7905	29.7263	29.7672	29.7897	29.7836
2 ,,	29.7266	29.8302	29.7254	29.8023	29.7813	29.8295	29.8099	29.7983	29.7857	29.7216	29.7647	29.7909	29.7806
3 ,,	29.7245	29.8256	29.7191	29.7993	29.7777	29.8265	29.8064	29.7946	29.7811	29.7158	29.7603	29.7899	29.7767
4 ,,	29.7207	29.8230	29.7157	29.7973	29.7757	29.8257	29.8059	29.7921	29.7775	29.7128	29.7571	29.7870	29.7742
5 ,,	29.7172	29.8229	29.7153	29.7975	29.7773	29.8275	29.8067	29.7933	29.7767	29.7118	29.7560	29.7843	29.7739
6 ,,	29.7164	29.8232	29.7177	29.8024	29.7800	29.8304	29.8089	29.7977	29.7810	29.7126	29.7558	29.7846	29.7759
7 ,,	29.7195	29.8275	29.7226	29.8075	29.7820	29.8344	29.8128	29.8020	29.7870	29.7176	29.7598	29.7872	29.7800
8 ,,	29.7262	29.8347	29.7266	29.8113	29.7844	29.8379	29.8163	29.8065	29.7929	29.7253	29.7667	29.7936	29.7851
9 ,,	29.7338	29.8398	29.7308	29.8153	29.7852	29.8386	29.8173	29.8098	29.7986	29.7287	29.7714	29.8010	29.7892
10 ,,	29.7398	29.8431	29.7327	29.8163	29.7839	29.8378	29.8169	29.8099	29.7991	29.7295	29.7745	29.8076	29.7909
11 ,,	29.7406	29.8452	29.7317	29.8138	29.7817	29.8362	29.8156	29.8074	29.7963	29.7278	29.7729	29.8048	29.7895
Noon	29.7318	29.8402	29.7286	29.8099	29.7784	29.8327	29.8126	29.8027	29.7930	29.7208	29.7645	29.7940	29.7841
1ʰ. p.m.	29.7234	29.8305	29.7215	29.8052	29.7738	29.8282	29.8085	29.7986	29.7879	29.7121	29.7567	29.7843	29.7776
2 ,,	29.7207	29.8238	29.7144	29.7998	29.7699	29.8248	29.8055	29.7950	29.7837	29.7083	29.7517	29.7803	29.7732
3 ,,	29.7243	29.8209	29.7093	29.7934	29.7652	29.8204	29.8016	29.7903	29.7785	29.7056	29.7513	29.7822	29.7702
4 ,,	29.7278	29.8210	29.7067	29.7909	29.7632	29.8174	29.7980	29.7877	29.7760	29.7062	29.7528	29.7844	29.7693
5 ,,	29.7312	29.8239	29.7073	29.7903	29.7616	29.8148	29.7947	29.7853	29.7757	29.7103	29.7569	29.7866	29.7699
6 ,,	29.7343	29.8302	29.7119	29.7919	29.7627	29.8152	29.7945	29.7856	29.7787	29.7168	29.7610	29.7889	29.7726
7 ,,	29.7373	29.8353	29.7175	29.7975	29.7668	29.8188	29.7979	29.7905	29.7853	29.7222	29.7636	29.7918	29.7770
8 ,,	29.7382	29.8373	29.7222	29.8052	29.7741	29.8245	29.8033	29.7989	29.7912	29.7257	29.7649	29.7937	29.7816
9 ,,	29.7380	29.8400	29.7270	29.8107	29.7829	29.8351	29.8125	29.8054	29.7945	29.7300	29.7673	29.7953	29.7866
10 ,,	29.7374	29.8405	29.7280	29.8129	29.7857	29.8378	29.8158	29.8080	29.7951	29.7304	29.7669	29.7961	29.7879
11 ,,	29.7362	29.8404	29.7280	29.8134	29.7870	29.8392	29.8166	29.8089	29.7938	29.7299	29.7663	29.7973	29.7881
Means	29.7294	29.8319	29.7217	29.8041	29.7772	29.8293	29.8087	29.7990	29.7873	29.7199	29.7626	29.7912	29.7802

In the months of November 1857, June 1864, and April 1868 the photographic records were not sufficiently complete to be used. The values given in the above table for April, June, and November, are, in each case, the means of the monthly values for the remaining nineteen years.

TABLE XIV.—MONTHLY MEAN DIURNAL INEQUALITY of the BAROMETER through the RANGE of YEARS 1854 to 1873.

Hour, Greenwich Mean Solar Time (Civil reckoning).	January.	February.	March.	April.	May.	June.	July.	August.	September.	October.	November.	December.	For the Year.
	in.	in.	in.	in.	in.	in.	in.	in.	in.	in.	in.	in.	in.
Midnight	+0·0029	+0·0029	+0·0100	+0·0048	+0·0108	+0·0070	+0·0084	+0·0069	+0·0071	+0·0089	+0·0088	+0·0010	+0·0066
1ʰ. a.m.	− 22	+ 6	+ 81	+ 20	+ 69	+ 40	+ 48	+ 35	+ 32	+ 64	+ 46	− 15	+ 34
2 ,,	−· 28	− 17	+ 37	− 18	+ 41	+ 2	+ 12	− 5	− 16	+ 17	+ 21	− 3	+ 4
3 ,,	− 49	− 63	− 26	− 48	+ 5	− 28	− 23	− 44	− 62	− 41	− 23	− 13	− 35
4 ,,	− 87	− 89	− 60	− 68	− 15	− 36	− 28	− 69	− 98	− 71	− 55	− 42	− 60
5 ,,	− 122	− 90	− 64	− 66	+ 1	− 18	− 20	− 57	− 106	− 81	− 66	− 69	− 63
6 ,,	− 130	− 87	− 40	− 17	+ 28	+ 11	+ 2	− 13	− 63	− 73	− 68	− 66	− 43
7 ,,	− 99	− 44	+ 9	+ 34	+ 48	+ 51	+ 41	+ 30	− 3	− 23	− 28	− 40	− 2
8 ,,	− 32	+ 28	+ 49	+ 72	+ 72	+ 86	+ 76	+ 75	+ 56	+ 54	+ 41	+ 24	+ 50
9 ,,	+ 44	+ 79	+ 91	+ 112	+ 80	+ 93	+ 86	+ 108	+ 113	+ 88	+ 88	+ 98	+ 90
10 ,,	+ 104	+ 112	+ 110	+ 122	+ 67	+ 85	+ 82	+ 109	+ 118	+ 96	+ 119	+ 164	+ 107
11 ,,	+ 112	+ 133	+ 100	+ 97	+ 45	+ 69	+ 69	+ 84	+ 90	+ 79	+ 103	+ 136	+ 93
Noon	+ 24	+ 83	+ 69	+ 58	+ 12	+ 34	+ 59	+ 37	+ 57	+ 9	+ 19	+ 28	+ 39
1ʰ. p.m.	− 60	− 14	− 2	+ 11	− 34	− 11	− 2	− 4	+ 6	− 78	− 39	− 69	− 26
2 ,,	− 87	− 81	− 73	− 43	− 73	− 45	− 32	− 40	− 56	− 116	− 109	− 109	− 70
3 ,,	− 51	− 110	− 124	− 107	− 120	− 89	− 71	− 87	− 88	− 143	− 113	− 90	− 100
4 ,,	− 16	− 109	− 150	− 132	− 140	− 119	− 107	− 113	− 115	− 137	− 98	− 68	− 109
5 ,,	+ 18	− 80	− 144	− 138	− 156	− 145	− 140	− 137	− 116	− 96	− 57	− 46	− 103
6 ,,	+ 49	− 17	− 98	− 122	− 145	− 141	− 142	− 134	− 86	− 31	− 16	− 23	− 76
7 ,,	+ 79	+ 34	− 42	− 66	− 104	− 105	− 108	− 85	− 20	+ 23	+ 10	+ 6	− 32
8 ,,	+ 88	+ 54	+ 5	+ 11	− 31	− 48	− 49	− 1	+ 39	+ 58	+ 23	+ 25	+ 14
9 ,,	+ 86	+ 81	+ 53	+ 66	+ 57	+ 58	+ 38	+ 64	+ 72	+ 101	+ 47	+ 41	+ 64
10 ,,	+ 80	+ 86	+ 63	+ 88	+ 85	+ 85	+ 71	+ 90	+ 78	+ 105	+ 43	+ 49	+ 77
11 ,,	+ 68	+ 85	+ 63	+ 93	+ 98	+ 99	+ 79	+ 99	+ 65	+ 100	+ 37	+ 61	+ 79

TABLE XV.—MAXIMA and MINIMA of the MEAN DIURNAL INEQUALITY of the BAROMETER in each MONTH, and for the YEAR, through the RANGE of YEARS 1854 to 1873, with the HOURS of their OCCURRENCE, as extracted from TABLE XIV.

Month.	First Minimum.	Time of Occurrence.	First Maximum.	Time of Occurrence.	Second Minimum.	Time of Occurrence.	Second Maximum.	Time of Occurrence.
	in.	h.	in.	h.	in.	h.	in.	h.
January	− ·0130	6 a.m.	+ ·0112	11 a.m.	− ·0087	2 p.m.	+ ·0088	8 p.m.
February	− ·0090	5 „	+ ·0133	11 „	− ·0110	3 „	+ ·0086	10 p.m.
March	− ·0064	5 „	+ ·0110	10 „	− ·0150	4 „	+ ·0100	midnight.
April	− ·0068	4 „	+ ·0122	10 „	− ·0138	5 „	+ ·0093	11 p.m.
May	− ·0015	4 „	+ ·0080	9 „	− ·0156	3 „	+ ·0108	midnight.
June	− ·0036	4 „	+ ·0093	9 „	− ·0145	5 „	+ ·0099	11 p.m.
July	− ·0028	4 „	+ ·0086	9 „	− ·0142	6 „	+ ·0084	midnight.
August	− ·0069	4 „	+ ·0109	10 „	− ·0137	5 „	+ ·0099	11 p.m.
September	− ·0106	5 „	+ ·0118	10 „	− ·0116	5 „	− ·0078	10 „
October	− ·0081	5 „	+ ·0096	10 „	− ·0743	3 „	+ ·0103	10 „
November	− ·0068	6 „	+ ·0110	10 „	− ·0113	3 „	+ ·0088	midnight.
December	− ·0069	5 „	+ ·0164	10 „	− ·0109	2 „	+ ·0061	11 p.m.
For the Year	− ·0063	5 a.m.	+ ·0107	10 a.m.	− ·0109	4 p.m.	+ ·0079	11 p.m.

TABLE XVI.—APPROXIMATE TIMES of the DAY at which, in each MONTH of the YEAR, through the RANGE of YEARS 1854 to 1873, the MEAN BAROMETER READING coincides with the MEAN READING for the MONTH, as deduced from TABLE XIV.

Month.	Times of Coincidence of Mean Reading with the Mean for the Month.			
	First.	Second.	Third.	Fourth.
	h. m.	h. m.	h. m.	h. m.
January	0. 34 a.m.	8. 25 a.m.	0. 17 p.m.	4. 28 p.m.
February	1. 16 „	7. 37 „	0. 51 „	6. 20 „
March	2. 35 „	6. 49 „	0. 58 „	7. 54 „
April	1. 32 „	6. 20 „	1. 12 „	7. 51 „
May	3. 15 „	4. 56 „	0. 16 „	8. 21 „
June	2. 4 „	5. 37 „	0. 45 „	8. 27 „
July	3. 21 „	5. 55 „	0. 37 „	8. 54 „
August	1. 53 „	6. 18 „	0. 54 „	8. 1 „
September	1. 40 „	7. 5 „	1. 0 „	7. 20 „
October	2. 18 „	7. 18 „	0. 6 „	6. 54 „
November	2. 30 „	7. 24 „	0. 15 „	6. 37 „
December	0. 24 „	7. 38 „	0. 17 „	6. 48 „

TABLE XVII.—MEAN READING of the BAROMETER in each MONTH, as deduced from the MEAN of the MEAN HOURLY DETERMINATIONS in each MONTH.

Year.	January.	February.	March.	April.	May.	June.	July.	August.	September.	October.	November.	December.	Yearly Means.	Difference of the Mean Reading in each Year from the Mean Reading throughout the Period 1854 to 1873, as deduced from the whole of the Observations.
	in.	in.	in.	in.	in.	in.	in.	in.	in.	in.	in.	in.	in.	in.
1854	29·676	30·038	30·190	29·989	29·672	29·734	29·808	29·885	30·037	29·696	29·693	29·765	29·849	+ 0·068
1855	30·008	29·596	29·540	29·936	29·700	29·857	29·735	29·855	29·975	29·527	29·863	29·776	29·781	0·000
1856	29·428	29·945	30·036	29·606	29·650	29·875	29·816	29·725	29·653	29·992	29·904	29·645	29·773	− 0·008
1857	29·634	29·043	29·724	29·628	29·802	29·876	29·824	29·837	29·786	29·703	29·042	30·217	29·826	+ 0·045
1858	30·177	29·845	29·760	29·781	29·764	29·924	29·789	29·828	29·811	29·837	29·756	29·775	29·838	+ 0·057
1859	30·043	29·810	29·771	29·613	29·703	29·764	29·942	29·820	29·703	29·522	29·827	29·642	29·771	− 0·010
1860	29·527	29·860	29·666	29·752	29·756	29·611	29·848	29·559	29·735	29·861	29·699	29·497	29·699	− 0·082
1861	30·011	29·689	29·620	29·999	29·924	29·780	29·622	29·868	29·697	29·873	29·568	29·975	29·802	+ 0·021
1862	29·715	29·909	29·545	29·858	29·773	29·730	29·786	29·787	29·874	29·665	29·794	29·851	29·774	− 0·007
1863	29·620	30·175	29·699	29·821	29·858	29·728	29·939	29·755	29·698	29·647	29·872	29·951	29·814	+ 0·033
1864	30·016	29·786	29·517	29·915	29·717	29·792	29·865	29·928	29·773	29·662	29·646	29·869	29·791	+ 0·010
1865	29·406	29·740	29·724	29·958	29·766	30·030	29·804	29·711	30·068	29·452	29·720	30·060	29·787	+ 0·006
1866	29·706	29·541	29·531	29·744	29·814	29·771	29·770	29·658	29·576	29·934	29·787	29·787	29·717	− 0·064
1867	29·508	29·910	29·627	29·634	29·736	29·937	29·752	29·830	29·903	29·734	30·106	29·824	29·792	+ 0·011
1868	29·747	29·974	29·822	29·782	29·854	29·978	29·893	29·757	29·699	29·794	29·837	29·385	29·794	+ 0·013
1869	29·860	29·808	29·638	29·831	29·652	29·920	29·924	29·968	29·642	29·869	29·765	29·624	29·792	+ 0·011
1870	29·822	29·659	29·867	30·001	29·896	29·946	29·818	29·806	29·906	29·541	29·635	29·738	29·806	+ 0·025
1871	29·648	29·850	29·878	29·649	29·905	29·767	29·689	29·858	29·715	29·788	29·815	29·928	29·791	+ 0·010
1872	29·461	29·647	29·632	29·737	29·714	29·736	29·758	29·800	29·681	29·537	29·511	29·407	29·635	− 0·146
1873	29·573	29·904	29·631	29·825	29·798	29·794	29·793	29·768	29·793	29·713	29·689	30·109	29·782	+ 0·001
Means	29·729	29·832	29·722	29·803	29·777	29·828	29·809	29·799	29·787	29·720	29·771	29·791	29·781	..

In the months of 1857, November; 1864, June; and 1868, April; the photographic records were not sufficiently complete to be used. The values inserted above are those derived from the eye observations.

TABLE XVIII.—GREATEST and LEAST MEAN READING of the BAROMETER in each MONTH through the ENTIRE PERIOD 1854 to 1873, as extracted from TABLE XVII.

Month.	Greatest Mean Monthly Reading.	In what Year.	Least Mean Monthly Reading.	In what Year.	Difference between the greatest and least.
	in.		in.		in.
January - -	30·177	1858	29·406	1865	0·771
February - -	30·175	1863	29·541	1866	0·634
March - -	30·190	1854	29·517	1864	0·673
April - -	30·001	1870	29·606	1856	0·395
May - -	29·924	1861	29·650	1856	0·274
June - -	30·030	1865	29·611	1860	0·419
July - -	29·942	1859	29·622	1861	0·320
August - -	29·968	1869	29·559	1860	0·409
September -	30·068	1865	29·576	1866	0·492
October - -	29·992	1856	29·452	1865	0·540
November -	30·106	1867	29·511	1872	0·595
December - -	30·217	1857	29·385	1868	0·832

c

TABLE XIX.—Mean of the Mean Monthly Readings of the Barometer

Year.	Aggregate Number of Days employed.	Midnight.	1^{h} a.m.	2^{h} a.m.	3^{h} a.m.	4^{h} a.m.	5^{h} a.m.	6^{h} a.m.	7^{h} a.m.	8^{h} a.m.	9^{h} a.m.	10^{h} a.m.	11^{h} a.m.
		in.	in.	in.	in.	in.	in.	in.	in.	in.	in.	in.	in.
1854	358	29·857	29·853	29·850	29·844	29·840	29·836	29·837	29·842	29·851	29·858	29·860	29·859
1855	351	29·790	29·787	29·784	29·780	29·776	29·772	29·772	29·778	29·786	29·791	29·793	29·792
1856	344	29·773	29·770	29·768	29·766	29·764	29·765	29·767	29·772	29·777	29·782	29·784	29·783
1857	319	29·821	29·819	29·815	29·811	29·808	29·809	29·810	29·814	29·819	29·823	29·826	29·825
1858	344	29·843	29·840	29·837	29·834	29·833	29·834	29·836	29·840	29·845	29·848	29·849	29·847
1859	354	29·779	29·776	29·773	29·770	29·768	29·767	29·768	29·771	29·775	29·779	29·780	29·780
1860	347	29·701	29·698	29·695	29·692	29·691	29·691	29·693	29·698	29·703	29·707	29·708	29·707
1861	338	29·806	29·803	29·801	29·798	29·796	29·797	29·800	29·802	29·807	29·811	29·812	29·811
1862	312	29·786	29·783	29·781	29·778	29·774	29·772	29·772	29·775	29·777	29·779	29·779	29·778
1863	347	29·825	29·824	29·821	29·816	29·814	29·812	29·812	29·813	29·816	29·819	29·820	29·819
1864	296	29·805	29·803	29·799	29·796	29·794	29·792	29·793	29·794	29·797	29·800	29·801	29·798
1865	362	29·792	29·789	29·787	29·783	29·781	29·781	29·784	29·788	29·793	29·798	29·800	29·798
1866	364	29·724	29·720	29·716	29·712	29·710	29·710	29·713	29·717	29·722	29·724	29·727	29·725
1867	350	29·794	29·791	29·788	29·784	29·782	29·783	29·785	29·791	29·796	29·801	29·805	29·804
1868	332	29·800	29·797	29·795	29·791	29·790	29·790	29·793	29·798	29·804	29·807	29·809	29·806
1869	365	29·798	29·793	29·789	29·784	29·781	29·781	29·783	29·791	29·797	29·801	29·804	29·803
1870	355	29·815	29·811	29·808	29·803	29·800	29·801	29·803	29·808	29·812	29·815	29·818	29·815
1871	363	29·799	29·794	29·790	29·784	29·781	29·781	29·785	29·790	29·795	29·800	29·803	29·801
1872	362	29·638	29·635	29·632	29·628	29·626	29·628	29·631	29·637	29·643	29·647	29·649	29·648
1873	361	29·790	29·786	29·783	29·778	29·776	29·776	29·779	29·785	29·790	29·792	29·794	29·792
Means	6924 sum.	29·787	29·784	29·781	29·777	29·774	29·774	29·776	29·780	29·785	29·789	29·791	29·790

In the months of November 1857, June 1864, and April 1868, the photographic records were not sufficiently complete to be used. The values given

TABLE XX.—Mean Diurnal Inequality of the

Year.	Midnight.	1^{h} a.m.	2^{h} a.m.	3^{h} a.m.	4^{h} a.m.	5^{h} a.m.	6^{h} a.m.	7^{h} a.m.	8^{h} a.m.	9^{h} a.m.	10^{h} a.m.	11^{h} a.m.
	in.	in.	in.	in.	in.	in.	in.	in.	in.	in.	in.	in.
1854	+0·008	+0·004	+0·001	−0·005	−0·009	−0·013	−0·012	−0·007	+0·002	+0·009	+0·011	+0·010
1855	+ 9	+ 6	+ 3	− 1	− 5	− 9	− 9	− 3	+ 5	+ 10	+ 12	+ 11
1856	0	− 3	− 5	− 7	− 9	− 8	− 6	− 1	+ 4	+ 9	+ 11	+ 10
1857	+ 5	+ 3	− 1	− 5	− 8	− 7	− 6	− 2	+ 3	+ 9	+ 10	+ 9
1858	+ 5	+ 2	− 1	− 4	− 5	− 4	− 2	+ 2	+ 7	+ 10	+ 11	+ 9
1859	+ 8	+ 5	+ 2	− 1	− 3	− 4	− 3	0	+ 4	+ 8	+ 9	+ 9
1860	+ 2	− 1	− 4	− 7	− 8	− 8	− 6	− 1	+ 4	+ 8	+ 9	+ 8
1861	+ 4	+ 1	− 1	− 4	− 6	− 5	− 2	0	+ 5	+ 9	+ 10	+ 9
1862	+ 12	+ 9	+ 7	+ 4	0	− 2	− 2	− 1	+ 3	+ 5	+ 5	+ 4
1863	+ 11	+ 10	+ 7	+ 2	0	− 2	− 2	− 1	+ 2	+ 5	+ 6	+ 5
1864	+ 14	+ 12	+ 8	+ 5	+ 3	+ 1	+ 2	+ 3	+ 6	+ 9	+ 10	+ 7
1865	+ 5	+ 2	0	− 1	− 6	− 6	− 3	+ 1	+ 6	+ 11	+ 13	+ 11
1866	+ 7	+ 3	− 1	− 5	− 7	− 7	− 4	0	+ 5	+ 7	+ 10	+ 8
1867	+ 2	− 1	− 4	− 8	− 10	− 9	− 7	− 1	+ 4	+ 10	+ 13	+ 12
1868	+ 6	+ 3	+ 1	− 3	− 4	− 4	− 1	+ 4	+ 10	+ 13	+ 15	+ 12
1869	+ 6	+ 1	− 3	− 8	− 11	− 11	− 7	− 1	+ 5	+ 9	+ 12	+ 11
1870	+ 9	+ 5	+ 2	− 3	− 6	− 5	− 3	+ 2	+ 6	+ 9	+ 12	+ 9
1871	+ 8	+ 3	− 1	− 7	− 10	− 10	− 6	− 1	+ 4	+ 9	+ 12	+ 10
1872	+ 3	0	− 3	− 7	− 9	− 7	− 4	+ 2	+ 8	+ 12	+ 14	+ 13
1873	+ 8	+ 4	+ 1	− 4	− 6	− 6	− 3	+ 3	+ 8	+ 10	+ 12	+ 10
For the whole Period }	+0·007	+0·004	+0·001	−0·003	−0·006	−0·006	−0·004	0·000	+0·005	+0·009	+0·011	+0·010

at every HOUR of the DAY for each YEAR from 1854 to 1873.

Noon.	1ʰ. p.m.	2ʰ. p.m.	3ʰ. p.m.	4ʰ. p.m.	5ʰ. p.m.	6ʰ. p.m.	7ʰ. p.m.	8ʰ. p.m.	9ʰ. p.m.	10ʰ. p.m.	11ʰ. p.m.	Yearly Means.	Year.
in.	in.	in.	in.	in.	in.	in.	in.	in.	in.	in.	in.	in.	
29·854	29·849	29·844	29·841	29·840	29·838	29·840	29·846	29·851	29·858	29·860	29·862	29·849	1854
29·788	29·782	29·777	29·773	29·771	29·768	29·768	29·774	29·780	29·786	29·790	29·790	29·781	1855
29·777	29·772	29·768	29·766	29·766	29·767	29·768	29·773	29·777	29·782	29·783	29·782	29·773	1856
29·820	29·813	29·809	29·806	29·805	29·806	29·809	29·812	29·818	29·824	29·826	29·827	29·816	1857
29·842	29·836	29·831	29·828	29·828	29·829	29·831	29·835	29·839	29·842	29·843	29·844	29·838	1858
29·776	29·769	29·765	29·762	29·761	29·762	29·764	29·767	29·770	29·776	29·777	29·776	29·771	1859
29·703	29·697	29·694	29·692	29·692	29·693	29·697	29·702	29·705	29·708	29·710	29·709	29·699	1860
29·807	29·802	29·796	29·794	29·794	29·794	29·795	29·799	29·803	29·807	29·809	29·809	29·802	1861
29·774	29·767	29·764	29·762	29·763	29·765	29·766	29·770	29·773	29·778	29·780	29·780	29·774	1862
29·814	29·805	29·802	29·800	29·800	29·802	29·805	29·809	29·813	29·820	29·822	29·823	29·814	1863
29·792	29·784	29·781	29·778	29·778	29·778	29·780	29·784	29·787	29·791	29·792	29·793	29·791	1864
29·792	29·785	29·780	29·777	29·775	29·775	29·778	29·781	29·785	29·792	29·792	29·793	29·787	1865
29·719	29·711	29·707	29·706	29·705	29·706	29·711	29·716	29·722	29·726	29·726	29·726	29·717	1866
29·798	29·791	29·787	29·785	29·783	29·784	29·786	29·790	29·794	29·799	29·799	29·798	29·792	1867
29·799	29·791	29·785	29·781	29·779	29·780	29·784	29·789	29·794	29·799	29·801	29·803	29·794	1868
29·796	29·791	29·786	29·783	29·782	29·782	29·787	29·791	29·796	29·800	29·800	29·792	29·792	1869
29·809	29·804	29·798	29·794	29·793	29·793	29·797	29·802	29·808	29·814	29·815	29·816	29·806	1870
29·795	29·789	29·784	29·780	29·779	29·780	29·783	29·789	29·795	29·801	29·801	29·800	29·791	1871
29·641	29·636	29·630	29·627	29·625	29·625	29·628	29·632	29·637	29·639	29·640	29·640	29·635	1872
29·785	29·778	29·774	29·770	29·769	29·770	29·774	29·780	29·785	29·790	29·792	29·792	29·782	1873
29·784	29·778	29·773	29·770	29·769	29·770	29·773	29·777	29·782	29·787	29·788	29·788	29·780	..

In the above table for the years 1857, 1864, and 1868, are, in each case, the means of the monthly values for the remaining eleven months of the year.

BAROMETER for each YEAR from 1854 to 1873.

Noon.	1ʰ. p.m.	2ʰ. p.m.	3ʰ. p.m.	4ʰ. p.m.	5ʰ. p.m.	6ʰ. p.m.	7ʰ. p.m.	8ʰ. p.m.	9ʰ. p.m.	10ʰ. p.m.	11ʰ. p.m.	Year.
in.	in.	in.	in.	in.	in.	in.	in.	in.	in.	in.	in.	
+0·005	0·000	−0·005	−0·008	−0·009	−0·011	−0·009	−0·003	+0·002	+0·009	+0·011	+0·013	1854
+ 7	+ 1	− 4	− 8	− 10	− 13	− 13	− 7	− 1	+ 5	+ 9	+ 9	1855
+ 4	− 1	− 5	− 7	− 7	− 6	− 5	0	+ 4	+ 9	+ 10	+ 9	1856
+ 4	− 3	− 7	− 10	− 11	− 10	− 7	− 4	+ 2	+ 8	+ 10	+ 11	1857
+ 4	− 2	− 7	− 10	− 10	− 9	− 7	− 3	+ 1	+ 4	+ 5	+ 6	1858
+ 5	− 2	− 6	− 9	− 10	− 9	− 7	− 4	− 1	+ 5	+ 6	+ 5	1859
+ 4	− 2	− 5	− 7	− 7	− 6	− 2	+ 3	+ 6	+ 9	+ 11	+ 10	1860
+ 5	0	− 6	− 8	− 8	− 8	− 7	− 3	+ 1	+ 5	+ 7	+ 7	1861
0	− 7	− 10	− 12	− 11	− 9	− 8	− 4	− 1	+ 4	+ 6	+ 6	1862
0	− 9	− 12	− 14	− 14	− 12	− 9	− 5	− 1	+ 6	+ 8	+ 9	1863
+ 1	− 7	− 10	− 13	− 13	− 13	− 11	− 7	− 4	0	+ 1	+ 2	1864
+ 5	− 2	− 7	− 10	− 12	− 12	− 9	− 6	− 2	+ 5	+ 5	+ 6	1865
+ 2	− 6	− 10	− 11	− 12	− 11	− 6	− 1	+ 5	+ 9	+ 9	+ 9	1866
+ 6	− 1	− 5	− 7	− 9	− 8	− 6	− 2	+ 2	+ 7	+ 7	+ 6	1867
+ 5	− 3	− 9	− 13	− 15	− 14	− 10	− 5	0	+ 5	+ 7	+ 9	1868
+ 4	− 1	− 6	− 9	− 10	− 10	− 5	− 1	+ 4	+ 8	+ 8	0	1869
+ 3	− 2	− 8	− 12	− 13	− 13	− 9	− 4	+ 2	+ 8	+ 9	+ 10	1870
+ 4	− 2	− 7	− 11	− 12	− 11	− 8	− 2	+ 4	+ 10	+ 10	+ 9	1871
+ 6	+ 1	− 5	− 8	− 10	− 10	− 7	− 3	+ 2	+ 4	+ 5	+ 5	1872
+ 3	− 4	− 8	− 12	− 13	− 12	− 8	− 2	+ 3	+ 8	+ 10	+ 10	1873
+0·004	−0·002	−0·007	−0·010	−0·011	−0·010	−0·007	−0·003	+0·002	+0·007	+0·008	+0·008	..

TABLE XXI.—MEAN READING of the BAROMETER, as deduced from the Twenty-four Hourly Readings on each Day, for every DAY of the YEAR, through the RANGE of YEARS 1854 to 1873.

Day of the Month.	January.	February.	March.	April.	May.	June.	July.	August.	September.	October.	November.	December.
	in.	in.	in.	in.	in.	in.	in.	in.	in.	in.	in.	in.
1	29·753	29·663	29·811	29·752	29·788	29·778	29·854	29·831	29·837	29·777	29·760	29·713
2	29·750	29·711	29·815	29·728	29·804	29·747	29·836	29·782	29·794	29·807	29·783	29·782
3	29·731	29·775	29·851	29·745	29·751	29·752	29·829	29·763	29·775	29·813	29·839	29·776
4	29·693	29·708	29·861	29·818	29·759	29·842	29·790	29·757	29·787	29·844	29·852	29·818
5	29·648	29·755	29·820	29·867	29·816	29·872	29·780	29·777	29·799	29·846	29·855	29·748
6	29·725	29·703	29·683	29·850	29·824	29·858	29·780	29·795	29·782	29·854	29·909	29·717
7	29·735	29·727	29·606	29·840	29·752	29·841	29·804	29·742	29·766	29·739	.29·958	29·761
8	29·664	29·710	29·617	29·736	29·736	29·843	29·823	29·714	29·801	29·691	29·879	29·795
9	29·675	29·804	29·731	29·736	29·730	29·791	29·855	29·753	29·758	29·698	29·902	29·844
10	29·748	29·858	29·719	29·749	29·718	29·757	29·854	29·807	29·768	29·716	29·844	29·869
11	29·759	29·849	29·618	29·777	29·679	29·767	29·837	29·827	29·849	29·694	29·843	29·881
12	29·839	29·829	29·600	29·805	29·698	29·735	29·805	29·847	29·894	29·756	29·911	29·880
13	29·804	29·935	29·605	29·800	29·763	29·728	29·805	29·823	29·835	29·742	29·819	29·814
14	29·788	29·964	29·632	29·799	29·814	29·728	29·822	29·806	29·770	29·792	29·673	29·817
15	29·815	29·900	29·678	29·790	29·771	29·759	29·792	29·799	29·781	29·728	29·686	29·869
16	29·839	29·857	29·736	29·804	29·781	29·795	29·799	29·782	29·795	29·679	29·714	29·835
17	29·811	29·848	29·753	29·806	29·802	29·799	29·827	29·780	29·813	29·659	29·793	29·853
18	29·721	29·871	29·726	29·844	29·788	29·829	29·795	29·747	29·840	29·622	29·906	29·773
19	29·839	29·839	29·774	29·774	29·839	29·823	29·796	29·750	29·818	29·603	29·936	29·771
20	29·571	29·851	29·741	29·723	29·875	29·840	29·825	29·785	29·821	29·643	29·892	29·763
21	29·635	29·889	29·728	29·756	29·832	29·896	29·814	29·802	29·778	29·706	29·778	29·768
22	29·621	29·899	29·799	29·791	29·804	29·896	29·771	29·799	29·746	29·693	29·578	29·794
23	29·638	29·938	29·779	29·820	29·752	29·903	29·758	29·807	29·738	29·656	29·534	29·813
24	29·610	29·931	29·678	29·854	29·765	29·928	29·780	29·820	29·749	29·648	29·587	29·744
25	29·728	29·903	29·685	29·888	29·769		29·754	29·839	29·813	29·678	29·595	29·684
26	29·837	29·806	29·682	29·909	29·774	29·921	29·777	29·871	29·870	29·662	29·577	29·641
27	29·839	29·817	29·754	29·839	29·775	29·913	29·803	29·887	29·788	29·721	29·671	29·697
28	29·840	29·795	29·727	29·810	29·811	29·859	29·816	29·828	29·695	29·789	29·725	29·793
29	29·774		29·746	29·836	29·832	29·830	29·825	29·804	29·730	29·761	29·717	29·804
30	29·703		29·747	29·819	29·811	29·802	29·837	29·836	29·741	29·710	29·662	29·809
31	29·665		29·749		29·782		29·828	29·827		29·729		29·810
Means	29·729	29·829	29·722	29·804	29·780	29·825	29·809	29·800	29·791	29·724	29·773	29·789

The Mean of the twelve monthly values is 29in·781.

TABLE XXII.—MEANS, for periods of FIVE DAYS, of the MEAN DAILY READINGS of the BAROMETER contained in Table XXI.

Period.		Mean Reading of the Barometer.	Period.		Mean Reading of the Barometer.	Period.		Mean Reading of the Barometer.
		in.			in.			in.
Jan. 1 to Jan.	5	29·715	May 6 to May 10		29·752	Sept. 8 to Sept. 12		29·814
6	10	29·709	11	15	29·745	13	17	29·798
11	15	29·801	16	20	29·817	18	22	29·801
16	20	29·718	21	25	29·784	23	27	29·792
21	25	29·646	26	30	29·801	28 Oct. 2		29·750
26	30	29·799	31 June 4		29·780	Oct. 3	7	29·819
31 Feb.	4	29·722	June 5	9	29·841	8	12	29·711
Feb. 5	9	29·740	10	14	29·743	13	17	29·720
10	14	29·887	15	19	29·801	18	22	29·653
15	19	29·863	20	24	29·892	23	27	29·673
20	24	29·902	25	29	29·888	28 Nov. 1		29·750
25 Mar.	1	29·826	30 July 4		29·822	Nov. 2	6	29·848
Mar. 2	6	29·806	July 5	9	29·808	7	11	29·885
7	11	29·660	10	14	29·825	12	16	29·761
12	16	29·650	15	19	29·862	17	21	29·861
17	21	29·732	20	24	29·790	22	26	29·574
22	26	29·725	25	29	29·795	27 Dec. 1		29·698
27	31	29·742	30 Aug. 3		29·808	Dec. 2	6	29·768
Apr. 1 Apr.	5	29·782	Aug. 4	8	29·757	7	11	29·830
6	10	29·790	9	13	29·811	12	16	29·847
11	15	29·794	14	18	29·783	17	21	29·786
16	20	29·790	19	23	29·789	22	26	29·735
21	25	29·822	24	28	29·853	27	31	29·783
26	30	29·843	29 Sept. 2		29·818			
May 1 May	5	29·784	Sept. 3	7	29·782			

TABLE XXIII.—LIST of DAYS on which the Wind blew THROUGHOUT THE DAY from EACH DIRECTION, referred to EIGHT POINTS of the AZIMUTHAL CIRCLE, as determined from OSLER'S ANEMOMETER, during the Period 1869–1873.

[This Table is a continuation of Table LXXXVIII. in the Thermometric Section, in which will be found similar information for the Period 1854–1868, completing the information in regard to the distribution of the Winds, 1854–1873, required for the formation of Tables XXIV. to XXXI.]

Days which, in the following Table referring to the Years 1869–1873, are printed in a slightly bolder type have been omitted in the formation of Tables XXIV. to XXXI. Days which have been omitted during the earlier Period, 1854–1868, are similarly indicated in Table LXXXVIII.

Year.	January.	February.	March.	April.	May.	June.	July.	August.	September.	October.	November.	December.
NORTH.												
1869			6	18	10	13			29	24		1
			11		19	19						2
			20		29							3
			27									27
1870		19	9	2		10				1		3
						11				10		7
						19				11		8
												23
1871	12		29	1	9	2		18		17	4	
	27		30			3		21		30		
	28					4						
						5						
						6						
						7						
						8						
						9						
						25						
						26						
1872	9		19	3	11	14	3			11	4	
	27		20	13		15	27			12	11	
			22	17		31				13		
				18						14		
				19								
1873	3		7	19	6		5	26				
	4		26	28								
	12			31								
	13											
NORTH-EAST.												
1869	22	13	27	4	20	1	17	1		5		
		14	28	12	25	2	19	2		6		
		15	29	13	27	20	30			8		
		21	30	15	30		31			23		
		22		16						24		
		23		27								
		24		28								
		25		29								
		29										
		30										
		31										

Year.	January.	February.	March.	April.	May.	June.	July.	August.	September.	October.	November.	December.
NORTH-EAST continued.												
1870	19	9	4	6	5	27	8	29	5	5	4	
	20	10	5		6	28	9	30			22	
	21	11	6		7	29	12				26	
	22	12	7				13				27	
	23	13	8				14				28	
	24	14	25				15				29	
	25	15	26				16				30	
	26	16	27								31	
		17	28									
		18	29									
1871	23		27	10	24		7	11	10	2	1	
	24		28	12			14	12	31	25		
	25			13				13		26		
	26			14				14		27		
	29			15				16		28		
	30			28				17		29		
				29				19				
				31				26				
1872	20		23	5	10		22	5	15	3		
			24	6	13		23	14				
			25		17		24	20				
					18							
1873	24	7	13	8	13	2		25	8			
		8	18	9	14	7		27	14			
		9	19	10	18				16			
		10	20	11					17			
				18					18			
				19								
				20								
				23								
				24								
EAST.												
1869	13		9	5	11	27	4		7			
	22		10	14		28			9			
			26									

TABLE XXIII.—List of Days on which the Wind blew THROUGHOUT THE DAY from EACH DIRECTION—*continued.*

EAST continued.

Year	January	February	March	April	May	June	July	August	September	October	November	December
1870			3 4 5 18	9 27 28			23 24	2	22 23 24 25 26	1 2		21
1871	20	1	23	6 7 8 9 10	7 22 23	11 12		8 9 10 12 13 15 16 29	8 15 20	11 12 30	1 3 4 5	
1872		15		20				14 15 18 19 20 21		17		2 14 19
1873	30 31			15 16 22 23 24 25 26 30	16 17			24	24			9 10 11 12 13 15 19

SOUTH.

Year	January	February	March	April	May	June	July	August	September	October	November	December
1869	20										11	30 31
1870	2 31	2 3 4 5 6 27 28		20							26	
1871	3	12	4 6						20	9	5 17 19 26 27	20 22
1872	16 25 31	1 3 4 5 8 10	5 7 14 27	22 23	20		24	9	2 3 4	21 24 25 26	21 30	1 28 29
1873	8		1		5		13	18	27		2 3 4	29 30

SOUTH-EAST.

Year	January	February	March	April	May	June	July	August	September	October	November	December
1869	10 11 12 14 19 23 24		17	25		4	21	29	6 7 10			
1870	17 28 29 30	7 8		1	10		7	19		28 29 30	11	
1871	1 2 4 21 31	4	1 3	11 25		13	11 17	10	14 18 23 28 29	6 21 24		
1872	22	11 12 13 14	6		14 24		16 17	19				20
1873	26 27 28 29	1		14	12 22			25		5 20		

SOUTH-WEST.

Year	January	February	March	April	May	June	July	August	September	October	November	December
1869	2 3 4 5 6 8 15 16 17 25 26 29 30 31	1 3 6 7 8 9 10 11 14 15 16 17 18 19		2 6 7 8 12 15 16 20 21 22	7 10 18 19 24 26 27 29 30 31	2 4 5 8 13 15 17 23 24	6 7 8 12 14 16 18 25	1 7 13 14 15 16 17 18 19 26 31	4 6 8 12 14 15 16 17 18 19 22 23 24 25 26 27	4 7 8 12 13 14 15 16 18 21 26	12 13 14 15 16 19 20	12 13 14 15 16 19 20 29
1870	1 3 4 5 6 7 8 11 12 13 14	23 26	14 15 16	7 8 9 13 17 22	12 13 14 15 17 18	12 13	4 5 10 17 18 22	5 6 18 19	1 4 5 6 7 9 11 12 13 19 20 21 30 31	16 18 19 22 23	17 21 24 25	

TABLE XXIII.—List of Days on which the Wind blew THROUGHOUT THE DAY from EACH DIRECTION—*concluded.*

SOUTH-WEST—continued. / WEST.

Year	January	February	March	April	May	June	July	August	September	October	November	December
1871	6 7 13 14 15 16 17 18	5 14 15 16 17 18 19 20 24 27	7 8 9 11 12 13 21	12 16 19 20 22 28	16 18 19 27 29 30	1 3 4 5 6 7 8 9 12 13 14 15 16 17 21 22 23 24 26 29 30 31	1 23 24 25 31	3 4 5 7	2 6 16 21		14	15 18 19 21 24 25 26 27 28 30
1872	1 2 3 4 6 7 11 12 13 17 18 23 24 29 30	2 6 17 18 19 20 21 22 24 25 29	2 3 8 16 17 28 29 30 31	10 11 24 25	4 6 7 8 22 23	2 5 6 7 8 9 11 15 21 25 27	5 9 12 20 27 28 29	1 10 25 30	1 5 6 9 10 11 23 27 28 30	1 2 7 10 23 27 30	1 2 4 5 6 18 20 22 23 24 25 26 27	5 6 8 13 22 23 24 25 26 30 31
1873	1 2 3 4 5 6 7 9 10 11 12 13 14 15 16 18 19 20	26	3 8 9 10 11	10 21	10 11 19 20 22 24	2 3 5 7 8 11 12 14 17 20 24 25 27 28 30 31	4 5 6 7 12 15 16 17 19 20 21 22 27 28 31	1 7 9 12 20	2 3 6 10 20	1 26 29		1 4 5 8 9 10 11 15 18 19 21 26 31
WEST.												
1869	28			20		9 12	9 21	16 23	14 23	1 2 7		17

WEST—continued. / NORTH-WEST.

Year	January	February	March	April	May	June	July	August	September	October	November	December
1870		21	10 11 24 25	1	10 11 26	6 16		10	11 17 24 27	12 13 16 18 23	9 19	
1871	5 8	6 8 23 25	10	13 21 23 27	4 26		25	5 19 26	22 28	3		8 9 10 11 12 13 14 31
1872	5 8 14	1 13 26	8 15	5 21 29 30	10 12 22 26 28	1 2 8 19	11 12 28 31	7 8 12 13 14 16 17 18 19 21 25 26 29	8 11 12 15 29 31	3 7 8 9 17	9 17 18	
1873				4	2 4 9 11 22 23	2 6 9 21 26	9 15 16 19 21 26	4 9 14 16 23	3 16 21 29 30	2 15 18	14 16 22	24 10 28
NORTH-WEST.												
1869		2	17					15	10 11		3 17 26 27 28	4 6 11
1870		21	11 12 23 24	23 27		25 30	2	23 25 29		28		
1871		9	31	30	1 5 20	20	20					
1872		18	4 16	26	3 20			22		10		
1873		14 27	5 6 28	1 8 12 24		9				22 23 30		

TABLE XXIV.—MONTHLY MEAN READING of the BAROMETER at every HOUR of the DAY through the RANGE of YEARS 1854 to 1873, during prevalence of NORTH WIND.

Hour, Greenwich Mean Solar Time (Civil reckoning).	January.	February.	March.	April.	May.	June.	July.	August.	September.	October.	November.	December.	Yearly Means.
	in.	in.	in.	in.	in.	in.	in.	in.	in.	in.	in.	in.	in.
Midnight	29·474	29·776	29·670	29·819	29·762	29·941	29·866	29·815	29·751	29·700	29·779	29·774	29·761
1, a.m.	29·478	29·780	29·676	29·821	29·763	29·941	29·867	29·818	29·750	29·703	29·778	29·775	29·763
2 ,,	29·493	29·783	29·678	29·821	29·765	29·938	29·866	29·818	29·750	29·700	29·779	29·780	29·764
3 ,,	29·506	29·785	29·681	29·823	29·766	29·937	29·866	29·818	29·749	29·700	29·779	29·785	29·766
4 ,,	29·517	29·788	29·686	29·826	29·767	29·939	29·870	29·822	29·748	29·701	29·780	29·787	29·769
5 ,,	29·530	29·794	29·696	29·831	29·772	29·942	29·873	29·830	29·750	29·710	29·782	29·790	29·775
6 ,,	29·545	29·800	29·711	29·841	29·779	29·947	29·880	29·839	29·736	29·716	29·787	29·793	29·785
7 ,,	29·562	29·809	29·725	29·851	29·783	29·954	29·889	29·850	29·764	29·726	29·748	29·802	29·793
8 ,,	29·583	29·819	29·739	29·861	29·788	29·958	29·898	29·860	29·774	29·738	29·815	29·809	29·803
9 ,,	29·605	29·832	29·752	29·870	29·793	29·963	29·901	29·870	29·783	29·744	29·823	29·821	29·813
10 ,,	29·630	29·830	29·758	29·874	29·745	29·967	29·907	29·880	29·787	29·749	29·834	29·831	29·821
11 ,,	29·645	29·844	29·761	29·876	29·797	29·966	29·911	29·887	29·790	29·751	29·837	29·835	29·825
Noon	29·642	29·845	29·766	29·878	29·797	29·964	29·912	29·886	29·791	29·747	29·834	29·834	29·825
1, p.m.	29·644	29·842	29·766	29·880	29·792	29·962	29·913	29·889	29·791	29·744	29·833	29·830	29·824
2 ,,	29·653	29·840	29·767	29·877	29·796	29·960	29·910	29·890	29·790	29·745	29·834	29·831	29·825
3 ,,	29·671	29·847	29·769	29·873	29·796	29·959	29·909	29·892	29·790	29·750	29·840	29·839	29·828
4 ,,	29·686	29·853	29·772	29·873	29·798	29·958	29·907	29·893	29·793	29·754	29·845	29·850	29·832
5 ,,	29·705	29·850	29·778	29·875	29·799	29·956	29·909	29·865	29·708	29·758	29·835	29·857	29·837
6 ,,	29·722	29·870	29·786	29·881	29·803	29·963	29·909	29·899	29·806	29·765	29·865	29·866	29·845
7 ,,	29·741	29·878	29·799	29·889	29·810	29·970	29·915	29·908	29·818	29·772	29·872	29·875	29·854
8 ,,	29·757	29·886	29·807	29·902	29·817	29·982	29·923	29·924	29·829	29·781	29·879	29·881	29·864
9 ,,	29·776	29·895	29·818	29·912	29·830	29·997	29·934	29·935	29·837	29·789	29·889	29·888	29·875
10 ,,	29·786	29·899	29·819	29·915	29·834	30·000	29·941	29·938	29·838	29·794	29·892	29·893	29·879
11 ,,	29·795	29·900	29·821	29·918	29·835	30·005	29·937	29·946	29·839	29·795	29·896	29·897	29·882
Means	29·631	29·836	29·750	29·866	29·793	29·961	29·900	29·875	29·786	29·743	29·829	29·830	29·817
Number of Days employed	14	22	29	22	32	41	21	20	13	19	34	30	..

TABLE XXV.—MONTHLY MEAN READING of the BAROMETER at every HOUR of the DAY through the RANGE of YEARS 1854 to 1873, during prevalence of NORTH-EAST WIND.

Hour, Greenwich Mean Solar Time (Civil reckoning).	January.	February.	March.	April.	May.	June.	July.	August.	September.	October.	November.	December.	Yearly Means.
	in.	in.	in.	in.	in.	in.	in.	in.	in.	in.	in.	in.	in.
Midnight	29·881	29·890	29·810	29·909	29·834	29·953	29·969	29·908	30·027	29·923	29·951	29·945	29·917
1, a.m.	29·881	29·887	29·811	29·908	29·831	29·940	29·967	29·907	30·024	29·926	29·951	29·946	29·916
2 ,,	29·884	29·888	29·810	29·906	29·828	29·946	29·964	29·904	30·021	29·926	29·951	29·950	29·915
3 ,,	29·886	29·885	29·806	29·904	29·824	29·950	29·956	29·902	30·017	29·926	29·949	29·953	29·913
4 ,,	29·887	29·884	29·805	29·904	29·821	29·943	29·959	29·899	30·015	29·927	29·949	29·953	29·912
5 ,,	29·888	29·885	29·807	29·907	29·822	29·943	29·956	29·901	30·013	29·932	29·949	29·955	29·914
6 ,,	29·891	29·887	29·813	29·912	29·824	29·944	29·963	29·907	30·010	29·936	29·950	29·961	29·917
7 ,,	29·898	29·893	29·822	29·918	29·825	29·948	29·967	29·910	30·006	29·945	29·958	29·970	29·923
8 ,,	29·911	29·901	29·827	29·926	29·827	29·950	29·971	29·915	30·031	29·956	29·967	29·980	29·930
9 ,,	29·924	29·907	29·830	29·836	29·829	29·940	29·973	29·911	30·041	29·963	29·974	29·996	29·937
10 ,,	29·933	29·910	29·829	29·842	29·829	29·946	29·971	29·911	30·041	29·966	29·979	30·007	29·940
11 ,,	29·940	29·912	29·844	29·838	29·828	29·941	29·969	29·917	30·037	29·967	29·980	30·010	29·940
Noon	29·933	29·907	29·844	29·835	29·825	29·967	29·962	29·914	30·033	29·966	29·973	30·000	29·936
1, p.m.	29·927	29·901	29·840	29·833	29·821	29·933	29·962	29·909	30·028	29·956	29·969	29·995	29·931
2 ,,	29·926	29·894	29·837	29·833	29·818	29·927	29·958	29·905	30·022	29·952	29·964	29·994	29·927
3 ,,	29·931	29·890	29·834	29·924	29·813	29·921	29·954	29·900	30·015	29·950	29·964	29·999	29·925
4 ,,	29·936	29·895	29·833	29·924	29·812	29·915	29·949	29·896	30·011	29·952	29·966	30·002	29·924
5 ,,	29·940	29·895	29·836	29·942	29·810	29·913	29·945	29·895	30·010	29·955	29·970	30·007	29·925
6 ,,	29·945	29·898	29·842	29·932	29·813	29·915	29·944	29·896	30·014	29·963	29·975	30·010	29·929
7 ,,	29·952	29·903	29·849	29·943	29·819	29·917	29·945	29·903	30·021	29·967	29·979	30·016	29·935
8 ,,	29·956	29·905	29·856	29·828	29·828	29·924	29·952	29·915	30·030	29·972	29·981	30·021	29·941
9 ,,	29·958	29·910	29·866	29·964	29·838	29·934	29·961	29·922	30·038	29·980	29·986	30·025	29·948
10 ,,	29·961	29·911	29·868	29·969	29·842	29·936	29·964	29·926	30·040	29·979	29·986	30·025	29·949
11 ,,	29·962	29·911	29·869	29·971	29·844	29·936	29·967	29·927	30·038	29·980	29·986	30·025	29·951
Means	29·922	29·898	29·834	29·929	29·825	29·936	29·961	29·909	30·026	29·953	29·967	29·989	29·929
Number of Days employed	64	55	84	76	96	47	40	41	53	46	72	39	..

TABLE XXVI.—MONTHLY MEAN READING of the BAROMETER at every HOUR of the DAY through the RANGE of YEARS 1854 to 1873, during prevalence of EAST WIND.

Hour, Greenwich Mean Solar Time (Civil reckoning).	January.	February.	March.	April.	May.	June.	July.	August.	September.	October.	November.	December.	Yearly Means.
	in.	in.	in.	in.	in.	in.	in.	in.	in.	in.	in.	in.	in.
Midnight	29·803	29·894	29·803	30·004	29·978	29·810	29·952	29·940	30·042	29·889	29·955	29·898	29·914
1ʰ. a.m.	29·796	29·894	29·803	30·002	29·973	29·805	29·943	29·931	30·036	29·887	29·949	29·895	29·909
2 ,,	29·796	29·893	29·796	29·999	29·967	29·796	29·936	29·924	30·027	29·880	29·947	29·896	29·905
3 ,,	29·795	29·891	29·789	29·995	29·959	29·793	29·930	29·913	30·017	29·874	29·942	29·893	29·899
4 ,,	29·792	29·888	29·786	29·992	29·955	29·788	29·927	29·910	30·010	29·870	29·939	29·888	29·895
5 ,,	29·788	29·889	29·784	29·993	29·953	29·789	29·924	29·909	30·005	29·869	29·939	29·884	29·894
6 ,,	29·789	29·887	29·786	29·997	29·953	29·791	29·924	29·911	30·004	29·870	29·939	29·885	29·895
7 ,,	29·795	29·890	29·785	30·001	29·952	29·789	29·926	29·911	30·005	29·872	29·943	29·889	29·897
8 ,,	29·805	29·894	29·786	30·003	29·948	29·792	29·922	29·912	30·005	29·877	29·947	29·895	29·899
9 ,,	29·816	29·899	29·786	30·005	29·943	29·792	29·915	29·909	30·007	29·881	29·947	29·894	29·899
10 ,,	29·823	29·898	29·783	30·004	29·933	29·793	29·904	29·902	30·002	29·877	29·948	29·898	29·897
11 ,,	29·827	29·898	29·777	29·995	29·922	29·789	29·892	29·897	29·990	29·877	29·945	29·894	29·892
Noon	29·816	29·896	29·776	29·988	29·916	29·784	29·882	29·888	29·980	29·869	29·934	29·883	29·884
1ʰ. p.m.	29·807	29·884	29·764	29·982	29·906	29·776	29·874	29·879	29·966	29·859	29·922	29·875	29·875
2 ,,	29·804	29·878	29·753	29·971	29·897	29·774	29·864	29·871	29·956	29·850	29·915	29·868	29·867
3 ,,	29·806	29·872	29·745	29·961	29·884	29·768	29·856	29·863	29·943	29·843	29·912	29·869	29·860
4 ,,	29·807	29·872	29·741	29·955	29·876	29·762	29·848	29·857	29·935	29·841	29·913	29·874	29·854
5 ,,	29·810	29·872	29·738	29·952	29·867	29·758	29·841	29·851	29·931	29·842	29·914	29·871	29·854
6 ,,	29·812	29·876	29·738	29·949	29·861	29·759	29·836	29·851	29·929	29·847	29·915	29·875	29·854
7 ,,	29·816	29·877	29·740	29·950	29·858	29·760	29·830	29·851	29·930	29·851	29·915	29·880	29·855
8 ,,	29·822	29·879	29·740	29·953	29·856	29·764	29·833	29·858	29·931	29·851	29·917	29·882	29·857
9 ,,	29·826	29·876	29·741	29·952	29·854	29·770	29·830	29·859	29·925	29·855	29·912	29·883	29·857
10 ,,	29·826	29·878	29·740	29·951	29·852	29·774	29·830	29·860	29·921	29·856	29·909	29·884	29·857
11 ,,	29·826	29·877	29·734	29·948	29·845	29·775	29·825	29·836	29·915	29·855	29·907	29·881	29·854
Means	29·808	29·885	29·767	29·979	29·913	29·781	29·885	29·888	29·976	29·864	29·930	29·885	29·880
Number of Days employed	10	22	34	53	28	13	10	31	23	35	35	21	..

TABLE XXVII.—MONTHLY MEAN READING of the BAROMETER at every HOUR of the DAY through the RANGE of YEARS 1854 to 1873, during prevalence of SOUTH-EAST WIND.

Hour, Greenwich Mean Solar Time (Civil reckoning).	January.	February.	March.	April.	May.	June.	July.	August.	September.	October.	November.	December.	Yearly Means.
	in.	in.	in.	in.	in.	in.	in.	in.	in.	in.	in.	in.	in.
Midnight	29·913	29·831	29·817	29·822	29·838	29·926	30·026	29·845	29·932	29·809	29·897	29·794	29·871
1ʰ. a.m.	29·905	29·826	29·813	29·815	29·833	29·921	30·023	29·837	29·927	29·803	29·886	29·790	29·865
2 ,,	29·903	29·820	29·807	29·808	29·825	29·915	30·018	29·831	29·920	29·796	29·886	29·784	29·858
3 ,,	29·901	29·811	29·802	29·801	29·818	29·906	30·012	29·821	29·914	29·787	29·863	29·780	29·851
4 ,,	29·897	29·806	29·795	29·795	29·815	29·902	30·007	29·816	29·808	29·784	29·853	29·777	29·846
5 ,,	29·892	29·801	29·793	29·792	29·813	29·899	30·007	29·816	29·808	29·780	29·845	29·765	29·842
6 ,,	29·887	29·794	29·794	29·794	29·815	29·897	30·010	29·818	29·897	29·778	29·834	29·761	29·841
7 ,,	29·887	29·794	29·796	29·799	29·810	29·893	30·012	29·818	29·894	29·785	29·834	29·760	29·840
8 ,,	29·888	29·795	29·797	29·795	29·808	29·890	30·015	29·818	29·894	29·792	29·833	29·759	29·840
9 ,,	29·892	29·794	29·801	29·793	29·808	29·882	30·014	29·812	29·889	29·793	29·831	29·738	29·839
10 ,,	29·892	29·794	29·798	29·787	29·804	29·871	30·006	29·806	29·884	29·789	29·828	29·736	29·835
11 ,,	29·886	29·791	29·792	29·781	29·796	29·866	30·004	29·798	29·873	29·784	29·816	29·734	29·828
Noon	29·837	29·784	29·784	29·776	29·787	29·857	29·994	29·791	29·863	29·777	29·797	29·742	29·818
1ʰ. p.m.	29·834	29·771	29·774	29·767	29·779	29·843	29·982	29·783	29·851	29·761	29·782	29·734	29·807
2 ,,	29·843	29·760	29·765	29·755	29·771	29·827	29·971	29·776	29·842	29·753	29·770	29·727	29·797
3 ,,	29·842	29·757	29·757	29·745	29·755	29·813	29·965	29·768	29·829	29·746	29·759	29·723	29·788
4 ,,	29·840	29·755	29·751	29·739	29·747	29·806	29·957	29·763	29·823	29·741	29·753	29·721	29·783
5 ,,	29·840	29·755	29·750	29·736	29·737	29·797	29·930	29·756	29·823	29·743	29·753	29·722	29·780
6 ,,	29·838	29·757	29·751	29·737	29·733	29·793	29·946	29·757	29·818	29·747	29·752	29·722	29·779
7 ,,	29·837	29·759	29·754	29·738	29·731	29·791	29·943	29·754	29·818	29·745	29·747	29·724	29·778
8 ,,	29·835	29·758	29·754	29·740	29·730	29·790	29·944	29·749	29·818	29·744	29·746	29·723	29·777
9 ,,	29·831	29·758	29·753	29·739	29·733	29·786	29·942	29·749	29·814	29·743	29·742	29·723	29·776
10 ,,	29·828	29·756	29·751	29·738	29·730	29·787	29·944	29·749	29·809	29·741	29·738	29·724	29·775
11 ,,	29·824	29·754	29·744	29·736	29·729	29·787	29·938	29·747	29·811	29·742	29·737	29·722	29·772
Means	29·868	29·783	29·779	29·772	29·781	29·852	29·985	29·791	29·864	29·769	29·803	29·748	29·816
Number of Days employed	49	26	24	25	14	13	8	17	23	39	34	29	..

D

TABLE XXVIII.—Monthly Mean Reading of the Barometer at every Hour of the Day through the Range of Years 1854 to 1873, during prevalence of South Wind.

Hour, Greenwich Mean Solar Time (Civil reckoning).	January.	February.	March.	April.	May.	June.	July.	August.	September.	October.	November.	December.	Yearly Means.
	in.	in.	in.	in.	in.	in.	in.	in.	in.	in.	in.	in.	in.
Midnight	29·734	29·663	29·573	29·594	29·691	29·853	29·685	29·752	29·624	29·701	29·715	29·704	29·699
1ʰ. a.m.	29·728	29·663	29·663	29·589	29·687	29·846	29·673	29·751	29·621	29·693	29·714	29·702	29·694
2 ,,	29·724	29·656	29·652	29·580	29·683	29·835	29·666	29·751	29·618	29·684	29·713	29·704	29·689
3 ,,	29·718	29·648	29·639	29·572	29·682	29·828	29·659	29·744	29·614	29·676	29·713	29·702	29·683
4 ,,	29·712	29·644	29·627	29·565	29·681	29·817	29·655	29·746	29·613	29·672	29·711	29·698	29·678
5 ,,	29·706	29·642	29·616	29·562	29·683	29·816	29·636	29·745	29·611	29·666	29·714	29·605	29·676
6 ,,	29·704	29·638	29·607	29·561	29·684	29·811	29·658	29·748	29·612	29·662	29·714	29·695	29·675
7 ,,	29·705	29·640	29·603	29·561	29·686	29·803	29·662	29·751	29·615	29·665	29·719	29·697	29·676
8 ,,	29·710	29·644	29·594	29·557	29·687	29·796	29·658	29·750	29·621	29·668	29·726	29·698	29·676
9 ,,	29·715	29·640	29·582	29·554	29·683	29·793	29·647	29·747	29·622	29·669	29·732	29·703	29·673
10 ,,	29·718	29·630	29·570	29·549	29·680	29·784	29·637	29·746	29·622	29·665	29·733	29·702	29·671
11 ,,	29·715	29·649	29·557	29·545	29·679	29·760	29·627	29·752	29·623	29·659	29·725	29·663	29·664
Noon	29·703	29·640	29·538	29·538	29·669	29·755	29·615	29·720	29·613	29·651	29·714	29·680	29·653
1ʰ. p.m.	29·645	29·627	29·519	29·528	29·664	29·748	29·600	29·711	29·610	29·640	29·703	29·667	29·643
2 ,,	29·690	29·621	29·500	29·520	29·654	29·739	29·582	29·608	29·608	29·635	29·694	29·638	29·633
3 ,,	29·690	29·617	29·481	29·511	29·647	29·734	29·553	29·608	29·600	29·631	29·601	29·656	29·625
4 ,,	29·691	29·618	29·472	29·507	29·641	29·730	29·543	29·675	29·601	29·631	29·649	29·653	29·621
5 ,,	29·692	29·619	29·461	29·505	29·635	29·713	29·522	29·670	29·601	29·653	29·689	29·632	29·616
6 ,,	29·689	29·619	29·436	29·504	29·630	29·707	29·504	29·663	29·607	29·638	29·690	29·630	29·613
7 ,,	29·692	29·616	29·454	29·506	29·629	29·694	29·497	29·660	29·619	29·638	29·683	29·653	29·612
8 ,,	29·693	29·613	29·448	29·318	29·628	29·687	29·498	29·662	29·621	29·637	29·684	29·653	29·612
9 ,,	29·689	29·612	29·443	29·524	29·630	29·687	29·506	29·650	29·623	29·639	29·677	29·655	29·612
10 ,,	29·690	29·609	29·430	29·529	29·627	29·683	29·517	29·653	29·622	29·639	29·675	29·654	29·611
11 ,,	29·690	29·609	29·438	29·533	29·622	29·681	29·532	29·630	29·622	29·640	29·668	29·630	29·611
Means	29·704	29·634	29·543	29·542	29·662	29·762	29·598	29·711	29·615	29·636	29·704	29·678	29·651
Number of Days employed	25	24	19	13	12	4	4	9	15	22	19	27	..

TABLE XXIX.—Monthly Mean Reading of the Barometer at every Hour of the Day through the Range of Years 1854 to 1873, during prevalence of South-west Wind.

Hour, Greenwich Mean Solar Time (Civil reckoning).	January.	February.	March.	April.	May.	June.	July.	August.	September.	October.	November.	December.	Yearly Means.
	in.	in.	in.	in.	in.	in.	in.	in.	in.	in.	in.	in.	in.
Midnight	29·713	29·829	29·608	29·719	29·675	29·736	29·765	29·749	29·707	29·682	29·686	29·765	29·727
1ʰ. a.m.	29·706	29·823	29·693	29·715	29·671	29·733	29·762	29·744	29·703	29·678	29·680	29·761	29·722
2 ,,	29·704	29·815	29·686	29·708	29·668	29·730	29·759	29·738	29·696	29·672	29·675	29·762	29·718
3 ,,	29·699	29·807	29·669	29·696	29·664	29·727	29·753	29·733	29·691	29·664	29·668	29·761	29·712
4 ,,	29·692	29·800	29·669	29·696	29·661	29·723	29·752	29·729	29·685	29·658	29·661	29·737	29·707
5 ,,	29·685	29·796	29·667	29·693	29·661	29·727	29·757	29·727	29·684	29·655	29·655	29·735	29·705
6 ,,	29·682	29·792	29·666	29·696	29·663	29·731	29·755	29·728	29·688	29·653	29·656	29·751	29·705
7 ,,	29·680	29·792	29·667	29·696	29·667	29·734	29·755	29·751	29·692	29·655	29·656	29·752	29·706
8 ,,	29·684	29·794	29·669	29·671	29·671	29·737	29·755	29·723	29·696	29·658	29·659	29·756	29·709
9 ,,	29·686	29·797	29·668	29·665	29·671	29·738	29·757	29·737	29·699	29·657	29·662	29·759	29·710
10 ,,	29·690	29·796	29·667	29·665	29·670	29·736	29·755	29·736	29·698	29·655	29·662	29·752	29·710
11 ,,	29·687	29·766	29·663	29·685	29·668	29·734	29·755	29·731	29·663	29·649	29·658	29·734	29·706
Noon	29·675	29·786	29·657	29·670	29·663	29·730	29·748	29·726	29·680	29·638	29·646	29·739	29·698
1ʰ. p.m.	29·662	29·773	29·646	29·671	29·658	29·726	29·743	29·720	29·683	29·625	29·635	29·723	29·689
2 ,,	29·657	29·761	29·638	29·663	29·654	29·723	29·740	29·717	29·677	29·618	29·626	29·716	29·683
3 ,,	29·638	29·754	29·630	29·636	29·630	29·718	29·736	29·711	29·670	29·612	29·622	29·713	29·678
4 ,,	29·653	29·751	29·626	29·646	29·646	29·712	29·732	29·705	29·666	29·612	29·622	29·711	29·674
5 ,,	29·660	29·751	29·623	29·646	29·646	29·712	29·737	29·705	29·666	29·612	29·622	29·711	29·674
6 ,,	29·650	29·756	29·629	29·644	29·648	29·712	29·726	29·705	29·668	29·616	29·624	29·710	29·674
7 ,,	29·659	29·756	29·632	29·646	29·632	29·714	29·728	29·708	29·671	29·618	29·624	29·709	29·676
8 ,,	29·657	29·756	29·637	29·660	29·652	29·719	29·730	29·715	29·675	29·618	29·622	29·707	29·676
9 ,,	29·650	29·754	29·636	29·649	29·669	29·727	29·738	29·719	29·675	29·619	29·622	29·704	29·680
10 ,,	29·645	29·752	29·638	29·648	29·655	29·730	29·739	29·721	29·675	29·617	29·620	29·703	29·680
11 ,,	29·641	29·751	29·637	29·645	29·674	29·730	29·730	29·720	29·674	29·614	29·618	29·703	29·679
Means	29·675	29·781	29·655	29·677	29·663	29·727	29·746	29·725	29·684	29·640	29·645	29·735	29·696
Number of Days employed	205	150	119	91	125	142	179	190	182	136	118	192	..

TABLE XXX.—MONTHLY MEAN READING of the BAROMETER at every HOUR of the DAY through the RANGE of YEARS 1854 to 1873, during prevalence of WEST WIND.

Hour, Greenwich Mean Solar Time (Civil reckoning).	January.	February.	March.	April.	May.	June.	July.	August.	September.	October.	November.	December.	Yearly Means.
	in.	in.	in.	in.	in.	in.	in.	in.	in.	in.	in.	in.	in.
Midnight	29·599	29·791	29·681	29·676	29·723	29·777	29·758	29·721	29·720	29·633	29·582	29·867	29·711
1ʰ. a.m.	29·591	29·787	29·679	29·678	29·721	29·779	29·758	29·723	29·721	29·635	29·580	29·866	29·710
2 ,,	29·588	29·785	29·677	29·678	29·720	29·781	29·759	29·724	29·722	29·638	29·582	29·867	29·710
3 ,,	29·581	29·785	29·670	29·677	29·720	29·781	29·760	29·726	29·723	29·636	29·581	29·869	29·709
4 ,,	29·578	29·783	29·666	29·679	29·721	29·783	29·762	29·729	29·725	29·639	29·587	29·867	29·710
5 ,,	29·574	29·793	29·667	29·682	29·726	29·791	29·769	29·736	29·731	29·644	29·591	29·867	29·714
6 ,,	29·572	29·794	29·670	29·691	29·733	29·798	29·775	29·745	29·740	29·650	29·595	29·870	29·719
7 ,,	29·575	29·798	29·678	29·701	29·736	29·804	29·780	29·757	29·753	29·662	29·603	29·876	29·727
8 ,,	29·583	29·807	29·682	29·706	29·740	29·800	29·789	29·764	29·764	29·673	29·612	29·887	29·735
9 ,,	29·586	29·811	29·684	29·716	29·744	29·810	29·796	29·773	29·774	29·687	29·617	29·896	29·742
10 ,,	29·600	29·819	29·686	29·722	29·743	29·813	29·799	29·778	29·779	29·693	29·626	29·907	29·747
11 ,,	29·600	29·825	29·681	29·722	29·743	29·815	29·800	29·778	29·781	29·698	29·628	29·908	29·748
Noon	29·595	29·821	29·678	29·721	29·740	29·813	29·799	29·773	29·781	29·698	29·621	29·898	29·745
1ʰ. p.m.	29·588	29·813	29·669	29·720	29·736	29·800	29·797	29·774	29·781	29·695	29·619	29·891	29·741
2 ,,	29·589	29·806	29·662	29·717	29·734	29·808	29·796	29·771	29·782	29·698	29·612	29·891	29·739
3 ,,	29·597	29·812	29·657	29·713	29·731	29·807	29·797	29·770	29·781	29·699	29·614	29·896	29·740
4 ,,	29·606	29·815	29·652	29·713	29·731	29·805	29·797	29·770	29·782	29·703	29·617	29·900	29·741
5 ,,	29·611	29·821	29·652	29·715	29·733	29·824	29·797	29·770	29·788	29·711	29·625	29·902	29·744
6 ,,	29·618	29·830	29·655	29·719	29·735	29·807	29·798	29·774	29·793	29·725	29·635	29·905	29·749
7 ,,	29·623	29·840	29·665	29·726	29·741	29·809	29·803	29·784	29·806	29·729	29·641	29·906	29·756
8 ,,	29·616	29·844	29·672	29·740	29·749	29·818	29·812	29·795	29·820	29·734	29·643	29·909	29·764
9 ,,	29·629	29·847	29·681	29·732	29·738	29·830	29·825	29·804	29·829	29·738	29·651	29·911	29·771
10 ,,	29·631	29·847	29·687	29·736	29·760	29·836	29·831	29·809	29·833	29·753	29·653	29·911	29·773
11 ,,	29·632	29·846	29·687	29·759	29·764	29·839	29·834	29·812	29·835	29·737	29·655	29·910	29·776
Means	29·599	29·814	29·672	29·712	29·737	29·805	29·791	29·765	29·773	29·687	29·615	29·891	29·738
Number of Days employed	32	34	38	54	29	39	58	61	57	40	31	59	..

TABLE XXXI.—MONTHLY MEAN READING of the BAROMETER at every HOUR of the DAY through the RANGE of YEARS 1854 to 1873, during prevalence of NORTH-WEST WIND.

Hour, Greenwich Mean Solar Time (Civil reckoning).	January.	February.	March.	April.	May.	June.	July.	August.	September.	October.	November.	December.	Yearly Means.
	in.	in.	in.	in.	in.	in.	in.	in.	in.	in.	in.	in.	in.
Midnight	29·372	29·693	29·672	29·670	29·745	29·782	29·777	29·724	29·717	29·678	29·709	29·700	29·687
1ʰ. a.m.	29·376	29·701	29·675	29·666	29·730	29·782	29·779	29·724	29·719	29·676	29·703	29·695	29·687
2 ,,	29·381	29·709	29·679	29·663	29·753	29·781	29·779	29·727	29·727	29·675	29·702	29·697	29·690
3 ,,	29·392	29·720	29·686	29·666	29·760	29·783	29·781	29·729	29·729	29·675	29·700	29·699	29·694
4 ,,	29·402	29·728	29·692	29·669	29·764	29·790	29·788	29·733	29·744	29·675	29·701	29·700	29·699
5 ,,	29·414	29·739	29·700	29·677	29·770	29·797	29·791	29·741	29·741	29·675	29·705	29·707	29·706
6 ,,	29·428	29·757	29·713	29·686	29·779	29·803	29·798	29·752	29·776	29·684	29·709	29·706	29·716
7 ,,	29·451	29·775	29·726	29·696	29·788	29·813	29·810	29·765	29·793	29·684	29·723	29·716	29·729
8 ,,	29·482	29·802	29·739	29·703	29·799	29·821	29·818	29·777	29·808	29·708	29·737	29·722	29·743
9 ,,	29·519	29·819	29·752	29·711	29·810	29·828	29·826	29·788	29·826	29·722	29·750	29·741	29·757
10 ,,	29·548	29·836	29·764	29·716	29·822	29·834	29·834	29·796	29·838	29·722	29·767	29·737	29·770
11 ,,	29·570	29·845	29·768	29·717	29·828	29·835	29·840	29·802	29·846	29·728	29·773	29·763	29·776
Noon	29·585	29·852	29·769	29·716	29·831	29·836	29·842	29·801	29·850	29·723	29·772	29·760	29·779
1ʰ. p.m.	29·592	29·851	29·769	29·716	29·833	29·837	29·846	29·801	29·851	29·718	29·773	29·759	29·779
2 ,,	29·614	29·850	29·765	29·713	29·834	29·838	29·849	29·801	29·861	29·723	29·782	29·764	29·783
3 ,,	29·636	29·854	29·764	29·713	29·829	29·840	29·849	29·801	29·862	29·730	29·791	29·777	29·787
4 ,,	29·655	29·860	29·765	29·712	29·828	29·840	29·849	29·805	29·868	29·745	29·818	29·783	29·792
5 ,,	29·676	29·870	29·773	29·716	29·827	29·841	29·847	29·805	29·868	29·745	29·818	29·796	29·798
6 ,,	29·702	29·882	29·782	29·722	29·833	29·841	29·807	29·807	29·874	29·767	29·830	29·806	29·805
7 ,,	29·702	29·894	29·790	29·730	29·840	29·847	29·835	29·816	29·883	29·767	29·838	29·817	29·815
8 ,,	29·710	29·903	29·801	29·740	29·828	29·850	29·830	29·830	29·830	29·734	29·844	29·827	29·821
9 ,,	29·723	29·915	29·808	29·749	29·877	29·865	29·874	29·844	29·914	29·790	29·853	29·837	29·837
10 ,,	29·727	29·919	29·808	29·755	29·889	29·878	29·878	29·850	29·919	29·790	29·855	29·843	29·842
11 ,,	29·726	29·920	29·810	29·759	29·893	29·875	29·881	29·854	29·920	29·800	29·858	29·852	29·846
Means	29·557	29·821	29·749	29·708	29·814	29·826	29·829	29·786	29·827	29·724	29·771	29·759	29·764
Number of Days employed	8	16	30	24	12	19	24	30	8	21	27	20	..

TABLE XXXII.—MEAN READING of the BAROMETER, at every HOUR of the DAY, during prevalence of WINDS referred to EIGHT POINTS of AZIMUTH, through the RANGE of YEARS 1854 to 1873.

Hour. Greenwich Mean Solar Time (Civil reckoning).	N.	N.E.	E.	S.E.	S.	S.W.	W.	N.W.
	in.	in.	in.	in.	in.	in.	in.	in.
Midnight	29·761	29·917	29·914	29·871	29·699	29·727	29·711	29·687
1ʰ. a.m.	29·763	29·916	29·909	29·865	29·694	29·722	29·710	29·687
2 ,,	29·764	29·915	29·905	29·858	29·689	29·718	29·710	29·690
3 ,,	29·766	29·913	29·899	29·851	29·683	29·712	29·709	29·694
4 ,,	29·769	29·912	29·895	29·846	29·678	29·707	29·710	29·699
5 ,,	29·775	29·914	29·894	29·842	29·676	29·705	29·714	29·706
6 ,,	29·783	29·917	29·895	29·841	29·675	29·705	29·719	29·716
7 ,,	29·795	29·923	29·897	29·840	29·676	29·706	29·727	29·729
8 ,,	29·803	29·930	29·899	29·840	29·676	29·709	29·735	29·743
9 ,,	29·813	29·937	29·899	29·830	29·675	29·710	29·742	29·757
10 ,,	29·821	29·940	29·897	29·835	29·671	29·710	29·747	29·770
11 ,,	29·825	29·940	29·892	29·828	29·664	29·706	29·748	29·776
Noon	29·825	29·936	29·884	29·818	29·653	29·698	29·745	29·778
1ʰ. p.m.	29·824	29·931	29·875	29·807	29·643	29·689	29·741	29·779
2 ,,	29·825	29·927	29·867	29·797	29·633	29·683	29·739	29·783
3 ,,	29·828	29·925	29·860	29·788	29·625	29·678	29·740	29·787
4 ,,	29·832	29·924	29·856	29·783	29·621	29·675	29·741	29·792
5 ,,	29·837	29·925	29·854	29·780	29·616	29·674	29·744	29·798
6 ,,	29·845	29·929	29·854	29·779	29·613	29·674	29·749	29·806
7 ,,	29·854	29·935	29·855	29·778	29·612	29·676	29·756	29·815
8 ,,	29·864	29·941	29·857	29·778	29·612	29·679	29·764	29·825
9 ,,	29·875	29·948	29·857	29·776	29·612	29·680	29·771	29·837
10 ,,	29·879	29·951	29·857	29·775	29·611	29·680	29·774	29·842
11 ,,	29·882	29·951	29·854	29·772	29·611	29·679	29·776	29·846
Means	29·817	29·929	29·880	29·816	29·651	29·696	29·738	29·764

TABLE XXXIII.—MEAN DIURNAL INEQUALITY of the BAROMETER for each WIND, referred to EIGHT POINTS of AZIMUTH, through the RANGE of YEARS 1854 to 1873.

Hour. Greenwich Mean Solar Time (Civil reckoning).	N.	N.E.	E.	S.E.	S.	S.W.	W.	N.W.
	in.	in.	in.	in.	in.	in.	in.	in.
Midnight	− 0·056	− 0·012	+ 0·034	+ 0·055	+ 0·048	+ 0·031	− 0·027	− 0·077
1ʰ. a.m.	− ·054	− ·013	+ ·029	+ ·049	+ ·043	+ ·026	− ·028	− ·077
2 ,,	− ·053	− ·014	+ ·025	+ ·042	+ ·038	+ ·022	− ·028	− ·074
3 ,,	− ·051	− ·016	+ ·019	+ ·035	+ ·032	+ ·016	− ·029	− ·070
4 ,,	− ·048	− ·017	+ ·015	+ ·030	+ ·027	+ ·011	− ·028	− ·065
5 ,,	− ·042	− ·015	+ ·014	+ ·026	+ ·025	+ ·009	− ·024	− ·058
6 ,,	− ·034	− ·012	+ ·015	+ ·025	+ ·024	+ ·009	− ·019	− ·048
7 ,,	− ·024	− ·006	+ ·017	+ ·024	+ ·025	+ ·010	− ·011	− ·035
8 ,,	− ·014	+ ·001	+ ·019	+ ·024	+ ·025	+ ·013	− ·003	− ·021
9 ,,	− ·004	+ ·008	+ ·019	+ ·023	+ ·024	+ ·014	+ ·004	− ·007
10 ,,	+ ·004	+ ·011	+ ·017	+ ·019	+ ·020	+ ·014	+ ·009	+ ·006
11 ,,	+ ·008	+ ·011	+ ·012	+ ·012	+ ·013	+ ·010	+ ·010	+ ·012
Noon	+ ·008	+ ·007	+ ·004	+ ·002	+ ·002	+ ·002	+ ·007	+ ·014
1ʰ. p.m.	+ ·007	+ ·002	− ·005	− ·009	− ·008	− ·007	+ ·003	+ ·015
2 ,,	+ ·008	+ ·002	− ·013	− ·019	− ·018	− ·013	+ ·001	+ ·019
3 ,,	+ ·011	− ·004	− ·020	− ·028	− ·026	− ·018	+ ·002	+ ·023
4 ,,	+ ·015	− ·005	− ·024	− ·033	− ·030	− ·021	+ ·003	+ ·028
5 ,,	+ ·020	− ·004	− ·026	− ·036	− ·035	− ·022	+ ·006	+ ·034
6 ,,	+ ·028		− ·026	− ·037	− ·038	− ·022	+ ·011	+ ·042
7 ,,	+ ·037	+ ·006	− ·025	− ·038	− ·039	− ·020	+ ·018	+ ·051
8 ,,	+ ·047	+ ·012	− ·023	− ·038	− ·039	− ·017	+ ·026	+ ·061
9 ,,	+ ·058	+ ·019	− ·023	− ·040	− ·039	− ·016	+ ·033	+ ·073
10 ,,	+ ·062	+ ·021	− ·023	− ·041	− ·040	− ·016	+ ·036	+ ·078
11 ,,	+ ·063	+ ·022	− ·026	− ·044	− ·040	− ·017	+ ·038	+ ·082

TABLE XXXIV.—MEAN READING of the BAROMETER in each MONTH through the RANGE of YEARS 1854 to 1873, under all ATMOSPHERIC CIRCUMSTANCES, and with each WIND.

Hour, Greenwich Mean Solar Time (Civil reckoning).	January.	February.	March.	April.	May.	June.	July.	August.	September.	October.	November.	December.	Yearly Mean.
Under all Atmospheric circumstances.	in. 29·729	in. 29·829	in. 29·722	in. 29·804	in. 29·780	in. 29·825	in. 29·809	in. 29·800	in. 29·791	in. 29·724	in. 29·773	in. 29·789	in. 29·781
N.	29·631	29·836	29·750	29·866	29·793	29·961	29·900	29·875	29·786	29·743	29·829	29·830	29·817
N.E.	29·922	29·898	29·834	29·929	29·825	29·936	29·961	29·909	30·026	29·953	29·967	29·989	29·929
E.	29·808	29·885	29·767	29·979	29·913	29·781	29·883	29·888	29·976	29·864	29·930	29·885	29·880
S.E.	29·868	29·783	29·779	29·772	29·781	29·852	29·985	29·791	29·864	29·769	29·803	29·748	29·816
S.	29·704	29·634	29·543	29·542	29·662	29·762	29·598	29·711	29·615	29·656	29·704	29·678	29·651
S.W.	29·675	29·781	29·655	29·677	29·663	29·727	29·746	29·725	29·684	29·640	29·645	29·735	29·696
W.	29·599	29·814	29·672	29·712	29·737	29·805	29·791	29·765	29·773	29·687	29·615	29·891	29·738
N.W.	29·557	29·821	29·749	29·708	29·814	29·826	29·829	29·786	29·827	29·724	29·771	29·759	29·764

TABLE XXXV.—EXCESS of the MEAN READING of the BAROMETER in each MONTH for each WIND, through the RANGE of YEARS 1854 to 1873, above the MEAN for the MONTH under ALL ATMOSPHERIC CIRCUMSTANCES.

Hour Greenwich Mean Solar Time (Civil reckoning).	January.	February.	March.	April.	May.	June.	July.	August.	September.	October.	November.	December.	Yearly Excess.
N.	in. −0·098	in. +0·007	in. +0·028	in. +0·062	in. +0·013	in. +0·136	in. +0·001	in. +0·075	in. −0·005	in. +0·019	in. +0·036	in. +0·041	in. +0·036
N.E.	+ ·193	+ ·069	+ ·112	+ ·125	+ ·045	+ ·111	+ ·152	+ ·109	+ ·235	+ ·229	+ ·194	+ ·200	+ ·148
E.	+ ·079	+ ·056	+ ·045	+ ·175	+ ·133	− ·044	+ ·076	+ ·088	+ ·185	+ ·140	+ ·157	+ ·096	+ ·099
S.E.	+ ·139	− ·046	+ ·057	− ·032	+ ·001	+ ·027	+ ·176	− ·009	+ ·073	+ ·045	+ ·030	− ·041	+ ·035
S.	− ·025	− ·195	− ·179	− ·262	− ·118	− ·063	− ·211	− ·089	− ·176	− ·068	− ·069	− ·111	− ·130
S.W.	− ·054	− ·048	− ·067	− ·127	− ·117	− ·098	− ·063	− ·075	− ·107	− ·084	− ·128	− ·054	− ·085
W.	− ·130	− ·015	− ·050	− ·092	− ·043	− ·020	− ·018	− ·035	− ·018	− ·037	− ·158	+ ·102	− ·043
N.W.	− ·172	− ·008	+ ·027	− ·096	+ ·034	+ ·001	+ ·020	− ·014	+ ·036	·000	− ·002	− ·030	− ·017

TABLE XXXVI.—MEAN READING of the BAROMETER at every HOUR in each LUNAR MONTH, through the RANGE of YEARS 1854 to 1873.

Nominal Solar Hours after Moon's Upper Meridian Passage.	For Lunar Month commencing in												Yearly Means.
	January.	February.	March.	April.	May.	June.	July.	August.	September.	October.	November.	December.	
	in.	in.	in.	in.	in.	in.	in.	in.	in.	in.	in.	in.	in.
1st	29·807	29·769	29·770	29·800	29·797	29·832	29·786	29·824	29·741	29·766	29·764	29·750	29·7838
2nd	29·807	29·769	29·769	29·799	29·798	29·833	29·785	29·823	29·740	29·766	29·763	29·751	29·7836
3rd	29·808	29·768	29·770	29·800	29·798	29·833	29·785	29·822	29·738	29·766	29·764	29·751	29·7836
4th	29·809	29·769	29·770	29·800	29·799	29·832	29·785	29·823	29·738	29·766	29·765	29·751	29·7839
5th	29·810	29·769	29·771	29·799	29·799	29·832	29·786	29·823	29·736	29·766	29·765	29·751	29·7839
6th	29·810	29·769	29·771	29·799	29·790	29·831	29·786	29·824	29·736	29·767	29·766	29·750	29·7840
7th	29·810	29·770	29·772	29·798	29·799	29·831	29·785	29·823	29·736	29·767	29·765	29·750	29·7840
8th	29·800	29·770	29·773	29·798	29·799	29·831	29·786	29·826	29·735	29·767	29·765	29·750	29·7841
9th	29·809	29·770	29·774	29·798	29·799	29·830	29·785	29·827	29·735	29·768	29·764	29·749	29·7840
10th	29·808	29·770	29·776	29·799	29·799	29·830	29·785	29·828	29·735	29·768	29·763	29·749	29·7843
11th	29·809	29·769	29·776	29·799	29·799	29·830	29·786	29·828	29·735	29·768	29·763	29·749	29·7844
12th	29·808	29·768	29·776	29·800	29·799	29·831	29·786	29·829	29·734	29·768	29·765	29·750	29·7845
13th	29·808	29·768	29·777	29·800	29·799	29·831	29·786	29·829	29·734	29·767	29·765	29·750	29·7845
14th	29·809	29·767	29·776	29·800	29·799	29·831	29·786	29·829	29·734	29·767	29·765	29·751	29·7845
15th	29·810	29·766	29·776	29·799	29·799	29·831	29·787	29·829	29·733	29·766	29·766	29·751	29·7843
16th	29·811	29·765	29·776	29·798	29·798	29·831	29·787	29·829	29·733	29·766	29·766	29·751	29·7843
17th	29·812	29·765	29·775	29·797	29·797	29·831	29·787	29·828	29·733	29·764	29·765	29·752	29·7839
18th	29·813	29·765	29·775	29·796	29·797	29·831	29·787	29·828	29·732	29·763	29·765	29·752	29·7837
19th	29·812	29·764	29·775	29·796	29·797	29·831	29·787	29·828	29·732	29·763	29·765	29·752	29·7834
20th	29·813	29·764	29·775	29·795	29·797	29·832	29·787	29·828	29·732	29·763	29·764	29·751	29·7834
21st	29·814	29·763	29·775	29·794	29·797	29·832	29·786	29·828	29·732	29·762	29·764	29·750	29·7831
22nd	29·815	29·762	29·775	29·794	29·797	29·832	29·786	29·827	29·731	29·761	29·765	29·748	29·7828
23rd	29·816	29·762	29·776	29·794	29·797	29·832	29·786	29·826	29·732	29·761	29·765	29·747	29·7829
24th	29·816	29·761	29·776	29·794	29·797	29·833	29·786	29·826	29·732	29·761	29·765	29·747	29·7828
25th	29·816	29·761	29·775	29·794	29·798	29·833	29·786	29·825	29·731	29·761	29·763	29·746	29·7826
Means	29·811	29·767	29·774	29·798	29·798	29·832	29·786	29·827	29·734	29·765	29·765	29·750	29·7838
Aggregate number of days employed	547	544	563	538	548	524	601	579	534	566	534	589	6667

TABLE XXXVII.—MEAN DIURNAL INEQUALITY of the BAROMETER in each LUNAR MONTH, through the RANGE of YEARS 1854 to 1873.

Nominal Solar Hours after Moon's Upper Meridian Passage.	For Lunar Month commencing in												For the Year.
	January.	February.	March.	April.	May.	June.	July.	August.	September.	October.	November.	December.	
	in.	in.	in.	in.	in.	in.	in.	in.	in.	in.	in.	in.	in.
1st	-0·004	+0·003	-0·003	+0·002	-0·001	0·000	0·000	-0·003	+0·007	+0·001	-0·001	0·000	0·0000
2nd	- 4	+ 2	- 5	+ 1	0	+ 1	- 1	- 4	+ 6	+ 1	- 2	+ 1	- 2
3rd	- 3	+ 1	- 4	+ 2	0	+ 1	- 1	- 4	+ 4	+ 1	- 1	+ 1	- 2
4th	- 2	+ 2	- 4	+ 2	+ 1	0	- 1	- 4	+ 4	+ 1	0	+ 1	- 1
5th	- 1	+ 2	- 3	+ 1	+ 1	0	0	- 1	+ 4	+ 1	0	+ 1	+ 1
6th	- 1	+ 2	- 3	+ 1	+ 1	- 1	0	- 3	+ 2	+ 2	+ 1	0	+ 2
7th	- 1	+ 3	- 2	0	+ 1	- 1	0	- 1	+ 2	+ 1	0	+ 1	+ 2
8th	- 1	+ 3	- 1	0	+ 1	- 1	- 1	0	+ 1	+ 2	0	0	+ 3
9th	- 2	+ 3	0	0	+ 1	- 1	0	0	+ 1	+ 3	- 1	- 1	+ 2
10th	- 3	+ 3	+ 2	+ 1	+ 1	- 1	0	+ 1	+ 1	+ 3	0	- 1	+ 5
11th	- 2	+ 2	+ 2	+ 1	+ 1	0	0	+ 2	0	+ 2	0	- 1	+ 6
12th	- 3	+ 1	+ 2	+ 2	+ 1	0	0	+ 2	0	+ 2	0	0	+ 7
13th	- 3	+ 1	+ 3	+ 2	+ 1	0	0	+ 2	0	+ 2	0	0	+ 7
14th	- 2	0	+ 2	+ 2	+ 1	0	+ 1	+ 1	0	+ 1	0	+ 1	+ 4
15th	- 1	- 1	+ 2	+ 1	+ 1	+ 1	+ 1	+ 1	- 1	0	+ 1	+ 1	+ 4
16th	0	- 2	+ 2	0	0	+ 1	+ 1	+ 1	- 1	- 1	+ 1	+ 1	+ 5
17th	+ 1	- 2	+ 1	- 1	- 1	+ 1	+ 1	- 1	- 1	- 1	0	0	+ 4
18th	+ 2	- 2	+ 1	- 1	- 2	+ 1	+ 1	- 1	- 2	0	+ 1	- 1	+ 4
19th	+ 1	- 3	+ 1	- 1	- 1	+ 1	+ 1	- 1	- 2	0	+ 1	- 1	+ 4
20th	+ 1	- 3	+ 1	- 1	- 3	+ 1	0	+ 1	- 2	0	+ 1	- 1	+ 4
21st	+ 3	- 4	+ 1	- 1	- 4	0	- 1	+ 1	- 3	- 1	0	- 1	+ 1
22nd	+ 4	- 5	+ 1	- 1	- 4	0	0	0	- 3	- 1	- 2	- 1	- 10
23rd	+ 5	- 5	0	+ 2	- 1	0	0	+ 1	- 3	- 2	+ 4	- 3	- 9
24th	+ 5	- 6	+ 2	- 1	- 4	+ 1	+ 1	0	- 1	- 2	0	- 3	- 10
25th	+ 5	- 6	+ 1	- 1	- 4	+ 1	+ 1	0	- 1	- 2	+ 4	- 3	- 12

Comparing together the numbers contained in the column "For the Year," there appears to be no trace of a semidiurnal period. There is slight indication of a diurnal period. The greatest value is + ·0007 inch at the 13th hour; the least is - ·0012 inch at the 25th hour: difference = ·0019 inch. But it is doubtful whether this indication has any significance, for the accidental irregularity is also relatively large, the last value in the column differing from the first value by ·0012 inch. Further the values in the separate months do not support the supposition of any definite diurnal period.

RESULTS

OF THE

OBSERVATIONS OF THE DRY-BULB AND WET-BULB THERMOMETERS,

1849 TO 1868.

TABLE XXXVIII.—MEAN TEMPERATURE of the Air at every Hour of the Day, in each YEAR from 1849 to 1868, for the MONTH of JANUARY.

Year	Midnight	1 a.m.	2 a.m.	3 a.m.	4 a.m.	5 a.m.	6 a.m.	7 a.m.	8 a.m.	9 a.m.	10 a.m.	11 a.m.	Noon	1 p.m.	2 p.m.	3 p.m.	4 p.m.	5 p.m.	6 p.m.	7 p.m.	8 p.m.	9 p.m.	10 p.m.	11 p.m.	Mean	Number of Days employed in forming the Mean
1849	42.1	42.1	41.8	41.5	41.2	41.0	40.9	40.9	41.1	41.7	42.6	43.6	44.7	43.2	43.5	43.1	44.5	43.6	43.1	42.8	42.7	42.4	42.2	42.1	42.7	27
1850	33.2	32.9	32.8	32.7	32.6	32.6	32.7	32.8	33.1	33.9	35.0	35.9	36.6	36.9	36.6	33.9	33.1	34.6	34.3	34.1	33.8	33.7	33.8	34.1	34.1	31
1851	42.0	42.0	42.0	41.9	41.6	41.2	41.1	41.0	40.8	41.4	42.9	44.3	43.3	46.4	46.3	46.0	45.2	44.2	43.5	43.1	42.7	42.6	42.4	42.0	43.0	31
1852	41.2	40.9	40.7	40.8	40.7	40.5	40.1	39.9	39.9	40.1	41.5	43.1	44.6	45.2	45.5	44.8	43.8	41.5	41.0	41.9	41.6	41.4	41.8	41.8	41.9	31
1853	39.9	39.9	40.0	39.9	39.9	40.2	40.1	40.0	39.9	40.2	41.1	42.4	43.6	44.2	44.1	43.5	42.8	42.1	41.6	41.1	40.6	40.1	39.8	39.3	41.1	21
1854	38.0	38.1	38.1	37.8	37.9	37.9	37.7	37.4	37.4	38.0	39.1	40.2	41.4	41.9	42.1	42.0	41.2	40.4	39.9	39.6	39.4	39.1	38.8	38.8	39.3	31
1855	34.2	34.2	34.1	34.0	33.9	33.9	33.7	33.7	33.8	34.2	35.1	36.1	37.2	37.5	37.5	37.1	36.2	35.5	35.0	34.5	34.3	34.1	33.8	33.7	34.9	31
1856	38.1	38.1	38.0	37.8	37.7	37.6	37.6	37.7	38.0	38.6	40.0	40.9	42.0	42.5	42.7	41.9	40.9	39.8	39.3	39.0	38.7	38.6	38.4	38.1	39.2	31
1857	36.5	35.0	35.9	35.8	35.5	35.5	35.3	35.4	35.9	36.4	37.4	38.1	38.9	39.3	39.8	39.2	38.3	37.3	36.8	36.7	36.2	35.9	35.8	35.7	36.8	31
1858	36.6	36.4	36.1	35.9	35.8	35.8	35.7	35.5	35.7	36.3	38.1	39.8	41.4	43.1	42.1	41.8	40.6	39.2	38.5	37.7	37.3	37.1	37.0	36.7	37.9	30
1859	39.5	39.5	39.4	39.2	39.2	39.1	39.1	39.0	39.2	39.8	40.9	41.9	42.8	43.8	43.5	42.3	41.4	40.7	40.3	40.0	40.0	39.7	39.4		40.5	31
1860	38.7	38.8	38.6	38.5	38.2	38.1	37.7	37.7	37.8	38.5	39.6	40.8	41.8	41.6	42.4	42.3	41.5	40.9	40.4	39.4	38.3	37.3	36.7	35.9	40.5	30
1861	35.7	35.9	36.0	35.8	35.2	35.0	34.9	35.1	34.8	35.3	36.7	38.5	40.0	40.8	40.9	40.4	39.4	38.3	37.3	36.7	35.9	35.4	35.1	34.8	36.8	19
1862	39.3	39.1	39.2	39.2	39.4	39.4	39.3	39.1	39.2	39.6	40.7	41.9	42.7	45.0	45.1	44.6	42.2	41.5	41.0	40.3	40.0	39.8	40.0	39.8	40.2	25
1863	41.1	41.2	41.2	41.3	41.4	41.5	41.4	41.4	41.4	41.7	42.6	43.5	44.7	45.0	45.1	44.6	43.6	42.9	42.1	41.7	41.4	41.0	40.9	40.9	42.2	31
1864	35.2	35.2	35.2	35.5	35.3	35.1	35.2	35.2	35.6	36.4	37.7	38.7	39.3	39.5	39.2	38.2	37.5	36.9	36.1	36.1	36.3	36.1	35.8		36.5	18
1865	35.9	35.5	35.6	35.5	35.6	35.5	35.1	35.2	34.9	34.7	35.2	36.3	37.5	38.6	39.1	39.2	38.7	38.0	37.5	36.8	36.6	36.3	36.4	36.4	36.5	31
1866	41.7	41.6	41.8	42.0	42.0	42.0	41.0	41.8	42.4	43.4	44.7	46.2	46.0	46.3	45.8	44.7	43.7	42.0	42.6	42.4	41.8		43.1		43.1	31
1867	33.1	33.1	33.1	32.8	32.8	33.1	33.1	33.1	33.6	34.0	35.0	36.1	37.1	37.8	38.0	37.2	36.4	35.6	35.2	34.6	34.1	33.7	33.6	33.7	34.6	31
1868	36.7	36.4	36.3	36.4	36.3	36.1	36.0	36.2	36.9	37.7	38.6	39.1	39.4	39.3	39.2	38.7	38.4	38.3	38.2	38.1	37.8	37.6	37.5	37.6	37.6	
Mean	37.93	37.84	37.79	37.70	37.61	37.55	37.43	37.36	37.47	37.96	39.05	40.23	41.32	41.89	41.99	41.55	40.71	39.85	39.20	38.90	38.58	38.34	38.20	38.03	38.94	..

TABLE XXXIX.—MEAN TEMPERATURE of the Air at every Hour of the Day, in each YEAR from 1849 to 1868, for the MONTH of FEBRUARY.

Year	Midnight	1 a.m.	2 a.m.	3 a.m.	4 a.m.	5 a.m.	6 a.m.	7 a.m.	8 a.m.	9 a.m.	10 a.m.	11 a.m.	Noon	1 p.m.	2 p.m.	3 p.m.	4 p.m.	5 p.m.	6 p.m.	7 p.m.	8 p.m.	9 p.m.	10 p.m.	11 p.m.	Mean	Number of Days employed in forming the Mean
1849	40.3	40.0	39.8	39.6	39.3	39.1	39.0	39.1	39.3	40.9	42.8	44.3	45.9	46.8	47.4	47.1	46.5	45.0	43.7	42.7	42.1	41.6	41.2	41.1	42.3	28
1850	42.4	42.2	42.3	42.2	42.4	42.4	42.2	42.5	43.0	44.7	46.0	48.2	48.6	48.5	47.8	48.5	46.5	45.0	44.4	43.6	43.0	42.5	43.3	44.5	29
1851	38.1	37.8	37.4	37.3	37.1	36.9	36.7	36.5	37.0	38.5	40.3	42.5	44.1	44.8	45.1	45.3	44.6	42.8	41.4	40.5	39.7	39.2	38.8	38.2	40.0	28
1852	30.9	30.8	30.6	30.5	30.4	30.2	30.1	30.1	30.8	32.6	34.0	34.9	36.3	36.5	36.8	36.1	35.7	34.4	33.6	33.3	33.5	33.3	32.0	31.5	33.3	25
1853	31.6	31.5	31.6	31.5	31.4	31.2	31.1	31.2	31.7	32.6	34.0	34.9	36.3	36.5	36.8	36.1	35.7	34.4	33.6	33.3	33.3	33.0	32.0	31.7	33.2	27
1854	37.7	37.5	37.4	37.1	36.7	36.8	36.5	36.4	37.0	38.3	40.2	41.7	43.2	44.0	44.4	44.0	43.1	41.7	40.6	39.7	38.7	38.1	37.8	37.3	39.4	28
1855	27.4	27.0	26.7	26.4	26.5	26.6	26.3	26.7	27.2	28.4	30.0	33.3	33.8	32.0	31.0	30.7	29.6	29.0	28.6	28.3	28.0		29.2		29.2	28
1856	40.4	40.4	40.4	40.1	40.0	40.0	40.1	40.2	40.4	41.2	42.5	43.6	44.8	45.6	45.0	45.7	44.8	43.6	41.6	41.0	41.6	41.3	40.0	41.1	42.1	28
1857	41.7	41.6	41.8	42.0	42.0	41.9	41.0	41.8	42.4	43.4	44.7	45.7	46.2	46.0	46.3	45.8	44.7	43.7	42.2	41.7	41.3	41.2	41.0	40.0	42.1	28
1858	34.1	33.6	33.4	33.4	33.2	33.0	32.9	32.8	33.5	35.0	36.5	36.3	37.7	38.9	39.7	39.9	39.2	38.0	36.7	35.7	35.4	35.1	34.7	34.0	33.8	35.4	20
1859	41.2	41.2	40.7	40.6	40.5	40.6	40.5	40.6	41.1	42.6	44.6	46.6	48.0	48.5	48.1	47.3	46.9	44.4	43.5	42.3	43.5	43.2	42.3	41.9	43.4	28
1860	34.1	33.9	33.6	33.5	33.1	32.9	32.7	32.9	33.9	35.0	36.8	38.8	37.8	36.5	35.3	34.3	35.3	34.8	34.6	34.3	34.3	34.6	34.3	33.7	34.7	29
1861	40.7	40.4	40.1	40.0	30.8	40.0	40.0	39.5	39.0	40.3	46.0	46.5	45.8	44.7	44.7	44.2	41.7	42.1	41.8	41.0	41.3	41.2	41.0	42.2	14
1862	39.6	30.7	30.5	39.4	39.2	38.9	38.5	38.4	38.6	39.6	40.8	41.9	43.3	43.6	44.5	44.6	43.7	41.7	40.8	40.2	39.7	39.2	38.8	40.3	24
1863	40.0	30.7	30.5	30.1	30.2	39.2	39.2	39.1	39.4	40.8	43.0	44.4	46.2	47.2	47.7	47.5	46.5	44.9	43.7	42.5	41.9	41.3	40.8	40.3	42.2	28
1864	34.6	34.5	34.2	34.1	34.1	34.0	33.9	33.8	34.5	35.8	35.7	37.0	38.3	39.5	39.7	39.6	36.9	36.3	35.9	35.1	36.3	36.7	36.6	37.0	28
1865	36.5	36.4	36.0	35.8	35.5	35.0	35.0	34.7	34.8	35.7	37.0	38.3	39.7	39.6	36.3	35.9	38.1	37.6	37.3	37.1	36.9	36.7	36.6	37.0	23
1866	39.8	39.8	39.8	30.7	30.6	30.8	30.9	30.0	40.6	40.8	45.8	45.3	44.1	47.8	46.8	45.8	45.1	44.7	44.3	43.8	43.5	43.1	44.5	50.5	41.7	23
1867	44.0	43.6	43.5	43.4	42.3	43.0	42.8	42.6	43.3	44.6	46.2	47.4	48.1	47.9	47.6	46.8	45.8	44.8	44.7	44.3	43.8	43.5	43.5	43.7	23
1868	41.6	41.5	41.3	41.3	41.2	41.2	40.8	40.8	41.0	42.1	44.0	45.6	47.1	47.7	47.9	47.6	46.7	45.4	44.1	42.5	41.8	41.6	41.3	43.3	27
Mean	38.07	37.86	37.68	37.49	37.31	37.20	37.10	37.07	37.50	38.74	40.46	41.90	43.22	43.90	44.07	43.76	42.94	41.68	40.59	39.86	39.31	38.80	38.46	38.15	39.71	..

TABLE XL.—MEAN TEMPERATURE of the Air at every HOUR of the DAY, in each YEAR from 1849 to 1868, for the MONTH of MARCH.

Year	Midnight	1 a.m.	2 a.m.	3 a.m.	4 a.m.	5 a.m.	6 a.m.	7 a.m.	8 a.m.	9 a.m.	10 a.m.	11 a.m.	Noon	1 p.m.	2 p.m.	3 p.m.	4 p.m.	5 p.m.	6 p.m.	7 p.m.	8 p.m.	9 p.m.	10 p.m.	11 p.m.	Mean	Number of Days employed in forming the Means
1849	40.3	39.9	39.8	39.7	39.8	39.6	39.7	40.4	41.3	42.9	44.3	45.3	46.7	47.5	47.7	47.5	46.9	45.7	44.1	42.8	41.9	41.2	40.9	40.8	42.8	30
1850	36.3	36.1	35.6	35.6	35.3	35.0	34.7	35.2	36.8	38.9	41.3	43.1	45.0	45.8	46.2	46.2	45.7	44.3	42.3	40.7	39.5	38.6	38.1	37.3	39.7	30
1851	40.0	39.0	30.8	39.7	30.7	39.4	39.4	39.8	41.1	42.9	44.3	45.4	46.6	46.6	46.9	46.7	46.2	45.3	44.4	43.2	42.5	41.9	41.3	40.9	42.7	31
1852	36.4	36.4	35.9	35.4	35.3	34.9	34.9	35.7	37.9	41.4	41.4	46.2	48.0	48.5	48.9	48.5	47.6	44.9	42.3	40.3	38.9	37.9	37.3	36.7	40.6	30
1853	33.9	33.4	33.0	31.9	32.7	32.7	32.7	33.4	34.9	37.3	39.0	40.2	41.9	42.2	42.5	41.9	41.3	39.8	37.8	36.7	35.9	35.1	34.5	33.8	36.6	19
1854	39.4	38.8	38.4	38.0	37.7	37.7	37.7	38.2	40.3	43.1	43.6	47.5	49.2	50.9	52.0	52.0	51.2	49.5	47.0	44.8	43.2	41.9	40.9	40.4	43.6	31
1855	34.6	34.5	34.3	34.3	34.4	34.2	34.2	34.6	35.9	38.1	40.3	41.5	42.7	43.2	43.8	43.1	42.7	41.3	39.3	37.8	36.7	35.9	35.2	34.6	37.8	31
1856	36.8	36.6	36.3	35.9	35.4	35.1	35.1	36.0	37.3	39.2	40.8	42.4	43.2	43.6	43.8	43.8	43.1	42.0	40.8	39.5	38.6	38.1	37.8	37.3	39.1	31
1857	39.4	39.1	39.0	38.6	38.3	38.0	37.7	38.1	39.8	42.1	43.8	45.5	46.8	46.0	47.0	46.9	46.1	44.7	43.4	42.4	41.6	40.9	40.4	40.1	41.9	31
1858	39.1	38.6	38.3	37.6	37.3	37.2	36.9	37.6	39.3	42.6	44.4	46.1	47.0	48.3	48.1	47.1	46.2	44.7	43.1	42.1	41.3	40.6	40.0		42.2	29
1859	44.3	44.5	44.3	44.1	44.0	43.9	43.9	44.0	45.2	47.1	48.6	50.2	51.2	51.8	52.0	52.0	51.0	49.5	47.8	46.7	45.2	44.6	44.2	44.0	46.8	31
1860	38.7	38.6	38.3	38.0	37.8	37.8	37.9	38.3	39.3	41.1	43.1	44.4	45.4	46.4	46.3	46.5	45.5	44.3	43.0	41.6	40.8	40.1	39.5	39.3	41.3	30
1861	41.1	40.7	40.7	40.6	40.7	40.7	41.0	42.5	44.1	45.9	47.3	48.9	49.4	49.7	49.7	48.8	47.4	46.1	44.5	43.4	42.4	41.8	41.2		44.1	31
1862	42.1	41.1	41.3	41.3	41.1	41.1	41.0	41.4	42.5	43.6	44.9	46.0	47.0	47.6	48.0	48.1	47.5	46.7	45.8	44.6	43.8	42.9	42.2	41.8	43.9	18
1863	40.6	40.0	39.6	39.5	39.0	38.5	38.5	39.2	41.2	43.9	45.3	48.1	49.4	50.4	51.1	50.8	49.5	48.1	46.3	44.9	43.9	42.8	41.8	40.9	43.9	31
1864	38.7	37.9	37.5	37.3	37.3	37.3	37.4	37.6	39.3	41.3	43.3	45.1	46.7	47.4	47.8	47.7	46.6	45.0	43.2	41.6	40.8	40.2	39.8	39.5	41.5	30
1865	34.8	34.4	34.0	33.8	33.5	33.3	33.3	33.7	35.0	36.8	38.5	39.5	41.3	43.0	43.7	44.3	43.6	42.6	41.1	39.9	39.0	38.3	37.9	37.5	38.0	29
1866	38.3	38.2	38.0	37.8	37.6	37.4	37.3	37.6	39.2	41.0	42.9	44.3	45.8	46.7	46.3	46.4	46.1	44.9	43.1	41.9	40.7	39.8	39.2	38.8	41.2	30
1867	35.7	35.6	35.4	35.2	35.1	35.0	35.7	36.8	38.3	39.7	41.0	42.4	41.7	42.1	42.4	41.7	41.0	39.0	37.7	37.1	36.6	36.3	35.6		38.0	31
1868	41.8	41.3	41.1	40.7	40.4	40.1	39.9	40.4	42.1	44.3	46.6	47.9	49.2	49.0	50.2	50.0	49.2	47.9	46.5	45.1	44.2	43.4	42.9	42.4	44.3	31
Means	38.57	38.29	38.03	37.80	37.63	37.45	37.40	37.89	39.40	41.51	43.40	44.89	46.19	46.81	47.12	46.91	46.17	44.85	43.23	41.85	40.87	40.08	39.52	39.04	41.43	..

TABLE XLI.—MEAN TEMPERATURE of the AIR at every HOUR of the DAY, in each YEAR from 1849 to 1868, for the MONTH of APRIL.

Year	Midnight	1 a.m.	2 a.m.	3 a.m.	4 a.m.	5 a.m.	6 a.m.	7 a.m.	8 a.m.	9 a.m.	10 a.m.	11 a.m.	Noon	1 p.m.	2 p.m.	3 p.m.	4 p.m.	5 p.m.	6 p.m.	7 p.m.	8 p.m.	9 p.m.	10 p.m.	11 p.m.	Mean	Number of Days employed in forming the Means
1849	42.1	41.8	41.4	41.0	40.6	40.3	40.8	42.5	44.9	46.9	48.2	49.1	50.6	50.2	50.1	49.4	48.3	47.1	45.0	43.3	42.7	42.0	45.1			25
1850	46.1	45.9	45.6	45.5	45.3	45.2	45.7	47.3	48.8	50.2	52.0	53.3	53.9	54.7	54.8	54.9	54.2	53.2	51.9	50.8	48.1	47.3	46.6	46.2	49.5	27
1851	41.1	40.7	40.7	40.6	40.4	40.3	41.0	42.6	44.9	46.8	49.8	50.9	51.8	51.5	51.5	50.4	49.2	47.8	45.9	44.6	43.3	42.4	41.8	41.2	45.5	30
1852	39.0	38.2	37.7	37.3	37.3	37.4	38.2	41.2	44.9	47.9	50.3	52.6	54.3	55.4	55.2	54.8	53.4	51.6	49.3	46.8	43.6	42.1	41.2	39.9	45.4	30
1853	40.5	40.0	40.2	40.3	39.0	38.9	40.1	42.5	45.7	45.0	45.9	46.4	46.9	47.3	48.0	48.3	48.1	46.8	45.5	44.1	41.2	41.2	39.9	43.6		10
1854	42.5	41.8	41.2	41.0	40.8	40.6	41.5	43.4	47.0	48.4	50.8	54.0	56.6	54.8	57.0	54.8	53.0	50.0	47.6	45.3	44.0	43.5	42.5	41.7	48.6	30
1855	41.0	40.4	39.9	39.4	38.9	39.0	39.5	41.4	43.7	46.5	48.9	51.0	53.3	54.4	54.7	54.6	54.1	52.9	50.7	47.6	45.9	44.7	44.1	43.5	45.7	30
1856	42.9	42.5	42.1	41.4	41.0	40.9	41.2	43.1	45.8	48.1	49.2	50.3	51.4	52.0	52.4	52.5	51.4	49.9	48.7	47.6	45.9	44.5	44.3	43.8	46.3	30
1858	41.4	41.0	40.7	40.0	40.1	40.3	42.1	44.7	47.6	50.8	53.4	54.6	56.2	57.0	56.7	56.0	54.7	52.9	50.5	48.9	46.7	45.9	45.4		47.0	24
1859	42.7	42.2	41.9	41.5	41.0	40.9	41.5	43.8	48.2	49.7	50.8	51.4	52.2	52.7	51.9	51.3	50.2	48.6	46.7	45.4	44.3	43.9	43.5		46.3	28
1860	38.9	38.4	38.0	37.5	37.4	37.3	37.9	39.6	42.1	44.5	45.9	47.4	48.6	49.8	50.1	49.9	48.9	47.5	45.9	43.4	41.8	40.6	39.8	39.2	42.9	24
1861	40.4	40.0	38.8	38.6	38.6	39.2	41.1	44.0	46.7	46.9	47.8	47.9	47.8	48.4	42.2	44.1	42.4	41.3	41.2	44.1					49.3	30
1862	43.0	44.6	43.9	43.6	43.5	43.4	44.3	47.7	49.5	50.7	51.5	52.5	53.3	53.6	53.5	53.1	52.4	51.0	49.4	48.2	47.1	46.6	46.1	48.3		25
1863	40.9	40.0	39.6	39.5	39.0	41.0	42.1	46.1	48.1	49.7	51.0	51.3	52.3	50.5	50.5	48.9	47.8	46.7	45.7	4.70					46.1	18
1864	43.8	43.3	43.1	42.9	42.7	42.5	43.1	45.4	47.9	50.2	52.5	54.2	55.6	55.9	56.0	56.0	55.3	54.3	52.6	49.4	47.5	46.3	45.3	44.2	48.7	29
1865	46.5	45.9	45.4	45.2	44.4	44.3	44.8	47.1	50.0	53.3	57.1	59.8	62.5	63.9	65.7	64.5	63.9	61.1	58.5	54.3	51.4	49.4	47.7	47.7	52.9	30
1866	44.6	44.0	43.8	43.5	43.4	43.3	43.4	45.6	49.0	51.9	52.0	54.0	54.8	55.1	54.1	53.6	52.7	51.7	50.3	48.1	46.3	45.5	44.8	48.6		30
1867	46.5	45.7	45.1	44.8	44.5	44.4	46.8	48.6	50.9	51.9	53.5	54.2	54.2	55.3	54.5	54.2	52.8	50.9	49.0	47.8	46.7	45.7	4.70		49.9	30
1868	44.0	43.8	43.6	43.5	43.2	43.2	43.2	44.7	46.8	47.6	50.0	51.2	53.5	56.2	55.6	55.5	55.3	54.2	52.6	51.1	49.0	47.8	46.7	45.7	48.7	30
Means	42.90	42.40	42.00	41.63	41.41	41.32	41.91	43.87	46.30	48.71	50.60	52.15	53.41	54.09	54.33	54.13	53.26	51.86	50.18	47.80	46.20	45.02	44.20	43.48	47.21	..

TABLE XLII.—MEAN TEMPERATURE of the Air at every HOUR of the Day, in each YEAR from 1849 to 1868, for the MONTH of MAY.

Year.	Midnight.	1 a.m.	2 a.m.	3 a.m.	4 a.m.	5 a.m.	6 a.m.	7 a.m.	8 a.m.	9 a.m.	10 a.m.	11 a.m.	Noon.	1 p.m.	2 p.m.	3 p.m.	4 p.m.	5 p.m.	6 p.m.	7 p.m.	8 p.m.	9 p.m.	10 p.m.	11 p.m.	Mean.	Number of Days employed in forming the Means.
1849	49·5	49·1	48·8	48·5	48·4	48·0	50·5	52·6	54·0	56·3	57·5	58·9	60·7	61·4	61·6	62·0	61·4	59·9	58·0	55·8	53·5	52·2	51·3	50·5	54·6	28
1850	46·7	46·3	45·9	45·7	45·6	46·2	47·5	49·8	52·5	54·8	55·5	56·4	57·5	58·0	58·2	57·9	57·3	56·2	54·5	52·7	50·5	49·1	48·5	47·5	51·6	31
1851	46·4	45·9	45·3	44·7	44·3	44·5	46·2	49·5	52·2	54·3	55·9	57·4	58·3	58·8	58·6	58·8	58·3	57·1	55·7	53·1	50·8	49·1	48·0	47·1	51·7	30
1852	47·7	47·1	46·4	45·9	45·8	45·9	47·2	49·0	51·6	53·6	55·6	56·6	57·0	58·7	58·9	58·6	58·2	57·4	55·6	53·5	51·4	50·0	48·0	52·1	51·7	31
1853	46·7	46·1	45·6	45·5	45·4	45·8	47·6	50·4	53·3	55·6	57·8	58·6	59·2	59·7	60·2	59·8	58·7	57·6	55·9	53·6	51·0	49·4	48·2	47·6	52·5	31
1854	45·5	45·2	44·8	44·5	44·2	44·9	46·7	49·0	50·9	53·7	55·2	56·9	57·9	58·5	59·1	58·8	57·8	56·5	54·5	52·3	49·8	48·0	46·8	46·2	51·2	31
1855	42·8	42·3	41·8	41·6	41·4	41·3	42·8	45·4	48·1	50·8	52·6	53·5	53·9	54·4	54·9	54·3	53·7	52·5	51·2	49·3	47·3	45·4	44·4	43·6	47·9	25
1856	45·8	45·6	44·9	44·4	45·1	44·7	46·1	47·0	46·8	52·2	53·3	54·5	55·3	56·0	56·2	55·9	54·8	54·1	52·6	50·4	48·8	47·5	46·9	46·5	49·9	28
1857	47·6	47·2	46·6	46·0	45·8	46·2	48·4	46·7	49·2	51·3	53·2	55·0	56·4	57·8	58·6	59·5	58·5	57·6	56·9	54·3	52·4	50·3	48·9	47·7	52·2	28
1858	45·3	44·7	44·3	44·2	44·0	44·3	46·7	49·2	51·3	53·2	55·0	56·4	57·8	58·6	59·5	58·5	57·6	56·9	54·3	52·4	50·3	48·9	47·7	46·8	51·1	26
1859	45·9	45·8	45·6	45·4	45·1	45·8	46·9	49·0	51·3	53·6	55·5	57·5	59·3	60·0	60·3	60·1	58·9	57·2	55·3	52·6	50·2	48·4	47·5	46·9	51·8	22
1860	49·9	48·8	48·0	47·7	47·3	47·8	49·8	52·3	54·8	56·9	59·1	60·3	61·2	63·0	63·7	63·0	61·8	59·3	56·7	55·8	51·7	50·7	50·0	55·0	53·6	18
1861	46·9	46·3	45·7	45·3	45·2	45·8	47·4	44·8	51·8	53·7	54·9	56·7	58·0	59·1	59·5	59·2	58·8	57·8	56·2	53·8	51·4	50·0	49·1	48·0	52·1	29
1862	51·7	51·5	51·1	50·8	50·6	51·2	52·4	53·8	55·5	57·4	59·1	60·6	62·1	62·6	62·5	62·4	61·7	60·4	58·9	57·3	55·5	54·1	53·3	52·6	56·2	23
1863	46·4	45·5	44·9	44·6	44·3	44·0	46·9	48·9	51·2	53·9	55·2	55·6	58·2	59·0	58·8	58·4	57·3	56·1	54·4	52·4	50·3	48·6	47·5	46·6	51·3	25
1864	49·3	48·5	47·9	47·5	47·5	48·1	50·0	52·3	54·6	56·6	58·4	59·0	61·0	61·1	61·2	61·2	60·8	60·0	58·1	55·9	53·5	51·9	50·7	49·7	54·4	28
1865	50·6	50·1	49·7	49·5	49·0	49·4	51·4	54·5	57·1	59·2	61·2	62·5	63·8	64·5	64·7	65·5	64·2	63·0	61·4	58·8	56·2	54·3	53·3	52·1	56·9	31
1866	45·1	44·5	43·6	43·1	42·8	43·0	45·7	49·2	52·0	54·3	56·6	58·9	60·1	61·2	62·0	62·2	61·0	59·6	56·4	52·2	49·6	48·4	47·8	46·9	53·3	31
1867	46·5	45·8	45·4	45·0	44·8	45·2	47·3	49·6	51·6	53·4	55·0	55·8	56·7	56·8	57·0	56·9	56·2	54·9	53·4	51·6	50·0	48·8	48·0	47·3	50·9	23
1868	51·1	50·4	49·9	49·7	49·5	50·2	52·7	56·8	59·3	62·4	64·5	65·8	66·8	67·3	67·4	67·8	66·6	65·2	62·6	60·1	56·6	54·5	53·2	52·2	58·4	30
Means	47·35	46·81	46·31	45·97	45·75	46·21	48·01	50·56	52·86	55·11	56·81	58·10	59·29	59·94	60·16	60·03	59·25	57·99	56·34	54·01	51·67	50·04	49·00	48·20	52·73	..

TABLE XLIII.—MEAN TEMPERATURE of the Air at every HOUR of the Day, in each YEAR from 1849 to 1868, for the MONTH of JUNE.

Year.	Midnight.	1 a.m.	2 a.m.	3 a.m.	4 a.m.	5 a.m.	6 a.m.	7 a.m.	8 a.m.	9 a.m.	10 a.m.	11 a.m.	Noon.	1 p.m.	2 p.m.	3 p.m.	4 p.m.	5 p.m.	6 p.m.	7 p.m.	8 p.m.	9 p.m.	10 p.m.	11 p.m.	Mean.	Number of Days employed in forming the Means.
1849	53·0	52·5	51·7	51·0	50·7	51·5	54·0	56·9	60·2	63·0	64·7	66·2	67·7	67·6	67·2	66·9	66·4	65·1	63·5	61·5	58·6	56·3	54·9	53·8	59·4	30
1850	54·3	53·5	53·0	52·6	52·3	51·8	52·8	56·4	59·8	63·0	66·2	68·1	69·6	70·6	71·2	71·3	71·6	70·6	69·0	66·6	64·0	60·7	58·8	55·8	63·0	18
1851	53·5	52·6	51·9	51·6	51·6	52·5	54·7	57·8	60·7	63·3	64·9	66·4	67·2	67·5	67·2	66·2	65·3	63·5	61·1	50·0	57·0	55·5	54·7	50·7	59·7	30
1852	51·7	52·1	51·8	51·7	51·7	52·3	53·5	55·2	56·7	58·7	60·5	62·7	63·7	64·0	62·0	60·5	59·8	56·3	56·3	54·8	53·3	53·0	53·8	50·9	56·9	30
1853	54·1	53·6	53·4	53·1	52·8	53·2	55·1	57·6	60·0	61·5	63·1	64·2	64·8	63·3	63·2	63·8	62·1	60·0	57·9	56·1	53·2	54·6	—	59·0	30	
1854	51·3	51·2	51·0	50·7	50·5	51·1	52·7	54·7	56·4	58·0	59·3	60·8	62·0	63·2	63·4	63·4	61·9	61·4	59·7	57·8	55·6	54·1	53·0	52·3	56·5	27
1855	52·3	51·4	50·9	50·6	50·4	50·9	53·0	56·8	60·9	63·2	65·8	67·5	68·9	69·0	70·0	70·8	70·4	69·9	69·4	67·5	64·3	60·8	58·2	56·8	58·2	28
1856	54·3	53·9	53·2	52·6	52·3	52·7	54·3	56·8	58·9	61·7	63·6	64·4	66·1	66·7	66·9	66·5	65·6	64·6	63·1	61·5	59·3	57·5	56·5	55·4	59·5	22
1857	54·5	53·6	53·0	52·7	52·5	53·5	55·7	59·2	61·7	63·6	64·4	66·1	66·7	64·7	74·7	74·7	73·6	72·0	69·9	67·4	64·0	61·6	59·6	58·4	61·4	23
1858	57·6	57·0	56·1	55·7	55·4	56·2	59·4	61·9	64·9	67·8	69·8	71·3	72·9	74·1	74·7	74·7	73·6	72·0	69·9	67·4	64·0	61·6	59·6	58·4	64·8	19
1859	56·8	56·3	55·9	55·6	55·2	55·8	57·5	59·5	61·2	63·5	65·6	67·7	69·5	70·2	70·6	70·3	69·6	68·2	66·3	64·3	61·3	59·5	58·4	57·3	62·5	29
1860	51·8	51·6	51·3	51·0	51·3	52·1	54·9	56·4	57·8	58·8	59·5	61·0	61·1	61·0	58·8	58·0	57·9	56·6	54·7	53·2	52·5	52·1	55·8	55·8	55·8	27
1861	54·7	54·1	53·8	53·5	53·4	54·2	56·0	58·4	60·1	62·4	63·6	64·9	66·3	66·6	66·8	66·7	66·1	65·1	63·5	61·8	59·8	57·8	56·7	55·6	60·1	28
1862	51·9	51·3	51·0	51·0	51·2	51·6	53·5	55·5	57·3	59·1	61·4	62·5	63·1	63·5	63·9	63·5	62·0	58·0	58·9	58·0	57·9	56·3	55·3	54·5	56·8	26
1863	53·8	53·2	52·5	52·2	52·2	53·0	54·8	57·4	59·1	61·4	62·5	63·5	63·9	66·1	65·6	64·7	63·3	61·6	60·0	57·9	56·3	55·2	54·5	53·8	55·8	30
1864	52·7	52·3	51·9	51·4	51·3	51·8	55·8	58·0	59·8	61·5	63·2	64·5	65·9	67·3	67·8	67·0	66·5	65·3	63·3	61·9	59·6	57·3	55·5	53·8	59·8	25
1865	54·9	54·2	53·4	53·1	52·7	53·8	56·1	60·0	61·2	63·7	66·1	68·0	69·6	70·8	70·8	70·4	69·9	69·4	67·5	64·3	60·6	58·2	56·8	55·7	61·7	28
1866	51·8	51·5	53·0	54·9	53·9	54·9	57·1	60·2	61·8	63·1	66·1	67·4	69·0	69·7	69·5	69·5	69·5	68·9	67·6	66·1	63·6	60·9	58·8	57·6	56·7	61·8	30
1867	52·5	52·0	51·8	51·6	51·4	52·1	54·8	57·0	59·0	61·1	63·1	64·3	65·2	66·2	65·9	64·0	62·0	60·6	58·3	56·3	54·9	54·0	58·8	24		
1868	56·1	55·0	54·2	53·5	53·2	53·9	57·0	61·8	63·7	66·2	68·3	70·2	71·6	72·3	72·3	71·3	71·6	71·1	68·5	63·9	61·0	60·0	58·6	57·3	63·2	30
Means	53·93	53·33	52·83	52·47	52·27	52·97	55·09	57·83	59·97	61·23	63·95	65·31	66·72	67·27	67·40	67·17	66·35	65·38	63·63	61·51	58·92	56·97	55·73	54·80	59·75	..

Year.	Midnight.	1ʰ a.m.	2ʰ a.m.	3ʰ a.m.	4ʰ a.m.	5ʰ a.m.	6ʰ a.m.	7ʰ a.m.	8ʰ a.m.	9ʰ a.m.	10ʰ a.m.	11ʰ a.m.	Noon.	1ʰ p.m.	2ʰ p.m.	3ʰ p.m.	4ʰ p.m.	5ʰ p.m.	6ʰ p.m.	7ʰ p.m.	8ʰ p.m.	9ʰ p.m.	10ʰ p.m.	11ʰ p.m.	Mean.	Number of Days employing in forming the Means.
1849	54·4	53·8	53·6	53·5	53·2	53·6	53·8	59·5	62·8	65·4	66·7	66·7	67·5	68·1	68·3	68·3	68·2	66·1	64·8	62·7	59·8	57·7	56·6	55·6	60·9	19
1850	57·0	56·4	56·2	55·9	55·5	55·9	57·6	59·8	62·0	64·0	66·0	67·6	68·7	69·2	69·3	69·0	68·1	67·1	65·3	63·5	61·5	59·9	58·5	57·7	62·2	31
1851	55·2	54·6	54·0	53·5	53·3	53·9	55·5	57·7	60·1	62·3	64·0	65·6	66·7	67·6	68·1	67·5	66·5	64·9	63·3	61·7	59·6	57·0	56·8	56·1	60·3	31
1852	50·4	48·9	58·3	57·7	57·5	58·0	60·0	63·1	65·6	68·6	70·8	72·6	74·4	75·3	75·2	75·2	74·6	72·6	70·0	67·3	64·4	62·3	61·0	60·1	66·0	23
1853	56·6	56·4	56·1	55·8	55·6	56·2	57·5	59·6	61·4	63·1	64·2	65·3	66·0	67·0	67·1	66·5	66·5	65·3	63·8	62·1	60·1	58·6	58·0	57·6	61·1	29
1854	55·6	54·9	54·1	53·7	53·6	53·9	55·8	58·7	61·3	63·5	65·1	66·5	67·4	68·4	68·6	68·6	67·9	66·8	63·0	62·7	59·8	57·6	56·4	61·0	31
1855	58·4	58·1	57·6	57·4	57·1	57·3	58·0	60·1	62·4	64·1	65·6	66·7	68·1	69·0	69·2	69·2	68·5	67·5	65·5	63·6	61·7	60·2	59·3	58·7	62·6	22
1856	56·4	55·6	54·9	54·4	54·4	54·7	56·4	58·9	60·9	63·2	64·9	66·0	68·0	68·3	69·3	69·6	68·0	67·2	65·5	63·8	61·5	59·5	58·2	57·5	61·6	30
1857	58·8	58·4	57·8	57·5	57·3	57·7	59·2	62·3	65·4	68·1	69·8	71·2	72·5	72·8	73·0	72·9	71·9	70·4	68·7	66·5	63·8	61·6	60·1	58·8	64·8	25
1858	57·2	56·3	55·5	55·2	55·0	55·3	57·2	59·4	62·0	64·3	66·2	67·5	68·5	69·9	70·1	70·1	69·0	67·9	66·2	64·3	61·9	59·9	58·5	57·8	62·3	27
1859	61·4	60·6	60·2	60·0	59·9	60·8	63·0	65·9	68·6	71·2	73·1	74·7	76·7	77·9	78·7	78·8	78·1	76·2	74·4	71·9	68·1	65·5	64·0	62·8	68·9	31
1860	53·8	53·1	52·5	52·2	52·1	52·4	53·7	55·6	57·3	59·2	60·2	61·5	63·2	64·8	65·2	65·5	64·2	63·1	61·7	59·8	57·8	56·2	55·3	54·6	58·1	29
1861	56·9	56·4	56·2	56·1	56·1	56·9	58·7	60·7	62·2	64·0	65·1	65·9	66·7	67·5	68·1	67·8	66·7	65·5	64·3	62·6	60·8	59·2	58·2	57·4	61·7	18
1862	54·2	53·8	53·1	52·8	52·6	53·2	54·7	57·1	59·3	61·2	63·8	64·3	65·4	66·0	66·2	66·6	66·0	64·8	63·2	61·2	59·1	57·3	56·2	55·0	59·4	27
1863	55·6	54·8	54·0	53·4	52·8	53·1	55·5	59·1	62·0	64·9	67·0	70·9	71·2	72·5	71·4	70·5	68·8	66·7	64·5	61·7	59·6	57·9	56·7	62·1	18
1864	56·5	55·8	55·2	54·7	54·5	54·8	56·1	58·4	61·2	63·9	65·9	68·2	71·3	72·2	72·6	72·6	71·2	69·8	67·3	64·7	62·1	60·4	59·4	57·9	62·8	28
1865	58·6	58·2	57·7	57·2	56·9	57·7	59·9	62·5	64·7	67·5	69·6	71·3	72·4	73·0	73·3	72·7	72·4	71·6	69·2	66·7	63·9	61·6	60·3	59·4	64·9	29
1866	56·9	56·4	55·5	54·4	53·1	56·9	59·7	61·9	63·6	65·3	66·8	68·0	69·0	69·2	69·4	68·8	68·3	66·1	63·4	61·4	60·0	58·9	58·0	57·4	61·7	18
1867	54·6	54·0	53·6	53·2	52·8	53·3	55·3	58·5	60·3	62·0	63·7	65·5	66·7	67·0	67·7	67·1	67·1	66·6	64·3	61·6	59·1	57·2	56·1	55·2	60·1	31
1868	60·0	59·9	59·0	58·4	58·1	58·7	60·6	64·4	67·1	70·6	72·1	73·5	73·5	77·3	77·9	78·3	78·4	77·8	77·0	73·9	70·6	67·3	64·7	63·3	62·2	68·1	31
Means	56·92	56·28	55·75	55·36	55·14	55·62	57·37	60·04	62·43	64·72	66·45	67·88	69·31	70·09	70·44	70·37	69·65	68·37	66·46	64·27	61·78	59·86	58·67	57·74	62·54	..

Year.	Midnight.	1ʰ a.m.	2ʰ a.m.	3ʰ a.m.	4ʰ a.m.	5ʰ a.m.	6ʰ a.m.	7ʰ a.m.	8ʰ a.m.	9ʰ a.m.	10ʰ a.m.	11ʰ a.m.	Noon.	1ʰ p.m.	2ʰ p.m.	3ʰ p.m.	4ʰ p.m.	5ʰ p.m.	6ʰ p.m.	7ʰ p.m.	8ʰ p.m.	9ʰ p.m.	10ʰ p.m.	11ʰ p.m.	Mean.	Numb of Days employing the Mean
1849	58·3	58·0	57·6	57·2	56·9	56·9	57·7	60·1	62·1	63·2	66·5	67·7	69·4	69·8	70·3	70·5	69·8	68·2	66·3	64·2	62·4	61·0	60·0	59·2	63·1	24
1850	56·6	56·2	55·7	55·3	54·8	54·5	55·2	57·8	60·2	62·6	64·5	65·8	67·5	67·5	68·1	67·6	66·8	65·4	63·8	61·5	60·8	59·5	58·9	58·1	61·8	31
1851	57·4	56·8	56·5	56·3	56·1	55·9	56·8	58·9	60·7	62·4	64·6	66·8	68·0	69·0	70·1	70·4	69·9	69·1	67·1	65·1	63·4	61·4	60·0	58·9	58·1	62·6	31
1852	57·7	57·3	57·0	56·9	56·8	56·7	57·0	59·0	61·8	64·0	67·1	69·3	61·9	63·8	64·8	66·2	67·2	67·6	67·4	66·8	65·4	63·1	61·0	58·7	57·5	56·5	55·9	62·3	31
1853	55·7	55·3	54·7	54·4	54·1	53·9	54·7	57·0	59·3	61·9	63·8	64·8	66·2	67·2	67·6	67·4	66·8	65·3	63·1	60·6	58·7	57·5	56·5	55·9	60·1	31
1854	56·4	55·6	55·1	54·6	54·3	54·0	54·8	57·2	62·0	62·9	64·9	66·6	67·7	68·4	68·7	68·3	67·2	65·7	64·3	61·6	59·7	58·5	57·4	56·7	60·8	29
1855	57·3	56·8	56·3	56·0	55·9	53·8	56·9	59·5	62·3	64·8	66·5	67·8	69·4	70·1	70·4	70·1	69·6	69·0	66·9	64·4	62·5	60·0	59·8	58·0	60·3	29
1856	58·4	57·6	57·1	56·7	56·4	56·2	57·2	59·7	62·1	65·2	66·9	68·8	70·4	71·3	71·5	71·3	70·5	68·6	67·1	64·9	62·2	60·8	59·8	59·0	65·3	29
1857	60·4	60·0	59·6	58·4	58·0	57·9	59·0	61·4	64·9	66·9	68·9	71·8	73·2	74·2	75·1	71·4	68·9	68·9	66·9	64·6	62·9	61·9	60·9	65·7	31
1858	56·6	55·9	55·4	55·0	54·7	54·6	55·7	58·2	61·0	63·9	66·5	68·9	71·1	71·2	71·7	71·7	70·6	68·2	65·8	63·3	61·1	58·9	57·8	56·7	62·2	29
1859	57·2	56·6	56·2	56·2	56·7	57·8	60·4	63·5	66·1	67·9	70·4	71·4	72·2	73·0	71·0	69·5	67·5	64·3	62·9	62·3	59·3	31
1860	54·9	54·6	54·5	54·5	54·4	54·7	55·3	57·0	58·5	59·5	60·8	61·9	63·2	63·3	63·1	63·0	62·1	61·0	60·0	58·6	57·3	56·4	55·9	55·3	58·3	30
1861	58·9	58·4	58·0	57·9	58·1	59·1	61·2	63·6	66·1	66·9	67·7	67·8	67·3	71·6	66·9	67·1	69·9	62·4	19
1862	55·0	54·3	53·8	53·4	53·0	53·0	53·2	56·3	59·4	61·7	63·2	64·7	66·6	66·8	67·0	66·8	66·1	66·0	58·9	57·4	56·3	55·6	59·7	29
1863	58·2	57·7	57·1	56·8	56·6	56·5	57·5	59·7	61·8	63·7	65·2	67·5	69·7	70·1	70·0	68·8	66·8	65·2	63·0	61·4	61·8	60·4	62·5	21
1864	54·6	53·8	53·0	52·2	51·6	51·4	52·8	56·3	59·2	62·4	66·1	68·5	69·0	69·6	69·6	68·4	66·6	64·4	61·8	59·5	57·9	56·6	55·3	60·2	31
1865	55·5	55·2	54·6	54·2	53·9	53·8	54·5	56·8	59·5	62·0	63·8	65·6	66·8	65·0	67·7	68·0	68·8	63·8	61·6	59·6	58·2	57·3	56·3	60·4	31
1866	55·5	55·2	54·6	54·2	53·9	53·8	54·5	56·6	59·0	61·1	63·1	64·5	66·6	65·5	64·6	63·1	60·6	58·1	60·6	61·1	60·6	58·2	57·3	56·3	59·7	31
1867	57·3	57·0	56·7	56·4	55·9	56·0	56·9	59·4	62·6	65·0	66·6	67·8	69·0	69·7	69·8	69·8	69·1	68·0	65·2	63·4	61·1	59·7	58·9	58·1	63·5	31
1868	59·0	58·4	58·2	58·0	57·3	57·4	58·7	61·2	64·0	66·0	67·6	69·1	71·3	71·5	71·9	71·6	70·6	68·8	66·9	64·2	62·2	60·8	60·0	59·4	63·9	31
Means	57·12	56·63	56·18	55·83	55·33	55·46	56·39	58·80	61·32	63·80	65·60	67·10	68·68	69·30	69·65	69·51	68·59	67·03	65·33	62·67	60·82	59·32	58·37	57·59	61·94	..

E 2

TABLE XLVI.—MEAN TEMPERATURE of the Air at every Hour of the Day, in each Year from 1849 to 1868, for the Month of SEPTEMBER.

Year.	Midnight.	1 a.m.	2 a.m.	3 a.m.	4 a.m.	5 a.m.	6 a.m.	7 a.m.	8 a.m.	9 a.m.	10 a.m.	11 a.m.	Noon.	1 p.m.	2 p.m.	3 p.m.	4 p.m.	5 p.m.	6 p.m.	7 p.m.	8 p.m.	9 p.m.	10 p.m.	11 p.m.	Mean.	Number of Days employed in forming the Means.
1849	54·3	54·3	54·1	54·1	54·2	54·2	54·3	55·7	57·8	60·2	62·5	64·2	64·7	65·1	64·9	64·8	63·4	61·4	59·3	57·7	56·4	55·4	55·0	54·4	58·4	28
1850	52·3	52·3	51·8	51·4	51·2	51·0	51·1	52·5	55·1	58·1	60·1	61·6	62·8	62·9	63·7	63·6	62·4	60·4	58·0	56·0	54·8	53·6	53·1	52·6	56·3	28
1851	51·3	50·7	50·1	49·9	49·7	49·7	50·0	51·7	54·6	58·1	60·4	62·5	63·7	65·1	63·4	65·0	63·2	61·0	58·2	55·8	54·4	53·3	52·3	51·7	56·2	30
1852	52·7	52·4	52·2	52·2	52·3	52·5	52·6	53·6	55·1	5·7	59·8	61·4	62·8	63·6	63·1	64·1	63·0	61·2	58·8	56·9	55·6	54·4	53·7	52·9	56·9	29
1853	52·0	51·9	51·6	51·3	51·1	50·9	51·0	52·0	54·0	56·8	58·4	59·6	61·0	61·5	61·5	61·1	60·1	58·9	56·9	55·1	54·1	53·4	52·5	52·0	55·4	30
1854	52·9	52·1	51·5	51·0	50·5	50·1	50·3	51·9	55·5	60·0	64·0	66·2	67·9	68·7	69·1	68·4	66·7	64·0	61·1	58·6	56·9	55·5	54·4	53·6	58·4	26
1855	52·8	52·5	52·2	51·7	51·5	51·2	51·0	52·0	54·8	58·5	61·8	63·9	65·7	66·4	66·3	65·6	64·4	62·5	60·0	57·7	56·0	54·6	53·8	53·2	57·3	29
1856	51·5	51·2	50·7	50·2	50·0	49·0	49·8	51·1	53·8	57·2	59·8	61·3	62·4	62·3	62·4	61·5	60·3	58·1	56·3	54·5	53·5	52·4	52·1	51·6	55·2	30
1857	56·0	55·8	55·4	55·3	55·3	55·1	55·0	56·3	58·7	61·1	63·2	65·0	66·9	66·9	66·7	65·8	63·9	61·6	59·4	58·1	57·0	56·6	56·1	59·9	30
1858	56·5	56·2	55·8	55·4	55·4	55·4	55·6	56·8	58·8	61·3	63·9	65·8	67·4	68·1	67·7	66·8	65·7	63·7	61·7	59·9	59·0	58·2	57·6	56·9	60·4	30
1859	53·2	53·0	52·8	52·7	52·7	52·7	53·0	54·2	56·6	59·2	61·5	63·0	63·6	63·7	63·6	63·6	62·7	61·1	58·8	57·1	55·9	55·0	54·5	53·8	57·4	27
1860	50·1	49·7	49·5	49·2	49·2	49·1	49·3	50·5	52·8	55·5	57·5	58·8	59·7	60·0	59·2	58·1	56·7	54·8	53·3	52·2	51·3	50·8	50·6	53·6	28
1861	53·3	52·7	52·4	52·1	51·8	51·7	51·9	53·2	55·9	58·9	61·0	62·5	64·1	64·3	64·4	64·4	63·3	61·5	59·6	57·3	56·0	55·0	54·5	53·9	57·3	23
1862																										
1863	50·0	49·7	49·3	49·2	49·2	49·1	49·6	51·4	53·7	55·9	57·3	58·5	59·9	60·3	60·6	60·2	58·6	57·0	55·2	53·9	52·8	51·8	51·1	50·4	53·9	26
1864	53·2	52·8	52·5	52·2	51·9	51·8	51·7	53·0	55·3	58·4	60·3	62·2	63·2	64·3	62·8	61·0	59·3	58·2	56·1	54·8	54·2	57·2	28			
1865	58·0	57·5	57·1	56·9	56·4	56·3	56·5	58·0	60·8	64·9	68·7	71·4	73·4	74·7	74·9	74·1	72·2	69·5	66·4	63·4	61·8	60·3	64·1	30		
1866	53·7	53·7	53·5	53·3	53·0	53·2	53·5	54·0	55·7	59·6	61·0	61·9	62·3	61·5	60·4	59·1	57·6	56·6	56·0	56·6	30					
1867	53·9	53·6	53·4	53·3	53·1	53·1	53·2	54·9	57·0	59·1	61·0	62·5	64·0	64·8	65·0	64·8	63·5	61·5	59·0	57·1	55·9	55·0	54·4	54·0	57·8	30
1868	55·4	54·7	54·1	53·9	53·6	53·6	53·9	55·7	59·2	62·3	65·4	67·6	69·0	69·0	69·3	68·6	67·4	65·1	62·3	60·1	58·7	57·3	56·4	55·9	60·4	30
Means	53·32	52·99	52·63	52·30	52·22	52·12	52·26	53·60	56·09	59·03	61·37	63·09	64·39	64·96	65·07	64·65	63·37	61·47	59·18	57·22	55·96	54·92	54·28	53·69	57·51	..

In the month of September 1862 the photographic records were not sufficiently complete to be used.

TABLE XLVII.—MEAN TEMPERATURE of the Air at every Hour of the Day, in each Year from 1849 to 1868, for the Month of OCTOBER.

Year.	Midnight.	1 a.m.	2 a.m.	3 a.m.	4 a.m.	5 a.m.	6 a.m.	7 a.m.	8 a.m.	9 a.m.	10 a.m.	11 a.m.	Noon.	1 p.m.	2 p.m.	3 p.m.	4 p.m.	5 p.m.	6 p.m.	7 p.m.	8 p.m.	9 p.m.	10 p.m.	11 p.m.	Mean.	Number of Days employed in forming the Means.
1849	49·1	49·2	48·9	48·7	48·8	48·7	48·8	49·0	49·8	51·5	53·7	55·1	56·6	57·2	57·0	56·2	54·6	52·9	51·4	50·3	49·6	49·0	49·0	48·9	51·4	28
1850	44·2	43·8	43·6	43·2	43·1	43·0	43·0	43·4	44·7	46·9	49·2	50·7	51·7	52·4	52·3	53·7	52·4	51·6	50·3	49·1	47·8	47·0	45·9	45·4	44·8	44·3	46·7	31
1851	50·5	50·4	50·1	50·0	49·9	49·7	49·8	50·3	50·4	51·4	53·1	54·9	56·4	55·2	53·7	52·4	51·6	50·8	50·1	49·4	51·6	52·3	31			
1852	50·0	43·1	45·1	45·1	45·1	44·8	45·1	46·1	48·3	50·1	51·4	52·4	51·8	52·0	52·1	51·0	49·2	48·0	47·3	46·3	45·7	45·4	45·1	47·7	29	
1853	48·8	48·7	48·7	48·4	48·3	48·4	48·2	48·5	49·0	50·1	51·4	52·4	52·8	52·0	52·1	51·0	49·2	48·0	47·3	46·3	45·7	45·4	45·1	47·7	51·3	31
1854	46·9	46·5	46·1	45·7	45·7	45·5	45·5	45·8	47·1	49·5	52·1	53·0	55·3	56·1	55·9	55·6	53·6	51·5	50·2	49·0	48·3	47·9	47·5	47·1	49·5	31
1855	49·3	49·2	49·1	48·9	48·9	48·5	48·6	49·0	50·0	52·0	53·9	55·5	56·6	56·7	56·5	55·5	54·1	52·9	51·8	50·6	50·2	49·9	49·5	49·0	50·3	31
1856	49·4	49·3	49·3	48·8	48·9	49·0	49·2	49·5	50·3	52·0	54·0	55·2	56·4	57·2	57·1	56·4	55·1	53·8	52·9	51·3	51·0	50·6	50·2	49·6	51·0	28
1857	50·4	50·4	50·1	50·0	50·3	50·3	50·3	50·6	51·6	53·0	55·1	56·8	55·1	53·8	52·9	52·1	50·7	50·0	49·0	48·3	55·3	31				
1858	48·2	48·1	47·8	47·7	47·5	47·5	47·4	47·9	49·3	51·6	54·1	56·1	57·2	57·6	57·3	56·3	54·2	52·1	50·7	50·0	49·0	48·3	47·9	51·2	31	
1859	48·8	48·6	48·2	48·0	47·7	47·6	47·7	47·9	49·0	50·4	51·8	53·3	54·7	55·4	55·5	55·0	53·7	52·2	51·3	50·7	50·2	49·9	49·6	49·2	50·7	24
1860	48·8	48·6	48·4	48·2	48·0	48·1	48·2	48·8	50·1	52·2	55·8	55·5	54·6	53·8	52·9	51·8	50·9	50·2	49·8	48·8	51·2	31				
1861	51·2	50·8	50·4	50·4	50·2	50·1	50·3	50·8	52·4	54·4	56·1	58·1	60·5	61·2	61·2	60·1	58·5	56·6	54·8	53·8	53·1	52·2	51·7	51·4	54·2	14
1862	50·5	50·3	50·3	50·1	50·0	49·9	49·9	50·6	52·5	54·0	55·5	56·3	56·8	56·9	56·3	54·7	52·9	51·7	50·9	50·4	50·2	50·0	49·6	52·3	29	
1863	49·7	49·6	49·5	49·3	49·3	49·3	49·0	49·5	50·6	52·5	54·0	55·5	56·3	56·6	56·9	56·3	54·7	52·9	51·7	50·9	50·4	50·2	50·0	49·6	51·8	28
1864	48·7	48·6	48·5	48·1	47·6	47·2	47·0	47·4	49·0	51·5	53·7	55·1	56·1	56·1	55·7	55·0	53·8	52·4	51·4	50·6	50·0	49·7	49·3	49·0	50·9	31
1865	48·4	48·0	47·7	47·6	47·7	47·3	47·3	47·4	48·0	49·5	51·2	57·3	57·8	58·7	57·2	55·9	54·2	52·9	51·9	50·9	49·9	48·9	48·4	51·3	31	
1866	49·9	49·4	49·2	49·0	48·9	48·7	48·8	49·8	52·1	52·5	53·9	54·6	55·2	55·0	54·7	53·8	52·7	51·6	50·7	50·0	49·6	49·1	48·7	49·3	51·8	29
1867	46·6	46·3	46·0	45·8	45·6	45·3	45·4	45·6	45·6	47·6	51·6	58·2	54·7	55·9	53·9	52·7	50·9	49·6	48·3	47·6	47·3	49·0	31			
1868	44·7	44·3	44·0	43·8	43·8	43·6	43·8	44·1	45·8	48·4	50·8	53·0	54·5	54·9	55·0	54·2	52·7	51·0	49·6	48·5	47·8	46·8	45·8	45·2	48·2	31
Means	48·46	48·28	48·05	47·84	47·78	47·64	47·64	47·99	49·24	51·36	53·28	54·87	56·04	56·49	56·46	55·71	54·33	52·76	51·44	50·51	49·80	49·28	48·90	48·51	50·94	..

TABLE XLVIII.—Mean Temperature of the Air at every Hour of the Day, in each Year from 1849 to 1868, for the Month of November.

Year	Midnight	1ʰ a.m.	2ʰ a.m.	3ʰ a.m.	4ʰ a.m.	5ʰ a.m.	6ʰ a.m.	7ʰ a.m.	8ʰ a.m.	9ʰ a.m.	10ʰ a.m.	11ʰ a.m.	Noon	1ʰ p.m.	2ʰ p.m.	3ʰ p.m.	4ʰ p.m.	5ʰ p.m.	6ʰ p.m.	7ʰ p.m.	8ʰ p.m.	9ʰ p.m.	10ʰ p.m.	11ʰ p.m.	Mean	Number of Days employed in forming the Means
1849	43·5	43·4	43·5	43·0	43·1	43·2	43·2	43·2	43·6	44·8	46·3	47·4	48·5	49·0	49·1	48·5	46·9	45·7	44·5	44·0	43·6	43·2	42·9	42·9	44·9	26
1850	44·9	44·9	44·8	44·6	44·4	44·6	44·6	44·7	45·9	47·6	49·0	49·9	50·4	50·3	49·6	48·4	47·6	46·7	46·2	45·8	45·5	45·1	44·6	46·4	46·4	30
1851	35·9	35·8	35·5	35·6	35·5	35·4	35·5	35·5	35·8	36·7	38·3	39·9	41·3	42·6	42·2	41·3	40·4	39·3	38·6	37·6	37·2	36·7	36·3	35·8	37·7	30
1852	48·0	47·8	47·7	47·7	47·4	47·5	47·2	47·3	47·6	48·5	49·6	50·9	51·4	51·8	51·8	51·2	50·5	50·0	49·6	49·2	49·1	48·8	48·2	47·8	49·0	30
1853	40·4	40·3	40·7	40·5	40·3	40·3	40·3	40·3	40·8	41·8	43·3	44·5	45·3	46·6	46·9	45·9	44·7	43·6	42·9	42·2	41·8	41·3	40·8	40·5	42·3	29
1854	39·3	39·0	39·0	38·8	38·6	38·4	38·3	38·3	38·7	39·7	41·3	42·6	43·6	44·4	44·3	43·8	42·8	41·6	41·1	41·0	40·6	40·0	39·7	39·6	40·6	30
1855	41·0	40·7	40·5	40·5	40·2	40·2	40·1	40·0	40·3	41·2	43·0	43·9	44·9	45·3	45·3	44·4	43·4	42·8	42·2	41·7	41·6	41·1	40·8	40·8	41·9	27
1856	40·0	39·8	39·6	39·5	39·3	39·1	38·8	39·0	39·3	40·4	41·9	42·9	44·2	45·0	45·2	44·1	42·9	42·0	41·4	40·8	40·3	39·8	39·8	39·5	41·0	30
1857	44·5	44·2	44·0	43·6	43·2	43·2	43·4	43·9	45·1	46·2	47·5	48·5	49·0	49·0	48·6	47·5	46·5	45·8	45·2	45·1	44·8	44·6	44·3	43·5	45·5	29
1858	37·2	37·1	37·0	37·1	37·0	37·0	36·9	37·1	37·8	39·1	40·8	42·4	43·6	44·0	44·1	43·4	42·1	40·8	40·1	39·3	38·9	38·5	37·9	37·8	39·5	30
1859	42·4	42·3	41·8	41·4	41·2	41·3	41·2	40·7	41·0	42·5	43·2	46·8	47·8	48·4	48·4	47·6	45·8	44·5	43·6	42·9	42·6	42·1	41·7	41·4	43·5	21
1860	39·7	39·3	39·3	39·4	39·1	38·9	38·9	39·7	39·5	40·6	42·1	43·3	44·5	44·6	44·5	43·9	42·7	41·7	41·2	40·6	40·3	40·2	39·9	39·6	41·0	30
1861	39·1	38·9	38·7	38·5	38·6	38·7	38·8	39·5	40·8	42·5	44·1	44·0	45·2	44·7	43·3	42·2	41·2	40·6	40·2	40·0	39·5	39·2	41·0	30	41·0	30
1862	38·2	38·1	38·1	38·0	37·8	37·9	37·8	37·8	38·3	39·5	41·0	42·3	43·4	43·9	43·8	43·3	42·4	41·7	41·1	40·4	39·8	39·5	38·8	38·4	40·1	24
1863	45·0	44·7	44·7	44·5	44·4	44·3	44·2	44·0	44·3	45·6	47·1	48·2	49·4	49·8	49·9	49·4	48·2	47·3	46·3	45·6	45·3	44·9	44·5	44·4	46·1	29
1864	40·4	40·1	39·9	39·6	39·2	39·3	39·4	39·4	40·0	41·4	43·4	45·4	46·5	46·9	47·1	46·2	45·1	44·2	43·4	42·8	42·0	41·3	40·9	40·6	42·3	30
1865	43·6	43·4	43·4	43·4	43·3	43·1	43·1	43·0	43·2	44·6	46·1	48·1	49·3	49·5	49·7	48·9	47·7	46·6	45·9	45·1	44·4	44·1	43·9	43·9	45·3	29
1866	43·2	42·9	43·1	42·6	42·8	42·9	42·9	43·2	44·3	46·1	48·1	49·3	49·5	49·7	48·9	47·7	46·6	45·9	45·1	44·4	44·1	43·9	43·9	45·3	42·3	29
1867	39·8	39·9	39·5	39·3	39·1	38·7	38·7	38·7	39·5	40·5	42·6	44·4	45·7	46·0	46·2	45·1	43·9	42·9	42·2	41·8	41·2	40·9	40·3	39·8	41·5	30
1868	40·7	40·7	40·5	40·2	40·2	40·2	40·2	40·3	40·5	41·5	42·8	44·1	45·1	45·5	45·4	44·7	43·7	42·9	42·3	41·8	41·4	41·0	40·5	40·1	41·9	29
Means	41·33	41·17	41·04	40·90	40·74	40·69	40·66	40·67	41·00	42·12	43·85	45·21	46·35	46·85	46·80	46·11	44·93	43·96	43·24	42·63	42·24	41·83	41·45	41·16	42·80	..

TABLE XLIX.—Mean Temperature of the Air at every Hour of the Day, in each Year from 1849 to 1868, for the Month of December.

Year	Midnight	1ʰ a.m.	2ʰ a.m.	3ʰ a.m.	4ʰ a.m.	5ʰ a.m.	6ʰ a.m.	7ʰ a.m.	8ʰ a.m.	9ʰ a.m.	10ʰ a.m.	11ʰ a.m.	Noon	1ʰ p.m.	2ʰ p.m.	3ʰ p.m.	4ʰ p.m.	5ʰ p.m.	6ʰ p.m.	7ʰ p.m.	8ʰ p.m.	9ʰ p.m.	10ʰ p.m.	11ʰ p.m.	Mean	Number of Days employed in forming the Means
1849	37·7	37·3	37·1	37·2	36·9	37·0	37·2	37·2	37·3	37·5	38·3	39·3	40·0	40·2	40·3	40·0	39·5	39·1	38·8	38·4	38·3	38·2	38·0	37·6	38·3	21
1850	36·7	36·9	36·7	38·7	38·6	38·4	38·4	38·3	38·0	39·0	40·1	41·7	42·4	42·8	42·9	42·4	41·7	41·4	41·1	40·9	40·7	40·8	40·5	40·5	40·6	31
1851	36·8	36·8	36·8	36·6	36·3	36·4	36·3	36·4	36·3	36·8	40·7	41·7	42·4	42·8	42·9	42·4	41·7	41·4	41·1	40·7	40·5	40·1	40·2	40·1	40·6	31
1852	46·5	46·6	46·3	46·2	46·1	45·9	46·1	46·3	46·0	46·7	47·0	47·4	48·0	48·7	49·0	48·7	47·7	47·2	47·3	47·6	47·6	47·7	47·8	47·6	47·2	22
1853	34·0	34·1	33·8	33·8	33·5	33·4	33·5	33·3	33·5	33·6	34·3	35·4	36·3	36·7	36·9	36·2	35·3	35·2	34·2	33·9	33·9	33·6	33·3	33·2	34·3	27
1854	40·9	40·7	40·8	40·7	40·4	40·3	40·1	40·0	40·1	40·8	41·0	43·1	44·0	44·6	44·4	43·8	43·0	42·7	42·3	42·0	41·9	41·6	41·3	41·2	41·8	27
1855	35·0	35·0	35·1	35·0	35·0	34·9	35·0	34·9	36·8	37·9	38·5	39·5	39·5	38·5	37·7	36·7	35·7	35·3	35·1	35·1	41·8	31	41·8	31	41·8	31
1856	38·3	38·1	37·9	37·6	37·5	37·2	37·1	37·1	37·2	37·8	39·0	40·2	41·2	41·7	41·8	41·3	40·6	40·2	39·9	39·8	39·6	39·5	39·4	39·5	39·2	29
1857	44·0	44·1	44·1	43·7	43·6	43·6	43·7	43·4	43·5	43·6	45·0	48·0	47·7	46·6	46·2	45·1	43·9	42·9	42·2	41·8	41·8	41·5	44·5	44·4	41·1	31
1858	40·5	40·3	40·3	40·0	39·8	39·8	39·6	39·5	39·7	40·1	41·0	42·1	42·6	43·1	43·5	43·0	42·4	41·9	41·8	41·6	41·4	41·3	41·2	40·8	41·1	31
1859	38·5	33·5	33·2	33·4	33·8	33·5	33·1	33·1	34·0	35·0	35·3	36·5	37·2	37·8	38·8	38·9	36·2	35·8	35·6	35·6	35·5	34·5	34·2	34·9	34·9	22
1860	37·8	37·7	37·5	37·5	37·5	37·3	37·1	37·1	37·4	38·5	39·7	40·4	40·6	40·6	40·1	39·4	39·0	38·6	38·4	38·2	38·0	37·6	38·4	25	38·4	25
1861	40·0	40·7	40·6	40·6	40·6	40·6	40·4	41·1	42·5	43·7	44·6	45·6	44·2	43·2	42·3	41·2	41·0	40·7	40·6	40·6	40·5	40·6	28	40·6	40·6	28
1862	42·8	42·7	42·6	42·7	42·5	42·6	42·6	42·3	42·4	42·8	44·0	45·0	45·9	46·2	45·8	45·0	44·0	43·6	43·4	43·3	43·2	42·2	42·2	43·7	43·7	31
1863	42·0	42·1	42·1	42·1	42·4	42·3	42·6	42·8	42·9	43·2	43·9	45·0	46·1	46·4	46·4	45·7	45·0	44·5	44·0	43·5	43·2	42·6	42·2	42·2	43·6	31
1864	37·7	37·7	37·4	37·4	37·1	37·4	37·6	38·0	38·8	40·0	40·8	41·1	40·4	39·3	38·5	38·3	38·8	38·1	38·0	37·8	37·6	43·5	31	43·5	43·5	31
1865	42·6	42·4	42·3	42·3	41·9	41·6	41·7	41·5	41·4	41·8	42·6	43·6	44·6	45·1	45·1	44·7	43·6	43·2	42·9	42·6	42·7	42·9	29	42·9	42·9	29
1866	41·9	41·7	41·6	41·7	41·7	41·7	41·9	42·4	43·6	44·5	45·1	44·7	44·1	43·6	43·3	42·8	42·3	41·4	40·7	40·2	42·7	29	42·7	42·7	29
1867	36·9	36·6	36·6	36·3	36·4	36·5	36·5	36·5	36·6	37·2	37·0	38·8	39·8	39·0	38·7	38·5	38·1	37·8	37·5	37·2	36·8	37·7	31	37·7	37·7	31
1868	44·9	44·9	44·9	44·8	44·7	44·8	44·9	44·9	45·0	45·4	46·3	47·3	48·1	48·6	49·0	48·3	47·4	46·8	46·2	45·9	45·5	45·6	45·2	46·0	46·0	29
Means	39·90	39·78	39·68	39·55	39·47	39·42	39·39	39·37	39·45	39·91	40·93	42·00	42·84	43·25	43·35	42·81	42·04	41·51	41·14	40·80	40·66	40·44	40·26	40·09	40·75	..

TABLE L.—MONTHLY MEAN TEMPERATURE of the Air at every Hour of the Day through the Range of Years 1849 to 1868.

Hour, Greenwich Mean Solar Time (Civil reckoning).	January.	February.	March.	April.	May.	June.	July.	August.	September.	October.	November.	December.	Yearly Means.
Midnight	37·03	38·07	38·5?	42·00	47·32	53·03	56·02	57·12	53·32	48·46	41·33	39·90	46·31
1h a.m.	37·84	37·86	38·20	42·40	46·81	53·32	56·28	56·63	52·90	48·28	41·17	39·78	45·97
2 „	37·79	37·68	38·03	42·00	46·31	52·83	55·7?	56·18	52·63	48·05	41·04	39·68	45·66
3 „	37·70	37·49	37·80	41·63	45·97	52·47	55·36	55·83	52·39	47·84	40·90	39·5?	45·41
4 „	37·61	37·32	37·63	41·41	45·73	52·27	55·14	55·5?	52·22	47·78	40·74	39·47	45·24
5 „	37·33	37·20	37·4?	41·32	46·21	52·07	55·62	55·46	52·12	47·64	40·69	39·42	45·31
6 „	37·43	37·10	37·40	41·91	48·01	53·09	57·37	56·36	52·26	47·64	40·60	39·39	45·89
7 „	37·39	37·0?	37·89	43·87	50·56	57·83	60·04	58·80	53·60	47·99	40·67	39·37	47·00
8 „	37·47	37·50	39·40	46·30	52·86	59·07	62·43	61·52	56·09	49·24	41·07	39·45	48·59
9 „	37·96	38·74	41·51	48·71	55·11	62·23	64·72	63·60	59·03	51·36	42·22	39·91	50·44
10 „	39·03	40·46	43·40	50·60	56·81	63·05	66·46	65·60	61·37	53·18	43·85	40·93	52·15
11 „	40·23	41·90	44·89	52·15	58·10	63·31	67·88	67·10	63·00	54·87	43·24	42·00	53·56
Noon	41·32	43·22	46·19	53·41	59·29	66·72	69·51	68·68	64·39	56·04	46·35	42·84	54·81
1h p.m.	41·89	43·90	46·81	54·00	59·94	67·27	70·09	66·58	64·06	56·49	46·85	43·25	55·49
2 „	41·89	44·07	47·12	54·33	60·16	67·40	70·44	66·66	65·07	56·46	46·89	43·35	55·58
3 „	41·55	43·76	46·91	54·13	60·03	67·17	70·37	66·51	64·65	55·71	46·11	42·81	55·23
4 „	40·71	42·94	46·17	53·26	59·35	66·35	69·63	68·59	63·37	54·33	44·93	42·04	54·30
5 „	39·85	41·68	44·85	51·86	58·00	65·38	68·37	67·03	61·47	52·70	43·96	41·51	53·03
6 „	39·29	40·59	43·25	50·18	56·24	63·63	66·46	65·22	59·18	51·44	43·24	41·14	51·66
7 „	38·90	39·86	41·85	47·80	54·01	61·51	64·27	62·78	57·22	50·51	42·65	40·80	50·18
8 „	38·58	39·31	40·87	46·20	51·67	58·02	61·78	60·82	55·96	49·80	42·24	40·66	48·90
9 „	38·84	38·80	40·08	45·02	50·04	56·97	59·86	59·32	54·92	49·28	41·83	40·44	47·91
10 „	58·20	38·46	39·52	44·20	49·00	55·73	58·67	58·37	54·28	48·90	41·45	40·26	47·25
11 „	38·03	38·13	39·04	43·48	48·20	54·86	57·74	57·59	53·69	48·51	41·16	40·09	46·71
Means	38·94	39·71	41·45	47·21	52·73	59·75	62·54	61·94	57·51	50·94	42·80	40·75	49·69

In the month of September 1862 the photographic records were not sufficiently complete to be used. The values given in the above table for September are the means of the monthly values for the remaining nineteen years.

TABLE LI.—MONTHLY MEAN DIURNAL INEQUALITY of the Temperature of the Air through the Range of Years 1849 to 1868.

Hour, Greenwich Mean Solar Time (Civil reckoning).	January.	February.	March.	April.	May.	June.	July.	August.	September.	October.	November.	December.
Midnight	− 1·01	− 1·64	− 2·88	− 3·31	− 5·41	− 5·82	− 5·62	− 4·82	− 4·19	− 2·48	− 1·47	− 0·85
1h a.m.	− 1·10	− 1·85	− 3·16	− 3·81	− 5·02	− 6·43	− 6·26	− 5·31	− 4·52	− 2·66	− 1·63	− 0·97
2 „	− 1·15	− 2·03	− 3·42	− 5·11	− 6·42	− 6·02	− 6·79	− 5·76	− 4·88	− 2·89	− 1·76	− 1·07
3 „	− 1·24	− 2·12	− 3·65	− 5·58	− 6·76	− 7·28	− 7·18	− 6·11	− 5·12	− 3·10	− 1·90	− 1·20
4 „	− 1·33	− 2·39	− 3·82	− 5·80	− 6·98	− 7·48	− 7·40	− 6·41	− 5·29	− 3·16	− 2·06	− 1·28
5 „	− 1·39	− 2·51	− 4·00	− 5·89	− 6·52	− 6·78	− 6·92	− 6·48	− 5·39	− 3·30	− 2·11	− 1·33
6 „	− 1·51	− 2·61	− 4·05	− 5·30	− 4·72	− 4·66	− 5·17	− 5·55	− 5·13	− 3·50	− 2·14	− 1·36
7 „	− 1·55	− 2·64	− 3·56	− 3·34	− 2·17	− 1·92	− 2·50	− 3·14	− 3·91	− 2·95	− 2·13	− 1·38
8 „	− 1·47	− 2·21	− 2·05	− 0·91	+ 0·13	+ 0·22	− 0·11	− 0·62	− 1·42	− 1·70	− 1·73	− 1·30
9 „	− 0·98	− 0·97	+ 0·06	+ 1·50	+ 2·38	+ 2·48	+ 2·18	+ 1·86	+ 1·52	+ 0·42	− 0·58	− 0·84
10 „	+ 0·11	+ 0·75	+ 1·93	+ 3·39	+ 4·08	+ 4·20	+ 3·92	+ 3·66	+ 5·86	+ 1·34	+ 1·05	+ 0·18
11 „	+ 1·20	+ 2·19	+ 3·44	+ 4·34	+ 4·57	+ 5·34	+ 5·16	+ 5·58	+ 3·93	+ 2·44	+ 1·25	+ 0·88
Noon	+ 2·38	+ 3·51	+ 4·74	+ 6·20	+ 6·56	+ 6·97	+ 6·77	+ 6·74	+ 6·88	+ 5·10	+ 3·53	+ 1·00
1h p.m.	+ 2·95	+ 4·19	+ 5·36	+ 6·88	+ 7·21	+ 7·52	+ 7·33	+ 7·36	+ 7·45	+ 5·55	+ 4·05	+ 2·50
2 „	− 3·05	+ 4·36	+ 5·67	+ 7·12	+ 7·43	+ 7·65	+ 7·90	+ 7·72	+ 7·36	+ 5·52	+ 4·09	+ 2·60
3 „	+ 2·61	+ 4·05	+ 5·46	+ 6·92	+ 7·30	+ 7·42	+ 7·83	+ 7·37	+ 7·14	+ 4·77	+ 3·31	+ 2·06
4 „	+ 1·77	+ 3·23	+ 4·72	+ 6·05	+ 6·52	+ 6·60	+ 7·11	+ 6·65	+ 5·86	+ 3·39	+ 2·13	+ 1·29
5 „	+ 0·91	+ 1·97	+ 3·40	+ 4·65	+ 5·26	+ 5·63	+ 5·83	+ 5·09	+ 3·96	+ 1·76	+ 1·16	+ 0·76
6 „	+ 0·35	+ 0·88	+ 1·80	+ 2·97	+ 3·51	+ 3·88	+ 3·92	+ 3·28	+ 1·67	+ 0·50	+ 0·44	+ 0·39
7 „	− 0·04	+ 0·15	+ 0·40	+ 0·59	+ 1·28	+ 1·76	+ 1·73	+ 0·84	− 0·29	− 0·43	− 0·13	+ 0·05
8 „	− 0·36	− 0·40	− 0·58	− 1·01	− 1·06	− 0·83	− 0·76	− 1·12	− 1·55	− 1·14	− 0·36	− 0·09
9 „	− 0·60	− 0·91	− 1·3?	− 2·10	− 2·60	− 2·78	− 2·68	− 2·62	− 2·59	− 1·66	− 0·97	− 0·31
10 „	− 0·74	− 1·25	− 1·53	− 3·01	− 3·73	− 4·02	− 3·87	− 3·57	− 3·23	− 2·04	− 1·33	− 0·49
11 „	− 0·91	− 1·56	− 2·41	− 3·73	− 4·53	− 4·95	− 4·80	− 4·35	− 3·82	− 2·43	− 1·64	− 0·65

TABLE LII.—Mean Temperature of the Air in each Month, as deduced from the Mean of the Mean Hourly Determinations in each Month.

Year.	January.	February.	March.	April.	May.	June.	July.	August.	September.	October.	November.	December.	Mean Annual Temperature	Difference of the Mean Temperature of each Year from the Mean Temperature over the whole of the Period (1849 to 1868, as deduced from the whole of the Observations.
	°	°	°	°	°	°	°	°	°	°	°	°	°	°
1849	42·7	42·3	42·8	45·1	54·6	59·4	60·0	63·1	58·4	51·4	44·9	38·3	50·32	+ 0·63
1850	34·1	41·5	39·7	49·3	51·6	62·0	62·2	60·8	56·3	46·7	46·4	40·4	49·52	− 0·17
1851	45·0	40·0	42·7	45·5	51·7	59·7	60·3	62·6	56·1	52·5	37·7	40·6	49·38	− 0·31
1852	41·9	41·3	40·6	45·4	51·1	56·9	66·0	62·3	56·9	47·7	49·0	47·4	50·63	+ 0·94
1853	41·1	33·2	36·6	43·6	52·5	59·0	61·1	60·1	53·4	51·3	42·3	34·3	47·54	− 2·13
1854	39·3	39·4	43·6	48·6	51·2	56·3	61·0	60·8	58·4	49·5	40·6	41·8	49·23	− 0·46
1855	34·9	29·2	37·8	45·9	47·9	58·2	62·6	62·5	57·5	51·5	41·9	36·2	47·17	− 2·52
1856	39·2	42·1	39·1	47·7	49·9	59·5	61·6	63·3	55·2	51·9	41·0	39·2	49·14	− 0·55
1857	36·8	40·0	41·9	46·3	54·2	61·4	64·8	65·7	59·9	53·3	45·5	45·1	51·24	+ 1·55
1858	37·9	35·4	42·2	45·9	51·1	64·8	62·3	61·2	60·4	51·2	39·5	41·1	49·50	− 0·19
1859	40·5	43·4	46·8	46·3	51·8	62·3	68·9	63·9	57·4	50·7	43·5	34·9	50·87	+ 1·18
1860	39·3	35·7	41·3	42·9	55·0	55·8	58·1	58·3	53·6	51·2	41·0	38·4	47·57	− 2·12
1861	36·8	42·2	44·1	44·9	52·1	60·1	61·7	64·2	57·3	54·2	41·0	41·8	50·03	+ 0·34
1862	40·5	40·5	43·9	48·3	56·2	56·8	59·4	59·7	57·7	52·5	40·1	45·7	49·94	+ 0·25
1863	42·2	42·2	43·9	49·5	51·3	58·8	62·1	62·5	53·9	51·8	46·1	43·6	50·66	+ 0·97
1864	36·3	36·2	41·5	48·7	54·4	58·2	62·8	60·2	57·2	50·9	42·5	38·6	48·96	− 0·73
1865	36·5	37·0	36·8	52·9	56·9	61·7	64·9	60·4	63·8	51·3	45·3	42·9	50·87	+ 1·18
1866	43·1	41·7	41·2	48·6	50·8	61·8	61·9	50·7	56·6	51·8	44·5	43·1	50·40	+ 0·71
1867	34·6	44·7	38·0	49·9	50·9	58·8	60·1	62·5	57·8	49·1	41·5	37·7	48·80	− 0·89
1868	37·6	43·3	44·5	48·7	58·4	63·2	68·1	63·9	60·4	48·2	41·9	46·0	52·02	+ 2·33
Means	38·94	39·71	41·45	47·21	52·73	59·73	62·54	61·94	57·51	50·94	42·80	40·75	49·69	....

In the month of September 1862, the photographic records were not sufficiently complete to give a trustworthy determination of the mean temperature of the air ; the value inserted above is approximate.

TABLE LIII.—Mean Temperature of Evaporation at every Hour of the Day in each Year from 1849 to 1868, for the Month of January.

Year.	Midnight.	1ʰ. a.m.	2ʰ. a.m.	3ʰ. a.m.	4ʰ. a.m.	5ʰ. a.m.	6ʰ. a.m.	7ʰ. a.m.	8ʰ. a.m.	9ʰ. a.m.	10ʰ. a.m.	11ʰ. a.m.	Noon.	1ʰ. p.m.	2ʰ. p.m.	3ʰ. p.m.	4ʰ. p.m.	5ʰ. p.m.	6ʰ. p.m.	7ʰ. p.m.	8ʰ. p.m.	9ʰ. p.m.	10ʰ. p.m.	11ʰ. p.m.	Mean.	Number of Days employed in forming the Means.
1849	40·8	40·7	40·5	40·2	40·0	39·7	39·8	39·8	39·8	40·1	40·7	41·3	42·2	42·4	42·5	42·3	41·7	41·2	40·9	40·7	40·7	40·6	40·6	40·8	40·8	17
1850	32·2	31·9	31·8	31·9	31·8	31·7	31·8	31·8	31·8	32·0	32·8	33·6	34·2	34·6	34·8	34·7	34·4	33·7	33·3	33·2	33·0	32·7	32·7	31·7	32·9	31
1851	41·1	40·9	41·0	40·9	40·5	40·2	40·1	39·7	39·6	41·0	42·2	43·5	43·6	43·4	43·0	42·4	42·0	41·7	41·5	41·3	41·0	41·4			41·4	31
1852	39·0	38·9	38·6	38·6	38·5	38·4	37·0	37·7	37·8	38·1	39·2	40·2	41·3	41·7	41·6	41·3	40·6	39·7	39·4	39·3	39·2	39·1	39·3	39·6	39·4	31
1853	37·9	37·9	37·9	38·0	37·9	37·9	37·8	37·8	37·6	37·8	38·2	39·4	40·0	40·4	40·2	40·1	39·7	39·1	38·9	38·5	38·3	37·8	37·5	37·3	38·5	21
1854	37·2	37·4	37·3	37·2	37·1	37·2	37·0	36·9	36·8	37·3	38·2	39·1	39·7	40·1	40·1	40·0	39·3	39·1	38·7	38·5	38·4	38·2	38·0	38·0	38·2	31
1855	33·4	33·3	33·1	33·1	33·0	33·0	32·8	32·9	33·2	34·0	34·8	35·5	35·7	36·0	35·7	35·1	34·7	34·2	33·8	33·5	33·3	33·1	33·0	33·9	33·9	31
1856	37·4	37·4	37·2	37·2	37·1	37·1	37·1	37·2	37·3	37·9	38·7	39·3	40·1	40·4	40·3	39·9	39·4	38·5	38·2	38·0	37·9	37·8	37·7	37·5	38·2	31
1857	35·5	35·5	35·1	35·1	34·9	34·8	34·7	34·6	35·1	35·6	36·2	36·6	37·2	37·6	37·7	37·5	36·8	36·1	35·8	35·6	35·3	35·1	35·0	34·8	35·8	31
1858	35·4	35·3	35·1	34·9	34·8	34·7	34·6	34·6	34·7	35·3	36·6	38·1	38·9	39·3	39·4	39·2	38·6	37·7	37·0	36·5	36·2	35·9	35·7	35·6	36·4	30
1859	38·4	38·4	38·3	38·2	38·1	38·0	38·0	38·1	38·2	38·7	39·4	40·7	40·8	41·4	41·6	41·3	40·6	39·9	39·4	39·0	38·8	38·7	38·6	38·2	39·2	31
1860	37·8	37·7	37·5	37·4	37·2	37·0	36·8	36·8	36·8	37·3	38·2	39·0	39·7	40·1	40·2	40·1	39·4	38·7	38·5	38·2	37·9	37·8	37·6	37·3	38·1	30
1861	35·1	35·4	35·3	35·2	34·6	34·3	34·2	34·2	34·1	34·5	35·3	37·1	38·4	38·6	38·8	38·7	37·9	37·3	36·5	35·8	35·0	34·6	34·3	34·1	35·8	19
1862	38·1	38·0	38·1	38·2	38·3	38·5	38·4	38·3	38·2	38·4	40·0	40·4	40·2	40·1	40·5	39·9	39·4	39·1	38·7	38·6	38·4	38·5	38·5	39·0	39·0	25
1863	39·6	39·6	39·6	39·7	40·0	40·1	40·1	40·1	40·0	40·1	40·7	41·3	42·0	42·3	42·0	41·7	41·1	40·5	40·1	39·8	39·7	39·4	39·3	39·4	40·3	31
1864	33·8	33·9	33·9	34·0	34·0	33·9	34·0	34·1	34·2	34·4	35·0	35·9	36·6	36·9	37·1	36·8	36·1	35·5	35·2	35·1	34·9	34·9	34·7	34·5	35·0	28
1865	34·7	34·4	34·5	34·3	34·1	33·9	33·7	33·6	33·7	36·6	36·8	36·8	36·6	36·1	35·3	35·2	35·0	33·3	35·2	35·2	35·2	35·1	33·0	33·9	31
1866	40·1	40·1	40·4	40·4	40·5	40·5	40·4	40·4	40·8	41·4	42·4	43·0	43·0	42·6	42·1	41·7	41·3	41·0	40·7	40·5	40·3	40·3	40·1	41·2	31
1867	31·9	31·9	31·8	31·6	31·8	31·9	32·1	32·6	33·0	33·5	35·8	35·7	35·3	34·6	34·1	33·8	33·3	32·9	32·4	32·3	32·2	33·2	31
1868	35·4	35·1	35·1	35·1	35·1	35·0	34·8	35·0	35·1	35·6	36·1	36·9	37·3	37·2	37·3	37·1	37·1	37·0	36·8	36·7	36·5	36·3	36·1	36·1	31
Means	36·74	36·67	36·60	36·57	36·49	36·40	36·33	36·30	36·34	36·70	37·49	38·37	39·12	39·44	39·46	39·26	38·68	38·10	37·73	37·44	37·21	37·02	36·91	36·80	37·42	..

TABLE LIV.—MEAN TEMPERATURE of EVAPORATION at every HOUR of the DAY in each YEAR from 1849 to 1868, for the MONTH of FEBRUARY.

Year.	Midnight.	1ʰ a.m.	2ʰ a.m.	3ʰ a.m.	4ʰ a.m.	5ʰ a.m.	6ʰ a.m.	7ʰ a.m.	8ʰ a.m.	9ʰ a.m.	10ʰ a.m.	11ʰ a.m.	Noon.	1ʰ p.m.	2ʰ p.m.	3ʰ p.m.	4ʰ p.m.	5ʰ p.m.	6ʰ p.m.	7ʰ p.m.	8ʰ p.m.	9ʰ p.m.	10ʰ p.m.	11ʰ p.m.	Mean.	Number of Days employed in forming the Means.
1849	38·9	38·8	38·7	38·5	38·1	38·2	37·9	38·0	38·3	39·5	40·9	42·1	43·3	44·1	44·4	44·1	43·7	42·9	41·8	40·8	40·4	40·0	39·7	39·6	40·5	13
1850	40·7	40·6	40·6	40·6	40·6	40·6	40·8	41·2	41·9	42·9	43·8	44·5	44·6	44·7	44·6	44·5	43·8	42·6	42·2	41·6	41·1	40·7	42·2	28
1851	37·0	36·6	36·2	36·1	36·1	35·9	35·6	35·6	35·9	37·3	38·5	40·1	41·3	41·6	41·9	41·9	41·6	40·5	39·4	38·6	38·1	37·8	37·3	36·8	38·2	28
1852	37·0	37·8	37·5	37·4	37·1	37·0	36·9	36·6	37·1	38·2	39·4	40·5	41·1	41·9	41·8	41·7	41·7	40·0	39·3	38·8	38·5	38·0	37·7	37·3	38·8	13
1853	30·0	30·0	30·0	30·1	30·1	30·1	39·9	30·1	30·2	31·0	32·1	32·3	33·3	33·3	33·4	33·3	33·0	32·3	31·7	31·4	30·9	32·5	30·3	30·1	31·2	17
1854	36·4	36·2	36·2	35·9	35·8	35·5	35·4	35·4	35·7	36·4	37·9	38·8	39·5	40·0	40·3	39·8	39·5	38·6	38·0	37·6	36·8	36·3	36·1	35·8	37·2	28
1855	26·9	26·6	26·2	26·0	25·9	26·0	26·0	26·1	26·1	26·6	27·9	29·6	30·8	31·9	31·8	32·0	31·6	31·2	30·2	29·3	28·8	28·3	28·1	27·8	27·5	28·5	28
1856	39·4	39·3	39·5	39·1	38·9	39·1	39·1	39·3	39·4	40·0	41·0	41·8	42·5	42·8	42·9	42·7	42·3	41·6	41·0	40·6	40·3	40·0	39·7	39·8	40·5	29
1857	36·3	35·9	35·5	35·1	34·9	34·8	34·8	35·1	36·0	35·7	39·6	41·0	42·1	42·6	42·7	42·4	41·7	40·8	39·6	38·9	38·3	37·8	37·4	37·0	38·3	15
1858	32·9	32·6	32·4	32·4	32·2	31·9	31·9	31·9	32·4	33·7	34·1	35·2	36·3	36·8	37·1	36·7	35·9	35·0	34·3	34·1	34·0	33·8	33·2	32·9	33·9	20
1859	39·7	39·5	39·1	39·0	39·0	38·8	38·9	39·0	39·5	40·6	42·0	42·9	43·6	44·0	44·2	44·0	43·5	42·7	41·9	41·1	40·7	40·4	40·2	40·1	41·0	28
1860	32·8	32·6	32·5	32·2	31·9	31·7	31·7	31·7	32·2	33·4	35·3	36·2	36·6	36·6	36·5	36·2	35·5	34·7	34·1	33·7	33·3	33·0	32·9	33·8	29
1861	40·0	40·0	39·7	39·5	39·3	39·2	39·3	39·5	39·6	40·5	41·6	42·5	43·3	43·8	43·9	43·7	43·0	42·3	41·6	41·1	40·6	40·4	40·4	40·1	41·0	28
1862	38·8	38·6	38·4	38·4	38·2	37·9	37·7	37·4	37·6	38·3	39·4	40·9	42·2	43·2	43·7	43·7	43·6	43·3	42·3	41·4	40·7	40·3	39·8	39·4	39·1	40·4	24
1863	38·8	38·8	38·8	38·5	38·5	38·4	38·4	38·1	38·5	39·4	40·9	42·2	43·2	43·7	43·7	43·6	43·3	42·3	41·4	40·7	40·3	39·8	39·4	39·1	40·4	28
1864	33·3	33·3	33·2	33·2	33·2	33·2	33·1	33·1	33·6	34·6	35·5	36·2	37·1	37·2	37·3	37·3	36·6	35·8	34·9	34·5	34·2	34·0	33·7	33·5	34·7	28
1865	33·4	33·3	34·0	34·8	34·6	34·3	34·0	33·8	33·9	34·4	33·4	36·1	36·8	37·2	37·0	36·8	36·8	36·3	35·8	35·5	35·5	35·3	35·3	35·1	35·4	28
1866	38·6	38·6	38·5	38·4	38·4	38·0	38·0	37·7	38·2	39·2	40·6	41·5	42·4	42·6	42·1	42·0	40·7	40·0	39·6	39·1	38·1	38·1	38·1	57·7	25
1867	42·5	42·4	42·3	42·3	42·2	41·8	41·9	41·7	41·5	42·0	42·9	43·8	44·2	44·3	44·1	43·9	43·6	43·0	42·7	42·5	42·3	42·0	42·0	41·9	42·7	15
1868	39·8	39·8	39·8	39·7	39·7	39·7	39·7	39·5	39·4	39·6	40·3	41·6	42·6	43·4	43·5	43·3	43·0	42·6	41·8	41·1	40·4	40·1	39·8	39·7	39·7	40·8	27
Means	36·80	36·67	36·46	36·36	36·24	36·10	36·04	36·03	36·35	37·32	38·50	39·47	40·33	40·67	40·73	40·52	40·11	39·28	38·54	38·02	37·65	37·29	37·03	36·80	37·89	..

TABLE LV.—MEAN TEMPERATURE of EVAPORATION at every HOUR of the DAY in each YEAR from 1849 to 1868, for the MONTH of MARCH.

Year.	Midnight.	1ʰ a.m.	2ʰ a.m.	3ʰ a.m.	4ʰ a.m.	5ʰ a.m.	6ʰ a.m.	7ʰ a.m.	8ʰ a.m.	9ʰ a.m.	10ʰ a.m.	11ʰ a.m.	Noon.	1ʰ p.m.	2ʰ p.m.	3ʰ p.m.	4ʰ p.m.	5ʰ p.m.	6ʰ p.m.	7ʰ p.m.	8ʰ p.m.	9ʰ p.m.	10ʰ p.m.	11ʰ p.m.	Mean.	Number of Days employed in forming the Means.
1849	38·3	38·1	38·1	37·9	38·1	38·0	38·1	38·5	39·3	40·4	41·2	42·0	42·4	42·8	43·0	43·1	42·6	42·1	41·2	40·2	39·7	39·3	38·9	38·8	40·1	30
1850	34·6	34·5	34·1	34·0	33·8	33·6	33·5	33·7	35·1	36·5	38·0	30·1	40·6	40·8	40·8	40·5	39·7	38·7	37·9	37·0	36·5	35·9	35·4	36·8	30
1851	38·3	38·2	38·1	38·0	38·0	37·9	37·7	38·1	39·3	40·7	41·8	42·5	43·1	43·0	43·1	42·7	42·3	42·1	41·5	40·7	40·2	39·7	39·4	39·0	40·2	31
1852	34·4	34·7	34·4	34·1	34·1	33·8	33·8	34·6	36·3	38·4	40·5	41·6	42·6	43·1	43·0	43·3	43·4	39·1	36·0	35·3	34·7	33·4	32·5	50
1853	33·8	33·5	33·2	32·0	31·9	32·0	32·0	32·6	32·6	33·5	36·5	37·1	37·6	38·0	38·1	37·9	37·3	36·5	35·4	34·6	34·0	33·4	33·1	32·5	34·6	19
1854	37·8	37·5	37·2	37·0	36·9	36·8	36·9	37·5	38·7	40·7	42·3	43·6	44·4	45·3	46·0	46·1	45·5	44·8	43·1	41·8	40·8	40·8	39·0	38·5	40·7	31
1855	33·3	33·3	33·2	33·2	33·2	33·1	32·7	34·7	36·4	37·9	38·6	38·8	38·5	38·3	38·5	34·0	34·3	35·8	30·0	38·3	38
1856	35·6	35·4	35·3	35·1	34·6	34·5	34·3	34·9	35·7	36·9	38·0	38·7	39·2	39·4	39·5	39·6	39·2	38·6	37·8	37·2	36·6	36·2	36·0	35·8	36·8	31
1857	38·1	37·9	37·5	37·3	37·2	36·9	36·1	35·8	35·5	36·1	37·4	40·3	40·5	41·5	43·0	42·4	42·6	42·0	41·8	41·0	40·3	39·7	39·3	38·7	38·3	31
1858	37·6	37·2	36·9	36·5	36·1	35·8	35·5	36·2	37·4	40·5	41·5	43·0	42·4	42·6	42·6	42·0	41·8	41·0	40·3	39·7	39·3	38·7	38·3	36·2	29
1859	42·4	42·6	42·6	42·6	42·5	42·4	42·5	43·2	44·5	45·1	45·8	46·3	46·8	46·9	46·9	46·5	45·6	44·6	43·9	43·2	42·6	42·3	42·1	44·0	31
1860	36·9	36·7	36·6	36·4	36·3	36·2	37·3	38·8	39·5	40·2	40·8	41·4	41·5	41·1	40·6	39·6	39·1	38·5	38·1	37·6	37·6	38·6	30
1861	40·2	40·1	40·1	40·2	40·4	40·5	40·6	40·9	41·4	42·6	44·0	45·4	46·9	47·1	47·1	46·4	44·5	44·3	43·4	42·2	41·3	40·7	40·4	42·8	31
1862	40·4	40·6	40·6	40·6	40·6	40·7	40·6	40·8	41·3	42·4	43·9	44·4	44·9	45·0	44·9	44·0	42·9	42·4	42·4	41·8	41·1	40·5	39·8	40·2	41·4	18
1863	38·9	38·5	38·3	38·1	38·0	37·6	37·7	38·0	39·5	41·5	42·8	44·1	44·6	44·8	45·0	45·0	44·0	42·0	42·0	41·4	40·5	39·8	30·2	41·1	31
1864	37·0	36·4	36·0	35·0	36·0	36·0	36·3	36·6	37·7	39·1	40·2	41·0	41·9	42·8	42·8	41·8	40·9	39·1	38·6	38·2	37·9	37·7	38·2	30
1865	33·3	33·2	32·9	32·8	32·5	32·5	32·4	32·7	33·7	35·8	37·0	37·5	37·5	37·3	37·2	36·7	36·1	35·6	35·8	34·8	34·9	34·0	33·7	33·6	34·7	29
1866	36·8	36·7	36·5	36·3	36·1	36·0	36·4	37·3	34·8	40·1	40·8	41·6	42·0	41·8	41·6	40·9	38·4	37·9	37·0	37·7	33·6	30
1867	34·7	34·6	34·7	34·4	34·5	34·3	34·3	34·7	35·5	36·3	37·1	37·6	38·3	38·4	38·3	38·0	37·3	36·6	35·9	35·6	35·2	35·0	34·8	36·0	31
1868	40·2	39·9	39·6	39·3	39·1	39·0	38·7	39·1	40·3	42·0	43·4	44·0	44·7	45·3	45·5	45·1	44·6	43·9	43·1	42·3	41·8	41·3	41·0	40·7	41·8	31
Means	37·08	36·93	36·76	36·61	36·56	36·42	36·35	36·76	37·82	39·20	40·44	41·34	42·04	42·35	42·48	42·41	41·93	41·21	40·25	39·41	38·74	38·18	37·76	37·48	39·02	..

TABLE LVI.—MEAN TEMPERATURE of EVAPORATION at every HOUR of the DAY in each YEAR from 1849 to 1868, for the MONTH of APRIL.

Year	Midnight	1ʰ a.m.	2ʰ a.m.	3ʰ a.m.	4ʰ a.m.	5ʰ a.m.	6ʰ a.m.	7ʰ a.m.	8ʰ a.m.	9ʰ a.m.	10ʰ a.m.	11ʰ a.m.	Noon	1ʰ p.m.	2ʰ p.m.	3ʰ p.m.	4ʰ p.m.	5ʰ p.m.	6ʰ p.m.	7ʰ p.m.	8ʰ p.m.	9ʰ p.m.	10ʰ p.m.	11ʰ p.m.	Mean	Number of Days employed in forming the Means
1849	40·3	40·2	40·0	39·8	39·5	39·1	39·4	40·7	42·4	43·9	44·3	44·8	45·9	45·7	45·5	45·4	45·0	44·4	43·9	42·6	41·7	41·1	40·5	40·1	42·4	25
1850	44·3	44·0	43·8	43·7	43·6	43·3	43·7	44·9	45·7	46·7	47·5	48·7	49·2	49·3	49·4	49·3	49·1	48·1	47·6	46·6	45·8	45·0	44·5	44·2	46·2	27
1851	40·0	39·6	39·2	39·0	38·9	38·0	39·3	40·6	42·3	43·8	44·6	45·4	46·1	46·9	47·3	46·7	46·1	45·4	44·5	43·1	43·4	41·5	40·7	40·3	42·6	30
1852	37·0	36·2	35·0	35·7	35·7	35·8	36·8	39·0	41·3	43·0	44·5	45·7	46·4	47·1	47·0	45·9	44·4	43·0	41·2	39·7	38·7	38·0	37·4	40·9		30
1853	39·2	38·9	38·3	37·5	37·1	37·3	38·0	39·8	42·1	42·5	43·1	43·4	43·8	44·2	44·6	44·5	43·7	43·1	42·1	41·2	40·5	40·2	39·8	41·1		10
1854	41·0	40·3	40·0	39·8	39·7	39·6	40·2	42·0	44·7	47·2	49·0	50·1	50·4	51·0	50·7	50·5	49·7	48·8	47·4	46·0	44·2	43·1	42·4	41·8	45·0	30
1855	39·5	39·0	38·7	38·2	37·9	38·0	38·5	39·8	41·5	43·3	44·7	46·0	47·2	47·9	48·2	48·1	47·3	46·4	44·8	43·3	42·0	41·1	40·5	40·0	42·6	30
1856	41·3	41·1	40·9	40·8	40·8	40·7	41·2	42·6	44·2	45·8	46·8	47·5	47·9	47·8	48·2	48·0	47·4	46·6	45·4	44·2	43·1	42·3	42·1	41·8	44·1	29
1857	41·3	41·0	40·8	40·2	40·0	39·9	40·3	41·8	43·7	44·9	45·8	46·1	46·5	46·0	47·2	47·1	46·6	45·8	44·8	43·8	42·9	42·3	41·8	41·5	43·5	30
1858	39·5	39·3	38·9	38·7	38·7	38·8	39·2	40·4	42·2	43·9	45·1	46·0	46·3	46·6	46·7	46·4	45·9	45·0	43·7	42·6	41·7	40·8	40·3	39·8	42·4	24
1859	41·0	40·8	40·5	40·2	39·9	39·7	40·1	41·5	43·1	44·6	45·0	45·4	45·6	46·2	46·8	46·5	46·1	45·5	44·6	43·7	42·9	42·3	42·0	41·6	43·1	28
1860	37·2	36·9	36·5	36·3	36·1	36·2	36·7	38·1	39·8	41·6	42·4	43·1	43·6	44·2	44·4	44·3	43·6	42·9	41·8	40·5	39·4	38·4	37·7	37·3	30·9	24
1861	39·5	39·1	38·9	38·6	38·3	38·2	38·5	40·1	42·2	44·0	45·2	46·5	47·3	47·5	47·5	47·5	46·6	45·7	44·6	43·2	42·2	41·2	40·6	40·1	43·6	28
1862	43·6	43·4	43·0	42·8	42·8	43·3	44·3	45·5	46·6	47·1	47·4	48·0	48·4	48·6	48·6	48·4	47·9	47·3	46·5	45·8	45·1	44·8	44·5	43·7	46·2	25
1863	43·2	43·0	42·7	42·4	42·1	42·3	42·7	44·3	46·1	47·5	48·6	49·3	49·9	50·2	50·5	50·6	49·8	49·1	48·1	47·0	46·0	45·0	44·4	43·7	46·2	29
1864	41·7	41·3	41·0	40·9	40·7	40·5	40·9	42·4	44·9	45·6	46·7	47·6	48·5	48·7	48·6	48·7	48·4	47·5	46·0	44·0	43·2	42·7	42·1	41·5	45·0	29
1865	44·6	44·0	43·6	43·1	43·0	42·9	43·3	44·9	46·8	48·9	51·0	52·7	53·8	54·5	55·1	54·7	53·0	53·0	51·5	49·4	47·4	46·4	45·6	44·9	48·3	30
1866	43·3	42·8	42·7	42·3	42·1	42·0	42·3	43·9	45·2	46·6	47·5	48·0	48·7	49·0	49·0	50·0	50·0	50·1	49·2	48·3	47·4	46·7	46·0	45·5	46·7	30
1867	44·6	44·3	44·0	43·9	43·9	43·8	44·1	45·2	46·4	47·5	48·0	48·7	49·2	49·6	50·0	50·0	50·1	49·2	48·3	47·4	46·7	46·0	45·5	45·1	46·7	30
1868	43·2	42·0	42·0	42·1	42·0	42·0	42·2	43·4	44·9	46·3	47·8	48·2	49·2	49·4	49·2	49·0	48·6	47·4	46·6	45·4	44·8	44·2	43·4	42·9	45·2	30
Means	41·22	40·86	40·57	40·30	40·14	40·09	40·54	41·98	43·64	45·20	46·20	47·03	47·66	48·03	48·21	48·03	47·54	46·70	45·71	44·46	43·44	42·61	42·07	41·61	43·91	..

TABLE LVII.—MEAN TEMPERATURE of EVAPORATION at every HOUR of the DAY in each YEAR from 1849 to 1868, for the MONTH of MAY.

Year	Midnight	1ʰ a.m.	2ʰ a.m.	3ʰ a.m.	4ʰ a.m.	5ʰ a.m.	6ʰ a.m.	7ʰ a.m.	8ʰ a.m.	9ʰ a.m.	10ʰ a.m.	11ʰ a.m.	Noon	1ʰ p.m.	2ʰ p.m.	3ʰ p.m.	4ʰ p.m.	5ʰ p.m.	6ʰ p.m.	7ʰ p.m.	8ʰ p.m.	9ʰ p.m.	10ʰ p.m.	11ʰ p.m.	Mean	Number of Days employed in forming the Means
1849	48·2	47·9	47·7	47·6	47·5	47·9	49·2	50·7	51·6	52·7	53·5	54·3	55·4	55·6	55·9	56·1	55·7	54·9	53·8	52·4	51·0	49·9	49·5	49·0	51·6	28
1850	45·2	44·9	44·5	44·4	44·2	44·7	45·8	47·5	49·0	49·9	50·5	51·0	51·4	51·6	51·6	51·3	51·1	50·6	49·7	48·8	47·7	46·9	46·5	45·8	48·1	31
1851	43·7	43·4	43·2	43·0	42·8	43·8	46·0	47·8	49·2	50·3	51·0	51·4	51·6	51·7	51·5	50·6	50·7	49·8	48·8	47·5	46·7	45·9	45·4	48·1		30
1852	43·3	43·0	44·6	44·3	44·2	44·3	45·2	46·7	47·9	49·1	50·2	50·9	52·0	52·4	52·6	52·6	52·2	51·5	50·1	48·7	47·5	46·7	45·9	45·4	48·1	31
1853	44·8	44·4	44·3	44·2	44·6	45·8	47·9	49·6	51·0	51·0	51·7	52·3	52·5	52·5	52·2	51·6	50·7	49·3	48·5	47·0	46·2	45·7				31
1854	44·9	44·5	44·2	44·0	43·8	44·2	45·7	47·2	48·7	50·4	51·3	52·1	52·6	52·8	53·0	53·1	52·6	51·9	50·7	49·1	47·5	46·3	45·5	45·2	48·4	31
1855	44·8	44·5	44·0	43·0	43·0	43·9	45·5	47·2	48·6	48·2	48·9	49·0	49·9	50·3	50·6	50·8	50·8	50·3	49·3	48·5	47·2	46·2	45·3	45·2	47·3	23
1856	44·5	44·2	43·8	43·5	43·4	43·7	44·8	46·5	48·3	48·6	49·3	49·9	50·3	50·6	50·8	50·8	49·8	49·3	48·5	47·2	46·2	45·5	45·0	46·9		28
1857	44·2	44·0	43·5	43·1	42·8	43·6	45·1	46·9	48·1	49·3	51·1	51·8	51·8	51·7	51·5	51·5	50·7	50·9	49·1	48·9	47·1	46·4	45·8	45·0	46·9	28
1858	44·2	43·5	43·1	42·8	42·6	43·0	44·4	46·2	47·6	48·5	49·4	50·3	50·9	51·3	51·6	51·4	50·7	49·9	48·9	47·9	47·0	46·2	45·7	45·1	47·2	26
1859	44·6	44·6	44·4	44·3	44·1	44·3	45·5	47·2	48·6	50·0	51·0	51·8	52·8	53·2	53·6	53·5	52·7	51·6	50·5	49·1	47·5	46·2	45·7	45·3	48·4	22
1860	42·6	42·4	42·1	41·9	41·4	42·5	43·3	44·7	46·9	48·1	49·3	50·0	50·7	51·3	51·8	51·8	51·7	51·5	50·0	49·1	48·0	47·1	46·4	45·8	48·0	18
1861	45·2	44·7	44·4	44·1	44·2	44·4	45·4	46·9	48·1	49·3	50·0	50·7	51·3	51·8	51·8	51·7	51·5	50·0	49·1	48·0	47·1	46·4	45·8	48·0		29
1862	43·6	43·0	42·8	42·7	43·0	43·8	45·5	46·7	51·9	53·0	54·3	55·1	55·4	55·2	54·7	55·1	54·2	53·2	52·2	51·5	49·7	48·6	47·6	46·5	45·7	25
1863	45·7	45·1	44·8	44·6	44·3	44·7	46·1	47·6	48·8	50·2	50·9	51·7	51·3	52·5	52·5	52·2	51·6	50·7	49·9	48·9	47·6	46·5	45·7	45·2	48·3	20
1864	47·7	47·1	46·6	46·3	46·2	46·7	47·9	49·3	50·6	51·9	52·7	53·5	53·7	53·6	53·4	53·4	53·3	52·8	52·0	50·9	50·0	49·0	48·7	48·0	51·1	28
1865	42·6	42·3	41·9	41·7	41·5	41·8	42·1	42·7	45·1	51·1	52·7	47·3	48·4	48·0	49·1	49·4	49·8	50·0	49·6	48·8	47·7	46·9	46·3	45·8	45·2	31
1866	42·6	42·3	41·9	41·7	41·5	41·6	42·5	43·9	47·3	48·4	48·9	49·1	49·4	49·8	50·0	49·9	49·6	48·8	47·7	46·9	46·3	45·8	45·2	47·2		31
1867	43·9	43·5	43·3	43·7	43·9	44·7	46·1	47·6	48·7	49·5	50·6	51·0	51·4	51·5	51·5	54·2	53·2	52·2	51·6	50·7	50·2	49·3	47·6	46·5	46·3	23
1868	49·6	49·1	48·9	48·7	48·6	49·2	50·9	53·2	54·9	56·6	57·4	57·9	58·3	58·7	59·0	58·9	58·3	57·3	56·2	54·7	53·9	51·9	50·9	50·4	53·9	30
Means	45·68	45·31	44·96	44·75	44·58	44·89	46·17	47·91	49·33	50·68	51·51	52·15	52·75	53·05	53·16	53·06	52·65	51·91	50·90	49·73	48·43	47·47	46·80	46·30	48·92	..

TABLE LVIII.—Mean Temperature of Evaporation at every Hour of the Day in each Year from 1849 to 1868, for the Month of June.

Year	Midnight	1 a.m.	2 a.m.	3 a.m.	4 a.m.	5 a.m.	6 a.m.	7 a.m.	8 a.m.	9 a.m.	10 a.m.	11 a.m.	Noon	1 p.m.	2 p.m.	3 p.m.	4 p.m.	5 p.m.	6 p.m.	7 p.m.	8 p.m.	9 p.m.	10 p.m.	11 p.m.	Mean	Number of Days employed in forming the Means
1849	51·0	50·3	49·8	49·3	49·1	49·6	51·3	53·0	54·8	55·9	56·7	57·6	58·1	57·7	57·6	57·4	57·4	56·9	56·1	55·2	54·1	52·9	52·0	51·4	54·0	30
1850	52·3	51·8	51·3	50·8	50·6	51·3	53·3	55·5	57·3	59·0	59·9	60·3	60·8	61·2	61·1	61·3	61·0	60·0	58·8	57·8	56·2	54·8	53·9	53·4	56·4	28
1851	51·1	50·3	49·8	49·5	50·1	51·7	53·9	55·4	57·2	58·0	58·5	59·1	59·6	59·5	59·1	58·6	57·9	56·9	55·9	54·6	53·3	52·6	51·9	54·7		30
1852	50·1	49·9	49·8	49·7	49·8	50·2	51·1	51·9	53·2	54·1	52·6	54·8	55·3	55·6	56·0	56·4	54·8	54·3	54·9	53·5	52·3	51·4	51·0	50·7	52·7	30
1853	51·4	51·2	50·9	50·6	50·4	50·7	51·1	53·6	54·8	55·7	56·5	57·2	57·5	57·7	57·7	57·4	57·0	56·8	56·0	55·0	53·8	52·8	51·2	51·9	54·2	30
1854	49·7	49·4	49·3	49·2	49·2	49·6	50·8	52·4	54·9	53·8	56·9	57·6	57·8	57·8	57·4	57·0	56·7	55·6	54·2	52·7	51·7	50·9	50·3	63·3		27
1855	50·2	49·7	49·5	49·2	49·1	49·5	50·9	52·7	54·2	53·0	55·5	55·8	56·4	56·7	56·9	57·1	56·8	56·3	55·4	54·5	53·2	52·2	51·6	51·2	53·3	28
1856	52·7	52·4	52·0	51·7	51·6	51·8	51·9	54·6	55·7	56·9	58·1	58·8	59·1	59·6	59·7	59·5	59·1	58·8	58·2	57·3	56·2	54·9	54·1	55·8		22
1857	53·7	52·0	52·5	52·1	51·9	52·6	52·4	56·3	57·6	59·0	60·2	60·9	61·5	61·6	61·7	61·5	60·7	50·7	58·7	57·4	56·1	54·9	54·0	53·5	56·9	23
1858	55·0	54·6	54·2	53·8	53·6	54·3	55·8	57·3	59·1	60·6	61·6	62·1	62·5	63·0	63·0	63·2	63·0	62·6	61·5	60·6	60·6	58·6	57·1	58·7		16
1859	55·3	54·8	54·6	54·3	54·2	54·6	55·6	56·8	57·8	59·2	60·0	60·7	61·5	61·9	61·2	62·0	61·8	61·0	60·0	59·1	57·7	56·8	55·9	55·4	58·1	19
1860	50·6	50·3	50·2	50·2	50·1	50·6	51·4	52·6	53·6	54·4	54·7	55·2	56·1	55·9	56·2	55·5	54·8	54·2	53·5	52·4	51·6	51·1	50·7	53·0		27
1861	53·8	53·5	53·2	52·9	53·6	54·7	56·1	57·3	58·4	59·0	59·5	60·2	60·2	60·1	60·2	59·8	59·4	58·8	57·7	56·7	55·8	55·1	54·4	56·8		28
1862	50·3	50·0	49·8	49·6	49·5	49·9	50·0	52·1	53·1	54·3	54·9	55·4	56·0	56·4	56·4	56·3	56·1	55·7	55·3	54·3	53·1	52·0	51·2	50·7	53·1	26
1863	52·4	52·0	51·7	51·7	51·6	52·2	53·3	54·3	55·5	56·4	56·9	57·1	57·8	58·1	58·0	57·8	57·5	56·8	55·9	55·1	54·2	52·5	52·7	54·8		30
1864	51·2	50·9	50·8	50·6	50·5	50·9	51·8	53·0	54·0	54·6	55·2	56·0	57·0	57·3	57·5	57·4	57·0	56·3	55·5	54·2	53·2	52·4	52·0	51·7	53·8	25
1865	51·6	51·2	51·7	51·5	51·2	51·7	52·1	53·9	57·3	58·4	59·2	59·9	60·3	60·9	59·6	58·3	57·1	55·3	54·2	53·5	53·1	55·9		30
1866	54·4	53·8	53·4	53·1	53·0	53·7	55·1	56·8	58·1	59·4	60·2	60·8	61·5	61·6	61·3	61·4	60·9	60·6	59·7	58·4	57·7	56·2	55·4	54·3	57·5	30
1867	51·0	50·7	50·5	50·2	50·6	52·0	53·5	54·7	55·9	56·7	57·4	58·0	58·1	57·7	57·1	56·2	55·3	52·3	53·3	52·3	51·6	54·3		24
1868	53·6	53·0	52·4	52·0	51·6	52·2	54·0	55·8	57·4	58·7	59·7	60·7	60·7	61·3	61·3	61·6	61·6	61·4	61·0	59·7	58·6	57·0	55·8	54·8	54·1	30
Means	52·12	51·69	51·37	51·11	50·98	51·48	52·81	54·38	55·67	56·85	57·63	58·25	58·88	59·08	59·13	59·01	58·65	58·09	57·24	56·23	54·94	53·88	53·13	52·61	55·22	..

TABLE LIX.—Mean Temperature of Evaporation at every Hour of the Day in each Year from 1849 to 1868, for the Month of July.

Year	Midnight	1 a.m.	2 a.m.	3 a.m.	4 a.m.	5 a.m.	6 a.m.	7 a.m.	8 a.m.	9 a.m.	10 a.m.	11 a.m.	Noon	1 p.m.	2 p.m.	3 p.m.	4 p.m.	5 p.m.	6 p.m.	7 p.m.	8 p.m.	9 p.m.	10 p.m.	11 p.m.	Mean	Number of Days employed in forming the Means
1849	52·4	52·0	51·7	51·4	51·2	51·4	53·0	55·0	56·8	57·7	58·1	58·1	58·6	59·0	59·4	59·6	59·0	58·3	57·4	56·3	55·1	54·3	54·0	53·2	55·5	19
1850	55·7	55·5	55·1	54·9	54·8	55·2	56·2	57·7	59·0	60·0	60·9	61·5	62·1	61·7	60·9	59·7	60·3	58·6	57·5	56·6	56·1	58·7		31
1851	53·0	52·6	52·2	51·8	51·7	52·2	53·2	54·6	55·8	56·9	58·1	58·8	59·6	60·1	60·1	60·4	59·9	59·3	58·7	57·9	57·1	56·0	54·0	54·1	53·6	31
1852	53·9	53·6	53·2	53·0	53·2	53·7	54·8	56·0	56·9	57·8	58·2	59·0	59·4	59·9	59·6	59·6	60·0	59·5	58·7	57·6	56·4	55·1	57·7		20
1853	53·8	53·7	53·5	53·3	53·1	53·7	54·8	56·0	56·9	57·8	58·2	59·0	59·4	59·9	59·6	59·6	60·0	59·5	58·7	57·6	56·4	55·1	54·9	54·7	56·6	29
1854	53·7	53·3	52·4	52·1	51·7	51·9	52·9	54·8	56·6	58·0	59·2	60·0	60·4	60·4	60·4	60·0	59·7	58·8	57·8	56·8	55·0	55·1	54·4	56·5		31
1855	57·1	56·7	56·5	56·2	56·2	56·8	57·8	59·2	60·6	60·6	61·0	61·6	61·0	62·0	61·4	62·3	62·0	61·3	60·6	60·6	59·2	58·2	57·5	56·8	59·0	27
1856	55·5	54·6	54·2	53·8	53·7	54·0	55·1	56·6	57·8	58·8	60·1	61·5	61·5	61·1	61·8	61·1	61·0	60·5	59·9	58·8	57·3	55·3	54·6	58·0		30
1857	56·6	56·4	56·3	56·2	56·2	56·5	57·8	59·4	60·8	61·8	62·3	62·8	63·1	63·7	63·8	63·4	62·7	61·8	61·0	60·1	58·8	57·8	57·1	56·6	59·7	25
1858	54·3	53·9	53·5	53·3	53·4	53·5	54·6	55·9	59·1	59·3	59·6	60·3	59·8	59·2	58·4	57·8	56·8	55·8	55·2	54·7	56·8		27
1859	59·3	58·8	58·6	58·4	58·2	58·6	60·1	61·9	63·5	64·7	65·5	66·0	66·7	67·1	67·2	67·0	66·1	65·4	64·6	63·1	61·7	60·9	60·0	62·9		31
1860	52·6	52·0	51·3	50·9	50·8	51·0	52·0	53·4	54·8	55·6	56·7	57·9	58·6	58·8	58·9	58·3	57·8	57·1	56·3	55·1	54·2	53·7	53·2	54·0		29
1861	54·4	54·1	53·9	53·6	54·0	54·1	55·6	56·8	58·7	58·7	59·4	59·1	58·7	58·0	57·3	56·6	56·0	55·4	55·0	53·9		13
1862	52·7	52·5	52·2	52·0	52·1	52·5	53·3	54·8	55·6	56·7	57·5	58·3	59·2	59·5	59·5	59·0	59·3	58·4	57·5	56·4	55·4	54·6	53·9	53·4	55·7	17
1863	52·4	52·0	51·7	51·7	51·9	52·2	53·9	55·8	57·4	58·9	60·2	60·5	60·1	59·0	58·7	57·6	56·4	55·4	54·3	52·3	51·8		18
1864	54·5	54·0	53·4	53·1	52·9	53·9	55·1	56·3	57·8	58·5	59·7	61·0	61·5	61·6	61·4	61·3	60·8	60·9	60·1	59·1	58·1	57·5	56·9	57·3		28
1865	56·0	56·1	55·8	55·6	55·9	57·1	58·6	59·9	61·1	61·8	62·1	62·5	62·7	62·7	62·4	61·9	60·9	60·0	59·1	58·1	57·5	56·9	59·3		29
1866	54·9	54·4	53·8	53·4	53·2	53·8	55·0	56·2	57·7	58·7	59·5	60·3	61·4	61·1	61·0	60·7	59·8	59·1	58·1	57·5	55·2	57·6		31
1867	53·0	52·6	52·1	52·1	52·5	53·6	55·0	56·7	57·3	57·7	58·3	58·3	58·4	58·3	57·6	56·4	54·9	54·3	52·3	51·6	55·2		31
1868	57·7	57·0	56·5	56·1	56·1	56·4	57·6	59·6	61·1	62·7	63·9	64·2	64·8	64·6	64·7	64·6	64·3	63·7	62·8	61·6	60·1	59·7	60·7	31
Means	54·88	54·47	54·10	53·83	53·72	54·06	55·20	56·71	58·05	59·18	59·90	60·48	61·12	61·43	61·54	61·52	61·17	60·56	59·70	58·73	57·52	56·87	55·95	55·43	57·74	..

TABLE LX.—MEAN TEMPERATURE of EVAPORATION at every HOUR of the DAY in each YEAR from 1849 to 1868, for the MONTH of AUGUST.

Year.	Midnight.	1ʰ a.m.	2ʰ a.m.	3ʰ a.m.	4ʰ a.m.	5ʰ a.m.	6ʰ a.m.	7ʰ a.m.	8ʰ a.m.	9ʰ a.m.	10ʰ a.m.	11ʰ a.m.	Noon.	1ʰ p.m.	2ʰ p.m.	3ʰ p.m.	4ʰ p.m.	5ʰ p.m.	6ʰ p.m.	7ʰ p.m.	8ʰ p.m.	9ʰ p.m.	10ʰ p.m.	11ʰ p.m.	Mean.	Number of Days employed in forming the Means.
1849	56·2	56·0	55·8	55·6	55·5	55·6	56·0	57·3	58·3	59·3	59·8	60·3	61·1	61·5	62·0	62·0	62·0	61·3	60·3	59·3	58·5	57·8	57·2	56·8	58·6	24
1850	55·3	55·1	54·7	54·2	55·0	55·6	54·0	55·8	57·0	58·3	59·3	60·0	60·7	61·0	61·5	60·0	60·5	59·8	59·0	57·8	56·9	56·1	55·7	55·2	57·3	31
1851	55·4	55·0	54·8	54·7	54·5	54·3	54·0	56·4	57·9	59·1	60·1	60·4	61·8	61·2	62·4	62·4	61·7	60·6	59·7	58·6	57·7	56·2	55·5	58·0	31	
1852	55·5	55·3	55·2	55·0	54·9	54·8	55·4	56·7	57·7	58·9	59·4	60·0	60·5	60·9	61·0	61·0	60·5	59·8	59·0	58·1	57·0	56·4	56·1	55·6	57·7	31
1853	54·1	53·7	53·3	53·0	52·8	52·6	53·3	54·8	56·1	57·6	58·4	58·9	59·5	59·9	60·0	59·7	59·4	58·4	57·7	56·8	55·6	55·0	54·3	54·1	56·2	31
1854	54·8	54·5	54·0	53·7	53·5	53·2	53·8	55·3	56·8	58·2	58·7	59·6	59·9	60·0	60·0	60·0	59·5	59·1	58·5	57·5	56·7	56·0	55·4	54·9	56·8	29
1855	55·6	55·5	55·2	54·7	54·6	54·6	55·3	56·9	58·6	60·0	61·0	61·0	61·6	61·8	62·0	61·6	61·6	60·8	59·8	58·2	57·2	56·4	56·0	55·8	58·2	25
1856	57·6	56·9	56·6	56·4	56·0	55·8	56·6	58·4	59·7	61·1	61·6	62·2	62·2	63·8	63·9	63·9	63·4	62·4	61·5	60·4	59·4	58·4	58·0	57·9	60·8	29
1857	59·1	58·9	58·7	58·5	58·2	58·1	58·6	59·9	61·1	62·6	64·0	64·8	65·6	66·2	66·1	66·0	65·6	64·8	63·4	62·1	61·0	60·1	59·5	59·2	61·8	31
1858	54·5	54·0	53·6	53·4	53·3	53·3	53·0	53·7	57·5	58·8	59·8	60·6	61·3	61·1	61·2	60·9	60·5	59·7	58·6	57·6	56·6	55·7	55·2	54·6	57·1	29
1859	56·6	56·4	55·8	55·5	55·3	55·1	55·9	57·7	59·4	60·7	61·5	61·8	62·2	62·6	62·4	62·3	61·9	61·6	60·8	59·8	58·8	57·9	57·3	56·8	59·0	31
1860	53·7	53·5	53·4	53·4	53·3	53·6	54·0	55·1	55·8	56·5	57·0	57·6	58·4	58·7	58·6	58·3	58·3	57·7	57·0	56·2	55·3	54·8	54·5	54·1	55·8	30
1861	57·5	57·4	57·1	57·1	57·2	57·4	58·1	59·3	60·5	61·8	62·5	63·1	63·5	63·9	64·3	64·5	64·2	63·6	62·5	61·2	60·1	59·2	58·5	57·9	60·5	18
1862	54·2	53·8	53·6	53·5	53·2	52·9	53·7	55·4	56·8	58·4	59·0	59·7	60·4	60·3	60·4	60·2	59·8	58·9	58·2	57·0	56·2	55·4	54·8	54·4	56·7	29
1863	56·2	55·9	55·6	55·2	55·0	55·1	55·5	57·1	58·4	59·2	60·0	61·4	61·5	61·2	61·2	60·9	60·5	59·9	58·8	57·9	56·9	56·3	56·0	58·2	24	
1864	51·7	51·0	50·4	49·9	49·6	49·6	50·3	52·1	53·8	55·4	56·2	57·0	57·8	57·8	57·9	57·8	57·5	56·8	55·7	54·9	53·9	53·1	52·4	51·9	53·9	31
1865	54·8	54·5	54·1	53·7	53·4	53·2	53·7	55·5	56·8	58·1	58·9	60·1	60·3	60·6	60·3	59·6	58·3	56·9	55·8	54·4	53·7	31				
1866	54·0	53·7	53·4	53·2	53·2	53·3	53·7	54·9	56·3	57·6	58·3	58·8	58·9	59·4	59·3	59·7	59·3	59·0	58·3	56·9	55·9	55·1	54·7	54·3	56·3	31
1867	56·1	55·7	55·5	55·3	55·1	55·8	57·7	59·4	60·8	60·6	61·2	62·0	62·8	62·8	62·6	62·5	61·8	61·1	60·5	59·6	58·4	57·6	57·2	56·7	58·9	31
1868	56·9	56·9	56·8	56·7	56·4	56·4	57·4	58·6	59·6	60·6	61·2	62·0	62·8	62·8	62·6	62·3	61·8	61·1	60·5	59·5	58·6	58·0	57·7	57·3	59·4	31
Means	55·49	55·20	54·88	54·62	54·43	54·38	55·01	56·52	57·87	59·15	59·92	60·52	61·16	61·41	61·31	61·41	61·07	60·35	59·51	58·41	57·44	56·65	56·15	55·72	57·87	..

TABLE LXI.—MEAN TEMPERATURE of EVAPORATION at every HOUR of the DAY in each YEAR from 1849 to 1868, for the MONTH of SEPTEMBER.

Year.	Midnight.	1ʰ a.m.	2ʰ a.m.	3ʰ a.m.	4ʰ a.m.	5ʰ a.m.	6ʰ a.m.	7ʰ a.m.	8ʰ a.m.	9ʰ a.m.	10ʰ a.m.	11ʰ a.m.	Noon.	1ʰ p.m.	2ʰ p.m.	3ʰ p.m.	4ʰ p.m.	5ʰ p.m.	6ʰ p.m.	7ʰ p.m.	8ʰ p.m.	9ʰ p.m.	10ʰ p.m.	11ʰ p.m.	Mean.	Number of Days employed in forming the Means.
1849	52·7	52·7	52·6	52·7	52·7	52·7	52·7	53·5	54·8	56·0	56·9	57·5	57·9	58·2	58·1	57·8	57·2	56·2	55·0	54·2	53·6	53·1	52·9	52·6	54·8	28
1850	50·6	50·4	50·0	49·9	49·7	49·9	50·9	52·5	54·2	55·6	55·0	56·0	56·6	57·0	57·1	57·1	56·1	55·8	55·0	53·9	52·7	52·1	52·3	51·9	53·8	28
1851	49·3	48·8	48·3	48·2	48·1	48·1	48·2	49·5	51·6	53·8	55·0	56·0	56·6	57·0	57·1	57·1	56·2	55·1	53·5	52·3	51·4	50·6	50·0	49·7	52·1	30
1852	50·6	50·4	50·6	50·3	50·5	50·6	50·8	51·6	51·6	54·0	56·0	56·4	56·5	56·5	55·3	54·2	52·1	53·5	51·5	51·1	50·9	53·1	29			
1853	51·0	50·9	50·6	50·4	50·3	50·1	50·4	51·3	52·7	54·2	55·2	55·8	56·5	56·6	56·4	55·9	55·4	54·3	53·3	52·6	51·5	51·1	50·9	53·1	30	
1854	51·9	51·5	50·9	50·1	49·6	49·9	51·3	53·7	56·8	58·3	58·9	59·8	59·7	59·2	58·9	58·8	57·7	56·5	55·2	54·6	53·8	53·6	53·4	53·1	55·2	26
1855	51·8	51·6	51·3	51·0	50·8	50·9	51·4	53·3	55·4	57·0	57·9	59·7	59·2	59·2	58·8	58·3	57·4	56·5	55·2	54·6	53·7	53·0	52·4	51·9	54·4	29
1856	50·1	49·9	49·7	49·2	48·9	48·8	49·6	51·5	53·3	55·4	57·0	58·9	59·2	59·2	58·3	57·4	56·2	55·6	54·6	54·5	53·5	51·6	51·0	50·6	53·0	30
1857	55·1	55·0	54·7	54·7	54·7	54·5	54·8	55·8	57·7	58·8	60·2	61·3	61·7	62·1	61·9	61·6	60·7	59·4	58·2	57·0	56·5	55·7	55·5	50·2	57·6	30
1858	55·1	54·9	54·5	54·3	54·3	54·3	54·4	55·3	56·6	58·1	59·2	60·3	60·7	61·0	60·6	60·4	59·8	58·8	57·9	56·9	56·1	55·9	55·8	55·3	57·1	30
1859	51·9	51·7	51·6	51·3	51·3	51·4	51·6	54·1	55·5	56·4	57·2	57·2	57·2	57·3	57·1	56·4	55·6	55·3	54·4	53·7	53·2	52·8	52·5	51·8	54·2	27
1860	40·8	49·5	49·3	49·2	49·1	48·9	49·0	49·9	51·6	53·6	54·6	55·3	55·7	55·7	55·8	55·5	54·9	54·0	53·1	52·2	51·3	50·6	50·1	50·1	52·0	28
1861	52·1	51·7	51·4	51·4	51·1	51·1	51·3	52·2	53·8	55·6	56·4	56·9	57·4	57·5	57·4	57·5	57·1	56·3	55·6	54·7	53·8	53·3	53·0	52·7	54·2	22
1862	..																								..	..
1863	48·1	48·1	47·9	47·9	48·0	48·1	48·3	49·1	51·2	52·4	54·2	54·8	55·2	55·2	55·2	54·9	53·7	53·3	52·6	51·7	50·7	50·1	49·2	48·8	48·7	26
1864	51·8	51·7	51·5	51·3	51·2	51·1	51·0	51·9	53·8	58·0	55·7	56·4	57·0	57·1	57·1	56·6	56·1	55·1	54·2	53·7	53·1	52·9	52·5	54·0	28	
1865	56·9	56·6	56·3	56·1	55·8	55·5	55·8	56·8	58·5	61·0	61·8	63·6	64·3	64·3	64·8	64·4	63·4	61·1	59·7	58·8	57·2	56·9	30			
1866	51·8	51·5	51·2	52·3	52·2	52·7	53·1	54·1	55·0	56·1	57·1	57·9	57·3	57·1	57·1	56·6	56·5	55·8	55·3	55·3	54·4	53·7	53·0	52·6	54·8	30
1867	51·8	51·3	52·1	52·3	52·2	52·1	52·5	52·6	54·9	56·1	57·1	57·9	59·6	60·1	60·4	60·6	60·5	60·6	58·5	57·7	56·8	55·3	54·4	53·7	53·0	30
1868	53·5	53·3	53·2	53·2	52·5	52·6	52·9	54·8	56·1	57·1	59·0	60·1	60·4	60·3	60·6	60·5	60·0	58·5	57·1	55·3	54·4	53·7	53·0	52·6	52·3	30
Means	51·01	51·79	51·54	51·38	51·26	51·18	51·29	52·29	53·95	55·65	56·72	57·48	57·96	58·08	58·11	57·85	57·37	56·44	55·31	54·29	53·62	52·96	52·58	52·26	54·31	..

In the month of September 1862 the photographic records were not sufficiently complete to be used.

TABLE LXII.—MEAN TEMPERATURE of EVAPORATION at every HOUR of the DAY in each YEAR from 1849 to 1868, for the MONTH of OCTOBER.

Year.	Midnight.	1h a.m.	2h a.m.	3h a.m.	4h a.m.	5h a.m.	6h a.m.	7h a.m.	8h a.m.	9h a.m.	10h a.m.	11h a.m.	Noon.	1h p.m.	2h p.m.	3h p.m.	4h p.m.	5h p.m.	6h p.m.	7h p.m.	8h p.m.	9h p.m.	10h p.m.	11h p.m.	Mean.	Number of Days employed in forming the Means.
1849	47·3	47·5	47·3	47·2	47·2	47·2	47·2	47·3	48·0	49·5	50·8	51·3	52·1	52·3	52·3	51·8	50·8	49·8	48·8	48·5	47·7	47·4	47·2	47·2	48·9	28
1850	42·8	42·5	42·3	42·0	41·8	41·7	42·0	43·0	44·5	46·1	47·1	47·8	47·9	47·8	47·5	46·7	46·0	45·4	44·9	44·1	43·7	43·3	42·9	44·4	31
1851	48·5	48·2	48·0	47·9	47·7	47·6	47·5	47·8	48·5	50·7	51·4	52·3	53·0	52·7	52·7	52·1	51·4	50·6	49·7	49·1	48·7	48·3	48·3	48·2	49·6	31
1852	45·1	45·2	45·3	45·2	45·4	45·3	45·2	45·5	44·1	45·5	46·6	47·2	47·7	47·8	47·5	46·8	45·9	45·1	44·7	44·1	43·5	43·3	43·1	44·9	29
1853	47·9	47·8	47·7	47·6	47·6	47·5	47·5	48·0	49·1	50·5	51·5	52·1	53·2	53·4	53·2	52·0	51·1	50·5	49·7	49·3	48·9	48·5	48·2	49·8	31
1854	43·8	45·3	44·8	44·7	44·7	44·4	44·3	44·5	45·9	47·7	49·1	50·2	50·9	51·1	50·9	50·6	49·5	48·3	47·6	47·0	46·6	46·4	46·2	45·9	47·2	31
1855	48·5	48·4	48·3	48·0	48·0	47·9	48·0	48·1	49·0	50·5	51·3	52·0	52·9	53·1	52·8	52·1	51·4	50·7	49·9	49·5	49·2	49·0	48·8	48·5	49·8	31
1856	48·7	48·7	48·7	48·4	48·3	48·4	48·5	48·9	49·7	50·8	51·2	53·0	53·7	54·1	53·8	53·4	52·7	51·7	50·8	50·4	50·0	49·8	49·5	49·0	50·3	28
1857	49·8	49·9	49·8	49·6	50·0	50·0	50·0	50·4	51·1	52·6	54·1	54·9	55·2	55·6	55·4	55·0	54·2	53·2	52·4	51·7	51·2	50·7	50·5	50·1	52·0	27
1858	47·1	46·9	46·7	46·7	46·6	46·5	46·4	46·7	47·8	49·5	51·0	52·1	52·6	52·8	52·6	51·9	51·1	50·3	49·5	48·8	48·3	47·7	47·3	46·8	48·9	31
1859	48·2	47·8	47·4	47·4	47·0	46·9	46·8	46·9	47·9	48·9	50·2	51·4	52·0	52·2	52·5	52·1	51·5	50·9	50·2	49·6	49·6	49·3	49·1	48·5	49·3	24
1860	48·0	47·9	47·7	47·5	47·5	47·5	47·4	47·6	48·5	50·0	51·1	51·8	52·0	52·1	52·2	52·2	51·8	51·0	50·3	49·7	49·0	48·4	48·0	47·9	49·5	31
1861	50·3	50·1	49·8	49·6	49·3	49·3	49·4	50·0	51·3	52·6	53·5	54·6	55·8	56·0	55·8	55·3	54·5	53·8	52·8	52·2	51·9	51·2	50·7	50·6	52·1	14
1862	49·7	49·5	49·4	49·2	49·1	49·2	49·1	49·2	50·0	51·4	51·5	53·1	53·6	53·5	53·5	53·0	52·1	51·4	50·8	50·2	49·8	49·4	49·2	49·1	50·7	29
1863	48·5	48·3	48·3	48·4	48·2	48·2	48·1	48·2	49·2	50·3	51·4	52·2	52·9	53·2	53·2	52·9	51·9	50·8	50·0	49·4	48·9	48·7	48·5	48·3	49·9	28
1864	46·4	46·3	46·3	46·1	45·9	45·7	45·5	45·8	47·0	48·5	49·4	50·1	50·3	50·5	49·9	49·6	49·0	48·2	47·8	47·4	47·0	46·8	46·6	46·5	47·6	31
1865	47·5	47·2	47·0	46·8	46·8	46·5	46·7	47·1	48·5	49·7	51·1	52·0	52·7	52·8	52·0	52·4	51·5	50·6	49·7	49·1	48·6	48·3	47·7	47·4	49·2	31
1866	49·4	49·2	49·0	48·8	48·5	48·3	48·2	48·4	49·5	50·9	51·8	52·4	52·7	53·1	53·0	52·1	51·5	50·9	50·3	49·9	49·5	49·4	48·9	50·4	29
1867	45·7	45·5	45·3	45·1	45·0	44·8	44·6	45·0	46·3	47·9	49·1	50·2	50·8	50·9	50·8	50·0	49·3	48·4	47·9	47·4	47·1	46·6	46·4	46·1	47·3	31
1868	44·1	43·7	43·4	43·3	43·2	43·2	43·2	43·5	44·8	46·9	48·3	49·6	50·4	50·4	50·4	50·0	49·2	48·3	47·6	46·9	46·3	46·6	45·0	44·5	46·3	31
Means	47·38	47·19	47·02	46·88	46·79	46·71	46·67	46·95	47·94	49·44	50·63	51·48	52·11	52·27	52·19	51·76	50·99	50·13	49·37	48·82	48·36	47·96	47·68	47·38	48·92	..

TABLE LXIII.—MEAN TEMPERATURE of EVAPORATION at every HOUR of the DAY in each YEAR from 1849 to 1868, for the MONTH of NOVEMBER.

Year.	Midnight.	1h a.m.	2h a.m.	3h a.m.	4h a.m.	5h a.m.	6h a.m.	7h a.m.	8h a.m.	9h a.m.	10h a.m.	11h a.m.	Noon.	1h p.m.	2h p.m.	3h p.m.	4h p.m.	5h p.m.	6h p.m.	7h p.m.	8h p.m.	9h p.m.	10h p.m.	11h p.m.	Mean.	Number of Days employed in forming the Means.
1849	41·9	41·9	41·6	41·4	41·6	41·7	41·7	42·0	42·3	43·1	44·0	44·6	45·6	45·9	46·1	45·7	44·3	43·5	42·7	42·5	42·1	41·9	41·6	41·4	43·0	26
1850	43·4	43·3	43·3	43·1	43·2	43·2	43·4	43·4	43·5	44·4	45·5	46·6	47·0	46·4	46·7	45·1	44·7	44·2	44·0	43·6	43·3	42·9	43·5	30
1851	34·2	34·1	33·9	34·0	33·8	33·9	33·9	33·9	34·2	34·9	36·0	36·9	38·1	38·9	38·6	38·1	37·5	36·8	36·0	35·5	35·3	34·8	34·3	34·1	35·5	30
1852	47·4	45·4	45·3	45·5	45·3	45·1	45·1	45·6	46·0	46·9	47·5	48·9	48·2	48·0	47·7	46·9	46·5	46·3	46·0	46·4	45·4	46·4	30
1853	39·8	39·8	39·9	39·8	39·8	39·6	39·6	39·6	40·0	40·8	42·0	42·3	43·9	44·6	44·7	44·3	43·2	42·5	41·9	41·5	41·1	40·6	40·1	40·0	41·3	29
1854	38·3	38·2	38·1	38·1	38·0	37·9	37·8	37·6	37·8	38·6	39·6	40·7	41·2	41·7	41·3	41·2	40·6	39·8	39·6	39·5	39·2	38·8	38·6	38·5	39·2	30
1855	40·2	39·9	39·6	39·5	39·4	39·4	39·2	39·3	36·3	39·6	40·7	42·4	43·1	43·3	43·0	42·5	41·9	41·3	40·7	40·6	40·3	40·2	39·9	40·7	27
1856	39·1	38·9	38·8	38·7	38·5	38·2	37·9	38·0	38·2	39·0	40·2	40·9	41·6	42·2	42·1	41·6	40·9	40·4	40·0	39·3	39·2	38·7	38·7	38·6	39·6	30
1857	44·3	44·0	44·0	43·8	43·4	43·1	43·0	43·1	43·5	44·3	44·8	45·8	47·4	47·1	46·4	47·1	46·6	45·7	45·5	44·8	44·8	44·4	44·8	44·9	29
1858	36·5	36·3	36·2	36·1	36·0	36·1	36·0	36·2	36·7	37·7	38·9	40·1	40·7	41·0	41·2	40·6	39·7	39·0	38·6	38·2	37·9	37·6	37·2	36·9	38·0	30
1859	41·2	41·1	40·8	40·6	40·2	40·2	40·0	39·5	39·8	40·9	42·3	43·7	44·3	45·1	45·0	44·1	43·1	42·0	41·4	41·0	40·9	40·7	40·4	40·2	41·6	21
1860	39·0	38·9	38·8	38·6	38·4	38·7	38·9	39·0	40·2	41·4	42·3	42·7	44·1	44·4	44·0	39·6	39·5	39·1	39·0	40·1	0·0	30
1861	37·9	37·9	37·6	37·6	37·5	37·5	37·7	37·7	38·3	39·5	40·7	41·7	42·5	42·5	42·1	41·2	40·4	39·7	39·2	38·9	38·6	38·2	37·9	39·4	30
1862	38·2	38·0	38·1	37·9	37·8	37·8	37·8	37·8	38·3	39·4	40·4	41·2	42·4	41·8	41·1	40·7	40·5	40·9	39·5	39·3	39·5	24
1863	43·7	43·5	43·4	43·4	43·4	43·2	43·0	43·3	44·2	45·0	46·2	46·9	47·3	47·1	46·8	46·1	45·3	44·9	44·2	43·9	43·6	43·5	43·1	44·3	29
1864	39·2	38·9	38·8	38·5	38·3	38·4	38·5	38·8	40·7	41·8	42·4	43·6	43·5	43·0	42·1	41·6	41·0	40·8	40·3	39·9	39·7	39·5	40·4	30
1865	43·4	42·2	42·3	42·2	42·1	42·1	42·0	41·9	42·3	43·3	44·4	45·6	46·2	46·5	46·3	46·0	46·1	44·6	44·1	43·0	42·9	42·7	42·8	43·6	29
1866	41·3	41·4	41·3	41·3	41·4	41·3	41·1	41·3	42·0	43·0	44·3	44·9	45·0	44·8	44·2	43·3	42·7	42·4	42·2	41·7	41·3	41·3	40·8	42·4	29
1867	38·0	38·8	38·6	38·2	38·1	37·7	37·7	37·6	38·3	39·2	40·6	41·8	42·7	42·9	42·6	42·3	41·6	40·8	40·1	39·6	39·2	38·9	39·9	30
1868	39·2	39·2	39·2	39·0	39·0	39·1	39·1	39·1	39·4	40·1	41·0	41·8	42·4	42·5	42·4	42·1	41·6	40·8	40·0	39·7	39·4	39·0	38·6	40·1	29
Means	40·23	40·09	39·99	39·88	39·76	39·70	39·65	39·66	40·00	40·89	42·05	43·03	43·71	44·04	43·97	43·50	42·71	42·04	41·57	41·16	40·87	40·57	40·26	40·04	41·22	..

TABLE LXIV.—MEAN TEMPERATURE of EVAPORATION at every HOUR of the DAY in each YEAR from 1849 to 1868, for the MONTH of DECEMBER.

Year	Midnight	1 a.m.	2 a.m.	3 a.m.	4 a.m.	5 a.m.	6 a.m.	7 a.m.	8 a.m.	9 a.m.	10 a.m.	11 a.m.	Noon	1 p.m.	2 p.m.	3 p.m.	4 p.m.	5 p.m.	6 p.m.	7 p.m.	8 p.m.	9 p.m.	10 p.m.	11 p.m.	Mean	Numb. of Days employ'd in forming the Mean
1849	36·1	35·9	35·8	36·0	35·8	35·8	35·9	35·9	36·0	36·2	36·7	37·4	37·9	38·4	38·1	37·7	37·4	37·1	36·9	36·7	36·6	36·4	36·1	36·7		21
1850	38·9	38·5	38·2	38·1	38·0	37·8	37·1	37·6	38·1	36·0	39·9	40·9	41·4	41·8	41·4	40·9	40·6	40·3	40·0	39·7	39·9	39·7	39·5	39·4		31
1851	38·1	38·1	38·0	37·9	37·7	37·7	37·6	37·7	38·0	38·7	39·3	39·9	40·2	40·1	39·8	39·3	39·1	38·8	38·7	38·5	38·5	38·4	38·3	38·6		31
1852	44·4	44·3	44·0	43·9	43·9	43·7	43·7	43·9	44·3	44·9	45·6	46·0	46·3	46·0	45·8	45·5	44·8	44·8	44·0	4·1	45·3	45·4	45·5	44·8		22
1853	33·2	33·3	33·1	33·2	33·0	32·8	32·7	32·6	32·8	33·6	34·7	35·1	35·9	35·7	35·2	34·5	34·0	33·6	33·3	33·2	32·8	32·6	32·4	33·6		27
1854	39·6	39·6	39·6	39·5	39·3	38·9	38·6	38·5	38·6	39·1	39·8	40·6	41·4	41·8	41·8	41·4	41·0	40·8	40·7	40·4	40·3	40·1	39·9	39·8	40·0	27
1855	34·0	34·1	33·8	33·9	34·0	34·0	34·1	34·1	34·0	34·5	35·2	35·9	36·3	36·6	36·6	36·1	35·5	35·1	34·9	34·6	34·3	34·0	33·9	33·8		31
1856	37·4	37·2	37·0	37·0	36·8	36·6	36·5	36·3	36·5	37·0	38·1	39·0	39·6	40·0	39·9	39·8	39·2	39·0	38·8	38·6	38·5	38·4	38·3	38·4	38·1	29
1857	43·0	42·9	42·8	42·7	42·6	42·6	42·5	42·5	42·6	43·0	44·0	44·9	45·0	46·0	46·0	45·7	45·0	44·6	44·1	43·7	43·6	43·5	43·3	43·0	43·8	31
1858	39·4	39·2	39·2	39·0	38·8	38·8	38·6	38·6	38·7	39·0	39·7	40·7	41·0	41·0	41·3	41·6	41·2	40·8	40·5	40·4	40·3	40·2	40·1	39·9	39·9	31
1859	32·4	32·2	32·1	32·1	32·4	32·5	32·3	31·2	32·3	33·1	33·8	34·8	35·6	35·8	36·0	35·9	35·5	35·0	34·7	34·5	34·1	33·7	33·3	33·5	33·7	22
1860	37·2	37·1	37·0	37·0	36·9	36·8	36·5	36·5	36·5	36·8	36·9	36·2	39·2	39·2	39·0	38·4	38·1	38·0	37·6	37·4	37·4	37·3	37·1	37·6	37·6	25
1861	39·6	39·6	39·4	39·4	39·4	39·2	39·0	39·2	39·6	40·7	41·6	42·2	42·3	42·1	41·9	41·2	40·7	40·3	39·8	39·6	39·5	39·4	39·4	40·2		28
1862	41·4	41·3	41·2	41·2	41·2	41·3	41·4	41·1	41·1	41·5	42·2	43·0	44·0	43·8	43·3	42·5	42·1	41·6	41·2	40·9	40·6	40·4	40·5	42·1		31
1863	40·3	40·3	40·3	40·5	40·7	41·1	41·2	41·4	41·4	41·4	41·9	42·5	43·1	43·4	43·3	42·5	42·1	41·6	41·2	40·9	40·6	40·4	40·5	41·5		31
1864	36·3	36·4	36·4	36·2	36·3	36·3	36·5	36·3	36·3	36·6	37·3	38·2	38·9	39·0	38·7	38·3	37·6	37·2	36·9	36·8	36·7	36·6	36·4	36·3	37·0	31
1865	41·5	41·2	41·1	41·0	40·8	40·5	40·4	40·4	40·7	41·3	42·9	43·0	42·6	42·3	42·0	41·8	41·6	41·8	41·7	41·5	41·5	29				
1866	41·1	40·8	40·6	40·4	40·4	40·4	40·5	40·6	40·8	41·5	42·3	42·9	43·2	43·3	42·9	42·5	42·3	42·2	41·9	41·7	41·6	41·4	41·2	41·5		31
1867	35·8	35·7	35·5	35·5	35·6	35·6	35·6	35·6	35·7	36·2	37·4	38·0	38·0	37·4	37·2	37·0	36·7	36·3	36·2	35·9	35·6	36·5				31
1868	43·5	43·4	43·3	43·2	43·2	43·4	43·5	43·6	43·7	44·0	44·9	45·7	46·3	46·6	46·7	46·3	45·6	45·2	44·8	44·6	44·5	44·3	44·1	43·8	44·5	29
Means	38·66	38·56	38·43	38·38	38·34	38·31	38·25	38·21	38·27	38·63	39·38	40·20	40·82	41·15	41·12	40·80	40·28	39·92	39·66	39·41	39·26	39·13	38·97	38·83	39·29	..

TABLE LXV.—MONTHLY MEAN TEMPERATURE of EVAPORATION at every HOUR of the DAY through the RANGE of YEARS 1849 to 1868.

Hour, Greenwich Mean solar Time (Civil reckoning).	January.	February.	March.	April.	May.	June.	July.	August.	September.	October.	November.	December.	Yearly Means.
Midnight	36·74	36·80	37·08	41·22	45·68	52·12	54·88	55·49	52·01	47·38	40·23	38·66	44·86
1ʰ. a.m.	36·67	35·67	36·93	40·86	45·31	51·69	54·47	55·20	51·79	47·19	40·09	38·56	44·62
2 „	36·60	36·49	36·76	40·46	44·96	51·37	54·10	54·88	51·54	47·02	39·99	38·43	44·39
3 „	36·57	36·36	36·61	40·30	44·75	51·11	53·85	54·61	51·38	46·88	39·88	38·38	44·22
4 „	36·49	36·24	36·50	40·14	44·58	50·98	53·72	54·43	51·26	46·79	39·76	38·34	44·14
5 „	36·40	36·10	36·42	40·09	44·89	51·48	54·06	54·38	51·18	46·71	39·70	38·31	44·14
6 „	36·33	36·04	36·35	40·34	45·59	52·58	55·01	55·20	51·29	46·67	39·65	38·25	45·31
7 „	36·30	36·03	36·76	41·98	47·91	54·38	56·71	56·61	52·29	46·95	39·66	38·21	45·31
8 „	36·34	36·35	37·82	43·69	49·53	55·85	58·05	57·87	53·95	47·94	40·00	38·27	46·27
9 „	36·70	37·32	39·29	45·20	50·68	56·85	59·18	59·15	55·63	49·44	40·89	38·63	47·41
10 „	37·49	38·50	40·44	46·20	51·51	57·63	59·90	59·92	56·72	50·63	42·05	39·38	48·36
11 „	38·37	39·47	41·34	47·03	52·15	58·25	60·48	60·52	57·48	51·48	43·03	40·10	49·15
Noon	39·12	40·33	42·04	47·66	52·75	58·88	61·12	61·16	57·96	52·11	43·71	40·82	49·80
1ʰ. p.m.	39·44	40·67	42·35	48·03	53·05	59·08	61·43	61·41	58·08	52·27	44·04	41·15	50·08
2 „	39·46	40·73	42·48	48·21	53·16	59·13	61·54	61·51	58·11	52·19	43·97	41·12	50·13
3 „	39·26	40·51	42·41	48·05	53·05	59·08	61·51	61·41	57·85	51·76	43·50	40·80	49·93
4 „	38·68	40·11	41·93	47·54	52·65	58·65	61·17	61·07	57·37	50·99	42·71	40·28	49·43
5 „	38·10	39·28	41·21	46·70	51·91	58·09	60·35	60·33	56·44	50·13	42·04	39·92	48·73
6 „	37·73	38·54	40·25	45·71	50·90	57·24	59·70	59·51	55·31	49·37	41·57	39·66	47·96
7 „	37·44	38·02	39·41	44·46	48·43	54·94	57·52	57·44	53·62	48·36	41·16	39·41	47·18
8 „	37·21	37·65	38·74	43·44	48·43	53·94	57·30	55·65	52·56	48·00	40·87	39·26	46·46
9 „	37·02	37·29	38·13	42·61	47·47	53·88	56·56	55·05	52·06	47·96	40·57	39·13	45·88
10 „	36·91	37·03	37·76	42·07	46·80	53·13	55·95	56·15	52·58	47·68	40·26	38·97	45·44
11 „	36·80	36·80	37·48	41·61	46·30	52·61	55·43	55·72	52·26	47·58	40·04	38·83	45·10
Means	37·42	37·89	39·02	43·91	48·92	55·22	57·74	57·87	54·31	48·92	41·22	39·29	46·81

In the month of September 1861 the photographic records were not sufficiently complete to be used. The values given in the above table for September are the means of the monthly values for the remaining 19 years.

TABLE LXVI.—Monthly Mean Diurnal Inequality of the Temperature of Evaporation through the Range of Years 1849 to 1858.

Hour, Greenwich Mean Solar Time (Civil reckoning).	January.	February.	March.	April.	May.	June.	July.	August.	September.	October.	November.	December.
	o	o	o	o	o	o	o	o	o	o	o	o
Midnight	− 0·68	− 1·09	− 1·94	− 2·69	− 3·24	− 3·10	− 2·86	− 2·38	− 2·30	− 1·54	− 0·99	− 0·63
1ʰ. a.m.	− 0·75	− 1·22	− 2·09	− 3·05	− 3·61	− 3·53	− 3·27	− 2·67	− 2·32	− 1·73	− 1·13	− 0·73
2 ,,	− 0·82	− 1·40	− 2·26	− 3·34	− 3·96	− 3·85	− 3·64	− 2·99	− 2·77	− 1·90	− 1·23	− 0·86
3 ,,	− 0·85	− 1·33	− 2·41	− 3·61	− 4·17	− 4·11	− 3·80	− 3·25	− 2·03	− 2·04	− 1·34	− 0·91
4 ,,	− 0·93	− 1·65	− 2·52	− 3·77	− 4·34	− 4·24	− 4·02	− 3·44	− 3·05	− 2·13	− 1·46	− 0·95
5 ,,	− 1·02	− 1·79	− 2·60	− 3·82	− 4·03	− 3·74	− 3·68	− 3·49	− 3·13	− 2·21	− 1·52	− 0·98
6 ,,	− 1·09	− 1·85	− 2·67	− 3·37	− 2·75	− 2·41	− 2·54	− 2·86	− 3·02	− 2·23	− 1·57	− 1·04
7 ,,	− 1·13	− 1·86	− 2·26	− 1·93	− 1·91	− 0·84	− 1·03	− 1·35	− 2·02	− 1·97	− 1·56	− 1·08
8 ,,	− 1·08	− 1·54	− 1·20	− 0·37	+ 0·41	+ 0·45	+ 0·31	0·00	− 0·36	− 0·98	− 1·22	− 1·02
9 ,,	− 0·72	− 0·57	+ 0·27	+ 1·19	+ 1·76	+ 1·63	+ 1·44	+ 1·28	+ 1·34	+ 0·52	− 0·33	− 0·66
10 ,,	+ 0·07	+ 0·61	+ 1·42	+ 2·20	+ 2·50	+ 2·41	+ 2·16	+ 2·05	+ 2·41	+ 1·71	+ 0·83	+ 0·09
11 ,,	+ 0·95	+ 1·58	+ 2·32	+ 3·12	+ 3·13	+ 3·03	+ 2·74	+ 2·65	+ 3·17	+ 2·56	+ 1·81	+ 0·91
Noon	+ 1·70	+ 2·44	+ 3·02	+ 3·72	+ 3·83	+ 3·66	+ 3·58	+ 3·29	+ 3·63	+ 3·19	+ 2·49	+ 1·33
1ʰ. p.m.	+ 2·02	+ 2·78	+ 3·53	+ 4·12	+ 4·13	+ 3·86	+ 3·60	+ 3·54	+ 3·77	+ 3·35	+ 2·85	+ 1·96
2 ,,	+ 2·04	+ 2·84	+ 3·46	+ 4·30	+ 4·24	+ 3·91	+ 3·80	+ 3·64	+ 3·80	+ 3·27	+ 2·75	+ 1·93
3 ,,	+ 1·84	+ 2·63	+ 3·39	+ 4·14	+ 4·14	+ 3·79	+ 3·78	+ 3·54	+ 3·54	+ 2·84	+ 2·28	+ 1·51
4 ,,	+ 1·26	+ 2·22	+ 2·91	+ 3·63	+ 3·73	+ 3·43	+ 3·43	+ 3·20	+ 3·06	+ 2·07	+ 1·40	+ 0·99
5 ,,	+ 0·68	+ 1·39	+ 2·19	+ 2·79	+ 2·99	+ 2·87	+ 2·81	+ 2·48	+ 2·13	+ 1·21	+ 0·82	+ 0·63
6 ,,	+ 0·31	+ 0·63	+ 1·23	+ 1·80	+ 1·98	+ 2·02	+ 1·96	+ 1·64	+ 1·00	+ 0·43	+ 0·33	+ 0·37
7 ,,	+ 0·02	+ 0·13	+ 0·30	+ 0·55	+ 0·81	+ 1·01	+ 0·99	+ 0·54	− 0·02	− 0·10	− 0·06	+ 0·12
8 ,,	− 0·21	− 0·24	− 0·28	− 0·47	− 0·49	− 0·28	− 0·22	− 0·43	− 0·69	− 0·56	− 0·35	− 0·03
9 ,,	− 0·40	− 0·60	− 0·84	− 1·30	− 1·45	− 1·34	− 1·17	− 1·22	− 1·35	− 0·96	− 0·65	− 0·16
10 ,,	− 0·51	− 0·86	− 1·26	− 1·84	− 2·12	− 2·00	− 1·79	− 1·72	− 1·73	− 1·24	− 0·96	− 0·32
11 ,,	− 0·62	− 1·09	− 1·54	− 2·30	− 2·62	− 2·61	− 2·31	− 2·15	− 2·05	− 1·54	− 1·18	− 0·46

TABLE LXVII.—Mean Temperature of Evaporation in each Month as deduced from the Mean of the Mean Hourly Determinations in each Month.

Year.	January.	February.	March.	April.	May.	June.	July.	August.	September.	October.	November.	December.	Mean Annual Temperature.	Difference of the Mean Temperature of Evaporation of each Year from the Mean Temperature throughout the Period 1849 to 1868, as deduced from the whole of the Observations.
	o	o	o	o	o	o	o	o	o	o	o	o	o	
1849	40·8	40·5	40·1	42·4	51·6	54·0	55·5	58·6	54·8	48·9	43·0	36·7	47·24	+ 0·43
1850	32·9	42·2	36·8	46·2	48·1	56·4	58·7	57·5	52·8	44·4	44·5	39·4	46·64	− 0·17
1851	41·4	38·2	40·2	42·6	47·3	54·7	53·9	58·0	52·1	40·6	35·5	38·6	46·18	− 0·63
1852	39·4	38·8	37·5	40·9	48·1	52·7	60·2	57·7	53·1	44·9	46·4	44·8	47·04	+ 0·23
1853	38·5	31·2	34·6	41·1	48·5	54·2	56·6	56·2	53·1	49·8	41·3	43·6	44·89	− 1·92
1854	38·2	37·2	40·7	45·0	48·4	53·3	56·5	56·8	54·8	47·2	39·2	40·0	46·44	− 0·37
1855	33·9	28·5	35·8	47·6	43·4	53·3	59·0	58·1	54·4	49·8	40·7	34·7	44·62	− 2·19
1856	38·2	40·5	36·8	44·1	46·9	55·8	58·0	59·8	51·8	50·5	39·6	38·1	46·67	− 0·14
1857	37·8	38·3	39·6	43·5	50·3	56·9	59·7	61·8	57·6	52·0	44·9	43·8	48·68	+ 1·87
1858	36·4	33·9	39·2	42·4	47·2	58·7	56·8	57·1	57·1	48·9	38·0	39·9	46·30	− 0·51
1859	39·2	41·0	44·0	43·1	48·4	58·1	62·9	59·0	54·2	49·3	41·6	33·7	47·87	+ 1·06
1860	38·1	33·8	38·6	38·9	50·1	53·0	54·9	55·8	52·0	49·5	40·0	37·6	45·27	− 1·54
1861	35·8	41·0	42·8	42·6	48·0	56·8	57·0	60·5	54·2	52·1	40·2	47·53	+ 0·72	
1862	39·0	38·9	42·4	46·7	55·2	53·1	55·7	56·7	54·4	50·7	30·5	42·1	47·62	+ 0·81
1863	40·5	40·4	41·1	46·2	48·3	54·8	56·8	58·2	50·7	49·9	44·5	41·5	47·73	+ 0·92
1864	35·0	34·7	38·9	44·5	50·2	53·8	57·3	53·9	54·0	47·6	40·4	37·0	45·61	− 1·20
1865	35·1	35·4	34·7	48·3	52·1	55·9	59·3	57·1	59·7	40·2	42·6	41·3	47·66	+ 0·83
1866	41·2	39·7	38·7	45·3	46·0	57·6	57·6	54·5	50·4	42·4	41·5	47·36	+ 0·78	
1867	33·2	42·7	36·0	46·7	47·2	54·3	55·7	58·9	54·8	47·3	39·9	36·5	46·10	− 0·71
1868	36·1	40·8	41·8	45·2	53·9	57·1	60·7	59·4	56·2	46·3	40·1	44·5	48·51	+ 1·70
Means	37·42	37·89	39·02	43·91	48·92	55·22	57·87	54·31	48·92	41·22	39·29	46·81		..

In the month of September 1862, the photographic records were not sufficiently complete to give a trustworthy determination of the mean temperature of evaporation; the value inserted above is approximate.

TABLE LXVIII.—MONTHLY MEAN TEMPERATURE of the DEW POINT at every HOUR of the DAY as deduced from the corresponding mean results of TEMPERATURE of the AIR and of EVAPORATION through the RANGE of YEARS 1849 to 1868.

Hour. Greenwich Mean Solar Time (civil reckoning).	January.	February.	March.	April.	May.	June.	July.	August.	September.	October.	November.	December.	Yearly Means.
Midnight	35·1	35·0	35·1	39·2	43·9	50·3	53·0	54·1	50·7	46·2	38·8	37·1	43·2
1ʰ. a.m.	35·2	35·1	35·0	39·1	43·6	50·1	52·8	53·9	50·6	46·0	38·7	37·0	43·1
2 ,,	35·0	34·9	35·1	38·9	43·6	50·0	52·5	53·7	50·4	45·8	38·7	36·7	42·9
3 ,,	35·1	34·9	35·0	38·7	43·4	49·7	52·3	53·5	50·4	45·9	38·7	36·8	42·9
4 ,,	35·0	34·7	35·0	38·5	43·2	49·7	52·3	53·4	50·4	45·7	38·7	36·7	42·8
5 ,,	34·9	34·7	34·9	38·6	43·5	50·0	51·7	53·4	50·3	45·7	38·5	36·9	42·8
6 ,,	34·8	34·5	34·8	38·8	44·2	50·6	53·2	53·7	50·3	45·7	38·5	36·7	43·0
7 ,,	34·8	34·3	35·3	39·7	45·1	51·4	53·8	54·4	51·0	45·7	38·5	36·7	43·4
8 ,,	34·7	34·7	35·7	40·5	45·7	51·9	54·3	53·0	51·0	46·5	38·6	36·7	43·9
9 ,,	34·9	35·4	36·7	41·4	46·5	52·3	54·6	53·2	51·7	47·4	39·3	36·9	44·4
10 ,,	35·5	35·9	36·8	41·6	46·6	52·5	54·6	55·3	51·6	47·9	39·7	37·5	44·7
11 ,,	36·1	36·5	37·1	41·8	46·9	52·6	54·7	55·2	52·8	48·2	40·5	38·0	45·0
Noon	36·4	36·8	37·2	42·0	47·1	51·6	54·8	55·4	51·7	48·4	40·7	38·5	45·2
1ʰ. p.m.	36·3	36·9	37·3	42·0	47·2	52·6	54·7	55·3	52·5	48·4	40·8	38·6	45·2
2 ,,	36·4	36·7	37·3	42·3	47·0	52·5	54·6	53·2	52·4	48·2	40·7	38·4	45·1
3 ,,	36·4	36·6	37·4	42·0	47·0	52·5	54·6	55·1	52·2	48·1	40·5	38·4	45·1
4 ,,	36·2	36·7	37·0	41·7	46·9	52·3	54·7	53·3	51·4	47·8	40·1	38·2	44·9
5 ,,	35·8	36·3	37·0	41·4	46·4	52·2	54·5	55·1	51·0	47·5	39·6	37·9	44·6
6 ,,	35·6	35·8	36·7	41·0	45·9	51·9	54·2	54·8	51·8	47·4	39·7	37·9	44·4
7 ,,	35·4	35·5	36·4	40·9	45·5	51·7	54·0	54·7	51·6	47·0	39·4	37·7	44·1
8 ,,	35·3	35·4	35·9	40·2	45·1	51·3	53·8	54·5	51·3	46·9	39·3	37·6	43·9
9 ,,	35·2	35·3	35·7	39·8	44·8	51·0	53·7	54·2	51·1	46·6	39·1	37·5	43·7
10 ,,	35·1	34·9	35·6	39·6	44·4	50·7	53·6	54·0	50·9	46·4	38·9	37·3	43·5
11 ,,	35·1	34·9	35·5	39·4	44·1	50·5	53·3	54·0	50·9	46·2	38·5	37·1	43·3
Means	35·4	35·5	36·1	40·4	45·3	51·4	53·8	54·5	51·5	46·9	39·4	37·4	44·0

TABLE LXIX.—MONTHLY MEAN DIURNAL INEQUALITY of the TEMPERATURE of the DEW POINT through the RANGE of YEARS 1849 to 1868.

Hour. Greenwich Mean Solar Time (civil reckoning).	January.	February.	March.	April.	May.	June.	July.	August.	September.	October.	November.	December.
Midnight	− 0·3	− 0·5	− 1·0	− 1·2	− 1·4	− 1·1	− 0·8	− 0·4	− 0·8	− 0·7	− 0·6	− 0·3
1ʰ. a.m.	− 0·2	− 0·4	− 1·1	− 1·3	− 1·7	− 1·3	− 1·0	− 0·6	− 0·9	− 0·9	− 0·7	− 0·7
2 ,,	− 0·4	− 0·6	− 1·0	− 1·5	− 1·7	− 1·4	− 1·3	− 0·8	− 1·1	− 1·1	− 0·7	− 0·7
3 ,,	− 0·3	− 0·6	− 1·1	− 1·7	− 1·9	− 1·7	− 1·5	− 1·0	− 1·1	− 1·0	− 0·7	− 0·6
4 ,,	− 0·4	− 0·8	− 1·1	− 1·9	− 2·1	− 1·7	− 1·5	− 1·1	− 1·1	− 1·2	− 0·7	− 0·7
5 ,,	− 0·5	− 0·8	− 1·2	− 1·8	− 1·8	− 1·4	− 1·1	− 1·1	− 1·2	− 1·2	− 0·9	− 0·5
6 ,,	− 0·6	− 1·0	− 1·3	− 1·6	− 1·1	− 0·8	− 0·6	− 0·8	− 1·2	− 1·2	− 0·9	− 0·7
7 ,,	− 0·6	− 1·0	− 0·8	− 0·7	− 0·2	0·0	0·0	− 0·1	− 0·5	− 1·2	− 0·9	− 0·7
8 ,,	− 0·7	− 0·8	− 0·4	+ 0·1	+ 0·4	+ 0·5	+ 0·3	+ 0·5	+ 0·4	− 0·4	− 0·8	− 0·7
9 ,,	− 0·5	− 0·1	+ 0·6	+ 1·0	+ 1·2	+ 0·9	+ 0·8	+ 0·7	+ 1·2	+ 0·5	− 0·1	− 0·5
10 ,,	+ 0·1	+ 0·4	+ 0·7	+ 1·2	+ 1·3	+ 1·1	+ 0·8	+ 0·8	+ 1·1	+ 1·0	+ 0·3	+ 0·1
11 ,,	+ 0·7	+ 1·0	+ 1·0	+ 1·4	+ 1·6	+ 1·2	+ 0·9	+ 0·7	+ 1·3	+ 1·3	+ 1·1	+ 0·6
Noon	+ 1·0	+ 1·3	+ 1·1	+ 1·6	+ 1·8	+ 1·2	+ 1·0	+ 0·9	+ 1·0	+ 1·5	+ 1·3	+ 1·1
1ʰ. p.m.	+ 0·9	+ 1·4	+ 1·2	+ 1·6	+ 1·9	+ 1·2	+ 0·9	+ 0·8	+ 1·0	+ 1·5	+ 1·4	+ 1·2
2 ,,	+ 1·0	+ 1·2	+ 1·2	+ 1·9	+ 1·7	+ 1·1	+ 0·8	+ 0·7	+ 0·9	+ 1·3	+ 1·3	+ 1·0
3 ,,	+ 1·0	+ 1·1	+ 1·3	+ 1·6	+ 1·7	+ 1·1	+ 0·8	+ 0·6	+ 0·7	+ 1·2	+ 1·1	+ 1·0
4 ,,	+ 0·8	+ 1·2	+ 0·9	+ 1·3	+ 1·6	+ 0·9	+ 0·9	+ 0·8	+ 0·9	+ 0·9	+ 0·7	+ 0·8
5 ,,	+ 0·4	+ 0·8	+ 0·9	+ 1·0	+ 1·1	+ 0·8	+ 0·7	+ 0·6	+ 0·5	+ 0·6	+ 0·2	+ 0·5
6 ,,	+ 0·2	+ 0·3	+ 0·6	+ 0·6	+ 0·6	+ 0·5	+ 0·4	+ 0·3	+ 0·5	+ 0·5	+ 0·3	+ 0·3
7 ,,	0·0	0·0	+ 0·3	+ 0·5	+ 0·2	+ 0·3	+ 0·2	+ 0·1	+ 0·1	0·0	0·0	+ 0·3
8 ,,	− 0·1	− 0·1	− 0·1	− 0·2	− 0·2	− 0·1	0·0	0·0	− 0·2	0·0	− 0·1	+ 0·1
9 ,,	− 0·2	− 0·2	− 0·4	− 0·6	− 0·3	− 0·4	− 0·1	− 0·3	− 0·4	− 0·3	− 0·3	+ 0·1
10 ,,	− 0·3	− 0·6	− 0·5	− 0·8	− 0·9	− 0·7	− 0·2	− 0·5	− 0·6	− 0·5	− 0·5	− 0·1
11 ,,	− 0·3	− 0·6	− 0·6	− 1·0	− 1·2	− 0·9	− 0·5	− 0·5	− 0·6	− 0·7	− 0·9	− 0·3

TABLE LXX.—MEAN TEMPERATURE of the DEW POINT in each MONTH, as deduced from the corresponding MEAN MONTHLY RESULTS of TEMPERATURE of the AIR and of EVAPORATION.

Year.	January.	February.	March.	April.	May.	June.	July.	August.	September.	October.	November.	December.	Mean Annual Temperature.
1849	38·6	38·3	36·9	39·3	48·7	49·2	50·8	54·8	51·6	46·3	40·8	34·5	44·1
1850	30·8	39·5	33·1	43·7	44·6	51·6	55·7	54·3	49·6	41·8	42·4	38·1	43·7
1851	39·5	35·9	37·2	39·5	42·8	50·3	52·1	54·1	48·2	46·7	32·4	36·1	42·9
1852	36·3	35·7	33·6	35·8	44·0	48·9	55·5	53·8	49·6	41·9	43·6	42·0	43·4
1853	35·2	27·3	31·7	38·2	44·5	49·9	52·7	52·8	50·9	48·3	49·1	32·4	43·0
1854	36·8	34·3	37·3	41·1	43·5	50·3	52·6	53·4	51·6	44·7	37·4	37·7	43·6
1855	32·5	26·1	33·1	38·8	40·8	48·9	55·9	54·6·	51·6	48·1	39·2	31·5	41·8
1856	36·9	38·5	33·8	40·1	43·7	52·5	54·9	56·9	48·5	40·1	37·8	36·7	44·1
1857	34·5	36·1	36·7	40·3	46·5	53·0	55·5	58·6	55·6	50·7	44·2	42·3	46·2
1858	34·4	34·6	35·5	38·4	43·1	53·6	52·1	52·7	54·3	46·5	36·0	38·4	43·0
1859	37·6	38·2	40·8	39·5	45·0	54·5	58·2	54·9	54·3	47·8	39·4	31·8	44·9
1860	36·3	30·9	33·5	36·3	45·4	50·4	52·0	53·5	50·4	47·8	38·7	36·5	42·8
1861	34·5	39·6	41·3	36·9	43·8	53·9	52·9	57·4	51·4	50·0	37·4	38·2	45·0
1862	37·1	36·9	40·6	42·9	50·4	49·7	51·4	54·1	51·4	48·9	38·7	40·2	45·3
1863	38·0	38·2	37·8	42·7	45·2	51·2	52·2	54·6	47·6	48·1	42·7	39·0	44·8
1864	32·8	32·5	35·7	40·0	46·1	49·9	52·6	48·4	51·0	44·2	38·1	34·8	42·2
1865	35·1	33·2	31·7	43·7	47·7	51·0	54·6	54·3	56·3	47·0	41·6	39·8	44·5
1866	38·9	37·2	35·6	41·7	41·0	53·8	53·0	53·3	52·6	49·0	39·9	39·6	44·7
1867	30·9	40·4	33·5	43·5	43·3	50·2	51·8	55·8	52·2	45·3	37·9	34·9	43·3
1868	34·1	37·8	38·6	41·4	49·9	51·9	54·9	55·6	52·6	44·2	37·8	42·8	45·1
Means	35·4	35·4	36·0	40·3	45·1	51·2	53·7	54·4	51·4	46·8	39·3	37·4	43·9

Hour, Greenwich Mean Solar Time (53=II reckoning).

TABLE LXXI.—MEAN TEMPERATURE of the AIR at every HOUR of the Day, in each Quarter, through the Range of Years 1849 to 1868, deduced from Table L.

	January, February, March.	April, May, June.	July, August, September.	October, November, December.
Midnight	38·2	48·0	55·8	43·2
1 a.m.	38·0	47·5	55·3	43·1
2 ,,	37·8	47·0	54·9	42·9
3 ,,	37·7	46·7	54·3	42·8
4 ,,	37·5	46·5	54·3	42·7
5 ,,	37·4	46·8	54·4	42·6
6 ,,	37·3	48·3	55·4	42·6
7 ,,	37·5	50·8	57·5	42·7
8 ,,	38·1	53·1	59·9	43·3
9 ,,	39·4	55·3	61·5	44·5
10 ,,	41·0	57·1	64·5	46·0
11 ,,	42·3	58·5	66·0	47·4
Noon	43·6	59·8	67·5	48·4
1 p.m.	44·2	60·1	68·1	48·8
2 ,,	44·4	60·6	68·4	48·9
3 ,,	44·1	60·4	68·2	48·9
4 ,,	43·3	59·6	67·2	47·1
5 ,,	42·1	58·4	65·6	46·1
6 ,,	41·1	56·7	63·6	45·2
7 ,,	40·2	54·4	61·4	44·7
8 ,,	39·6	52·3	59·5	44·2
9 ,,	39·1	50·7	58·0	43·8
10 ,,	38·7	49·6	57·1	43·5
11 ,,	38·4	48·8	56·3	43·3
Means	40·0	53·2	60·7	44·8

TABLE LXXII.—MEAN TEMPERATURE of EVAPORATION at every HOUR of the Day, in each Quarter, through the Range of Years 1849 to 1868, deduced from Table LXV.

	January, February, March.	April, May, June.	July, August, September.	October, November, December.
Midnight	36·9	46·3	54·1	42·1
1 a.m.	36·8	46·0	53·8	42·0
2 ,,	36·6	45·7	53·5	41·8
3 ,,	36·5	45·4	53·3	41·7
4 ,,	36·4	45·3	53·1	41·6
5 ,,	36·3	45·5	53·2	41·6
6 ,,	36·2	46·5	53·8	41·5
7 ,,	36·4	48·1	55·2	41·6
8 ,,	36·8	49·5	56·6	42·1
9 ,,	37·8	50·9	58·0	43·0
10 ,,	38·8	51·8	58·8	44·0
11 ,,	39·7	52·3	59·5	44·9
Noon	40·5	53·1	60·1	45·5
1 p.m.	40·8	53·4	60·3	45·8
2 ,,	40·9	53·5	60·4	45·9
3 ,,	40·7	53·4	60·3	45·4
4 ,,	40·2	52·9	59·9	44·7
5 ,,	39·5	52·1	59·1	44·0
6 ,,	38·8	51·3	58·2	43·6
7 ,,	38·3	50·1	57·1	43·1
8 ,,	37·8	48·9	56·1	42·9
9 ,,	37·5	48·0	55·4	42·5
10 ,,	37·2	47·3	54·9	42·3
11 ,,	37·0	46·8	54·3	42·1
Means	38·1	49·3	56·6	43·1

TABLE LXXIII.—MEAN TEMPERATURE of the DEW POINT at every HOUR of the Day, in each Quarter, through the Range of Years 1849 to 1868, deduced from Table LXVIII.

	January, February, March.	April, May, June.	July, August, September.	October, November, December.
Midnight	35·1	44·5	52·6	40·7
1 a.m.	35·1	44·3	52·4	40·6
2 ,,	35·0	44·2	52·2	40·4
3 ,,	35·0	43·9	52·1	40·5
4 ,,	34·9	43·8	52·0	40·4
5 ,,	34·8	44·0	52·1	40·4
6 ,,	34·7	44·5	52·4	40·3
7 ,,	34·9	45·4	53·1	40·3
8 ,,	35·0	46·0	53·8	40·6
9 ,,	35·7	46·7	54·2	41·2
10 ,,	36·1	46·9	54·2	41·7
11 ,,	36·6	47·1	54·2	42·2
Noon	36·8	47·2	54·3	42·5
1 p.m.	36·8	47·3	54·1	42·4
2 ,,	36·8	47·1	54·0	42·3
3 ,,	36·6	47·0	54·0	42·0
4 ,,	36·4	46·7	53·9	41·7
5 ,,	36·0	46·3	53·6	41·7
6 ,,	35·8	46·0	53·4	41·4
7 ,,	35·5	45·5	53·2	41·3
8 ,,	35·4	45·2	53·0	41·1
9 ,,	35·2	44·9	52·8	40·9
10 ,,	35·1	44·7	52·7	40·6
Means	35·7	45·7	53·3	41·2

4

Year.	TABLE LXXIV.—MEAN TEMPERATURE of the Air in each QUARTER of every Year, deduced from Table LII.				TABLE LXXV.—MEAN TEMPERATURE of EVAPORATION in each QUARTER of every Year, deduced from Table LXVII.				TABLE LXXVI.—MEAN TEMPERATURE of the DEW POINT in each QUARTER of every Year, deduced from Table LXX.			
	January, February, March.	April, May, June.	July, August, September.	October, November, December.	January, February, March.	April, May, June.	July, August, September.	October, November, December.	January, February, March.	April, May, June.	July, August, September.	October, November, December.
1849	42.6	53.0	60.8	44.0	40.5	49.3	56.3	42.9	37.9	45.7	52.4	40.5
1850	39.4	54.4	59.8	44.5	37.3	50.2	56.3	42.8	34.5	46.3	53.2	40.8
1851	41.9	52.3	59.7	43.6	39.9	48.2	55.3	41.2	37.5	44.1	51.5	38.4
1852	41.3	51.5	61.7	48.0	38.6	47.2	57.0	45.4	35.2	42.9	53.0	42.5
1853	37.0	51.7	58.9	42.6	34.8	47.9	55.3	41.6	31.4	44.2	52.1	40.3
1854	40.8	52.1	60.1	44.0	38.7	48.9	56.0	42.1	36.1	45.6	52.5	39.9
1855	34.0	50.7	60.9	43.1	32.7	46.8	57.2	41.7	30.5	42.8	54.0	39.9
1856	40.1	52.4	60.0	44.0	38.5	48.0	56.3	42.7	36.4	45.4	53.4	41.2
1857	39.6	54.0	63.5	48.0	37.9	50.2	59.7	46.9	35.8	46.6	56.6	45.7
1858	38.5	53.9	61.6	43.9	36.5	49.4	57.0	42.3	33.8	45.0	53.0	40.3
1859	43.6	53.5	63.4	43.0	41.4	49.9	58.7	41.5	38.9	46.3	54.8	39.7
1860	38.8	51.2	56.7	43.5	36.8	47.7	54.2	42.4	34.2	44.0	52.0	41.0
1861	41.0	51.4	61.1	43.7	39.9	49.1	57.2	43.9	38.5	45.9	53.9	41.9
1862	41.6	53.8	58.9	45.4	40.1	50.7	55.6	41.6	38.2	47.7	52.6	42.6
1863	42.8	53.2	59.5	47.2	40.6	49.8	55.2	45.3	38.0	46.4	51.5	43.3
1864	38.1	53.8	60.1	43.9	36.2	49.5	55.1	41.7	33.7	45.3	50.7	39.0
1865	36.8	57.2	63.0	46.5	35.1	52.1	58.7	44.8	32.7	47.5	55.1	42.8
1866	42.0	53.7	59.4	46.5	39.9	49.6	56.1	44.8	37.1	45.5	53.3	42.8
1867	39.1	53.1	60.1	42.8	37.3	49.1	56.5	41.2	34.9	45.6	53.5	39.4
1868	41.8	56.8	64.1	45.4	39.6	52.1	58.8	43.6	36.8	47.7	54.4	41.6
Means	40.0	53.2	60.7	44.8	38.1	49.3	56.6	43.1	35.6	45.5	53.2	41.2

TABLE LXXVII.—MEAN TEMPERATURE of the Air, as deduced from the Twenty-four Hourly Readings on each Day, for every DAY of the YEAR, through the RANGE of YEARS 1849 to 1868.

Day of the Month.	January.	February.	March.	April.	May.	June.	July.	August.	September.	October.	November.	December.
1	38.9	40.7	39.6	45.4	48.4	57.2	60.1	63.0	59.9	54.1	47.8	40.9
2	37.5	40.8	40.7	45.6	49.2 M	58.3	61.0	63.1	59.9	53.7	47.4	40.3
3	36.6	39.9	40.6	46.8	49.8 M	58.9	61.1	62.8	60.0	54.6	45.9	41.2
4	37.4	40.2	40.8	47.1	49.5 M	58.4	61.0	63.1	60.2	54.1	46.1	42.6
5	36.9	42.4	40.8	47.4	49.4 M	58.2	61.8	62.7	59.5	53.0	46.5	45.9
6	35.3	42.7	41.8	48.5	50.3	59.4	62.2	61.3	59.1	51.0	45.6	45.2
7	37.0	41.0	41.3	48.5	50.4	58.9	61.9	62.6	59.4	53.7	45.0	45.1
8	38.7	40.6	40.6	47.5	50.2	59.3	61.4	62.9	59.2	53.5	43.1	43.1
9	38.3	39.0	39.0	46.1	50.7	58.8	61.8	62.1	58.9	50.9	43.4	41.6
10	38.8	39.0	39.3	46.9	51.3	58.8	62.1	62.4	58.0	52.1	42.4	42.0
11	38.6	37.4	39.6	45.9	51.9	58.9	62.6	63.5	56.8	51.8	42.6	40.9
12	38.3	37.9	40.7	45.6	51.7	58.2	64.0	63.5	57.8	51.6	41.0	41.1
13	38.4	37.1	42.3	45.3	51.6	58.5	64.1	64.2	57.8	51.0	41.9	41.7
14	38.1	37.6	41.8	46.0	51.8	58.4	64.0	61.9	57.1	52.5	41.9	42.3
15	37.8	39.3	41.3	47.0	52.6	58.4	65.2 H	61.9	57.3	51.6	41.6	42.2
16	38.2	38.8	41.5	48.3	53.9	59.2	63.8	61.9	58.5	50.5	41.9	41.1
17	38.6	39.7	41.1	48.8	53.8	58.0	63.2	61.2	57.6	51.1	40.5	40.4
18	39.0	39.0	40.8	48.7	54.8	58.0	62.3	60.9	56.6	50.3	41.1	39.3
19	39.8	38.7	43.1	48.8	55.8	59.2	62.3	61.7	57.0	51.5	41.1	38.5
20	40.2	38.6	41.8	40.1	56.2	60.0	63.0	61.8	56.3	50.8	41.1	38.2
21	38.7	39.0	40.8 E	48.8	55.3	61.6 T	61.8	61.1	55.6	50.6	42.2	39.6
22	38.9	40.2	40.4	48.5	54.6	61.1	64.0	61.2	56.0	51.2	42.5	39.8 T
23	39.9	39.9	41.9	48.0	54.8	62.4	63.8	60.8	56.1	49.7 M	40.9	39.0
24	39.7	39.8	42.4	47.5	54.7	62.4	62.2	61.3	56.1	49.4 M	40.9	39.2
25	40.7	40.3	41.4	48.6	55.1	61.6	62.0	61.2	54.7	49.0 M	40.6	39.0
26	39.8	40.1	43.0	49.1	56.1	63.7	61.6	61.2	54.5	49.0 M	41.8	39.3
27	40.1	39.4	42.8	47.6	56.9	63.6	62.4	61.6	53.8	46.4	40.7	38.9
28	39.6	40.4	43.4	47.2	56.2	62.3	62.6	60.8	56.5	46.1	39.9	37.8
29	40.3		43.8	47.4	56.5	61.0	62.4	61.0	56.1	46.4	39.7	39.1
30	40.1		44.0	47.7	56.9	61.0	62.7	60.4	55.9	47.6	40.2	39.6
31	40.4		44.6		56.4		62.9	60.3		48.1		39.0
Means	38.73	39.66	41.48	47.46	53.14	59.82	62.55	61.91	57.47	51.02	42.67	40.78

The mean of the twelve monthly values is 49°.72.

TABLE LXXVIII.—LIST of WAVES of HIGH and LOW MEAN TEMPERATURE during the Period 1849 to 1868.

Days or groups of days in this Table marked † have been omitted in the reductions referring to the Temperature of the Air only, and those marked ‡ in the reductions referring to the Temperature of Evaporation only.

Limits of Waves of High Temperature.	Days omitted in the Reductions.	Limits of Waves of Low Temperature.	Days omitted in the Reductions.	Limits of Waves of High Temperature.	Days omitted in the Reductions.	Limits of Waves of Low Temperature.	Days omitted in the Reductions.
1849.				**1851 continued.**			
Jan. 8 to Mar. 8	Feb. 15, 19 to 22, Mar. 6.	Mar. 9 to Mar. 11		Jun. 25 to Jul. 2		Jun. 22 to Jun. 24	
		Mar. 18 to Mar. 30		Jul. 20 to Jul. 22		Jul. 5 to Jul. 19	
Mar. 12 to Mar. 17		Apr. 2 to Apr. 4		Aug. 29 to Aug. 8		Jul. 23 to Jul. 28	
Mar. 31 to Apr. 1		Apr. 9 to Apr. 28	Apr. 15, 19‡,	Aug. 12 to Aug. 17		Aug. 9 to Aug. 11	
Apr. 5 to Apr. 8	Apr. 5‡.		21‡, 22.	Aug. 20 to Aug. 25		Aug. 18 to Aug. 19	
Apr. 29 to May 5		May 6 to May 12	May 6.	Sep. 1 to Sep. 4		Aug. 26 to Aug. 31	
May 13 to May 26	May 15‡, 24.	May 27 to May 28		Sep. 16 to Sep. 19		Sep. 5 to Sep. 15	
May 29 to Jun. 5		Jun. 6 to Jun. 20		Sep. 23 to Sep. 25		Sep. 16 to Sep. 21	
Jun. 21 to Jun. 27		Jun. 28 to Jun. 30		Oct. 3 to Oct. 15		Sep. 26 to Oct. 2	
Jul. 1 to Jul. 3	Jul. 1 to 3‡.	Jul. 4 to Jul. 5	Jul. 4‡, 5‡.	Oct. 18 to Oct. 28		Oct. 16 to Oct. 17	
Jul. 6 to Jul. 17	Jul. 7, 8, 9, 15, 16.	Jul. 18 to Aug. 5	Jul. 28 to 30, Aug. 1, 5.	Dec. 5 to Dec. 11		Oct. 29 to Dec. 4	
Aug. 6 to Aug. 12	Aug. 6, 9.	Aug. 13 to Aug. 19	Aug. 17, 18.	Dec. 19 to Dec. 24		Dec. 12 to Dec. 18	
Aug. 20 to Sep. 7	Aug. 23‡, Sep. 1.	Sep. 8 to Sep. 21				Dec. 25 to Jan. 2	
Sep. 22 to Sep. 30	Sep. 28.	Oct. 1 to Oct. 16					
Oct. 17 to Nov. 14	Oct. 29 to Nov. 1.	Nov. 15 to Nov. 17		**1852.**			
		Nov. 20 to Dec. 4	Nov. 28 to Dec. 4.				
Nov. 18 to Nov. 19		Dec. 9 to Dec. 13	Dec. 9, 10.	Jan. 3 to Feb. 9		Feb. 10 to Feb. 14	
Dec. 5 to Dec. 8	Dec. 5 to 8.	Dec. 20 to Jan. 2		Feb. 15 to Feb. 18		Feb. 19 to Mar. 19	Feb. 24 to Mar. 1.
Dec. 14 to Dec. 19				Mar. 20 to Mar. 24			
				Mar. 29 to Mar. 30		Mar. 25 to Mar. 28	
1850.				Apr. 5 to Apr. 6		Mar. 31 to Apr. 4	
				Apr. 13 to Apr. 14		Apr. 7 to Apr. 12	
Jan. 3 to Jan. 4		Jan. 5 to Jan. 24		Apr. 21 to Apr. 23		Apr. 15 to Apr. 21	
Jan. 25 to Mar. 13		Mar. 14 to Mar. 30		Apr. 29 to Apr. 30		Apr. 24 to Apr. 28	
Mar. 31 to Apr. 21	Mar. 31, Apr. 1.	Apr. 22 to May 17	Apr. 28, 29.	May 7 to May 10		May 1 to May 6	
		May 24 to May 28		Jul. 3 to Aug. 2	Jul. 4 to 9, 11, 12.	May 11 to May 14	
May 18 to May 23		Jun. 6 to Jun. 8				May 21 to Jul. 2	
May 29 to Jun. 5		Jun. 12 to Jun. 17	Jun. 15, 16.			Aug. 3 to Aug. 16	
Jun. 9 to Jun. 11		Jun. 27 to Jul. 11		Aug. 17 to Sep. 11		Sep. 12 to Sep. 22	
Jun. 18 to Jun. 26		Jul. 25 to Jul. 28		Sep. 23 to Sep. 25	Oct. 21.	Sep. 26 to Oct. 19	Sep. 27, Oct. 17.
Jul. 12 to Jul. 24		Aug. 1 to Aug. 2		Oct. 20 to Oct. 24			
Jul. 29 to Jul. 31		Aug. 19 to Sep. 17	Sep. 13, 14.	Oct. 25 to Nov. 17		Oct. 25 to Oct. 29	
Aug. 3 to Aug. 18		Sep. 30 to Oct. 5		Nov. 26 to Nov. 28		Nov. 23 to Nov. 25	
Sep. 18 to Sep. 29		Oct. 9 to Oct. 16		Dec. 2 to Jan. 31	Dec. 5, 6, 20, 21, Dec. 27 to Jan. 10.	Nov. 29 to Dec. 1	
Oct. 6 to Oct. 8		Oct. 21 to Oct. 30					
Oct. 17 to Oct. 20		Nov. 13 to Nov. 15					
Oct. 31 to Nov. 12		Nov. 26 to Dec. 3		**1853.**			
Nov. 16 to Nov. 25		Dec. 8 to Dec. 10					
Dec. 4 to Dec. 7		Dec. 17 to Dec. 24		Mar. 5 to Mar. 13	Mar. 5 to 7.	Feb. 1 to Mar. 4	Feb. 28, Mar. 2 to 4.
Dec. 11 to Dec. 16				Mar. 30 to Apr. 7	Mar. 30 to Apr. 7.	Mar. 14 to Mar. 29	Mar. 26 to 29.
Dec. 25 to Jan. 23				Apr. 10 to Apr. 12	Apr. 10 to 12.	Apr. 8 to Apr. 9	Apr. 8 to 9.
				Apr. 16 to Apr. 19	Apr. 16 to 19.	Apr. 13 to Apr. 15	Apr. 13 to 15.
1851.				Apr. 30 to May 2		Apr. 20 to Apr. 29	Apr. 20.
				May 16 to May 27		May 3 to May 15	
Jan. 27 to Feb. 14		Jan. 24 to Jan. 26		Jun. 7 to Jun. 11		May 28 to Jun. 6	
Feb. 18 to Feb. 22		Feb. 15 to Feb. 17		Jun. 13 to Jun. 17		Jun. 12 to Jun. 16	
Mar. 18 to Apr. 3		Feb. 23 to Mar. 17		Jun. 24 to Jun. 25		Jun. 18 to Jun. 23	
Apr. 17 to Apr. 24		Apr. 4 to Apr. 16		Jul. 6 to Jul. 9		Jun. 26 to Jul. 5	
May 10 to May 11		Apr. 25 to May 9		Aug. 5 to Aug. 9		Jul. 10 to Aug. 1	Jul. 29, 30.
May 22 to May 25		May 12 to May 21		Aug. 19 to Aug. 22		Aug. 5 to Aug. 18	
Jun. 2 to Jun. 5		May 26 to Jun. 1	May 27.	Sep. 10 to Sep. 12		Aug. 23 to Sep. 9	
Jun. 19 to Jun. 21		Jun. 4 to Jun. 18		Sep. 16 to Sep. 19		Sep. 13 to Sep. 15	

TABLE LXXVIII.—List of Waves of High and Low Mean Temperature—continued.

Left columns

1853 continued.

Limits of Waves of High Temperature.	Days omitted in the Reductions.	Limits of Waves of Low Temperature.	Days omitted in the Reductions.
Sep. 28 to Sep. 29		Sep. 20 to Sep. 27	
Oct. 8 to Oct. 15		Sep. 30 to Oct. 7	
Oct. 21 to Nov. 8		Oct. 16 to Oct. 20	
		Nov. 9 to Jan. 6	Nov. 25, Dec. 8, 17 to 19.

1854.

Limits of Waves of High Temperature.	Days omitted in the Reductions.	Limits of Waves of Low Temperature.	Days omitted in the Reductions.
Jan. 7 to Feb. 2		Feb. 5 to Feb. 4	
Feb. 5 to Feb. 9		Feb. 10 to Feb. 19	
Feb. 20 to Mar. 2		Mar. 3 to Mar. 7	
Mar. 8 to Mar. 17		Mar. 18 to Mar. 25	
Mar. 26 to Apr. 21		Apr. 22 to May 11	
May 12 to May 15		May 16 to Jun. 21	Jun. 10 to 12.
Jun. 22 to Jun. 25		Jun. 26 to Jul. 19	
Jul. 20 to Jul. 26		Jul. 27 to Aug. 10	
Aug. 11 to Aug. 14		Aug. 15 to Aug. 18	
Aug. 19 to Sep. 7	Aug. 19, 20, Sep. 7.	Sep. 8 to Sep. 11	Sep. 8.
Sep. 12 to Sep. 20		Sep. 21 to Sep. 23	Sep. 21 to 23.
Sep. 24 to Oct. 10		Oct. 11 to Oct. 27	
Oct. 28 to Nov. 2		Nov. 3 to Nov. 28	
Nov. 29 to Dec. 5		Dec. 6 to Dec. 12	
Dec. 13 to Dec. 16		Dec. 17 to Dec. 19	Dec. 17 to 19.
Dec. 20 to Dec. 26	Dec. 20.	Dec. 27 to Dec. 29	
Dec. 30 to Jan. 9			

1855.

Limits of Waves of High Temperature.	Days omitted in the Reductions.	Limits of Waves of Low Temperature.	Days omitted in the Reductions.
Feb. 28 to Mar. 5		Jan. 10 to Feb. 27	
Mar. 16 to Mar. 20		Mar. 6 to Mar. 15	
Apr. 6 to Apr. 17		Mar. 21 to Mar. 25	
May 24 to May 27	May 24 to 27.	Apr. 18 to May 23	May 15, 16. May 29, 30, Jun. 2.
Jun. 5 to Jun. 8		May 28 to Jun. 4	
Jun. 26 to Jul. 4		Jun. 9 to Jun. 25	Jun. 19.
Jul. 8 to Jul. 15	Jul. 12. 13.	Jul. 5 to Jul. 7	Jul. 5 to 7.
Jul. 22 to Jul. 23	Jul. 22, 23.	Jul. 16 to Jul. 21	Jul. 16, 20, 21.
Jul. 29 to Aug. 2		Jul. 24 to Jul. 28	
Aug. 15 to Aug. 31	Aug. 18, 19, 30.	Aug. 3 to Aug. 14	Aug. 5 to 7.
Sep. 11 to Sep. 13		Sep. 1 to Sep. 10	Sep. 6.
Sep. 16 to Sep. 23		Sep. 14 to Sep. 15	
Sep. 28 to Oct. 8		Sep. 24 to Sep. 27	
Oct. 11 to Oct. 15		Oct. 9 to Oct. 10	
Oct. 17 to Oct. 23		Oct. 14 to Oct. 16	
Nov. 6 to Nov. 12		Oct. 24 to Nov. 5	Nov. 1 to 3.
Dec. 23 to Jan. 8		Nov. 13 to Dec. 22	

1856.

Limits of Waves of High Temperature.	Days omitted in the Reductions.	Limits of Waves of Low Temperature.	Days omitted in the Reductions.
Jan. 16 to Jan. 27		Jan. 9 to Jan. 15	
Feb. 5 to Feb. 16		Jan. 28 to Feb. 4	
Feb. 23 to Mar. 3		Feb. 17 to Feb. 22	
Mar. 18 to Mar. 20		Mar. 4 to Mar. 10	
Apr. 1 to Apr. 15		Mar. 21 to Mar. 31	
Apr. 25 to Apr. 26		Apr. 16 to Apr. 24	
May 10 to May 13	May 10 to 13.	Apr. 27 to May 9	Apr. 30, May 1.
May 26 to May 28			

Right columns

1856 continued.

Limits of Waves of High Temperature.	Days omitted in the Reductions.	Limits of Waves of Low Temperature.	Days omitted in the Reductions.
Jun. 2 to Jun. 4		May 14 to May 25	
Jun. 7 to Jun. 11		May 29 to Jun. 1	
Jun. 25 to Jun. 28	Jun. 25 to 28.	Jun. 5 to Jun. 6	Jun. 5, 6.
Jul. 19 to Aug. 16	Jul. 21, Aug. 3, 4.	Jun. 12 to Jun. 24	Jun. 15 to 18.
Aug. 25 to Aug. 31		Jun. 29 to Jul. 18	
Sep. 9 to Sep. 12		Aug. 17 to Aug. 24	
Sep. 30 to Oct. 24	Oct. 19 to 21.	Sep. 1 to Sep. 8	
Oct. 31 to Nov. 2		Sep. 13 to Sep. 29	
Nov. 20 to Nov. 24		Oct. 25 to Oct. 30	
Dec. 5 to Dec. 14	Dec. 8, 9.	Nov. 3 to Nov. 19	
Dec. 18 to Dec. 22		Nov. 25 to Dec. 4	
Dec. 30 to Jan. 4		Dec. 23 to Dec. 29	

1857.

Limits of Waves of High Temperature.	Days omitted in the Reductions.	Limits of Waves of Low Temperature.	Days omitted in the Reductions.
Jan. 9 to Jan. 20		Jan. 5 to Jan. 8	
Feb. 6 to Feb. 12		Jan. 21 to Feb. 5	Feb. 3 to 5.
Feb. 16 to Feb. 24		Feb. 13 to Feb. 15	
Feb. 27 to Mar. 7		Feb. 25 to Feb. 26	
Mar. 14 to Mar. 20		Mar. 8 to Mar. 13	
Mar. 28 to Apr. 10		Mar. 21 to Mar. 27	
Apr. 17 to Apr. 21		Apr. 11 to Apr. 16	
May 11 to Jun. 8	May 17, 24, Jun. 1, 2, 3, 6.	Apr. 22 to May 10	May 10.
Jun. 17 to Jun. 30	Jun. 19, 20,	Jun. 9 to Jun. 16	
Jul. 10 to Aug. 6	Jul. 10, 18, 19, 22, 23.	Aug. 7 to Aug. 9	Jul. q.
Aug. 10 to Sep. 1		Sep. 2 to Sep. 4	
Sep. 5 to Oct. 3		Oct. 4 to Oct. 9	Oct. 9.
Oct. 10 to Nov. 11	Oct. 25, 27, 28, Nov. 3.	Nov. 12 to Nov. 13	
Nov. 14 to Nov. 23		Nov. 24 to Nov. 30	
Dec. 1 to Jan. 2			

1858.

Limits of Waves of High Temperature.	Days omitted in the Reductions.	Limits of Waves of Low Temperature.	Days omitted in the Reductions.
Jan. 8 to Jan. 20		Jan. 3 to Jan. 7	Jan. 5.
Jan. 28 to Jan. 31		Jan. 21 to Jan. 27	
Feb. 3 to Feb. 6	Feb. 3.	Feb. 1 to Feb. 2	Feb. 1, 2.
Mar. 13 to Mar. 31		Feb. 7 to Mar. 12	Feb. 11, 12.
Apr. 15 to Apr. 26	Apr. 23 to 26.	Apr. 1 to Apr. 14	
May 16 to May 22		Apr. 27 to May 15	May 1.
May 29 to Jun. 26	May 29 to Jun. 4, 8, 9, 12 to 14, 17, 18, 19 to 21.	May 23 to May 28	May 24.
Jul. 11 to Jul. 12		Jun. 27 to Jul. 10	Jul. 1, 2, 3, 8, 9.
Aug. 3 to Aug. 5	Aug. 3.	Jul. 13 to Jul. 31	
Aug. 9 to Aug. 19		Aug. 1 to Aug. 2	
Aug. 22 to Aug. 24		Aug. 6 to Aug. 8	
Sep. 3 to Sep. 5		Aug. 20 to Aug. 21	
Sep. 8 to Oct. 1		Aug. 25 to Sep. 2	
Oct. 15 to Oct. 28		Sep. 6 to Sep. 7	
Nov. 25 to Dec. 5		Oct. 2 to Oct. 14	
Dec. 18 to Jan. 1		Oct. 29 to Nov. 24	
		Dec. 6 to Dec. 17	

TABLE LXXVIII.—LIST of WAVES of HIGH and LOW MEAN TEMPERATURE—*continued.*

Limits of Waves of High Temperature.	Days omitted in the Reductions.	Limits of Waves of Low Temperature.	Days omitted in the Reductions.	Limits of Waves of High Temperature.	Days omitted in the Reductions.	Limits of Waves of Low Temperature.	Days omitted in the Reductions.
1859.				**1862.**			
Jan. 4 to Jan. 5		Jan. 2 to Jan. 5		Jan. 4 to Jan. 15	Jan. 8, 9.	Jan. 16 to Jan. 21	Jan. 16 to 19.
Jan. 10 to Mar. 29		Jan. 6 to Jan. 9		Jan. 22 to Feb. 6	Feb. 1 to 3.	Feb. 7 to Feb. 16	Feb. 11.
Apr. 2 to Apr. 11	Apr. 6, 7.	Mar. 30 to Apr. 1		Feb. 17 to Feb. 21		Feb. 24 to Mar. 5	Mar. 1, 2.
Apr. 25 to Apr. 29		Apr. 12 to Apr. 24		Mar. 6 to Mar. 15	Mar. 11, 12.	Mar. 16 to Mar. 23	Mar. 19 to 23.
May 7 to May 16		Apr. 30 to May 6		Mar. 24 to Apr. 7	Mar. 24, 25,	Apr. 8 to Apr. 16	Apr. 11.
May 24 to Jun. 13	May 24 to 29,	May 17 to May 23	May 21, 22.		26, 31.	May 13 to May 15	May 13.
	31, Jun. 1.	Jun. 14 to Jun. 21		Apr. 17 to May 12	Apr. 24 to 27,	May 21 to May 22	
Jun. 22 to Jun. 28		Jun. 29 to Jul. 1			May 10 to	Jun. 9 to Sep. 6	Jun. 15, 16,
Jul. 2 to Aug. 8		Aug. 9 to Aug. 10			12.		Jul. 1¾, 2¾,
Aug. 11 to Aug. 14		Aug. 15 to Aug. 17		May 16 to May 20	May 18¾, 19.		13, 14, 17,
Aug. 18 to Aug. 29		Aug. 30 to Sep. 5		May 23 to Jun. 8	May 31¾.		18, 19 to
Sep. 6 to Sep. 9		Sep. 10 to Sep. 22	Sep. 14, 19,		Jun. 6, 7.		23¾, 29 to
Sep. 23 to Oct. 20	Oct. 3 to 5,	Oct. 21 to Oct. 31	20.	Sep. 7 to Sep. 9	Sep. 7 to 9.		31¾, Aug. 30
	13, 14.	Nov. 9 to Nov. 22	Oct. 21, 22.	Sep. 13 to Sep. 20	Sep. 13 to 20.	Sep. 10 to Sep. 12	to Sep. 4.
Nov. 1 to Nov. 8		Nov. 28 to Dec. 4	Nov. 15, 22.	Sep. 24 to Oct. 17	Sep. 24 to 28,	Sep. 21 to Sep. 23	Sep. 10 to 12,
Nov. 23 to Nov. 27	Nov. 23.	Dec. 9 to Dec. 23	Dec. 1 to 4.		29¾, Oct. 1.	Oct. 18 to Oct. 21	Sep. 21 to 23,
Dec. 5 to Dec. 8	Dec. 5 to 8.			Oct. 22 to Oct. 23		Oct. 24 to Oct. 25	Oct. 19.
Dec. 24 to Jan. 27	Dec. 31, Jan. 1.			Oct. 26 to Oct. 27		Oct. 28 to Oct. 30	
				Oct. 31 to Nov. 5		Nov. 6 to Dec. 2	Nov. 9 to 14.
				Dec. 3 to Mar. 7			
1860.				**1863.**			
Feb. 16 to Mar. 5		Jan. 28 to Feb. 25				Mar. 8 to Mar. 19	
Mar. 16 to Mar. 21		Mar. 6 to Mar. 15		Mar. 20 to Mar. 30	Apr. 25.	Mar. 31 to Apr. 2	
Mar. 28 to Apr. 1	Mar. 31 to Apr. 1.	Mar. 22 to Mar. 27		May 3 to May 17	May 3 to 5¾,	Apr. 28 to May 2	May 1¾, 2¾.
Apr. 5 to Apr. 8		Apr. 2 to Apr. 4			9 to 11.	May 18 to May 26	
Apr. 26 to May 4	Apr. 30 to May 2.	Apr. 9 to Apr. 29	Apr. 19, 20,	May 27 to May 30	May 27 to 30.	May 31 to Jun. 1	
			28, 29.	May 27 to May 30		Jun. 3 to Jun. 19	
May 8 to May 26	May 8 to 12,	May 5 to May 7	May 5 to 7,	Jun. 2 to Jun. 4		Jun. 26 to Jul. 4	
	17, 18, 25,	May 27 to Oct. 4	Jul. 13, 16.	Jun. 20 to Jun. 25		Jul. 16 to Jul. 31	Jul. 16, 17,
	26.		Aug. 7,	Jul. 5 to Jul. 15	Jul. 14, 15.		22 to 30,
Oct. 5 to Oct. 7			Sep. 2, 3.	Aug. 2 to Aug. 16	Aug. 2, 14,		Aug. 1.
Oct. 17 to Nov. 1		Oct. 8 to Oct. 16			15, 16.		
Nov. 14 to Nov. 16		Nov. 3 to Nov. 13		Aug. 23 to Aug. 29		Aug. 17 to Aug. 26	Aug. 18, 19.
Nov. 27 to Dec. 13		Nov. 17 to Nov. 26		Oct. 1 to Oct. 4	Oct. 10, 11.	Sep. 1 to Sep. 30	Sep. 1, 2, 6.
Dec. 30 to Jan. 1	Dec. 30 to Jan. 1.	Dec. 14 to Dec. 29	Dec. 24, 25,	Oct. 7 to Oct. 27			24.
			28, 29.	Nov. 4 to Nov. 8		Oct. 5 to Oct. 6	Oct. 5 to 6.
				Nov. 14 to Nov. 27		Oct. 23 to Nov. 3	
				Dec. 1 to Dec. 30		Nov. 9 to Nov. 13	Nov. 13.
						Nov. 24 to Nov. 30	
1861.						Dec. 31 to Jan. 9	
Jan. 20 to Feb. 9	Jan. 20.	Jan. 2 to Jan. 19	Jan. 4, 8 to				
Feb. 15 to Mar. 15			16, 19.	**1864.**			
Mar. 22 to Mar. 30		Feb. 10 to Feb. 14		Jan. 10 to Jan. 14		Jan. 15 to Jan. 16	
Apr. 11 to Apr. 18	Apr. 12¾, 14¾.	Mar. 16 to Mar. 21		Jan. 17 to Jan. 28	Jan. 28.	Jan. 29 to Jan. 31	Jan. 29 to 31,
May 15 to May 16		Mar. 31 to Apr. 10		Feb. 1 to Feb. 3		Feb. 4 to Feb. 11	Feb. 9.
May 20 to Jun. 1	May 30 to Jun. 1.	Apr. 19 to May 14		Feb. 12 to Feb. 16		Feb. 17 to Mar. 3	
		May 17 to May 19		Mar. 4 to Mar. 10	Mar. 5.	Mar. 9 to Mar. 10	
Jun. 11 to Jun. 24		Jun. 2 to Jun. 10	Jun. 2.	Mar. 11 to Mar. 15		Mar. 16 to Mar. 18	
Jul. 20 to Jul. 23	Jul. 20 to 23.	Jun. 25 to Jul. 19	Jul. 14 to 17,	Mar. 19 to Mar. 30		Mar. 21 to Mar. 30	
Aug. 1 to Aug. 19	Aug. 1, 2, 18,		18¾, 19¾.	Mar. 31 to Apr. 4		Apr. 5 to Apr. 8	
	19¾.	Jul. 24 to Jul. 31	Jul. 24, 25¾,	Apr. 9 to May 5	Apr. 17.	May 4 to May 8	
Aug. 23 to Sep. 19	Aug. 24, 25,		26¾, 27 to	May 6 to May 7		May 8 to May 11	
	Aug. 27 to		31.	May 12 to May 22	May 20.	May 23 to Jun. 5	May 25, 26.
	Sep. 1, 2¾,	Aug. 20 to Aug. 22	Aug. 20 to 22.	Jun. 6 to Jun. 10		Jun. 11 to Jun. 21	Jun. 12 to 14,
Sep. 2d to Oct. 31	10.	Sep. 11, 19 to		Jul. 1 to Jul. 9	Jun. 20, 21.	Jun. 22 to Jul. 16	Jul. 1, 5, 6.
	Oct. 1 to 6,		22.	Aug. 4 to Aug. 8		Aug. 2 to Aug. 3	
	8 to 11, 23	Nov. 1 to Nov. 20		Aug. 13 to Aug. 15		Aug. 9 to Aug. 13	
	to 29.	Nov. 23 to Nov. 30		Aug. 29 to Sep. 9		Aug. 16 to Aug. 28	
Nov. 21 to Nov. 22		Dec. 2 to Dec. 5				Sep. 10 to Sep. 20	Sep. 10, 11.
Nov. 25 to Dec. 1		Dec. 25 to Jan. 3	Dec. 25 to 27.				
Dec. 6 to Dec. 24							

TABLE LXXVIII.—LIST OF WAVES OF HIGH AND LOW MEAN TEMPERATURE—*concluded*.

Limits of Waves of High Temperature.	Days omitted in the Reductions.	Limits of Waves of Low Temperature.	Days omitted in the Reductions.	Limits of Waves of High Temperature.	Days omitted in the Reductions.	Limits of Waves of Low Temperature.	Days omitted in the Reductions.

1864 continued.

Limits of Waves of High Temperature	Limits of Waves of Low Temperature
Sep. 21 to Sep. 28	Sep. 29 to Oct. 15
Oct. 16 to Oct. 29	Oct. 30 to Nov. 12
Nov. 13 to Nov. 23	Nov. 24 to Nov. 26
Nov. 27 to Dec. 13	Dec. 14 to Dec. 19
Dec. 20 to Dec. 21	Dec. 22 to Dec. 27
Dec. 28 to Dec. 30	Dec. 31 to Jan. 3

1866 continued.

Limits of Waves of High Temperature	Limits of Waves of Low Temperature
Nov. 11 to Nov. 16	Nov. 9 to Nov. 10
Nov. 22 to Nov. 27	Nov. 17 to Nov. 21
Dec. 3 to Dec. 7	Nov. 28 to Dec. 2
Dec. 12 to Dec. 19	Dec. 8 to Dec. 11
Dec. 23 to Dec. 29	Dec. 20 to Dec. 22
	Dec. 30 to Jan. 5

1865.

Limits of Waves of High Temperature	Days omitted	Limits of Waves of Low Temperature	Days omitted
Jan. 4 to Jan. 16		Jan. 17 to Jan. 30	
Jan. 31 to Feb. 3		Feb. 4 to Feb. 22	Mar. 22, 23.
Feb. 23 to Mar. 2		Mar. 3 to Apr. 4	
Apr. 5 to Apr. 28		Apr. 29 to May 1	
May 2 to May 9		May 10 to May 16	
May 17 to May 31		Jun. 1 to Jun. 2	
Jun. 3 to Jun. 10		Jun. 11 to Jun. 19	
Jun. 20 to Jun. 23		Jun. 26 to Jul. 1	
Jul. 2 to Jul. 9		Jul. 10 to Jul. 13	
Jul. 14 to Jul. 30	Jul. 18, 19.	Jul. 31 to Aug. 19	
Aug. 20 to Oct. 17		Oct. 18 to Oct. 23	Nov. 3.
Oct. 24 to Oct. 27		Oct. 28 to Nov. 13	
Nov. 14 to Dec. 11		Dec. 12 to Dec. 16	
Dec. 17 to Jan. 8	Dec. 17, 18.		

1867.

Limits of Waves of High Temperature	Days omitted	Limits of Waves of Low Temperature	Days omitted
Jan. 6 to Jan. 10		Jan. 11 to Jan. 22	
Jan. 23 to Feb. 26	Feb. 12 to 16.	Feb. 27 to Mar. 22	
Mar. 23 to Mar. 27		Mar. 28 to Mar. 31	
Apr. 1 to Apr. 24		Apr. 25 to May 1	
May 2 to May 12	May 6 to 11.	May 13 to May 26	May 19.
May 27 to Jun. 2	May 31 to Jun. 2.	Jun. 3 to Jun. 8	Jun. 23, 24.
Jun. 9 to Jun. 12	Jun. 9.	Jun. 13 to Jun. 29	
Jun. 30 to Jul. 2		Jul. 3 to Aug. 7	
Aug. 8 to Aug. 23		Aug. 26 to Aug. 28	
Aug. 29 to Sep. 14		Sep. 15 to Sep. 26	
Sep. 27 to Sep. 30		Oct. 1 to Oct. 13	
Oct. 14 to Nov. 1		Nov. 2 to Nov. 13	
Nov. 14 to Nov. 16		Nov. 17 to Dec. 10	
Dec. 11 to Dec. 17		Dec. 18 to Dec. 21	
Dec. 22 to Dec. 25		Dec. 26 to Dec. 31	

1866.

Limits of Waves of High Temperature	Days omitted	Limits of Waves of Low Temperature	Days omitted
Jan. 13 to Feb. 16		Jan. 9 to Jan. 12	
Feb. 23 to Feb. 25	Feb. 25.	Feb. 17 to Feb. 22	Feb. 22.
Mar. 16 to Mar. 19		Feb. 26 to Mar. 15	Mar. 1.
Mar. 24 to Mar. 31		Mar. 20 to Mar. 23	
Apr. 10 to Apr. 28		Apr. 1 to Apr. 9	
May 7 to May 11		Apr. 29 to May 6	
Jun. 2 to Jun. 4		May 12 to Jun. 1	
Jun. 7 to Jun. 11		Jun. 5 to Jun. 6	
Jun. 21 to Jun. 30		Jun. 12 to Jun. 20	
Jul. 9 to Jul. 17		Jul. 1 to Jul. 8	
Aug. 24 to Aug. 28		Jul. 18 to Aug. 23	
Sep. 4 to Sep. 10		Aug. 29 to Sep. 3	
Oct. 19 to Oct. 24	Oct. 30, Nov. 7.	Sep. 11 to Sep. 25	Oct. 29.
Oct. 30 to Nov. 8		Oct. 12 to Oct. 18	
		Oct. 25 to Oct. 29	

1868.

Limits of Waves of High Temperature	Days omitted	Limits of Waves of Low Temperature	Days omitted
Jan. 12 to Jan. 19		Jan. 20 to Jan. 27	
Jan. 28 to Feb. 7	Feb. 21, 22.	Feb. 8 to Feb. 9	
Feb. 10 to Mar. 25		Mar. 13 to Mar. 25	
Mar. 26 to Mar. 28		Mar. 29 to Mar. 31	
Apr. 1 to Apr. 7		Apr. 8 to Apr. 13	
Apr. 14 to May 4		May 5 to May 7	May 6.
May 8 to Jun. 21		Jun. 22 to Jun. 24	Nov. 9.
Jun. 25 to Jul. 3		Jul. 4 to Jul. 5	
Jul. 6 to Aug. 29		Aug. 20 to Aug. 29	
Aug. 30 to Sep. 12		Sep. 13 to Sep. 15	
Sep. 16 to Sep. 29		Sep. 30 to Oct. 30	
Oct. 31 to Nov. 4		Nov. 5 to Nov. 21	
Nov. 22 to Nov. 23		Nov. 24 to Nov. 30	
Dec. 1 to Dec. 29	Dec. 8, 9.	Dec. 30 to Jan. 1	

TABLE LXXIX.—MEAN TEMPERATURE of the Air at every Hour of the Day

Year.	Number of Waves treated in each Year.	Midnight.	1h. a.m.	2h. a.m.	3h. a.m.	4h. a.m.	5h. a.m.	6h. a.m.	7h. a.m.	8h. a.m.	9h. a.m.	10h. a.m.	11h. a.m.
1849	16	50·9	50·5	50·2	50·0	50·0	50·3	51·3	53·1	55·1	57·2	58·7	60·0
1850	18	49·4	49·0	48·8	48·5	48·5	48·8	49·8	51·2	52·8	54·6	56·4	58·0
1851	20	51·7	51·2	50·7	50·3	50·4	50·7	51·6	53·8	55·9	58·2	59·9	61·5
1852	17	46·8	46·7	46·3	46·1	46·0	46·2	46·5	47·9	50·0	52·3	54·8	56·8
1853	14	52·9	52·3	52·1	52·1	52·0	51·8	51·9	52·9	54·9	57·3	59·8	63·3
1854	17	48·7	48·3	47·9	47·5	47·2	47·1	47·3	48·6	50·3	52·8	55·0	56·3
1855	13	51·2	51·0	50·7	50·3	50·4	50·3	50·7	51·9	53·7	56·0	57·9	59·5
1856	18	49·0	48·6	48·3	48·2	48·0	48·0	48·6	49·7	51·2	53·2	54·9	56·1
1857	15	48·0	47·6	47·2	46·9	46·7	46·6	47·0	48·3	50·1	52·3	54·3	56·0
1858	16	50·6	50·3	50·0	49·7	49·6	49·6	50·2	51·5	53·5	55·5	57·4	59·3
1859	15	50·8	50·7	50·4	50·1	49·9	50·1	50·8	52·2	53·7	55·7	57·3	58·8
1860	10	45·5	45·4	45·2	45·0	44·9	44·9	45·3	46·1	47·6	49·6	51·4	52·6
1861	13	48·4	48·2	47·9	47·8	47·8	48·0	48·6	49·9	51·4	53·2	54·7	56·2
1862	13	47·2	47·1	47·0	47·0	46·9	47·1	47·5	47·9	48·9	50·4	51·8	53·0
1863	13	51·6	51·2	50·9	50·6	50·3	50·6	51·5	53·0	54·8	56·8	58·3	59·8
1864	23	47·2	46·8	46·5	46·3	46·1	46·1	46·7	48·0	49·7	51·8	53·6	55·3
1865	14	50·1	50·6	49·3	49·0	48·8	49·0	50·1	51·9	53·4	55·5	57·6	59·2
1866	20	49·6	49·4	49·3	49·1	49·0	49·2	49·8	51·1	52·4	54·2	55·9	57·3
1867	15	50·0	49·7	49·5	49·5	49·1	49·3	50·5	51·3	53·5	55·2	56·7	58·1
1868	14	49·4	49·0	48·7	48·5	48·3	48·4	48·9	50·4	52·0	54·0	55·9	57·4
Means	15·8	49·45	49·14	48·86	48·63	48·50	48·61	49·28	50·60	52·35	54·41	56·22	57·73

TABLE LXXX.—MEAN TEMPERATURE of Evaporation at every Hour of the Day

Year.	Number of Waves treated in each Year.	Midnight.	1h. a.m.	2h. a.m.	3h. a.m.	4h. a.m.	5h. a.m.	6h. a.m.	7h. a.m.	8h. a.m.	9h. a.m.	10h. a.m.	11h. a.m.
1849	15	48·7	48·5	48·3	48·2	48·3	48·5	49·1	50·3	51·6	52·7	53·4	54·1
1850	18	48·1	47·8	47·6	47·4	47·4	47·6	48·2	49·2	50·1	51·2	52·4	53·3
1851	20	49·6	49·2	48·9	48·8	48·7	48·9	49·6	50·9	52·3	53·8	54·8	55·5
1852	17	44·5	44·3	44·4	44·2	44·2	44·3	44·6	45·6	46·9	48·4	50·0	51·2
1853	14	51·2	51·0	50·7	50·5	50·3	50·4	51·2	52·0	54·2	55·9	36·8	57·7
1854	17	47·0	46·8	46·5	46·2	46·0	45·8	46·1	46·8	47·9	49·6	50·7	51·5
1855	15	46·7	46·7	46·6	46·3	46·2	46·1	46·5	50·2	51·6	52·9	54·0	54·8
1856	18	47·7	47·6	47·4	47·3	47·1	47·1	47·5	48·3	49·2	50·3	51·2	51·9
1857	15	46·8	46·5	46·3	46·1	45·9	45·9	46·2	47·1	48·2	49·6	50·9	51·8
1858	16	49·1	48·9	48·7	48·6	48·4	48·4	48·7	49·6	50·8	52·1	53·2	53·9
1859	15	49·4	49·3	49·0	48·8	48·6	48·7	49·2	50·1	51·1	52·3	53·0	53·8
1860	10	44·3	44·1	44·0	44·0	43·9	43·8	44·2	44·7	45·6	47·1	48·0	48·8
1861	13	47·2	47·0	46·9	46·8	46·9	47·0	47·5	48·3	49·3	50·5	51·3	52·2
1862	13	46·4	46·2	46·2	46·1	46·1	46·3	46·5	47·0	47·6	48·6	49·4	50·0
1863	13	50·2	49·9	49·8	49·7	49·5	49·6	50·1	51·0	52·0	53·0	53·8	54·6
1864	23	45·5	45·3	45·1	45·0	44·9	44·9	45·2	46·0	47·0	48·3	49·3	50·2
1865	14	48·4	48·1	47·8	47·6	47·4	47·4	48·1	49·1	50·2	51·4	52·4	53·4
1866	20	48·2	48·1	48·0	47·9	47·8	47·9	48·4	49·2	50·1	51·3	52·2	52·9
1867	15	48·5	48·3	48·3	48·2	48·2	48·0	48·6	49·8	50·8	51·9	52·8	53·4
1868	14	47·7	47·4	47·1	47·1	47·0	47·1	47·4	48·3	49·3	50·3	51·5	52·3
Means	15·7	47·91	47·71	47·53	47·39	47·28	47·34	47·79	48·70	49·79	51·07	52·06	52·87

In each of the Years 1849 to 1868, for Waves of High Mean Temperature.

Noon.	1ʰ. p.m.	2ʰ. p.m.	3ʰ. p.m.	4ʰ. p.m.	5ʰ. p.m.	6ʰ. p.m.	7ʰ. p.m.	8ʰ. p.m.	9ʰ. p.m.	10ʰ. p.m.	11ʰ. p.m.	Yearly Means.	Number of Days used in Waves.	Number of Days rejected in Waves.
61·7	62·0	62·4	62·3	61·6	60·0	58·5	56·6	54·9	53·6	52·8	52·2	55·7	175	20
58·9	59·7	60·0	59·8	58·9	57·7	56·0	54·4	52·8	51·6	51·0	50·4	53·6	210	2
62·8	63·4	63·3	62·8	61·4	60·1	58·6	56·6	54·9	53·7	52·8	52·1	56·2	143	0
58·5	59·3	59·2	58·7	57·6	55·9	54·2	51·9	50·4	49·3	48·6	48·0	51·6	192	28
64·9	65·5	65·7	65·2	64·4	63·2	60·9	58·7	56·8	55·4	54·3	53·8	58·0	78	3
58·0	58·8	59·0	58·5	57·4	56·1	54·5	52·8	51·4	50·4	49·7	49·2	52·2	176	4
61·0	61·9	62·0	61·5	60·4	59·2	57·4	55·7	54·3	53·1	52·3	51·6	55·2	117	5
57·4	57·8	57·9	57·4	56·6	55·4	54·1	52·7	51·7	50·8	50·3	49·8	52·3	151	8
57·6	58·5	58·5	58·1	57·0	55·6	54·0	52·4	51·1	50·0	49·3	48·6	51·7	244	18
60·6	61·4	61·6	61·3	60·1	58·6	56·8	54·9	53·5	52·2	51·4	50·9	54·6	170	20
60·0	60·6	60·9	60·6	59·7	58·2	56·7	55·0	53·5	52·4	51·8	51·2	54·6	250	18
53·9	54·8	55·3	55·3	54·3	53·0	51·4	49·6	48·2	47·3	46·7	46·2	49·1	73	14
57·8	58·4	58·6	58·4	57·5	56·1	54·5	52·9	51·4	50·4	49·8	49·2	52·4	163	33
54·7	54·9	54·9	54·6	53·7	52·5	51·4	50·4	49·3	48·6	47·9	47·4	50·1	208	29
61·3	61·8	62·1	61·7	60·6	59·1	57·4	55·9	54·6	53·3	52·4	51·8	55·5	148	12
56·9	57·6	58·0	57·6	56·5	55·1	53·4	51·7	50·4	49·3	48·7	48·0	51·1	176	6
60·7	61·4	61·6	61·1	60·2	59·4	57·6	55·6	53·7	52·4	51·5	50·9	54·6	221	4
58·4	59·0	59·1	58·5	57·6	56·5	55·3	53·7	52·3	51·2	50·5	49·9	53·3	174	3
59·1	59·4	59·3	59·1	58·3	57·2	55·7	54·2	53·0	51·9	51·3	50·7	53·9	151	15
58·8	59·4	59·6	59·4	58·5	57·2	55·5	53·8	52·3	51·3	51·2	50·4	53·2	251	4
59·13	59·76	59·95	59·60	58·61	57·30	55·70	53·97	52·33	51·40	50·69	50·08	53·44	173·5	12·3

in each of the Years 1849 to 1868, for Waves of High Mean Temperature.

Noon.	1ʰ. p.m.	2ʰ. p.m.	3ʰ. p.m.	4ʰ. p.m.	5ʰ. p.m.	6ʰ. p.m.	7ʰ. p.m.	8ʰ. p.m.	9ʰ. p.m.	10ʰ. p.m.	11ʰ. p.m.	Yearly Means.	Number of Days used in Waves.	Number of Days rejected in Waves.
53·1	53·2	53·4	53·3	54·9	53·1	53·2	52·2	51·3	50·5	50·0	49·6	51·6	169	23
53·8	54·2	54·2	53·9	53·5	52·9	52·1	51·2	50·3	49·6	49·1	48·6	50·6	210	2
56·2	56·6	56·6	56·0	55·3	54·6	53·6	52·6	51·7	51·0	50·4	49·8	52·3	143	0
52·2	52·5	52·4	52·1	51·3	50·2	49·1	48·0	47·0	46·3	45·8	45·5	47·7	192	28
58·5	58·7	58·7	58·3	58·0	57·1	56·1	55·0	53·8	52·9	52·3	51·8	54·3	78	3
52·2	52·4	52·6	52·3	51·7	51·1	50·4	49·5	48·8	48·2	47·7	47·3	49·0	176	4
55·5	55·9	55·8	55·5	54·9	54·2	53·5	52·5	51·6	50·9	50·4	50·0	52·1	151	5
52·4	52·5	52·5	52·2	51·8	51·3	50·6	50·0	49·3	48·8	48·6	48·3	49·6	151	8
51·5	51·9	52·9	52·6	52·0	51·1	50·2	49·4	48·7	48·0	47·6	47·2	49·0	244	18
54·5	54·8	54·8	54·5	53·9	53·2	52·2	51·5	50·7	50·0	49·5	49·2	51·2	167	23
54·3	54·8	54·9	54·6	54·2	53·6	52·5	51·7	50·9	50·3	49·9	49·5	51·4	250	18
49·3	49·8	49·9	49·9	49·3	48·6	47·7	46·9	46·0	45·4	44·9	44·6	46·4	73	14
53·1	53·3	53·3	53·2	52·6	51·9	51·1	50·2	49·4	48·7	48·0	49·7	—	159	37
50·8	51·0	51·0	50·8	50·3	49·6	49·0	48·4	47·8	47·2	46·8	46·4	48·1	207	30
55·2	55·4	55·4	55·3	54·7	53·9	53·1	52·3	51·6	50·9	50·4	50·1	52·1	145	15
50·9	51·1	51·2	50·9	50·4	49·7	48·9	48·0	47·4	46·9	46·5	46·2	47·7	176	6
54·0	54·1	54·1	53·8	53·2	52·6	51·8	51·0	50·1	49·5	49·1	48·7	50·6	221	4
53·3	53·5	53·5	53·2	52·7	52·0	51·3	50·5	49·8	49·1	48·6	48·1	50·3	174	3
53·9	53·9	53·8	53·6	53·3	52·4	51·7	51·1	50·3	49·8	49·3	49·0	50·8	151	15
52·8	53·1	53·1	53·0	52·5	51·8	50·9	50·1	49·4	48·7	48·2	47·8	49·8	251	4
53·55	53·78	53·80	53·55	53·03	52·28	51·44	50·60	49·79	49·14	48·67	48·30	50·22	172·7	13·0

TABLE LXXXI.—MEAN TEMPERATURE of the Air at every Hour of the Day

Year.	Number of Waters treated in each Year.	Midnight.	1h. a.m.	2h. a.m.	3h. a.m.	4h. a.m.	5h. a.m.	6h. a.m.	7h. a.m.	8h. a.m.	9h. a.m.	10h. a.m.	11h. a.m.
1849	17	44·0	44·6	44·3	44·1	43·8	43·8	44·4	45·8	47·2	49·3	50·3	51·4
1850	17	45·1	44·6	44·3	43·8	43·6	43·7	44·4	45·4	46·6	48·0	49·6	50·8
1851	21	45·4	44·8	44·4	44·1	43·8	43·8	44·4	45·8	47·7	49·9	51·7	53·3
1852	16	41·8	41·2	40·7	40·4	40·3	40·2	40·7	42·2	44·2	46·5	48·3	49·7
1853	16	47·2	47·0	46·7	46·4	46·2	46·2	46·9	48·3	49·9	51·5	52·8	53·8
1854	14	42·0	41·5	41·3	41·0	40·6	40·6	41·2	42·2	43·6	45·6	47·5	49·1
1855	16	43·5	43·0	44·8	44·4	44·2	44·1	44·4	45·3	47·1	49·2	51·2	52·7
1856	19	41·1	40·9	40·5	40·1	39·9	39·8	40·5	41·5	42·6	44·4	46·0	47·5
1857	15	41·5	41·2	40·8	40·4	40·0	39·8	40·1	41·2	42·8	44·2	45·8	47·0
1858	15	44·7	44·2	43·7	43·4	43·2	43·2	43·8	45·2	46·9	48·7	50·6	52·0
1859	16	43·8	43·4	43·1	42·8	42·6	42·6	42·9	43·7	45·1	46·9	48·7	50·0
1860	10	39·0	38·7	38·5	38·2	38·0	37·9	38·1	38·7	39·9	41·4	42·9	44·2
1861	14	41·9	41·4	41·1	40·8	40·7	40·8	41·3	42·1	43·4	44·9	45·4	47·7
1862	12	40·7	40·4	40·0	39·8	39·7	39·6	39·9	40·5	41·9	43·2	44·4	45·4
1863	14	44·3	43·6	43·1	42·8	42·6	42·8	43·6	44·9	46·3	48·8	50·3	52·1
1864	22	42·0	41·5	41·1	40·7	40·4	40·5	41·0	42·0	43·4	44·9	46·4	47·9
1865	13	44·7	44·3	43·8	43·5	43·3	43·4	44·3	46·0	47·0	48·3	49·9	51·4
1866	21	42·1	41·7	41·3	40·9	40·7	40·8	41·2	42·1	43·2	44·7	46·1	47·5
1867	15	42·2	41·7	41·5	41·2	41·0	41·0	41·5	42·7	44·1	45·6	47·2	48·4
1868	14	42·6	42·2	42·0	41·8	41·5	41·5	42·0	43·1	44·7	47·0	48·4	49·9
Means	15·8	43·13	42·70	42·35	42·03	41·81	41·81	42·32	43·42	44·89	46·63	48·25	49·58

TABLE LXXXII.—MEAN TEMPERATURE of EVAPORATION at every Hour of the Day

Year.	Number of Waters treated in each Year.	Midnight.	1h. a.m.	2h. a.m.	3h. a.m.	4h. a.m.	5h. a.m.	6h. a.m.	7h. a.m.	8h. a.m.	9h. a.m.	10h. a.m.	11h. a.m.
1849	16	42·7	42·4	42·2	42·0	41·8	41·8	42·1	42·9	43·8	44·9	45·4	46·0
1850	17	43·6	43·3	43·0	42·6	42·5	42·6	43·0	43·6	44·3	45·2	46·3	47·0
1851	21	43·5	43·1	42·7	42·5	42·2	42·1	42·5	43·5	44·8	46·3	47·4	48·2
1852	16	39·8	39·5	39·2	39·0	38·9	38·8	39·3	40·4	41·6	43·0	44·1	44·9
1853	16	45·5	45·3	45·0	44·8	44·6	44·7	45·2	46·3	47·2	48·3	49·0	49·6
1854	14	40·9	40·6	40·3	40·1	39·8	39·7	40·1	40·9	41·9	43·1	44·2	45·2
1855	16	44·2	43·8	43·6	43·3	43·2	43·2	43·5	44·0	45·2	46·7	47·7	48·5
1856	19	40·2	40·0	39·7	39·4	39·2	39·1	39·4	40·1	40·9	42·0	43·0	43·7
1857	15	40·6	40·0	40·0	39·7	39·5	39·2	39·5	40·2	41·3	42·1	43·1	43·7
1858	15	43·1	42·7	42·4	42·1	41·9	41·9	42·3	43·2	44·1	45·2	46·1	46·9
1859	16	42·7	42·5	42·1	41·9	41·7	41·7	41·8	42·3	43·1	44·4	45·3	45·8
1860	10	37·8	37·6	37·4	37·2	37·0	36·0	37·0	37·4	38·3	39·3	40·3	41·2
1861	13	39·5	39·1	38·8	38·6	38·4	38·4	38·7	39·3	40·1	41·1	42·2	43·2
1862	12	39·8	39·4	39·2	38·9	38·8	38·8	39·1	39·4	40·2	41·3	42·1	42·8
1863	14	42·7	42·3	42·0	41·8	41·6	41·7	42·2	43·0	44·1	45·4	46·2	47·2
1864	22	40·4	40·1	39·8	39·5	39·3	39·3	39·6	40·1	40·0	41·8	42·6	43·4
1865	13	43·3	42·9	42·7	42·5	42·3	42·4	42·9	43·8	44·5	45·2	46·1	46·8
1866	21	40·9	40·6	40·2	40·0	39·8	39·9	40·1	40·6	41·4	42·3	43·3	44·0
1867	15	41·0	40·7	40·3	40·2	40·2	40·1	40·4	41·1	42·1	43·1	43·9	44·6
1868	14	40·9	40·6	40·5	40·3	40·1	40·2	40·4	41·1	42·3	43·6	44·6	45·2
Means	15·7	41·65	41·33	41·06	40·82	40·64	40·63	40·94	41·67	42·60	43·72	44·66	45·40

in each of the YEARS 1849 to 1868, for WAVES of LOW MEAN TEMPERATURE.

Noon.	1ʰ. p.m.	2ʰ. p.m.	3ʰ. p.m.	4ʰ. p.m.	5ʰ. p.m.	6ʰ. p.m.	7ʰ. p.m.	8ʰ. p.m.	9ʰ. p.m.	10ʰ. p.m.	11ʰ. p.m.	Yearly Means.	Number of Days used in Waves.	Number of Days rejected in Waves.
52·4	52·9	51·8	52·6	51·9	50·8	49·3	48·0	46·7	45·7	45·1	44·6	47·8	142	19
51·9	52·4	52·5	52·3	51·5	50·4	49·4	48·3	47·1	46·3	45·4	44·8	47·6	168	6
54·4	55·2	55·4	55·3	54·6	53·2	51·6	50·0	48·5	47·3	46·6	46·0	49·1	200	1
50·9	51·8	51·9	51·6	50·7	49·4	48·0	46·1	44·6	43·6	43·0	42·2	45·4	166	9
54·6	55·1	55·3	54·8	54·2	53·1	51·7	50·4	49·2	48·2	47·6	47·2	50·2	222	16
50·3	51·3	51·7	51·5	50·2	48·9	47·5	45·9	44·7	43·7	43·1	42·9	45·3	178	4
53·9	54·5	54·6	54·2	53·4	52·2	50·7	49·1	47·8	46·8	46·2	45·8	48·6	217	16
48·3	49·1	49·3	48·8	47·7	46·7	45·5	44·3	43·3	42·4	42·0	41·6	43·9	187	6
47·8	48·4	48·8	48·7	47·9	46·5	45·2	44·1	42·9	42·3	41·9	41·6	43·8	95	6
53·1	53·8	53·9	53·5	52·5	51·2	49·9	48·7	47·3	46·4	45·5	44·8	47·9	134	18
51·2	51·9	52·0	51·8	50·9	49·9	48·5	47·2	46·0	45·0	44·4	43·9	46·6	100	19
45·1	45·6	45·7	45·5	44·8	43·7	42·6	41·5	40·7	40·1	39·6	39·3	41·2	231	16
48·7	49·0	49·1	48·9	47·8	47·0	46·0	44·5	43·3	42·5	41·9	41·3	44·3	134	30
46·6	46·9	47·0	46·7	45·8	44·8	44·0	43·2	42·4	41·8	41·5	41·2	42·8	141	33
53·5	54·1	54·4	54·0	52·7	51·2	49·7	48·2	46·7	45·5	44·5	43·7	47·7	123	19
49·2	49·6	49·6	49·1	48·5	47·4	46·3	45·1	44·0	43·2	42·6	42·2	44·5	164	11
52·6	53·1	53·0	52·7	52·1	51·3	50·2	48·6	47·2	46·2	45·6	45·0	47·8	143	3
48·7	49·4	49·4	49·1	48·2	47·4	46·2	44·9	43·9	43·0	42·6	42·2	44·5	179	6
49·5	49·9	50·0	49·7	48·9	48·0	46·9	45·4	44·3	43·5	42·9	42·3	45·0	201	4
51·3	51·3	51·2	50·9	50·4	49·5	48·1	46·6	45·5	44·6	43·6	43·1	45·9	99	2
50·70	51·27	51·38	51·09	50·24	49·13	47·86	46·51	45·31	44·41	43·78	43·29	46·00	163·2	12·2

in each of the YEARS 1849 to 1868, for WAVES of LOW MEAN TEMPERATURE.

Noon.	1ʰ. p.m.	2ʰ. p.m.	3ʰ. p.m.	4ʰ. p.m.	5ʰ. p.m.	6ʰ. p.m.	7ʰ. p.m.	8ʰ. p.m.	9ʰ. p.m.	10ʰ. p.m.	11ʰ. p.m.	Yearly Means.	Number of Days used in Waves.	Number of Days rejected in Waves.
46·6	46·8	46·9	46·6	46·4	45·8	45·0	44·2	43·5	43·0	42·7	42·4	44·1	138	21
47·7	47·9	48·1	48·0	47·6	47·0	46·5	45·8	45·0	44·4	43·8	43·3	45·1	168	6
49·1	49·6	49·7	49·6	49·2	48·4	47·5	46·6	45·6	44·7	44·2	43·8	45·7	200	1
45·7	46·1	46·1	46·0	45·3	44·5	43·4	42·4	41·5	40·9	40·5	40·1	42·1	166	9
50·1	50·2	50·3	50·1	49·7	49·2	48·5	47·7	46·9	46·1	45·8	45·5	47·3	222	16
45·9	46·6	46·7	46·7	46·0	45·4	44·5	43·6	42·8	42·2	41·9	41·7	43·0	178	4
49·2	49·4	49·7	49·3	49·0	48·3	47·2	46·3	45·5	44·6	44·3	44·0	46·0	217	16
44·4	44·8	45·0	44·8	44·1	43·5	42·8	42·1	41·5	41·0	40·7	40·4	41·7	187	6
44·5	45·0	45·1	45·0	44·7	43·8	43·0	42·2	41·5	41·1	40·8	40·6	41·9	95	6
47·4	47·8	47·8	47·7	47·1	46·6	45·8	45·1	44·3	43·9	43·5	43·0	44·7	134	18
46·5	46·9	47·1	47·0	46·5	46·0	45·1	44·4	43·8	43·2	42·8	42·5	44·0	100	19
41·7	41·9	41·9	41·8	41·5	40·9	40·2	39·0	38·6	38·2	38·0	39·2	42·4	231	16
43·9	44·1	44·1	44·0	43·3	42·6	41·8	41·0	40·2	39·6	39·2	38·9	40·8	130	26
43·6	43·9	43·6	43·3	43·7	42·2	41·8	41·4	40·9	40·6	40·5	40·3	41·0	131	43
47·9	48·4	48·4	48·2	47·5	46·7	45·8	45·0	44·0	43·2	42·6	42·0	44·6	121	21
44·1	44·2	44·1	44·0	43·5	42·9	42·4	41·7	41·2	40·7	40·4	40·2	41·5	164	11
47·5	47·7	47·8	47·4	47·4	46·8	46·3	45·5	44·3	41·4	41·2	40·9	43·2	142	3
44·3	45·4	45·4	45·3	44·8	44·2	43·6	42·8	42·2	41·4	41·0	41·2	42·5	201	4
46·0	46·1	46·1	45·7	45·3	44·8	43·9	43·1	42·5	42·0	41·6	41·2	42·8	99	2
46·09	46·39	46·44	46·29	45·79	45·17	44·41	43·64	42·94	42·38	42·00	41·68	43·26	161·2	12·7

TABLE LXXXIII.—LIST of WAVES of HIGH and LOW MEAN ATMOSPHERIC PRESSURE during the Period 1849 to 1868.

Days or groups of days in this Table marked † have been omitted in the reductions referring to the Temperature of the Air only, and those marked ‡ in the reductions referring to the Temperature of Evaporation only.

Limits of Waves of High Atmospheric Pressure.	Days omitted in the Reductions.	Limits of Waves of Low Atmospheric Pressure.	Days omitted in the Reductions.	Limits of Waves of High Atmospheric Pressure.	Days omitted in the Reductions.	Limits of Waves of Low Atmospheric Pressure.	Days omitted in the Reductions.
1849.				**1851 continued.**			
Jan. 6 to Jan. 7		Jan. 3 to Jan. 5	Jan. 3 to 5.	Mar. 31 to Apr. 19	May 27.	Apr. 20 to May 11	
Jan. 15 to Jan. 23		Jan. 8 to Jan. 14		May 12 to Jun. 2		Jun. 3 to Jun. 13	
Jan. 30 to Feb. 19	Feb. 15, 19.	Jan. 26 to Jan. 29		Jun. 14 to Jul. 7		Jul. 8 to Jul. 29	
Mar. 2 to Mar. 6	Mar. 6.	Feb. 20 to Mar. 1	Feb. 20 to 22.	Jul. 30 to Aug. 22		Aug. 23 to Aug. 29	
Mar. 10 to Mar. 24		Mar. 7 to Mar. 9		Aug. 30 to Sep. 24		Sep. 25 to Oct. 7	
Apr. 29 to May 2		Mar. 25 to Apr. 28	Apr. 3‡, 13,	Oct. 8 to Oct. 14		Oct. 15 to Oct. 16	
May 7 to May 13			19‡, 21‡,	Oct. 17 to Oct. 28		Oct. 29 to Nov. 10	
May 23 to Jun. 8	May 24.		22.	Nov. 11 to Nov. 23		Nov. 24 to Nov. 26	
Jun. 12 to Jun. 14		May 3 to May 6	May 6.	Nov. 27 to Dec. 20		Dec. 21 to Dec. 22	
Jun. 17 to Jul. 2	July 1‡, 2‡.	May 14 to May 22	May 13‡.	Dec. 23 to Dec. 31			
Jul. 6 to Jul. 16	July 7, 8, 9,	Jun. 9 to Jun. 11					
	15, 16.	Jun. 15 to Jun. 16					
Aug. 1 to Aug. 7	Aug. 1, 5, 6.	Jul. 3 to Jul. 5	Jul. 3 to 5‡.		**1852.**		
Aug. 18 to Aug. 26	Aug. 18, 23‡.	Jul. 17 to Jul. 31	Jul. 28 to 30.				
Sep. 4 to Sep. 8		Aug. 8 to Aug. 17	Aug. 9, 17.				
Sep. 14 to Sep. 22		Aug. 27 to Sep. 3	Sep. 1.	Jan. 17 to Jan. 19		Jan. 1 to Jan. 16	
Oct. 14 to Oct. 30	Oct. 29, 30.	Sep. 9 to Sep. 13		Jan. 23 to Jan. 26		Jan. 20 to Jan. 24	
Nov. 7 to Nov. 12		Sep. 25 to Oct. 13	Sep. 28.	Feb. 2 to Feb. 7		Jan. 27 to Feb. 1	
Nov. 16 to Nov. 22		Oct. 31 to Nov. 6	Oct. 31,	Feb. 11 to Feb. 16	Feb. 24 to 27.	Feb. 8 to Feb. 10	
Nov. 26 to Dec. 1	Nov. 28 to Dec. 1.		Nov. 1.	Feb. 20 to Feb. 27		Feb. 17 to Feb. 19	Feb. 28 to Mar. 2.
Dec. 9 to Dec. 12	Dec. 9, 10.	Nov. 13 to Nov. 15		Mar. 3 to Mar. 31		Feb. 28 to Mar. 2	
Dec. 19 to Dec. 26		Nov. 23 to Nov. 25		Apr. 1 to Apr. 21		Mar. 26 to Mar. 31	
Dec. 30 to Jan. 3		Dec. 2 to Dec. 8	Dec. 2 to 8.	Apr. 25 to Apr. 28		Apr. 22 to Apr. 24	
		Dec. 13 to Dec. 18		May 2 to May 11		Apr. 29 to May 1	
		Dec. 27 to Dec. 29		May 20 to May 25		May 12 to May 19	
1850.				Jul. 1 to Jul. 14	Jul. 4 to 9,	May 26 to Jun. 30	
					11, 12.	Jul. 15 to Jul. 18	
Jan. 7 to Jan. 13		Jan. 4 to Jan. 6		Jul. 19 to Aug. 1		Aug. 2 to Aug. 19	
Jan. 20 to Jan. 31		Jan. 14 to Jan. 19		Aug. 20 to Sep. 4		Sep. 5 to Sep. 21	Sep. 27.
Feb. 13 to Mar. 22		Feb. 1 to Feb. 12		Oct. 7 to Oct. 21	Oct. 17, 21.	Sep. 27 to Oct. 6	
Mar. 28 to Mar. 29	Apr. 28, 29.	Mar. 23 to Mar. 27	Mar. 31,	Nov. 7 to Nov. 10		Oct. 22 to Nov. 6	
Apr. 22 to May 3		Mar. 30 to Apr. 21	Apr. 1.	Nov. 30 to Dec. 5	Dec. 5.	Nov. 11 to Nov. 29	Dec. 6.
May 10 to May 17		May 4 to May 9		Dec. 18 to Dec. 21	Dec. 20, 21.	Dec. 6 to Dec. 17	Dec. 27 to Jan. 10.
May 28 to Jun. 4		May 18 to May 27				Dec. 22 to Jan. 22	
Jun. 8 to Jun. 10	Jun. 16.	Jun. 5 to Jun. 7					
Jun. 16 to Jun. 27		Jun. 11 to Jun. 15	Jun. 15.		**1853.**		
Jul. 3 to Jul. 22		Jun. 28 to Jul. 2					
Jul. 30 to Aug. 3		Jul. 23 to Jul. 29		Jan. 23 to Jan. 24		Jan. 25 to Jan. 30	
Aug. 14 to Aug. 17		Aug. 4 to Aug. 13		Jan. 31 to Feb. 2		Feb. 3 to Mar. 8	Feb. 28, Mar. 2 to 7.
Aug. 23 to Sep. 18	Sep. 13, 14.	Aug. 18 to Aug. 22		Mar. 9 to Mar. 11			
Oct. 9 to Oct. 22		Sep. 19 to Oct. 8		Mar. 18 to Mar. 20		Mar. 12 to Mar. 17	
Oct. 31 to Nov. 17		Oct. 23 to Oct. 30		Mar. 26 to Mar. 29	Mar. 26 to 29.	Mar. 21 to Mar. 25	
Nov. 28 to Dec. 12		Nov. 18 to Nov. 27		Apr. 5 to Apr. 19	Apr. 5 to 19.	Mar. 30 to Apr. 4	Mar. 30 to Apr. 4.
Dec. 20 to Dec. 29		Dec. 13 to Dec. 19		May 4 to May 6			
		Dec. 30 to Jan. 8		May 10 to May 14		Apr. 20 to May 3	Apr. 20.
				May 18 to May 24		May 7 to May 9	
				May 30 to Jun. 9		May 15 to May 17	
1851.				Jun. 14 to Jun. 30		May 25 to May 29	
				Jul. 3 to Jul. 8		Jun. 10 to Jun. 13	
Jan. 9 to Jan. 12		Jan. 13 to Jan. 21		Jul. 31 to Aug. 15		Jun. 19 to Jul. 1	
Jan. 22 to Jan. 27		Jan. 28 to Feb. 5		Sep. 3 to Sep. 7		Jul. 13 to Jul. 30	Jul. 29, 30.
Feb. 6 to Feb. 18		Feb. 19 to Feb. 25		Sep. 17 to Sep. 21		Aug. 16 to Sep. 2	
Feb. 26 to Mar. 4		Mar. 5 to Mar. 30		Sep. 27 to Oct. 4		Sep. 8 to Sep. 16	
				Oct. 22 to Oct. 24		Sep. 22 to Sep. 26	

TABLE LXXXIII.—List of Waves of High and Low Mean Atmospheric Pressure.—*continued.*

Left side

Limits of Waves of High Atmospheric Pressure.	Days omitted in the Reductions.	Limits of Waves of Low Atmospheric Pressure.	Days omitted in the Reductions.
1853 continued.			
Oct. 29 to Nov. 12		Oct. 5 to Oct. 21	
Nov. 17 to Dec. 11	Nov. 25,	Oct. 25 to Oct. 28	
Dec. 21 to Dec. 29	Dec. 8.	Nov. 13 to Nov. 16	
		Dec. 12 to Dec. 20	Dec. 17 to 19.
		Dec. 30 to Jan. 13	
1854.			
Jan. 16 to Feb. 16		Feb. 17 to Feb. 20	
Feb. 21 to Apr. 19		Apr. 20 to Apr. 22	
Apr. 23 to Apr. 26		Apr. 27 to May 9	
May 10 to May 20		May 21 to Jun. 3	
Jun. 4 to Jun. 9		Jun. 10 to Jun. 20	Jun. 10 to 12.
Jun. 21 to Jun. 24		Jun. 25 to Jul. 15	
Jul. 16 to Jul. 30		Jul. 31 to Aug. 3	
Aug. 4 to Aug. 12		Aug. 13 to Aug. 16	
Aug. 17 to Sep. 11	Aug. 19. 20,	Sep. 12 to Sep. 17	
	Sep. 7⅞, 8,	Oct. 4 to Oct. 6	
Sep. 18 to Oct. 5	Sep. 21, 22.	Oct. 17 to Oct. 26	
Oct. 7 to Oct. 16		Nov. 14 to Nov. 18	
Oct. 27 to Nov. 13		Nov. 21 to Dec. 1	
Nov. 19 to Nov. 20		Dec. 5 to Dec. 9	
Dec. 2 to Dec. 4		Dec. 16 to Dec. 27	Dec. 17 to 20.
Dec. 10 to Dec. 15			
Dec. 28 to Jan. 28			
1855.			
Mar. 28 to Apr. 2		Jan. 29 to Mar. 27	
Apr. 5 to Apr. 8		Apr. 3 to Apr. 4	
Apr. 14 to May 2		Apr. 9 to Apr. 13	
May 17 to May 19		May 3 to May 16	May 15, 16.
Jun. 8 to Jun. 12		May 20 to Jun. 7	May 24 to 27, 29, 30, Jun. 2.
Jun. 17 to Jul. 7	Jun. 19, Jul. 5 to 7.	Jun. 13 to Jul. 20	Jul. 12, 13, 16, 20.
Jul. 21 to Jul. 23	Jul. 21 to 23.	Jul. 24 to Aug. 9	Aug. 5 to 7.
Aug. 10 to Aug. 18	Aug. 18.	Aug. 19 to Aug. 24	Aug. 19.
Aug. 25 to Sep. 27	Aug. 30, Sep. 6.	Sep. 28 to Oct. 17	
Oct. 18 to Oct. 24		Oct. 25 to Nov. 3	Nov. 1 to 3.
Nov. 4 to Nov. 6		Nov. 7 to Nov. 10	
Nov. 11 to Dec. 3		Dec. 4 to Dec. 8	
Dec. 9 to Dec. 20		Dec. 21 to Dec. 29	
Dec. 30 to Dec. 31			
1856.			
Jan. 11 to Jan. 16		Jan. 1 to Jan. 10	
Jan. 31 to Feb. 10		Jan. 17 to Jan. 30	
Feb. 21 to Mar. 16		Feb. 11 to Feb. 20	
Mar. 20 to Apr. 1		Mar. 17 to Mar. 19	
Apr. 15 to Apr. 23		Apr. 2 to Apr. 14	
May 2 to May 5		Apr. 24 to May 1	Apr. 30, May 1.
May 8 to May 10		May 6 to May 7	
Jun. 3 to Jun. 11	Jun. 5, 6.		

Right side

Limits of Waves of High Atmospheric Pressure.	Days omitted in the Reductions.	Limits of Waves of Low Atmospheric Pressure.	Days omitted in the Reductions.
1856 continued.			
Jun. 21 to Jul. 6	Jun. 26, 27.	May 11 to Jun. 2	May 11, 12.
Jul. 17 to Jul. 21	Jul. 21.	Jun. 12 to Jun. 20	Jun. 15 to 18.
Jul. 26 to Aug. 7	Aug. 3, 4.	Jul. 7 to Jul. 16	
Aug. 12 to Aug. 15		Jul. 22 to Jul. 25	
Sep. 2 to Sep. 4		Aug. 8 to Aug. 11	
Sep. 11 to Sep. 16		Aug. 16 to Sep. 1	
Oct. 5 to Nov. 9	Oct. 19 to 21.	Sep. 5 to Sep. 10	
Nov. 14 to Nov. 25		Sep. 17 to Oct. 4	
Dec. 1 to Dec. 4		Nov. 10 to Nov. 13	
Dec. 15 to Dec. 23		Nov. 26 to Nov. 30	
Dec. 29 to Jan. 1		Dec. 5 to Dec. 14	Dec. 8, 9.
		Dec. 24 to Dec. 28	
1857.			
Jan. 5 to Jan. 9		Jan. 2 to Jan. 4	
Jan. 14 to Jan. 19		Jan. 10 to Jan. 13	
Feb. 4 to Feb. 6	Feb. 4 to 6.	Jan. 20 to Feb. 3	Feb. 3.
Feb. 11 to Mar. 1		Feb. 7 to Feb. 10	
Apr. 17 to May 8		Mar. 6 to Apr. 16	
May 12 to May 19	May 17.	May 9 to May 11	May 9 to 11.
May 29 to Jun. 6	Jun. 1, 2, 5, 6.	May 20 to May 28	May 24.
Jun. 12 to Jun. 20	Jun. 19, 20.	Jun. 7 to Jun. 11	
Jul. 11 to Aug. 4	Jul. 18, 19, 22, 23.	Jun. 21 to Jul. 10	Jun. 28, Jul. 1.
Aug. 10 to Aug. 12		Aug. 5 to Aug. 9	
Aug. 17 to Aug. 30		Aug. 13 to Aug. 16	
Sep. 14 to Oct. 3		Aug. 31 to Sep. 13	
Oct. 11 to Oct. 17		Oct. 4 to Oct. 10	Oct. 9.
Oct. 23 to Nov. 1	Oct. 25, 27, 28.	Oct. 18 to Oct. 22	Nov. 3.
Nov. 6 to Nov. 9		Nov. 2 to Nov. 5	
Nov. 28 to Jan. 31	Jan. 5.	Nov. 23 to Nov. 27	
1858.			
Feb. 5 to Feb. 19	Feb. 7 to 10.	Feb. 1 to Feb. 4	Feb. 2, 3.
Feb. 24 to Feb. 26	Feb. 24 to 26.	Feb. 20 to Feb. 25	
Mar. 16 to Mar. 29		Feb. 27 to Mar. 15	Mar. 11, 12.
Apr. 11 to Apr. 28	Apr. 23 to 26.	Mar. 30 to Apr. 10	
May 5 to May 11		Apr. 29 to May 1	Apr. 29 to May 1.
May 17 to May 20		May 12 to May 16	
May 27 to Jul. 1	May 29 to Jun. 8, 9, 12 to 14, 17, 18.	May 21 to May 26	May 24.
Jul. 11 to Jul. 19	Aug. 2, 3.	Jul. 5 to Jul. 10	Jul. 8, 9.
Jul. 28 to Aug. 16		Jul. 20 to Jul. 27	
Aug. 23 to Aug. 26		Aug. 17 to Aug. 22	
Sep. 11 to Sep. 21		Sep. 22 to Sep. 23	
Sep. 24 to Oct. 6		Oct. 7 to Oct. 11	
Oct. 12 to Oct. 15		Oct. 16 to Oct. 20	
Oct. 21 to Nov. 12		Nov. 13 to Nov. 15	
Nov. 19 to Nov. 21		Nov. 24 to Dec. 2	
Dec. 3 to Dec. 17		Dec. 18 to Dec. 29	
Dec. 30 to Jan. 22			

TABLE LXXXIII.—LIST of WAVES of HIGH and LOW MEAN ATMOSPHERIC PRESSURE—*continued.*

Limits of Waves of High Atmospheric Pressure.	Days omitted in the Reductions.	Limits of Waves of Low Atmospheric Pressure.	Days omitted in the Reductions.
1859.			
Feb. 13 to Mar. 10		Jan. 23 to Feb. 12	
Mar. 19 to Mar. 25		Mar. 11 to Mar. 18	
Mar. 31 to Apr. 7	Apr. 6, 7.	Mar. 26 to Mar. 30	
May 5 to May 16		Apr. 8 to May 4	
May 21 to May 26	May 21 to 26.	May 17 to May 20	
Jun. 17 to Jul. 17		May 27 to Jun. 16	May 27 to 29, 31, June 1.
Jul. 24 to Aug. 23			
Sep. 10 to Sep. 12		Jul. 18 to Jul. 23	
Oct. 1 to Oct. 8	Oct. 3 to 5.	Aug. 24 to Sep. 9	
Nov. 9 to Nov. 28	Nov. 15 to 23.	Sep. 13 to Sep. 30	Sep. 14, 19, 20.
Dec. 2 to Dec. 3	Dec. 2, 3.		
Dec. 7 to Dec. 15	Dec. 7, 8.	Oct. 9 to Nov. 8	Oct. 13, 14, 21, 22.
		Nov. 29 to Dec. 1	Dec. 1.
		Dec. 4 to Dec. 6	Dec. 4 to 6.
		Dec. 16 to Jan. 6	Dec. 31, Jan. 1.
1860.			
Jan. 7 to Jan. 17		Jan. 18 to Feb. 1	
Feb. 2 to Feb. 18		Feb. 19 to Feb. 21	
Feb. 22 to Feb. 25		Feb. 26 to Feb. 28	
Feb. 29 to Mar. 9		Mar. 10 to Mar. 15	
Mar. 16 to Mar. 19		Mar. 20 to Apr. 10	Mar. 31, Apr. 1.
Apr. 11 to Apr. 19	Apr. 19.		
Apr. 25 to May 6	Apr. 28 to May 2, May 5.	Apr. 20 to Apr. 24	Apr. 20.
		May 7 to May 19	May 7 to 12, 17, 18.
May 20 to May 24		May 25 to Jun. 29	May 25, 26, Jun. 11 to 13.
Jun. 30 to Jul. 12			
Jul. 29 to Aug. 2			
Sep. 3 to Sep. 12	Sep. 3.	Jul. 13 to Jul. 28	Jul. 15, 16.
Sep. 29 to Oct. 10		Aug. 3 to Sep. 2	Aug. 7, Sep. 2.
Oct. 20 to Nov. 10			
Nov. 18 to Nov. 20		Sep. 13 to Sep. 28	
Dec. 12 to Dec. 15		Oct. 11 to Oct. 19	
		Nov. 11 to Nov. 17	
		Nov. 21 to Dec. 11	
		Dec. 16 to Jan. 1	Dec. 24, 25, 28 to 31.
1861.			
Jan. 2 to Feb. 4	Jan. 4, 8 to 16, 19, 20.	Feb. 5 to Feb. 24	
		Feb. 28 to Mar. 3	
Feb. 25 to Feb. 27		Mar. 10 to Mar. 13	
Mar. 4 to Mar. 9		Mar. 17 to Apr. 4	
Mar. 14 to Mar. 16		May 8 to May 12	
Apr. 5 to May 7	Apr. 12 ‡, 14 ‡.	Jun. 7 to Jun. 10	
		Jun. 20 to Jul. 27	Jul. 14 to 17, 18 to 20‡, 21 to 24, 25‡, 26‡, 27.
May 13 to Jun. 6	May 30 to June 2.		
Jun. 11 to Jun. 19			
Jul. 28 to Sep. 1	Jul. 28 to Aug. 2, Aug. 18, 19 ‡, 20, 21, 24, 25, Aug. 27 to Sep. 1.	Sep. 2 to Sep. 16	Sep. 2‡, 10, 11.
		Sep. 20 to Oct. 1	Sep. 20 to 22, Oct. 1.
		Oct. 31 to Nov. 16	
		Nov. 21 to Nov. 27	
1861 *continued.*			
Sep. 17 to Sep. 19	Sep. 19.	Dec. 5 to Dec. 13	
Oct. 2 to Oct. 30	Oct. 2 to 6, 8 to 11, 23 to 29.		
Nov. 17 to Nov. 20			
Nov. 28 to Dec. 4			
Dec. 14 to Jan. 7	Dec. 25 to 27.		
1862.			
Jan. 15 to Jan. 18	Jan. 15 to 18.	Jan. 8 to Jan. 14	Jan. 8, 9.
Jan. 26 to Jan. 27		Jan. 19 to Jan. 25	Jan. 19.
Feb. 1 to Feb. 13	Feb. 1 to 3, 11.	Jan. 28 to Jan. 31	
		Feb. 16 to Feb. 22	
Feb. 23 to Feb. 28		Mar. 1 to Apr. 3	Mar. 1, 2, 11, 12, 19 to 26, 31.
Apr. 4 to Apr. 16	Apr. 11.		
Apr. 27 to May 6	Apr. 27.		
May 13 to May 19	May 13, 18‡, 19.	Apr. 17 to Apr. 26	Apr. 24 to 26.
		May 7 to May 12	May 10 to 12.
May 24 to May 26		May 20 to May 23	May 20.
Jun. 1 to Jun. 4		May 27 to May 31	May 31‡.
Jun. 16 to Jun. 19	Jun. 16.	Jun. 5 to Jun. 15	Jun. 6, 7, 15.
Jul. 18 to Aug. 4	Jul. 18, 19 to 23‡, 29 to 31‡.	Jun. 20 to Jul. 17	July 1‡, 2‡, 13, 14, 17.
		Aug. 5 to Aug. 9	
Aug. 10 to Aug. 13		Aug. 14 to Aug. 17	
Aug. 18 to Aug. 31	Aug. 30, 31.	Sep. 1 to Sep. 15	Sep. 1 to 4, 7, 8, 10 to 15.
Sep. 16 to Oct. 11	Sep. 16 to 28, 29†, Oct. 1.	Oct. 12 to Nov. 1	Oct. 19.
Nov. 2 to Nov. 8		Nov. 9 to Nov. 11	Nov. 9 to 11.
Nov. 12 to Nov. 22	Nov. 12 to 14.	Nov. 23 to Dec. 4	
Dec. 3 to Dec. 18		Dec. 19 to Dec. 21	
Dec. 22 to Dec. 27		Dec. 28 to Jan. 10	
1863.			
Jan. 11 to Jan. 17		Jan. 18 to Jan. 24	
Jan. 25 to Jan. 28		Jan. 29 to Feb. 3	
Feb. 4 to Feb. 28		Mar. 1 to Mar. 16	
Mar. 17 to Apr. 4		Apr. 5 to Apr. 11	
Apr. 12 to Apr. 19		Apr. 20 to Apr. 22	
Apr. 23 to May 2	Apr. 25, May 1‡, 2‡.	May 3 to May 5	May 3 to 5‡.
		May 12 to May 17	
May 6 to May 11	May 9 to 11.	Jun. 5 to Jun. 13	
May 18 to Jun. 4	May 27 to 29.	Jun. 17 to Jun. 20	
Jun. 14 to Jun. 16		Jul. 18 to Jul. 23	Jul. 22, 23.
Jun. 21 to Jul. 17	Jul. 14 to 17.	Aug. 13 to Aug. 19	Aug. 15 to 19.
Jul. 24 to Aug. 14	Jul. 24 to 30, Aug. 1, 2, 14.	Aug. 23 to Sep. 10	Sep. 1, 2, 6.
		Sep. 19 to Sep. 25	Sep. 24.
		Sep. 30 to Oct. 2	
Aug. 20 to Aug. 22		Oct. 7 to Oct. 15	Oct. 10, 11.
Sep. 11 to Sep. 18		Oct. 28 to Nov. 3	
Sep. 26 to Sep. 29		Nov. 10 to Nov. 12	
Oct. 3 to Oct. 6	Oct. 6.	Dec. 1 to Dec. 3	
Oct. 16 to Oct. 27			
Nov. 4 to Nov. 9			
Nov. 13 to Nov. 30	Nov. 13.		
Dec. 4 to Feb. 6	Jan. 28 to 30.		

TABLE LXXXIII.—LIST of WAVES of HIGH and LOW MEAN ATMOSPHERIC PRESSURE—*concluded.*

Limits of Waves of High Atmospheric Pressure.	Days omitted in the Reductions.	Limits of Waves of Low Atmospheric Pressure.	Days omitted in the Reductions.	Limits of Waves of High Atmospheric Pressure.	Days omitted in the Reductions.	Limits of Waves of Low Atmospheric Pressure.	Days omitted in the Reductions.
1864.				**1866** *continued.*			
Feb. 14 to Feb. 19		Feb. 7 to Feb. 13	Feb. 9.	Nov. 14 to Nov. 30		Dec. 1 to Dec. 7	
Mar. 12 to Mar. 17		Feb. 20 to Mar. 11	Mar. 5.	Dec. 8 to Dec. 11		Dec. 12 to Dec. 16	
Apr. 2 to Apr. 13		Mar. 18 to Apr. 1		Dec. 17 to Dec. 25		Dec. 26 to Jan. 25	
Apr. 17 to May 1	Apr. 17.	Apr. 14 to Apr. 16					
May 13 to May 29	May 20, 23, 26.	May 2 to May 12				**1867.**	
		May 30 to Jun. 16	Jun. 12 to 14.				
Jun. 17 to Jun. 29	Jun. 20, 21.	Jun. 30 to Jul. 3	Jul. 1.				
Jul. 4 to Jul. 20	Jul. 5, 6.	Jul. 21 to Jul. 28					
Jul. 29 to Aug. 17		Aug. 18 to Aug. 23		Jan. 26 to Feb. 3		Feb. 4 to Feb. 8	
Aug. 24 to Aug. 29		Aug. 30 to Sep. 22	Sep. 10, 11.	Feb. 9 to Mar. 5	Feb. 12 to 16.	Mar. 6 to Mar. 30	
Sep. 23 to Oct. 15		Oct. 16 to Oct. 29		Mar. 31 to Apr. 6		Apr. 7 to Apr. 30	
Oct. 30 to Nov. 10		Nov. 11 to Nov. 28		May 1 to May 9	May 6 to 9.	May 10 to May 14	May 10, 11.
Nov. 29 to Dec. 6		Dec. 7 to Dec. 21		May 15 to May 18		May 19 to May 21	May 19.
Dec. 22 to Dec. 29		Dec. 30 to Jan. 3		May 22 to May 25		May 26 to May 29	
				May 30 to Jun. 1	May 30 to Jun. 1.	Jun. 2 to Jun. 7	Jun. 2.
		1865.		Jun. 8 to Jun. 30	Jun. 8, 9, 23, 24.	Jul. 1 to Jul. 4	
				Jul. 5 to Jul. 11		Aug. 6 to Aug. 9	
Jan. 4 to Jan. 7		Jan. 8 to Feb. 7		Jul. 27 to Aug. 5		Aug. 15 to Aug. 17	
Feb. 8 to Feb. 14		Feb. 15 to Feb. 19		Aug. 10 to Aug. 14		Aug. 31 to Sep. 15	
Feb. 20 to Feb. 23		Feb. 24 to Mar. 26	Mar. 22, 23.	Aug. 18 to Aug. 30		Oct. 7 to Oct. 8	
Mar. 27 to May 2		May 3 to May 16		Sep. 16 to Oct. 6		Oct. 12 to Oct. 19	
May 17 to May 26		May 27 to Jun. 2		Oct. 10 to Oct. 11		Nov. 14 to Nov. 16	
Jun. 3 to Jun. 28		Jun. 29 to Jul. 1		Oct. 20 to Oct. 29		Nov. 30 to Dec. 2	
Jul. 2 to Jul. 4		Jul. 5 to Jul. 23	Jul. 18, 19.	Nov. 17 to Nov. 29		Dec. 14 to Dec. 22	
Jul. 24 to Jul. 30		Jul. 31 to Aug. 6		Dec. 3 to Dec. 13			
Aug. 4 to Aug. 6		Aug. 7 to Aug. 24		Dec. 23 to Jan. 16			
Aug. 25 to Oct. 7		Oct. 8 to Nov. 1					
Nov. 2 to Nov. 18	Nov. 3.	Nov. 19 to Dec. 5				**1868.**	
Dec. 6 to Dec. 27	Dec. 17, 18.	Dec. 28 to Jan. 14					
				Jan. 24 to Jan. 30		Jan. 17 to Jan. 23	
		1866.		Feb. 3 to Feb. 18		Jan. 31 to Feb. 6	
				Feb. 23 to Feb. 27		Feb. 19 to Feb. 22	Feb. 21, 22.
Jan. 15 to Jan. 18		Jan. 19 to Jan. 22		Mar. 2 to Mar. 4		Feb. 28 to Mar. 1	
Jan. 23 to Jan. 30		Jan. 31 to Feb. 17		Mar. 13 to Apr. 6		Mar. 5 to Mar. 12	
Feb. 18 to Feb. 22	Feb. 22.	Feb. 23 to Mar. 25	Feb. 25 to Mar. 1.	Apr. 10 to Apr. 17		Apr. 7 to Apr. 9	
Mar. 26 to Mar. 30		Mar. 31 to Apr. 4		Apr. 25 to May 7	May 6.	Apr. 18 to Apr. 24	
Apr. 5 to Apr. 9		Apr. 10 to Apr. 13		May 12 to May 21		May 8 to May 11	
Apr. 14 to Apr. 26		Apr. 27 to May 8		May 26 to Jun. 20		May 22 to May 25	
May 5 to May 8		May 9 to May 12		Jun. 24 to Aug. 4		Jun. 21 to Jun. 23	
May 13 to May 23		May 24 to Jun. 11		Jul. 30 to Aug. 4		Jul. 27 to Jul. 29	
Jun. 6 to Jun. 11		Jun. 12 to Jun. 22		Aug. 25 to Sep. 10		Aug. 5 to Aug. 24	
Jun. 23 to Jun. 26		Jun. 27 to Jul. 6		Oct. 5 to Oct. 15		Sep. 11 to Oct. 4	
Jul. 7 to Jul. 26		July 27 to Aug. 21		Oct. 26 to Nov. 2		Oct. 16 to Oct. 25	
Aug. 22 to Aug. 25	Oct. 29, 30, Nov. 7.	Aug. 26 to Sep. 24		Nov. 9 to Nov. 20	Nov. 9.	Nov. 3 to Nov. 8	
Sep. 25 to Nov. 7		Nov. 8 to Nov. 13		Nov. 27 to Nov. 29		Nov. 21 to Nov. 26	
						Nov. 30 to Jun. 5	Dec. 8, 9.

TABLE LXXXIV.—Mean Temperature of the Air at every Hour of the Day

Year.	Number of Waves treated in each Year.	Midnight.	1ʰ. a.m.	2ʰ. a.m.	3ʰ. a.m.	4ʰ. a.m.	5ʰ. a.m.	6ʰ. a.m.	7ʰ. a.m.	8ʰ. a.m.	9ʰ. a.m.	10ʰ. a.m.	11ʰ. a.m.
1849	22	45·4	45·0	44·7	44·4	44·3	44·3	45·2	46·6	48·0	49·8	51·3	52·6
1850	17	45·2	44·8	44·4	44·2	44·1	44·3	45·4	46·0	48·7	50·7	52·6	53·9
1851	14	44·4	44·1	43·7	43·6	43·3	43·2	43·6	44·5	45·8	47·5	49·3	50·9
1852	18	45·0	44·6	44·0	43·8	43·7	43·6	44·0	45·2	46·7	48·7	51·0	52·8
1853	18	45·6	44·7	44·4	44·1	44·0	44·0	44·6	45·9	47·7	49·6	51·3	52·7
1854	16	45·6	45·3	45·0	44·8	44·5	44·5	45·0	46·2	47·9	50·0	51·9	53·6
1855	13	44·9	44·4	43·9	43·6	43·5	43·3	44·0	45·4	47·1	49·4	51·6	52·8
1856	19	44·5	44·2	43·8	43·4	43·2	43·3	43·9	45·4	47·0	49·1	51·0	52·6
1857	15	48·6	48·2	47·0	47·6	47·4	47·5	48·3	49·7	51·5	53·9	56·0	57·4
1858	16	46·8	46·3	45·8	45·5	45·3	45·3	46·0	47·4	49·4	51·7	53·9	55·7
1859	10	47·1	46·8	46·3	46·1	45·7	45·6	46·2	47·5	49·4	51·8	54·0	55·8
1860	15	42·4	42·1	41·7	41·3	41·5	41·4	41·9	42·9	44·4	46·3	48·1	49·3
1861	13	44·0	43·5	43·0	42·7	42·5	41·6	43·1	44·0	45·5	47·7	49·6	51·5
1862	17	46·5	46·1	45·8	45·6	45·4	43·5	46·3	47·6	49·1	50·8	52·3	53·7
1863	19	47·4	46·9	46·5	46·2	46·0	46·1	46·8	48·2	49·8	51·7	53·2	54·7
1864	13	46·1	45·7	45·3	44·9	44·7	44·7	45·4	46·8	48·6	50·7	52·6	54·4
1865	12	46·8	46·4	46·0	45·8	45·5	45·7	47·0	48·9	50·4	52·6	54·7	56·7
1866	16	46·2	45·8	45·5	45·0	44·8	45·0	45·8	47·4	49·1	50·8	52·5	53·9
1867	17	45·2	44·8	44·5	44·2	43·9	44·0	46·0	46·9	48·5	50·5	52·3	53·7
1868	16	47·1	46·7	46·4	46·2	45·9	46·0	46·7	48·3	50·1	52·3	54·3	55·9
Means	15·8	45·74	45·32	44·93	44·66	44·44	44·49	45·21	46·58	48·23	50·28	52·17	53·74

TABLE LXXXV.—Mean Temperature of Evaporation at every Hour of the Day

Year.	Number of Waves treated in each Year.	Midnight.	1ʰ. a.m.	2ʰ. a.m.	3ʰ. a.m.	4ʰ. a.m.	5ʰ. a.m.	6ʰ. a.m.	7ʰ. a.m.	8ʰ. a.m.	9ʰ. a.m.	10ʰ. a.m.	11ʰ. a.m.
1849	22	43·7	43·4	43·3	43·1	42·9	42·9	43·5	44·4	45·2	46·2	46·9	47·7
1850	17	43·8	43·5	43·2	43·1	43·0	43·1	43·8	44·8	46·0	47·2	48·4	49·1
1851	14	42·6	42·3	42·1	42·0	41·8	41·7	42·0	42·5	43·4	44·6	45·7	46·7
1852	18	43·0	42·7	42·2	42·0	42·0	41·9	42·3	43·1	44·1	45·3	46·7	47·9
1853	18	43·8	43·5	43·2	43·0	42·8	42·8	43·3	44·3	45·4	46·7	47·6	48·7
1854	16	44·2	44·0	43·7	43·6	43·3	43·3	43·6	44·5	45·6	47·0	48·1	49·1
1855	13	43·4	43·1	42·7	42·6	42·3	42·2	42·7	43·8	44·8	46·4	47·6	48·2
1856	19	43·4	43·2	42·9	42·7	42·6	42·6	43·0	44·0	45·0	46·1	47·2	48·1
1857	13	47·7	47·4	47·2	46·9	46·8	46·9	47·4	48·4	49·5	50·9	52·2	53·1
1858	16	45·3	45·0	44·6	44·4	44·2	44·3	44·7	45·7	47·0	48·4	49·6	50·5
1859	10	45·6	45·3	44·9	44·7	44·5	44·3	44·7	45·7	46·9	48·3	49·4	50·3
1860	15	41·2	40·9	40·6	40·4	40·3	40·3	40·7	41·3	42·4	43·8	44·8	45·6
1861	13	43·0	42·6	42·3	42·0	41·8	41·8	42·2	42·8	43·9	45·4	46·6	47·7
1862	17	43·5	43·2	43·0	42·9	44·7	44·8	45·4	46·3	47·1	48·1	49·1	49·7
1863	19	45·8	45·6	45·4	45·2	45·0	45·2	45·6	46·4	47·5	48·5	49·4	50·2
1864	13	43·9	43·7	43·4	43·2	43·0	43·1	43·5	44·4	45·4	46·7	47·6	48·6
1865	12	45·3	45·0	44·8	44·6	44·4	44·4	45·0	46·1	47·3	48·5	49·4	50·5
1866	16	44·8	44·5	44·2	43·9	43·7	43·8	44·4	45·4	46·5	47·6	48·5	49·2
1867	17	43·8	43·5	43·3	43·1	41·9	42·0	43·4	44·4	45·4	46·5	48·0	48·7
1868	16	45·4	45·2	45·0	44·9	44·7	44·8	45·3	46·2	47·2	48·6	49·6	50·4
Means	15·8	44·26	43·98	43·70	43·51	43·34	43·35	43·83	44·73	45·80	47·06	48·12	49·00

in each of the YEARS 1849 to 1868, for WAVES of HIGH MEAN ATMOSPHERIC PRESSURE.

Noon.	1ʰ. p.m.	2ʰ. p.m.	3ʰ. p.m.	4ʰ. p.m.	5ʰ. p.m.	6ʰ. p.m.	7ʰ. p.m.	8ʰ. p.m.	9ʰ. p.m.	10ʰ. p.m.	11ʰ. p.m.	Yearly Means.	Number of Days used in Waves.	Number of Days rejected in Waves.	Mean Reading of the Barometer.
															in.
54·0	54·7	54·8	54·5	53·5	52·2	50·6	49·5	48·0	47·0	46·4	45·9	48·8	174	21	30·017
55·3	55·9	56·3	55·9	55·1	54·1	52·5	50·8	49·2	48·0	47·1	46·5	49·7	208	5	29·987
52·2	52·9	53·0	52·8	51·9	50·7	49·4	48·0	46·9	46·1	45·5	45·0	47·4	210	1	30·002
54·3	55·2	55·3	54·9	53·9	52·2	50·6	49·1	47·7	46·7	46·2	45·6	48·5	150	17	29·971
54·3	55·0	55·0	54·6	53·6	52·6	50·9	49·4	48·0	46·8	46·0	45·5	48·7	136	2	29·938
55·0	55·7	55·9	55·5	54·6	53·4	51·0	50·4	49·0	48·0	47·1	46·6	49·5	247	5	29·997
54·4	55·0	55·5	54·7	53·9	52·6	50·9	49·2	47·8	46·6	45·8	45·2	48·6	141	7	30·003
54·0	54·5	54·6	54·0	53·7	52·3	50·8	49·2	47·8	46·7	46·1	45·6	48·4	182	10	29·970
55·1	59·9	60·1	56·7	58·6	57·2	55·5	53·8	52·3	51·0	50·2	49·5	52·9	235	15	29·988
57·4	58·3	58·4	58·0	56·8	55·2	53·5	51·8	50·3	49·0	48·0	47·4	51·0	199	26	29·977
57·2	58·1	58·5	58·2	57·1	55·5	53·7	51·8	50·1	49·0	48·4	47·7	51·2	139	16	29·095
50·9	51·9	51·9	51·7	50·5	49·3	47·8	46·4	44·9	44·0	43·4	42·9	45·8	133	8	29·987
53·0	53·8	54·1	53·7	51·7	51·5	50·0	48·4	47·2	46·3	45·5	44·8	47·3	164	53	29·989
55·2	55·7	55·8	55·4	54·5	53·4	52·2	50·6	49·3	48·3	47·6	47·1	50·0	134	30	29·938
55·9	56·6	56·9	56·7	55·5	54·1	52·7	51·3	50·1	49·0	48·1	47·5	50·7	243	26	29·961
56·0	56·6	56·7	56·4	55·3	54·1	52·4	50·6	49·0	47·8	47·1	46·3	49·9	155	8	30·001
58·2	58·9	59·1	58·8	57·8	56·7	55·2	53·1	51·2	49·0	48·2	51·8	181	3	30·019
55·3	55·9	56·0	55·7	55·0	54·0	52·8	51·0	49·5	48·4	47·7	47·1	50·0	159	4	29·964
55·0	55·5	55·8	55·5	54·8	53·7	52·1	50·5	49·0	47·8	47·1	46·3	49·4	200	13	29·967
57·2	58·0	58·3	58·0	57·0	55·6	54·0	52·3	50·8	49·6	48·7	48·0	51·4	201	2	29·975
55·19	55·90	56·11	55·76	54·79	53·52	51·98	50·35	48·90	47·79	47·05	46·43	49·56	179·6	13·6	29·983

in each of the YEARS 1849 to 1868, for WAVES of HIGH MEAN ATMOSPHERIC PRESSURE.

Noon.	1ʰ. p.m.	2ʰ. p.m.	3ʰ. p.m.	4ʰ. p.m.	5ʰ. p.m.	6ʰ. p.m.	7ʰ. p.m.	8ʰ. p.m.	9ʰ. p.m.	10ʰ. p.m.	11ʰ. p.m.	Yearly Means.	Number of Days used in Waves.	Number of Days rejected in Waves.	Mean Reading of the Barometer.
															in.
48·5	48·9	49·0	48·9	48·2	47·5	46·6	46·0	45·3	44·8	44·4	44·1	45·6	171	24	30·017
49·9	50·1	50·2	50·0	49·6	49·0	48·2	47·3	46·5	45·6	45·1	44·7	46·5	208	5	29·987
47·6	48·0	48·1	47·9	47·5	46·7	45·9	45·2	44·5	43·9	43·4	43·1	44·6	210	1	30·002
48·8	49·3	49·5	49·2	48·4	47·5	46·5	45·5	44·7	44·0	43·7	43·4	45·1	150	17	29·971
49·4	49·7	49·7	49·4	48·9	48·2	47·3	46·4	45·5	44·7	44·2	43·9	45·9	136	2	29·938
49·8	50·1	50·2	50·0	49·5	48·9	48·2	47·4	46·5	45·9	45·4	45·1	46·5	246	6	29·997
49·0	49·4	49·6	49·2	48·6	47·8	46·8	46·0	45·2	44·5	44·0	43·7	45·6	141	7	30·003
48·8	49·1	49·4	49·2	48·7	47·8	47·1	46·2	45·3	44·8	44·5	44·3	45·8	132	10	29·970
53·7	54·2	54·3	54·0	53·4	52·6	51·6	50·7	49·9	49·1	48·6	48·3	50·2	235	15	29·988
51·3	51·7	51·7	51·5	50·8	50·0	49·0	48·2	47·3	46·7	46·1	45·6	47·8	196	29	29·976
51·0	51·3	51·8	51·6	51·0	50·3	49·2	48·3	47·3	46·7	46·3	45·8	47·7	139	16	29·997
46·4	46·9	47·0	46·9	46·3	45·6	44·6	43·7	42·9	42·3	41·8	41·5	43·5	133	8	29·987
48·6	48·9	49·1	49·0	48·4	47·6	46·9	46·0	45·2	44·7	44·2	43·7	45·2	161	56	29·989
50·6	50·9	50·9	50·6	50·1	49·5	48·9	48·1	47·4	46·8	46·3	45·9	47·6	126	38	29·953
50·8	51·1	51·1	51·0	50·5	49·7	48·9	48·1	47·4	46·7	46·1	45·7	47·8	241	28	29·960
49·3	49·4	49·3	49·1	48·5	47·8	47·0	46·3	45·5	44·9	44·5	44·0	45·9	155	8	30·001
51·2	51·4	51·4	51·3	50·8	50·3	49·9	48·7	47·8	47·2	46·7	46·7	47·8	181	3	30·019
50·0	50·3	50·2	50·1	49·9	49·3	48·4	47·6	46·9	46·3	45·9	45·5	47·0	159	4	29·964
49·4	49·6	49·7	49·5	49·3	48·6	47·9	47·1	46·4	45·7	45·2	44·7	46·2	200	13	29·967
51·0	51·2	51·4	51·2	50·7	50·0	49·2	48·3	47·6	46·9	46·4	46·0	47·8	201	2	29·975
49·76	50·09	50·18	49·98	49·46	48·72	47·89	47·06	46·28	45·61	45·14	44·76	46·48	178·5	14·6	29·983

TABLE LXXXVI.—MEAN TEMPERATURE of the Air at every Hour of the Day

Year	Number of Waves treated in each Year	Midnight	1ʰ. a.m.	2ʰ. a.m.	3ʰ. a.m.	4ʰ. a.m.	5ʰ. a.m.	6ʰ. a.m.	7ʰ. a.m.	8ʰ. a.m.	9ʰ. a.m.	10ʰ. a.m.	11ʰ. a.m.
1849	20	47·1	46·8	46·6	46·5	46·3	46·6	47·2	48·4	49·8	51·5	53·0	53·9
1850	18	47·0	46·7	46·4	46·0	45·8	45·9	46·6	47·6	48·9	50·2	51·7	53·0
1851	13	45·2	45·0	44·6	44·6	44·5	44·6	45·0	45·8	46·9	48·7	49·8	50·8
1852	18	47·2	47·1	46·9	46·7	46·5	46·7	46·9	47·8	48·9	50·4	52·0	53·1
1853	19	44·9	44·7	44·5	44·4	44·3	44·4	45·0	46·1	47·4	48·9	50·2	51·1
1854	15	47·2	46·9	46·6	46·4	46·3	46·5	47·2	48·2	49·7	51·6	53·0	54·4
1855	14	45·9	45·8	45·6	45·5	45·5	45·5	46·0	47·1	48·6	50·1	51·6	52·8
1856	19	46·6	46·3	45·9	45·6	45·5	45·4	45·7	46·8	48·0	49·8	51·3	52·2
1857	13	48·6	48·4	48·1	48·0	47·8	47·7	48·0	49·1	50·3	51·6	53·0	54·2
1858	17	46·2	45·7	45·7	45·5	45·5	45·6	46·2	47·0	48·5	50·0	51·3	52·6
1859	12	47·8	47·7	47·5	47·4	47·3	47·4	47·8	48·5	49·8	51·5	53·0	54·4
1860	15	43·1	42·9	42·7	42·5	42·3	41·3	42·7	43·5	44·6	46·1	47·6	48·8
1861	12	45·4	45·2	45·2	45·1	45·1	45·3	45·6	46·4	47·6	48·9	50·4	51·7
1862	18	47·6	47·4	47·2	47·2	47·1	47·2	47·7	48·3	49·5	50·7	51·9	52·9
1863	17	46·9	46·7	46·4	46·3	46·3	46·5	47·2	48·6	50·2	52·1	53·3	54·4
1864	14	45·0	44·6	44·3	44·0	43·8	43·9	44·4	45·6	47·2	49·0	50·6	52·1
1865	12	47·3	47·0	46·7	46·6	46·5	46·6	47·2	48·2	49·1	50·4	52·2	53·5
1866	16	46·5	46·1	45·9	45·8	45·7	45·8	46·5	47·5	48·6	50·0	51·4	52·7
1867	17	49·6	49·3	49·1	48·9	48·7	48·7	49·3	50·5	51·8	53·0	54·2	55·1
1868	17	47·6	47·2	46·9	46·6	46·5	46·6	47·1	48·3	49·6	51·3	53·0	54·6
Means	15·9	46·64	46·38	46·14	45·98	45·86	45·96	46·46	47·48	48·75	50·29	51·72	52·91

TABLE LXXXVII.—MEAN TEMPERATURE of EVAPORATION at every Hour of the Day

Year	Number of Waves treated in each Year	Midnight	1ʰ. a.m.	2ʰ. a.m.	3ʰ. a.m.	4ʰ. a.m.	5ʰ. a.m.	6ʰ. a.m.	7ʰ. a.m.	8ʰ. a.m.	9ʰ. a.m.	10ʰ. a.m.	11ʰ. a.m.
1849	19	45·2	45·1	44·8	44·6	44·5	44·8	45·3	46·0	46·8	47·7	48·5	49·2
1850	18	45·5	45·3	45·0	44·8	44·6	44·7	45·1	45·7	46·4	47·3	48·2	48·9
1851	13	43·4	43·1	42·9	42·8	42·8	42·9	43·1	43·6	44·4	45·6	46·3	46·9
1852	18	44·8	44·8	44·6	44·5	44·4	44·4	44·7	45·3	45·8	46·7	47·7	48·3
1853	19	43·3	43·2	43·1	43·0	43·0	43·1	43·5	44·3	45·1	46·0	46·8	47·3
1854	15	46·0	45·7	45·5	45·5	45·4	45·4	46·0	46·8	47·7	48·8	49·5	50·3
1855	14	44·6	44·6	44·5	44·3	44·3	44·4	44·8	45·6	46·6	47·7	48·5	49·1
1856	19	45·5	45·3	45·1	44·9	44·7	44·6	44·8	45·3	46·3	47·3	48·0	48·5
1857	13	47·7	47·5	47·3	47·2	47·1	47·1	47·3	48·0	48·8	49·5	50·4	51·0
1858	17	44·5	44·3	44·2	44·1	44·0	44·1	44·4	45·0	45·8	46·8	47·5	48·2
1859	12	46·4	46·3	46·3	46·2	46·1	46·2	46·5	47·0	47·8	48·8	49·6	50·3
1860	13	42·1	41·9	41·7	41·6	41·3	41·3	41·5	42·2	42·9	44·0	44·8	45·5
1861	12	44·4	44·3	44·2	44·2	44·2	44·5	44·7	45·3	45·9	46·8	47·7	48·5
1862	18	46·4	46·2	46·1	46·0	45·9	46·1	46·5	46·9	47·5	48·4	49·1	49·6
1863	16	45·4	45·3	45·2	45·2	45·2	45·4	45·8	46·7	47·8	48·7	49·4	50·0
1864	14	43·6	43·3	43·1	42·9	42·8	42·8	43·1	43·8	44·7	45·7	46·5	47·3
1865	12	46·0	45·7	45·5	45·4	45·3	45·4	45·7	46·2	46·8	47·5	48·5	49·2
1866	16	44·9	44·8	44·7	44·6	44·5	44·6	45·0	45·8	46·5	47·3	48·1	48·8
1867	17	48·3	48·2	48·1	48·0	47·9	47·8	48·2	48·9	49·7	50·5	51·1	51·6
1868	17	45·9	45·6	45·6	45·2	45·2	45·3	45·7	46·4	47·2	48·1	49·1	50·0
Means	15·8	45·20	45·02	44·87	44·75	44·65	44·74	45·09	45·75	46·52	47·46	48·26	48·92

In each of the YEARS 1849 to 1868, for WAVES of LOW MEAN ATMOSPHERIC PRESSURE.

Noon.	1ʰ. p.m.	2ʰ. p.m.	3ʰ. p.m.	4ʰ. p.m.	5ʰ. p.m.	6ʰ. p.m.	7ʰ. p.m.	8ʰ. p.m.	9ʰ. p.m.	10ʰ. p.m.	11ʰ. p.m.	Yearly Means.	Number of Days used in Waves.	Number of Days rejected in Waves.	Mean Reading of the Barometer.
55·1	55·3	55·4	55·2	54·3	53·0	51·6	50·1	48·8	47·8	47·2	46·7	50·2	146	15	29·557
53·9	54·4	54·4	54·2	53·4	52·3	51·1	49·8	48·6	47·7	47·1	46·6	49·4	134	3	29·520
51·8	52·4	52·3	51·5	50·4	49·3	48·1	46·9	46·1	45·5	45·0	44·3	47·5	146	0	29·566
54·0	54·7	54·5	54·2	53·3	52·2	51·1	49·0	48·9	48·0	47·6	47·0	49·8	200	17	29·524
51·9	52·4	52·7	52·2	51·5	50·3	49·0	47·7	46·7	46·0	45·4	45·0	47·8	182	13	29·575
55·4	55·9	55·6	55·2	53·9	52·8	51·6	50·2	49·1	48·2	47·7	47·2	50·3	119	7	29·548
53·7	54·5	54·6	54·3	53·4	52·3	50·9	49·3	48·2	47·2	46·7	46·3	49·2	166	20	29·537
53·4	54·0	54·1	53·5	52·6	51·6	50·5	49·3	48·4	47·7	47·2	46·0	49·1	165	10	29·517
55·0	55·4	55·6	55·1	54·3	52·9	51·6	50·5	49·6	48·8	48·5	48·0	50·8	132	7	29·512
53·6	53·9	53·9	53·4	52·5	51·5	50·3	49·2	48·2	47·5	46·7	46·2	49·0	118	10	29·549
55·3	55·8	55·9	55·7	54·9	53·6	52·4	51·2	49·9	49·0	48·4	47·9	50·8	168	15	29·545
49·6	50·0	50·2	49·9	49·1	48·1	46·9	45·9	45·0	44·3	43·8	43·4	47·9	194	26	29·504
52·8	53·3	53·4	53·2	51·9	50·8	49·8	48·4	47·4	46·7	46·3	45·8	48·4	139	15	29·575
54·0	53·9	54·0	53·7	53·2	52·3	51·3	50·2	49·4	48·7	48·2	47·7	50·1	155	42	29·578
55·6	55·9	56·2	55·8	54·8	53·6	52·4	51·0	49·8	48·9	48·4	47·9	50·6	110	8	29·502
53·3	53·6	54·1	53·8	52·8	51·6	50·2	48·7	47·7	46·9	46·3	45·7	48·5	161	8	29·579
54·5	55·0	54·6	54·6	53·7	52·8	51·6	50·4	49·4	48·6	48·0	47·6	50·1	188	4	29·515
53·8	54·1	54·3	53·8	52·9	52·1	50·8	49·4	48·3	47·4	46·8	46·3	49·3	208	3	29·552
55·9	56·2	56·1	55·9	55·3	54·3	53·0	51·7	50·8	49·9	49·4	49·1	51·9	136	4	29·552
55·9	55·9	55·6	55·2	54·3	53·3	52·0	50·5	49·2	48·2	47·6	47·1	50·4	148	4	29·543
53·93	54·34	54·38	54·02	53·13	52·02	50·81	49·53	48·47	47·65	47·12	46·64	49·44	156·8	11·6	29·543

In each of the YEARS 1849 to 1868, for WAVES of LOW MEAN ATMOSPHERIC PRESSURE.

Noon.	1ʰ. p.m.	2ʰ. p.m.	3ʰ. p.m.	4ʰ. p.m.	5ʰ. p.m.	6ʰ. p.m.	7ʰ. p.m.	8ʰ. p.m.	9ʰ. p.m.	10ʰ. p.m.	11ʰ. p.m.	Yearly Means.	Number of Days used in Waves.	Number of Days rejected in Waves.	Mean Reading of the Barometer.
49·7	49·8	49·8	49·5	49·0	48·3	47·5	46·8	46·0	45·4	45·0	44·7	46·8	139	19	29·555
49·4	49·8	49·7	49·6	49·2	48·6	47·9	47·2	46·4	45·8	45·4	45·0	46·9	154	3	29·510
47·4	47·7	47·7	47·1	46·5	45·8	45·0	44·4	43·9	43·4	43·0	42·5	44·7	146	0	29·566
48·8	49·1	49·0	48·8	48·3	47·5	46·9	46·3	45·7	45·2	44·9	44·6	46·3	200	17	29·524
47·8	48·1	48·2	47·9	47·5	46·7	46·0	45·3	44·6	44·0	43·6	43·3	45·2	182	13	29·575
50·7	51·0	50·8	50·5	49·9	49·4	48·6	47·9	47·2	46·6	46·2	45·9	47·8	119	7	29·548
49·5	49·9	49·9	49·7	49·3	48·6	47·8	46·9	45·4	45·1	44·7	44·7	46·7	166	20	29·537
49·1	49·4	49·5	49·3	48·7	48·2	47·6	47·1	46·5	46·0	45·8	45·7	46·8	165	10	29·517
51·4	51·7	51·6	51·2	50·7	49·8	49·1	48·5	47·9	47·4	47·2	46·9	48·8	132	7	29·512
48·7	48·9	49·1	48·7	48·2	47·6	47·0	46·5	46·0	45·5	45·1	44·7	46·2	118	10	29·549
50·7	51·0	51·1	50·9	50·5	49·2	48·5	47·9	47·3	46·7	46·5	48·2	168	15	29·545
46·0	46·3	46·3	46·1	45·7	45·0	44·4	43·8	43·2	42·8	42·5	43·5	194	26	29·504
49·2	49·4	49·5	49·4	48·7	48·0	47·3	46·5	45·8	45·2	44·9	44·6	46·4	133	21	29·576
50·4	50·5	50·5	50·3	50·0	49·4	48·8	48·2	47·6	47·2	46·9	46·6	48·0	152	43	29·576
50·5	50·8	50·8	50·6	50·0	49·2	48·5	47·9	47·2	46·7	46·4	46·2	47·7	107	8	29·489
48·0	48·2	48·3	48·1	47·6	47·0	46·2	45·4	45·0	44·5	44·3	44·0	45·3	161	8	29·579
49·7	49·8	49·9	49·7	49·3	48·7	48·2	47·6	47·1	46·6	46·3	46·1	47·3	188	4	29·515
49·3	49·5	49·3	49·1	48·5	47·9	47·2	46·5	45·9	45·4	45·0	44·7	46·6	208	5	29·552
51·9	51·9	51·8	51·6	51·2	50·5	49·8	49·1	48·4	48·0	47·7	47·6	49·5	136	4	29·552
50·7	50·7	50·6	50·2	49·6	48·9	48·2	47·5	46·8	46·2	45·8	45·6	47·5	148	4	29·543
49·45	49·68	49·67	49·41	48·92	48·25	47·56	46·89	46·26	45·73	45·39	45·10	46·81	155·8	12·3	29·542

TABLE LXXXVIII.—LIST of DAYS on which the Wind blew THROUGHOUT THE DAY from EACH DIRECTION, referred to EIGHT POINTS of the AZIMUTHAL CIRCLE, as determined from OSLER'S ANEMOMETER, during the Period 1849–1868.

Days in this Table marked * have been omitted in the reductions, and those marked ‡ in the reductions referring to the Temperature of Evaporation only.

[The printing of certain days in this Table in a slightly bolder type has reference to the Wind Reductions of the Barometric Section. See heading to Table XXIII. in that Section.]

From 1853, Nov. 22 to Dec. 2, and from 1858, May 9 to 31, the Anemometer was under repair.

Year.	January.	February.	March.	April.	May.	June.	July.	August.	September.	October.	November.	December.	Year.	January.	February.	March.	April.	May.	June.	July.	August.	September.	October.	November.	December.
			NORTH.													NORTH continued.									
1849	26	10 24 25 26 27	10 11 20 11 28	1 8 9 17	11 16 17		4 19	18 19 20		26 27	11 21 22 30 31		1856 cont.							8 9 10 11* 12*				
1850	7 16 17	4 20 21 23	23	1 15 16		20 28 29 30	15 16	5 8 9	12 26	14 27	22	1857				30			17 18		21 22	7 8 14		
1851		2 9 27 28	1 2 6 10 7	8 9 11 23 26 27*	2 25	4 9 10 18	5 7 8 8	30	7 12 17 18 20	23			1858			11	4	3* 11 29					7 8	14
1852	10 11 19 20 27*	2 11 16 26		21 22 23 24 27 23 29	28 29 30	6 10 19	12 18	22 30					1859	13	3	10 22 31	21	9 10 14 30		21	15 16 17	21*	1* 13 14
1853	23 24 29	11 16 17 18 20 21		31	1 2 4 12 22 23		3 7 8		21	24 28			1860	6 31	1 2 3 9 10	5 16	20*	30	2 3 6 23 30		29		12 13 15 17 21 22
1854	10	2	1*	25 26	7		4 5 6		12	12 17 24 25 26	10		1861	25 26		24 29	2 4 8 9	3 30			17		
1855		14	23	25 26 29 30	14 15* 22 16* 21 29* 30*	19* 23	3	13 13	6* 29 30 31	28 24 27 28	4	10	1862	9				18		17		7 16	15 21
1856				17	2 4	3* 6*		14 20	9 25	14 15	14		1863		17 21	29		25	20		23		
													1864	5 6 7 8 21 22		17*	10 12 13 26* 27		8 26	23	9* 10 11	
													1865	27		8 9 12 15 22*		10	11 17	1	4 29 30		6	13 15

TABLE LXXXVIII.—LIST of DAYS on which the Wind blew THROUGHOUT THE DAY from EACH DIRECTION—continued.

NORTH continued.

Year	January	February	March	April	May	June	July	August	September	October	November	December
1865 cont.		23* / 24 / 27			1							1
1866		8 / 22	13 / 15					1 / 5*				
1867	11 / 15 / 16		6 / 20	22 / 23	13 / 16 / 23* / 24* / 25 / 26 / 27 / 28	26	2	17 / 20	4 / 10	5 / 18 / 20 / 21 / 23	3 / 6 / 7 / 29	
1868	23		28	9 / 10 / 11 / 12 / 13	28 / 30	1 / 2 / 3 / 4 / 6	20	22	18	7 / 9* / 14		

NORTH-EAST.

Year	January	February	March	April	May	June	July	August	September	October	November	December
1849	1* / 2* / 3* / 4* / 5 / 6	28		2 / 3 / 4 / 5 / 6' / 7	3 / 4 / 6 / 7 / 9 / 15 / 24	10 / 12 / 13 / 14 / 15' / 16'	5*	5 / 6 / 7 / 8 / 17 / 21 / 22 / 23 / 27	1 / 2 / 11 / 12 / 13 / 14 / 15 / 16	2 / 3 / 20 / 28*		23
1850	13 / 14 / 15 / 20		11 / 12 / 14 / 15 / 17	26 / 27 / 28* / 29* / 30	6 / 7 / 20 / 21	1 / 27 / 28	13 / 14 / 15	14 / 14* / 15 / 16 / 17 / 18	25	28 / 29		
1851	1 / 21 / 23 / 26		6 / 7 / 12 / 14 / 15	12 / 13 / 14 / 15	3	5 / 6 / 7 / 8 / 30	3 / 13 / 14 / 16 / 17 / 18 / 19 / 20	25				
1852	23 / 24* / 25* / 26*	7 / 8 / 9 / 12 / 14 / 17 / 18	1 / 4 / 6 / 7 / 8 / 9 / 20	1 / 3 / 5 / 6 / 13 / 14 / 24		6* / 7* / 11* / 12* / 13 / 14 / 24	27	8 / 9	13 / 14 / 15 / 16 / 17	10 / 12		

NORTH-EAST—continued.

Year	January	February	March	April	May	June	July	August	September	October	November	December
1852 cont.		25 / 28	10 / 16 / 17	25 / 26	27							
1853	26 / 27 / 28	4 / 5 / 10	3* / 16 / 17	13* / 6 / 7 / 17 / 18 / 19 / 21 / 22 / 23 / 24 / 25	5 / 6 / 7	3	8	11 / 12 / 13 / 23	4 / 5 / 6 / 17		12 / 13 / 14	3 / 10 / 11 / 12 / 13 / 14 / 20 / 21 / 22
1854	3		4 / 5 / 20	11 / 12 / 13 / 15 / 16 / 22 / 23 / 24	13 / 16 / 17	1 / 3 / 4 / 5 / 6	25 / 26 / 27 / 28	7	5 / 8* / 9	7 / 10 / 20		
1855	13 / 14 / 17 / 20 / 23 / 24 / 30 / 31	6 / 7 / 8 / 9 / 10 / 12 / 17 / 20	8 / 22 / 24 / 29 / 31	4 / 18 / 21 / 22 / 27*	1 / 3 / 20 / 4 / 21 / 26*	11 / 12	5*	1 / 2 / 3 / 4 / 5 / 14 / 23 / 24				3* / 13 / 16 / 17 / 18 / 19 / 20 / 25 / 26	9 / 17
1856	8 / 9 / 10 / 11 / 12 / 22	18 / 19 / 20 / 21 / 6 / 7 / 12 / 22 / 23	14 / 15 / 16 / 19 / 20 / 21 / 27	1* / 5 / 7 / 30 / 31	28			17 / 18 / 19	11	8 / 11 / 20* / 24* / 26 / 27	7 / 12	
1857	5 / 6 / 7 / 26 / 27 / 28	4* / 21	26 / 27 / 28 / 29 / 30 / 9 / 10* / 29 / 31	3 / 4 / 5 / 7 / 8	16 / 17 / 18 / 19*	19 / 20 / 27 / 28 / 29	19 / 20	20	9 / 10 / 15 / 26 / 27 / 28		
1858	5* / 14 / 15 / 16 / 25* / 26 / 27 / 28	11 / 11*	3 / 17	10 / 3 / 7 / 8	7	9* / 28	8 / 9 / 10 / 22 / 23	13 / 14 / 18 / 19 / 21	18 / 23 / 24 / 29 / 30 / 31	2 / 4 / 5 / 6 / 9 / 14 / 16 / 17 / 18

TABLE LXXXVIII.—List of Days on which the Wind blew THROUGHOUT THE DAY from EACH DIRECTION—continued.

NORTH-EAST continued.

Year	January	February	March	April	May	June	July	August	September	October	November	December
1859	5, 7, 8			22, 28	1, 2, 3, 4, 5, 10, 11, 12, 13, 14, 15, 16, 17, 18, 19, 20, 21*, 22', 23, 27*, 30	2, 3, 8	1, 2, 24	9, 10		10	16*, 17*	2*, 3*, 11
1860		13, 14, 15, 16, 17	8, 9	5, 6, 14, 15, 16, 17, 18, 19*, 24, 25, 26, 27	2*, 3		7, 8, 9, 10, 11	7, 8, 9, 10			1, 2, 7, 8	14, 28*
1861	2, 3, 4*, 16*, 17, 18	10, 11, 24		13, 14, 15, 22, 23	5, 6, 7, 18, 28	6, 7, 8, 9, 15, 16		10*	17, 27*, 28*, 29*, 30			19, 20, 21, 22, 23, 31
1862	2, 15	8, 13	14, 15, 14, 21*	8, 9, 16, 11*	13*, 14, 15, 12	1	16, 27, 28, 29, 31*	1*, 15*, 16*, 17*, 18*, 19*, 20*, 21*, 22*	8, 9, 29	17, 18, 19, 20, 24, 25		
1863	11, 14, 15, 16		16	16, 30	1, 2, 3, 19, 20, 21, 22, 23, 24, 25, 26	4, 5, 13, 16*, 30*			26	9		

NORTH-EAST continued.

Year	January	February	March	April	May	June	July	August	September	October	November	December
1864	1, 2, 3, 4	18, 19, 20, 23, 24, 25, 26	2, 21, 22, 23	26, 27, 28		3	9, 10, 11, 13	22		2, 7, 8, 29, 30	2, 6, 9	14, 13, 16, 22, 24, 26
1865	1, 24, 25, 26	9, 10, 12	14, 21	15, 20, 25			16, 18		25	22, 23, 29, 30	22, 23	7, 8, 9, 12
1866		21	1*, 2, 9, 10, 20, 21	7, 9, 29, 30	1, 24, 25	25, 26	18, 22		4, 6, 7, 8, 9, 10, 11			
1867		28	1, 2, 3, 4, 5, 7, 8, 9, 10, 11, 12, 14, 15, 19	13, 14, 15, 16	19, 30, 21, 22		1	18, 19	25	6, 10, 11, 12, 16, 17		27, 28, 30, 31
1868	1, 2, 3, 8, 9					4, 5	18, 19, 29	11, 12, 24, 25, 26	16, 17	9, 11, 12, 13, 14, 15, 21	1, 2	10, 11, 12, 13, 16, 17, 18, 19, 26, 27

EAST.

Year	January	February	March	April	May	June	July	August	September	October	November	December
1849					14	11			26		21, 22	12
1850	30			30	2, 3, 4, 24, 25, 26	12			11, 12, 13*			

TABLE LXXXVIII.—LIST OF DAYS on which the Wind blew THROUGHOUT THE DAY from EACH DIRECTION—*continued.*

EAST continued.

Year	January	February	March	April	May	June	July	August	September	October	November	December
1851		13, 24	16			28, 29, 30			10, 11			13, 14
1852				4, 6, 10, 13, 15, 19, 20	2, 11, 12, 13, 15, 22, 23, 24, 25, 26	7	9*		3, 4			13
1853	25	9, 12, 28*	11	29	3, 4, 12, 15, 16			3		12, 13		
1854				10, 14, 17, 18	15, 16			8				
1855		2, 16	7, 21	20	29	8, 9		25				18, 19, 20, 21
1856		17	11, 13, 14, 15, 16, 18, 25, 26, 27, 28, 29, 30	6				5, 10	25, 28	5, 6		
1857		2		2, 14	15, 25			22, 30	22	24	11, 18	
1858		10*, 13, 18, 19, 22, 23, 24*	1, 2	6, 7, 9, 19, 22, 23*				16, 29	19, 20, 21, 22, 23	3, 11, 12, 13, 15, 22, 23		
1859				20, 27, 30	9				9, 14*, 15	24	9, 10	
1860				30*	1*, 4, 6, 7*	16				3, 4, 5, 6	3	4

EAST continued.

Year	January	February	March	April	May	June	July	August	September	October	November	December
1860 cont.										9, 10, 11, 12, 13		
1861		15*			7, 8, 9, 10, 11, 17, 18, 20, 27		14			19, 26*	24, 26*, 28	
1862	21	26, 27, 28	1*							25, 26	5, 10	1
1863		15		12, 13	8, 9*			1*	13	7, 8, 24, 25	29, 30	31
1864	5	27	3, 5*, 13, 18, 19, 20	5, 8, 14, 17, 22	8, 16, 17, 19		16	19		3, 4, 5, 6	1, 10, 11, 12	23, 25, 31
1865			4, 5	19, 20	16, 29, 30	1				24, 25	1, 2, 3, 4, 8	
1866				6, 8, 23, 24, 25, 26	20, 21, 22	1, 3, 24	16, 19		28	17, 18		1
1867	20, 21	14*, 18, 27	13, 17, 18	26	12, 19*, 25		11, 12	13, 31	3			
1868				2, 3	6*, 7	17, 18				2, 3, 4, 10	6, 10, 16, 17	

SOUTH-EAST.

Year	January	February	March	April	May	June	July	August	September	October	November	December
1849	8				5*, 6, 7, 8		25			19	29*	7*, 13

TABLE LXXXVIII.—List of Days on which the Wind blew throughout the Day from each Direction—*continued*,

SOUTH-EAST *continued*.

Year	January	February	March	April	May	June	July	August	September	October	November	December
1850	11 21		29 30 31*	1* 25					20			2 7 8 9
1851	14 25 26	14	12 22				12					30
1852		13 14	5 21 22		6 8	4* 5*			22	21	23	
1853		1 2 3 8	29*		2 13 14			10	16	12	19 24 1 4 5	18*
1854	7 12 21 22		2	19 20				13	27 28	30	14	
1855		3 4	10 15	3	24* 25*	6		18* 23	8 26			
1856	2 6	3	17 24	1 11 23 24	21			2 4 6 9 27	14 22			
1857		2	17 18 24 29	4 5 9	25	13 14		13 23 30	7 14 18 19 27* 30	1 2 17 19		31
1858	26	6 7* 8* 9* 20 21	22	5 14						24 25		8 10 16 17
1859		8		24 25	6	7 25	11			4* 7 8	11 12 13 20* 21* 23* 25	17 18 19
1860	11 12 13 18					19			12 26	30		2 27
1861	10*									4* 7 15		2 3 4 25*
1862	17* 18*	15 16	29 30	3						31		1 2

SOUTH-EAST *continued*.

Year	January	February	March	April	May	June	July	August	September	October	November	December
1862 *cont.*	19* 20	22 24 25										3
1863		14 16 20	3 4 31	1	1 2	6				9 10* 12	26 27 28	
1864	9 10 11 12 15 16 17 18		1	17 21	4					21	13 20	10 19 20
1865	30		17 18 29	3 12		21 28	25			15 19 26 27	5 6 7	13 25 28 2 3 4 19
1866		16 18	5	17 19			12	28	23	19 20 21		
1867	22	15*					4 5 10*		31	12 11	14 13 23 24 14 15	
1868	10 11			24						15 19	19 10 25 29 30	20 1 13 20

SOUTH.

Year	January	February	March	April	May	June	July	August	September	October	November	December
1849	16 20 21	2 12	1	2			7*		2 29			2* 6* 14
1850				2 16					22		6 23 26	3
1851	12 13 16	3 5 15	9 21	8 9	5				30	1 2 3		16 17
1852	6 19 20 27			15 16 19	2 3 4 17 18 21 22 25 27	3 19	3 5 6 7	29	20	1 2 3	16 17 26	11 12 14 15 19 29*

TABLE LXXXVIII.—LIST of Days on which the Wind blew THROUGHOUT THE DAY from EACH DIRECTION.—continued.

SOUTH—continued.

Year	January	February	March	April	May	June	July	August	September	October	November	December
1853	4*, 6*, 19	7	10		19	7, 22, 24		25	1, 10, 11	4, 5, 27, 28, 31	19	
1854	8, 17, 18, 23, 24, 27, 28		12, 13		25, 28					28, 31	2	
1855				5, 17	13	9, 23				3	11	31
1856	1, 3, 4, 5, 19, 20	6, 11, 13, 15		2, 5, 8	23			8, 9		2, 3		
1857		8, 9, 17	13	16	26	5*			4	22	1, 3	
1858	7, 26, 27			13			24		23	26	11, 12, 18	
1859	9, 13						18	6, 7	24	3*, 22*	7*	
1860		24				12*			22, 28, 29	21	1, 6, 8	
1861		13, 18										
1862	23, 27	19							29*	3	5	
1863			5							3, 24*	13, 19, 20	18
1864					19, 20	5, 6, 30	12*			22	19	8, 9, 11
1865						26		12				5, 6, 23
1866			6, 15, 23							25, 26	24	2, 24
1867	23	16*	23	18, 27	6*, 28		15		8	21, 30	23	24

SOUTH—continued.

Year	January	February	March	April	May	June	July	August	September	October	November	December
1868		11, 14	19	11		21		14		20, 26		2, 14

SOUTH-WEST.

Year	January	February	March	April	May	June	July	August	September	October	November	December
1849	7, 9, 13, 14, 15, 17, 18, 19, 22, 23, 24, 25, 26, 28	1, 4, 6, 8, 9, 10, 17, 18, 19*, 20*, 22*, 23, 28	2, 3, 4, 5, 7, 11	27, 28	14, 15*, 17, 18	1, 19	3*, 6, 20, 22, 23, 24, 25, 26, 28*, 29*, 30*, 31	9*, 10, 11, 12, 13, 14, 15, 16, 17*, 22	10, 11, 30	5, 20, 21, 22, 23, 24, 25, 26, 27	5, 6, 7, 8, 9, 10, 11, 12, 13, 14, 18	15, 16, 17, 18
1850	4, 5, 13, 24, 25, 28	1, 2, 3, 4, 8, 9, 11, 12, 15, 17, 18, 19, 20, 23	2, 6, 7	3, 4, 6, 7, 9	4, 11, 16, 27, 28, 13, 17, 18, 19, 20	6, 7, 9, 12, 13, 14, 30	1, 2, 3, 4, 9, 10, 11	3, 4, 5, 8	27, 28, 29, 30, 10, 16, 19, 20, 23, 24	7, 8, 9, 13, 14, 16, 17, 18, 19, 20	1, 2, 3, 4, 5, 7	12, 13, 14, 15, 16, 17, 23, 24, 30, 31
1851	1, 2, 4, 8, 9, 11, 17, 18, 21, 22, 23, 24, 27, 28, 29, 30	6, 11, 12, 18, 19, 20	13, 14, 19, 20, 23, 24, 25, 26, 27, 29	2, 18, 19, 21, 23	7, 17, 18, 25	3, 6, 7, 8, 12, 13, 15, 16, 20, 25	13, 14, 20, 28, 29	14, 16, 17, 22, 13, 24, 26	27	4, 5, 6, 7, 9, 10, 11, 12, 13, 14, 16, 18, 19, 20	1, 2, 3	5, 6, 7, 8, 9, 10, 11, 21
1851	1, 2, 3, 7	2, 3, 4, 8	30	20, 29	9, 10, 11, 12	1, 11, 12, 13	1, 2, 18, 20	1, 2, 4, 8	22, 23	3, 5, 23, 30	2, 3, 6, 7	2, 3, 4, 5*

TABLE LXXXVIII.—LIST OF DAYS on which the Wind blew THROUGHOUT THE DAY from EACH DIRECTION—*continued*.

SOUTH-WEST *continued*.

Year	January	February	March	April	May	June	July	August	September	October	November	December
1852 cont.	8 11 12 14 15 18 24 25 26 31	15 16		13 14 31	14 15 19 23 24 28 29 30		9 10 12 14 18 25 29 30 31		31	8 18 27 28	6° 8 9 10 16 17 20° 21° 24 25 26 27° 28° 30° 31°
1853	1° 2° 3° 5° 8° 9° 11 12 13 15 20 21 30		5° 7° 9	1° 3° 6° 19°	9 23	8 9 15 17 18 24 27 28 29 30	1 20 21 25 26 27 28 14 30 31	1 19 22 25 28 29 16	14	15 17 21 22 23	2 10 18	31
1854	25 26 30 31	5 6 7 14 17 24	7 8 9 10 11 15 29 30 31	1 8 30	1 2 3 4 6 7 8 20 21 22 23 24 25 26 27 28 29 30	11° 12° 13 14 16 17 19 21 24 27 31	3 4 5 11 12 14 15 17 18 19° 21 23	1 9 11 16 17 18 20°	13 14 15 16 17 19	4 5	7 10 21 27 28 29 30	5 8 11 12 13 14 15 16
1855	4 5 6 7 8	24 25	1 2 3 4 18 19	6 7 9 15	6 10 18	1 3 7 9	1 13° 3 15 10 22°	1 3 6° 7°	18 20	1 5 6 7 8	8 23	4 24 25 26

SOUTH-WEST *continued*.

Year	January	February	March	April	May	June	July	August	September	October	November	December
1855 cont.			27		14 15 16 18	24 25 26 27 28	19° 20 24 25 26 27 28 30 31		26		27 28 29 30
1856	16 18 24 25 26 28	7 8 9 10 12 14 25		3 4 6 9 26	13 14 15 17 18 19 20 22 24 25 26 27°	2 8 9 11 12 13 23 24° 28 25	7 11 15 16 18 23 21 24°	7 11 12 13 14	4 5	3 17	2 6 7 8° 9° 10 11 12 24 31
1857	1 2 3 9 17 30	5° 6 7 10 11 13 18 21 22 27	14 15 23 30	7 12 19	12 18 19 20 21 24° 27	3 4 8 12 19° 30	3 5 9 18° 7 8 9 21	1 2 3 7 8 9	5 6 7 10 14 15 16 17 27	3 13 29 31	23	2 4 5 6 7 8 9 10 11 12 14 15 16 17 18
1858	8 9 10 14 15 18 19 29 30	4 5	29 30 31	30°	4° 17° 19 20	6 13 14 22 23 25	4 15 16 19 29 30 31	1 3 5 6 7 8 9 10 11 18 25 27	1 3 5 6 7 9 10 13	28 29 30	3 4 19 20 21 22 23 24 25 26 30
1859	10 15 16 17 18	4 5 7 10	1 2 3 4 6	2 3 5 6°	22 23 27	5 6 17 19 22	2 3 4 9	6 8 21	2 3 26 27	1 2 3 5 6	4° 5° 6° 20 24

TABLE LXXXVIII.—LIST of DAYS on which the Wind blew THROUGHOUT THE DAY from EACH DIRECTION—*continued.*

SOUTH-WEST *continued.*

Year	January	February	March	April	May	June	July	August	September	October	November	December
1859 cont.	19 20 21 22 23 24 25 27 28 29 30 31	11 12 15 16 17 21 24 25 26 28	7 10 11 12 13 14 15 16 17 20 27 28 29	8 9 10			27 28 31	13 14 17 26 27 29	22 23 26 28 29 30	28 29	7 18* 19* 29	27 28 29 30 31*
1860	1* 2 3 4 5 8 15 16 21 23 24 29 30	+ 5 26	1 2 3 11 17 20 21 23 31*	2 8	8' 9* 10* 11* 12' 16 17* 18* 19 22 23 25* 26*	1 3 4 5 6 7 8 11* 13' 14 15' 20 21 22 23 24 25 27	14 15* 18 19 21 23 27	3 5 6 8 11 13 16 17 18 22 24 25 27 28 29 30	1 14 15 16 17 20 22 23 24 25 26 27 28 29 30 31	5 6 13 15 16	16 20	7
1861	12* 20* 21 22 23 24 25 26 27 28 29 30 31	3 4 5 6 7 16 19 20 21 22	6 16 17 23 27 30 31	3	25 26	11 12 23 24 25 26	4 5 11 16* 17* 18‡ 19‡ 20‡ 21* 22* 23* 24‡ 25‡ 27* 29* 30* 31*	1* 3 5 7 8 11 12 13 16 17 18* 22 31*	3 6 9 13 19' 20* 24 27 28	11* 12 13 31*	4 3 6 11 12 18 20	8 9 11 12 13
1862	7 8* 9* 10 24 26 29	2* 3* 20 21	5 6 7 9 10 11*	1 2 5 6 18 19 20 21 22 24*	5 8 19* 20* 21 23 28	5 6* 7* 8 10 12 14 29	6 9 15 17* 19‡ 21 24 26 31‡	1 5 7 9 12 13 14 30 19*	3' 7' 8' 9 11* 13* 14 16 17 19*	3' 1* 8' 12 14 26* 30 19* 32 23 25 27	1* 2 9* 10* 13 17 26* 28 29 31	8 6 7 9 11 12 14 16 18 27 28 29 31

SOUTH-WEST *continued.*

Year	January	February	March	April	May	June	July	August	September	October	November	December
1863	1 2 3 4 5 22 23 24 26 28 19 30	1 2 7 10 11 18 25 16 27	1 2 6 7 14	3 4 5 6	12 13 15 16 17	5 6 7 8 21 22*	1 2 4 7 9 16	3 4 6* 7 8 9 13* 19 16* 22 23 24 25 26 27 28 29 30	2* 4 6* 8 7 9 10 12 16* 15 18 22 23 24	3 5 16 7 18 8 19 11 15 17 19 20 21 22 23	1 2 4 5 7 8 14 16 17 18 30 31	4 5 6 7 8 10 11 14 15 25 26 29
1864	19 20 21 23 24 25 26 27 31	1 3 13 14 15 16	4 7 11 12 13 14 31	3 18	5 6 11 14* 15 17 20* 21 22 23 25	2 20 21 22 13 24 25 28 30 31	4 5 8 28 19 24 31	2 18 6 13 7 8 9 10* 13 14 17	16 18 20 23 24 25 26 27 28 29 30	4 2 3 4 5 6 7 8
1865	4 7 8 10 11 12 18 21	1 2 7 18 23 26 28	4	6 18	2 3 4 6 12 13 16 17 23 24 25 27 28 29 30 31	3 4 5 7 8 13 14 16 18* 19* 20	2 6 9 10 11 13 14 16	10 11 13 17 21 30	17 19 20 21 22 23 24 26 29	7 10 20 21 22 23 25 26 29 30 31
1866	2 3 4 6 7 14 15 18 19	1 9 10 11 25*	7 24 26 28 16 19	13 14 15 16	8 11 28	5 6 7 8 9 10 11 12 15	2 3 5 8 9 25 27 31	6 7 8 9 10 13 14	1 2 23 29* 31 13 14	3 4 5 6 7* 8 12 15 14 15

K

TABLE LXXXVIII.—List of Days on which the Wind blew throughout the Day from each Direction—continued.

SOUTH-WEST continued.

Year	January	February	March	April	May	June	July	August	September	October	November	December
1866 cont.	20, 21, 25								18, 19, 20, 21	15, 16, 18, 19, 20, 21		16, 17, 18, 21, 23, 25, 26, 30
1867	4, 7, 8, 9, 24, 27, 28, 29	1, 3, 4, 6, 8, 9, 10, 12b	24, 26, 27, 18, 29	1, 7, 10, 13, 31b	3, 27, 30	1*, 4, 5, 6	4, 14, 16, 17, 18	5, 6, 7, 8, 9, 10, 13, 17, 18	4, 5, 6, 7, 10, 13, 16, 27, 28, 29	2, 11, 16, 17, 26, 19, 20, 22, 26, 27, 29, 30, 31	3, 8, 25, 26, 28	10, 14, 16, 17, 29
1868	12, 13, 14, 15, 16, 17, 18, 19, 21, 27, 30, 31	1, 5, 7, 10, 14, 15, 16, 17, 18, 24, 26, 28, 29	4, 5, 12, 13, 15, 19, 20, 21, 22	7, 20, 21, 22, 23, 27, 28, 29	1, 9, 10, 14, 12, 13, 20, 21	4, 6, 20, 21, 28	16, 20, 23, 24, 25	6, 7, 8, 12, 22, 26	3, 4, 6, 9, 13, 19, 30, 27	4, 6, 8, 13, 16, 17, 22, 23, 24, 28, 31	1, 3, 4, 5, 6	

WEST.

Year	January	February	March	April	May	June	July	August	September	October	November	December
1849		5, 14, 15*, 16				21, 27	4*, 27	14				
1850	1, 2	6, 7, 10	5			22	5, 26	19	31	6, 25	26	27, 28
1851	4	4, 28	30		18, 19	7, 11, 3, 12, 15	1, 26	8	19, 29			

WEST continued.

Year	January	February	March	April	May	June	July	August	September	October	November	December
1851 cont.									15, 21, 27	25, 27		
1852	9, 16	7, 17, 21	1*	30	8		21	13	14, 21		9	
1853	14	22	4*, 6*	2*, 4*, 5*, 7*, 17*					28	20, 24	2	
1854		8			5	23	13	17, 22, 24	24			1, 2, 3, 4, 17*, 22, 24, 25, 29, 30, 31
1855	1, 15			8, 10, 11, 12		25	11*, 17, 22	21	16	25		
1856					1, 3	6, 10, 12, 31	15, 28, 30	17	17, 19, 26, 27, 30			20, 21, 22, 30
1857	18, 21, 23	7, 8, 31					17, 26, 30, 31		2, 9*, 10			19, 21, 28, 30
1858	24		16, 17, 18				26		12, 13, 14			6, 27
1859	2, 3, 11	2, 19	5, 18, 26			19	26	30, 31	1, 3, 7, 10, 11	22*	8	21, 22
1860	22	7, 8, 19, 27, 28	4, 18, 19, 22, 24, 28, 29	1*, 3	13, 24, 27, 28	10, 18, 28, 29, 30	20	1, 2, 4, 7*, 10, 19, 20, 21, 23, 26	2*, 30, 3, 4, 7, 8, 14, 20	3, 4, 7, 8, 14, 20	15	10, 23

TABLE LXXXVIII.—LIST of DAYS on which the Wind blew THROUGHOUT THE DAY from EACH DIRECTION—*continued.*

WEST *continued.*

Year	January	February	March	April	May	June	July	August	September	October	November	December
1861			8 10 11 18 20 21	4		1* 10 28* 19‡ 20* 20* 30*	1 10 9 10 14 15	6 5 7 14 15	2‡ 22		7 8 23	7 14 15
1862	3 30 31	1* 4 5	17 23 27*	10* 22 24	5 9 13 15* 21 25 7 10 12 14* 16 18* 20‡ 25 27	1‡ 2‡ 3 7	8 22 23		3 20 24			25 26
1863	20 21 25	3 4 6	8	21 22 27	28* 29* 30	3 13 14 15 21 23 28 30	24*	5	1* 13 14 16 17 26	2	15	12 19 20 23 24
1864		9*		1	2	16 24 28	4 29	1 8	12	17		
1865	9 14 15 16 17 20		5	5 7	25	2 9 29	16 17 21 24 31	2 3 5 9 10 11	12 10			
1866	8 9 17 26 29	3 4 5 6 7 8	12 29	17 18 20	9 10	14	4 9 10	4 15 17	3		9 22 25	27 28 29
1867		2 7 11	30	6 8 9 15	4 9*	20		30		4	15 18	
1868		3 4 6 13 25	1 2 3 17 23		5		29 30	23 24 25 28 30 31	1 23	7 29 30	5	

NORTH-WEST.

Year	January	February	March	April	May	June	July	August	September	October	November	December
1849	11 29		9 14	17	10		2* 5	20			16 17 25	19 20 27 28
1850			24		17		9	29	3	2 11		
1851			31		5 6 20	17 23			1 2		6 15 27	2
1852		18 29*					20 21 22 23		28			
1853	17 18	23	20	15* 16* 20*	29	13			26			6 7 15 16 23 27
1854	11	10 11 19	21 22 23				12		25	18	3 9	9 27
1855	3		13	8 12	17 24	20*	5* 9		9 11 12 19 20 21 23 24			6 7
1856				29 16	3 25	5 8 9	26	18 19	16 9 15 10 22 23 24 27 29 30	1		17
1857			22 13				7 8 9*					
1858		1	8 15		27	1 30	20 25 26 27		11			5 29
1859	18 23 27	23 24 25	13 15		13 29		23					

Table LXXXVIII.—List of Days on which the Wind blew throughout the Day from each Direction—*concluded.*

NORTH-WEST *continued.*

Year	January	February	March	April	May	June	July	August	September	October	November	December
1860	7 23	6 20 21	6 15 23 22	9 11 21			1 24	12		1	18 19	16
1861			7	6 25			24* 25*	17 26			2 3	16 17
1862				15	17 10 22 28	21	9 10 11					19 20
1863	19		27 28 29	23 24 25* 26 28	4?		18* 21	10 11				17 22 27

NORTH-WEST *continued.*

Year	January	February	March	April	May	June	July	August	September	October	November	December
1864		17	29		27			10 11 24			12 13	
1865		20	1 3 7			24 26	12 28 30	8 18				14
1866	23		25				24 25 30	3 5 21			19 26 27	
1867	10 17		31			14	5 27			8	19 22	2 11 12 13 19
1868				24 27			8		29			

TABLE LXXXIX.—MONTHLY MEAN TEMPERATURE of the Air at every Hour of the Day, through the RANGE of YEARS 1849 to 1868, during prevalence of SOUTH WIND.

Hour, Greenwich Mean Solar Time (civil reckoning).	January.	February.	March.	April.	May.	June.	July.	August.	September.	October.	November.	December.	Yearly Means.
Midnight	33·6	32·0	36·3	36·0	48·1	52·4	56·3	55·2	50·8	45·9	38·7	35·3	43·38
1 a.m.	34·0	31·8	35·0	38·8	44·6	51·8	55·7	54·8	50·8	45·6	38·4	35·2	43·12
2 „	34·1	31·7	35·6	38·4	44·0	51·4	55·5	54·4	50·8	45·4	38·0	35·0	42·86
3 „	34·0	31·5	35·6	38·1	43·6	51·1	55·0	54·1	50·7	5·1	37·8	34·7	42·61
4 „	34·0	31·2	35·6	37·8	43·2	51·2	54·9	53·7	50·6	1·9	37·6	34·5	42·43
5 „	33·9	31·2	35·3	38·0	43·4	51·8	55·0	53·2	50·5	44·6	37·4	34·4	42·39
6 „	33·8	31·0	35·2	38·3	44·3	53·3	55·7	53·7	50·7	44·4	37·3	34·4	42·67
7 „	33·8	31·0	35·5	39·6	45·9	55·7	57·3	55·6	51·9	44·5	37·2	34·3	43·53
8 „	33·8	31·3	36·3	41·1	47·6	57·5	59·1	56·8	54·1	45·4	37·6	34·2	44·58
9 „	34·1	32·2	38·4	42·9	49·3	59·5	61·2	58·7	56·5	47·8	38·7	34·4	46·14
10 „	34·8	33·7	39·9	45·1	50·6	61·3	61·9	60·4	57·9	50·1	40·0	35·1	47·63
11 „	35·7	33·3	41·3	46·8	51·9	63·1	63·0	62·1	59·0	51·2	41·3	36·1	49·07
Noon	36·3	36·7	42·4	48·0	52·8	64·8	66·5	63·1	60·1	51·9	42·3	37·1	50·18
1 p.m.	37·0	37·5	43·0	48·4	53·4	65·5	67·7	63·7	60·6	51·9	43·3	37·5	50·79
2 „	36·8	37·7	43·1	49·1	53·8	65·2	68·3	64·2	61·1	52·2	43·0	37·7	51·02
3 „	36·5	37·4	42·7	49·2	55·7	64·5	68·1	64·3	60·7	51·5	42·1	37·2	50·65
4 „	35·7	36·6	42·3	48·7	53·6	63·6	67·3	64·0	59·3	50·3	41·1	36·6	49·96
5 „	35·0	35·3	41·2	47·4	52·4	62·5	67·0	62·9	58·2	49·0	40·3	36·1	48·94
6 „	34·4	34·4	39·8	46·2	51·0	60·8	65·2	61·3	56·1	47·8	39·8	35·8	47·72
7 „	33·9	33·6	38·3	43·0	49·0	59·1	62·7	59·2	54·3	47·1	39·0	35·3	46·28
8 „	33·6	33·0	37·3	41·5	47·3	56·6	59·9	57·2	53·4	46·3	38·6	35·0	45·06
9 „	33·3	32·5	36·4	41·2	46·3	54·5	58·0	55·9	52·5	45·4	38·1	34·6	44·05
10 „	32·9	31·9	36·0	40·3	45·7	53·1	56·9	54·9	51·7	44·9	37·6	34·1	43·33
11 „	32·6	31·2	35·3	39·6	45·0	52·2	56·3	54·1	51·4	44·2	37·1	33·7	42·73
Means	34·5	33·4	38·3	42·9	48·2	57·6	60·7	58·2	54·7	47·4	39·3	35·3	45·88
Number of Days employed	13	32	37	27	42	32	25	24	26	22	40	29	..

TABLE XC.—MONTHLY MEAN TEMPERATURE of the Air at every Hour of the Day, through the RANGE of YEARS 1849 to 1868, during prevalence of NORTH-EAST WIND.

Hour, Greenwich Mean Solar Time (civil reckoning).	January.	February.	March.	April.	May.	June.	July.	August.	September.	October.	November.	December.	Yearly Means.
Midnight	32·1	31·7	34·7	40·6	44·3	52·8	56·4	56·4	53·8	47·4	40·2	35·6	43·83
1 a.m.	31·8	31·4	34·6	40·1	43·7	52·2	55·6	56·0	53·2	47·1	40·2	35·4	43·44
2 „	31·7	31·5	34·2	39·7	43·1	51·5	55·3	55·5	52·7	46·8	40·1	35·3	43·11
3 „	31·7	31·3	33·9	39·4	42·9	51·1	55·0	55·4	52·5	46·7	39·8	35·1	43·02
4 „	31·7	31·3	33·8	39·4	42·6	51·0	55·2	55·2	52·2	46·7	39·7	35·1	42·83
5 „	31·7	31·2	33·7	39·2	43·0	51·7	55·8	55·1	52·1	46·7	39·7	35·1	42·92
6 „	31·6	31·1	33·7	39·9	44·6	53·5	57·4	55·9	52·3	46·7	39·6	35·0	43·44
7 „	31·5	31·0	34·2	41·5	47·1	56·0	59·7	57·6	53·9	46·8	39·6	34·7	44·47
8 „	31·7	31·4	35·3	43·6	49·5	58·5	62·3	59·9	56·7	47·9	40·0	34·7	45·96
9 „	32·0	32·4	37·1	45·7	51·9	60·7	64·8	62·1	59·9	50·0	41·1	34·9	47·72
10 „	32·8	33·9	38·7	47·7	53·6	62·5	67·2	64·2	62·6	52·1	42·7	35·4	49·45
11 „	33·6	34·9	40·0	49·4	54·9	64·2	69·0	66·1	64·4	53·4	44·1	36·1	50·98
Noon	34·2	36·0	41·1	50·6	56·3	65·7	70·8	67·6	65·8	54·5	45·2	36·5	52·02
1 p.m.	34·6	36·4	41·5	51·6	57·0	65·9	72·3	68·2	66·3	55·0	45·5	36·7	52·58
2 „	34·4	36·4	41·8	51·9	57·0	66·4	72·8	68·6	66·2	54·9	45·3	36·7	52·70
3 „	34·0	35·8	41·6	51·5	56·9	66·2	72·8	68·1	65·6	54·0	44·5	36·3	52·28
4 „	33·2	34·9	40·9	50·6	56·1	65·3	71·8	67·4	64·1	52·6	43·4	35·7	51·35
5 „	32·7	33·6	39·4	49·2	54·7	64·7	70·2	66·0	61·9	51·1	42·3	35·4	50·10
6 „	32·3	32·7	37·6	47·5	53·0	62·4	67·8	64·0	59·3	49·8	41·7	35·2	48·61
7 „	31·9	32·2	36·5	45·0	50·7	59·9	65·0	61·6	57·1	48·8	41·3	34·8	47·07
8 „	31·9	31·7	35·6	43·2	48·4	57·7	62·1	59·6	55·8	48·0	40·7	34·8	45·75
9 „	31·7	31·4	35·0	42·0	46·7	55·3	59·8	58·1	54·8	47·9	40·6	34·6	44·73
10 „	31·4	31·1	34·6	41·0	45·6	54·0	58·5	57·3	53·9	47·0	39·8	34·5	44·06
11 „	31·0	31·0	34·2	40·1	44·7	53·0	57·3	56·6	53·2	46·8	39·5	34·3	43·47
Means	32·4	32·8	36·8	44·6	49·5	58·4	63·1	60·9	57·9	49·5	41·5	35·3	46·90
Number of Days employed	57	58	74	78	100	49	43	37	66	53	71	31	..

TABLE XCI.—MONTHLY MEAN TEMPERATURE of the Air at every Hour of the Day, through the RANGE of YEARS 1849 to 1868, during prevalence of EAST WIND.

Hour, Greenwich Mean Solar Time (Civil reckoning).	January.	February.	March.	April.	May.	June.	July.	August.	September.	October.	November.	December.	Yearly Means.
Midnight	31·1	34·5	34·0	41·3	46·8	54·0	54·6	58·1	52·7	48·7	38·8	34·8	44·05
1ʰ. a.m.	31·2	34·4	33·9	40·8	46·1	53·2	53·0	57·5	52·4	48·4	37·5	34·5	43·63
2 ,,	31·2	34·2	33·7	40·4	45·6	52·7	53·6	5—1	51·8	48·3	37·0	33·8	43·28
3 ,,	31·6	33·7	33·3	40·1	45·3	52·3	53·4	56·0	51·5	48·2	37·1	33·7	43·09
4 ,,	31·8	33·5	33·1	39·8	45·0	52·0	53·3	56·5	51·6	48·0	36·7	33·5	42·90
5 ,,	31·7	33·5	32·9	39·5	45·7	53·3	54·1	56·5	51·9	47·6	36·9	33·6	43·10
6 ,,	31·4	33·4	32·9	40·2	48·2	56·9	56·7	58·2	52·0	47·8	37·0	33·6	44·03
7 ,,	31·2	33·4	33·6	42·6	51·5	61·2	59·7	62·7	53·7	48·4	37·2	33·3	45·71
8 ,,	31·0	33·8	35·4	45·5	54·5	64·4	62·8	66·9	57·0	49·9	37·6	33·3	47·68
9 ,,	31·2	35·0	37·6	48·4	56·8	67·2	65·3	70·5	61·0	52·5	39·2	33·8	49·88
10 ,,	31·9	36·1	39·7	50·8	58·8	69·4	67·5	72·8	63·2	54·6	41·4	34·8	51·92
11 ,,	33·0	37·0	41·2	52·4	50·7	71·0	69·4	74·6	67·7	56·9	43·2	36·1	53·32
Noon	33·6	37·9	42·2	53·5	60·9	71·9	71·2	76·1	69·2	58·2	44·8	36·9	54·70
1ʰ. p.m.	33·9	38·0	43·9	54·2	60·9	72·4	72·4	76·6	69·7	59·1	45·1	37·2	55·20
2 ,,	33·7	38·2	43·5	53·9	61·1	71·8	72·4	76·7	69·6	59·1	44·7	37·1	55·15
3 ,,	33·0	37·9	42·8	53·5	60·5	71·2	72·1	76·3	68·5	58·3	43·8	36·4	54·53
4 ,,	31·0	37·3	41·9	52·4	59·5	70·5	71·0	75·2	66·5	56·5	42·5	35·5	53·57
5 ,,	31·3	36·3	40·3	50·8	58·3	69·1	69·6	72·4	63·8	54·7	40·9	35·0	51·88
6 ,,	30·7	35·8	38·2	48·8	56·0	66·2	66·4	69·6	60·7	53·4	40·1	34·6	50·04
7 ,,	30·1	35·4	36·8	45·9	53·7	63·6	63·7	66·5	58·5	52·4	39·4	34·5	48·39
8 ,,	29·5	35·1	36·1	44·3	51·0	60·2	60·6	64·0	56·9	51·6	38·9	34·2	46·87
9 ,,	29·3	35·0	35·5	43·2	49·6	58·0	58·4	62·5	55·9	51·2	38·6	34·1	45·93
10 ,,	28·9	34·8	35·0	42·4	48·7	56·6	57·0	61·1	54·9	50·8	38·1	33·8	45·17
11 ,,	28·9	34·7	34·6	41·6	48·0	55·8	56·1	60·0	54·2	50·3	37·9	33·6	44·64
Means	31·4	35·4	37·1	46·1	53·0	62·3	62·3	66·1	59·0	52·3	39·7	34·6	48·28
Number of Days employed	6	20	35	51	26	22	9	13	21	32	31	17	..

TABLE XCII.—MONTHLY MEAN TEMPERATURE of the Air at every Hour of the Day, through the RANGE of YEARS 1849 to 1868, during prevalence of SOUTH-EAST WIND.

Hour, Greenwich Mean Solar Time (Civil reckoning).	January.	February.	March.	April.	May.	June.	July.	August.	September.	October.	November.	December.	Yearly Means.
Midnight	35·1	35·1	36·7	42·6	46·0	51·4	58·7	61·1	50·7	51·3	41·9	36·3	45·58
1ʰ. a.m.	35·0	34·7	36·5	42·3	45·2	50·7	56·6	60·4	50·3	51·2	41·8	36·0	45·14
2 ,,	34·8	34·5	36·3	42·1	44·7	50·4	56·9	60·1	50·3	50·8	42·0	35·8	44·80
3 ,,	34·9	34·7	36·1	42·1	44·1	49·9	56·4	59·6	49·3	50·7	42·0	35·6	44·63
4 ,,	34·7	34·8	36·1	41·8	43·7	50·0	56·1	59·3	49·4	50·4	41·9	35·6	44·53
5 ,,	34·6	34·8	35·9	41·8	44·5	51·1	56·9	59·3	48·9	50·3	41·8	35·8	44·68
6 ,,	34·4	34·4	35·7	42·6	46·9	54·9	60·5	60·5	49·0	50·3	41·9	35·2	45·53
7 ,,	34·4	34·4	36·1	45·4	50·4	58·7	65·1	63·6	50·7	50·9	42·3	35·5	47·29
8 ,,	34·4	34·5	38·7	48·9	54·0	60·8	69·7	66·7	54·5	51·6	42·5	35·7	49·33
9 ,,	34·8	35·5	41·9	51·8	57·0	63·4	71·7	70·5	59·3	55·2	43·9	36·4	51·78
10 ,,	35·7	37·2	44·3	54·1	59·0	65·4	74·0	73·0	62·8	57·3	45·3	37·8	53·84
11 ,,	36·7	38·5	46·8	55·6	59·8	67·7	75·4	74·4	64·9	59·2	46·5	39·2	55·31
Noon	37·6	40·2	48·6	56·8	60·4	69·2	77·1	75·4	66·5	60·7	47·2	40·4	56·67
1ʰ. p.m.	38·2	40·7	49·1	57·0	60·9	70·8	77·1	76·1	67·2	61·3	47·6	41·0	57·25
2 ,,	38·4	41·0	49·2	56·9	61·0	71·3	77·5	76·8	67·1	61·4	47·5	40·9	57·42
3 ,,	38·0	40·6	49·1	56·6	60·5	70·6	77·2	76·5	66·5	60·9	46·9	40·1	56·91
4 ,,	37·5	39·6	48·0	55·8	59·3	69·1	76·2	75·1	64·2	58·8	41·6	39·0	55·70
5 ,,	37·0	38·4	45·8	54·5	58·2	67·5	74·7	73·7	61·9	56·6	44·5	38·2	54·23
6 ,,	36·8	37·4	43·9	51·3	56·1	63·7	71·1	71·7	59·0	55·1	44·5	37·8	52·67
7 ,,	36·8	36·9	42·0	49·3	53·3	63·5	69·3	68·5	56·5	54·1	42·7	37·4	52·05
8 ,,	37·0	36·4	41·0	47·9	50·7	60·3	65·1	65·9	55·3	53·4	42·3	37·4	49·47
9 ,,	37·1	35·9	40·0	47·0	49·3	58·2	62·6	64·6	54·1	53·1	42·3	37·2	48·53
10 ,,	37·1	35·4	39·1	46·4	48·8	56·7	61·2	63·7	53·6	53·0	42·9	37·2	47·93
11 ,,	37·1	35·4	38·6	45·8	48·2	55·1	59·3	61·5	53·1	52·5	42·8	37·3	47·32
Means	36·2	36·7	41·5	49·0	52·6	60·5	67·0	67·4	56·9	54·6	43·9	37·4	50·31
Number of Days employed	30	23	27	27	12	14	5	12	22	31	30	33	..

TABLE XCIII.—MONTHLY MEAN TEMPERATURE of the Air at every Hour of the Day, through the Range of Years 1849 to 1868, during prevalence of SOUTH WIND.

Hour, Greenwich Mean Solar Time (Civil reckoning).	January.	February.	March.	April.	May.	June.	July.	August.	September.	October.	November.	December.	Yearly Means.
Midnight	40.8	39.9	39.3	45.4	46.9	53.5	57.4	56.7	55.1	49.5	45.2	43.3	47.75
1h. a.m.	40.6	39.9	39.3	45.3	46.1	53.1	57.1	56.2	54.7	49.6	45.3	43.5	47.37
2 „	40.5	39.8	38.9	45.2	45.6	52.8	57.0	55.5	54.7	49.3	45.2	43.4	47.32
3 „	40.5	39.9	38.7	45.0	45.1	52.6	57.1	55.1	54.8	49.1	45.4	43.8	47.26
4 „	40.6	39.7	38.9	45.2	44.5	52.4	57.3	54.8	54.6	49.2	45.3	44.0	47.21
5 „	40.7	39.7	39.0	45.4	45.5	53.0	57.6	54.8	54.4	48.9	45.7	44.0	47.39
6 „	40.6	39.5	39.2	46.0	48.7	54.8	59.4	56.5	54.6	48.9	45.8	44.2	48.17
7 „	40.6	39.5	39.8	48.3	52.3	57.4	61.7	59.2	56.2	49.7	46.2	44.4	49.61
8 „	40.7	40.1	41.9	51.1	54.8	59.1	64.0	62.3	58.7	51.3	46.8	44.3	51.28
9 „	41.6	41.5	44.5	53.3	57.4	61.2	66.8	64.6	61.1	54.2	48.1	45.0	53.27
10 „	43.3	43.3	47.4	54.8	59.4	62.5	68.0	65.6	62.8	56.4	49.7	45.9	54.93
11 „	44.3	44.9	48.9	56.0	61.0	63.0	69.6	66.4	63.9	57.9	50.9	47.0	56.15
Noon	45.3	46.3	50.1	56.5	61.4	64.1	72.3	67.3	65.4	58.5	51.9	47.8	57.24
1h. p.m.	46.0	47.1	50.1	56.5	61.8	64.6	71.8	67.9	65.4	58.9	52.3	47.9	57.52
2 „	46.0	47.8	50.3	56.5	62.0	64.2	71.7	67.6	65.0	58.5	52.4	47.9	57.49
3 „	45.7	47.6	49.7	56.4	62.0	63.9	71.3	68.1	64.4	57.6	51.4	47.3	57.12
4 „	44.8	46.8	48.8	55.2	61.7	62.9	70.6	67.5	63.8	56.3	50.2	46.6	56.27
5 „	43.9	45.3	47.8	54.4	60.6	62.3	69.7	65.9	61.9	55.0	49.3	46.1	55.20
6 „	43.5	44.1	46.1	53.4	58.7	61.3	67.8	65.0	60.0	53.8	48.5	45.9	54.01
7 „	43.2	43.2	44.8	51.0	56.7	59.2	67.0	63.5	58.4	52.9	48.2	45.4	52.79
8 „	43.0	42.8	43.7	49.3	53.7	57.1	64.9	62.1	57.5	51.4	47.9	45.2	51.63
9 „	42.8	42.5	43.6	48.4	51.6	55.4	63.5	61.0	56.7	52.1	47.4	45.2	50.76
10 „	42.8	42.0	41.8	47.7	50.1	54.4	62.3	60.2	56.0	51.9	47.3	45.0	50.13
11 „	42.5	41.9	41.6	46.8	49.5	53.9	61.2	59.4	55.5	51.7	47.3	44.6	49.66
Means	42.7	42.7	43.8	50.6	54.0	58.3	64.5	61.8	59.0	53.1	48.1	45.3	51.99
Number of Days employed }	32	19	15	15	15	14	8	11	17	22	19	31	..

TABLE XCIV.—MONTHLY MEAN TEMPERATURE of the Air at every Hour of the Day, through the Range of Years 1849 to 1868, during prevalence of SOUTH-WEST WIND.

Hour, Greenwich Mean Solar Time (Civil reckoning).	January.	February.	March.	April.	May.	June.	July.	August.	September.	October.	November.	December.	Yearly Means.
Midnight	41.9	42.0	42.5	46.5	49.6	53.5	57.1	57.4	54.3	49.7	44.4	44.0	48.58
1h. a.m.	41.9	41.9	42.3	46.2	49.2	53.0	56.7	57.0	54.1	49.6	44.3	44.1	48.37
2 „	41.8	41.8	42.3	46.0	48.9	52.6	56.2	56.7	53.8	49.4	44.5	44.1	48.18
3 „	41.8	41.8	42.2	45.8	48.7	52.4	55.9	56.5	53.7	49.4	44.4	43.8	48.03
4 „	41.7	41.8	42.1	45.7	48.5	52.3	55.8	56.2	53.7	49.4	44.4	43.8	47.95
5 „	41.6	41.9	42.0	45.6	49.1	53.0	56.3	56.3	53.6	49.6	44.3	43.8	48.03
6 „	41.8	42.0	42.6	46.1	51.0	55.1	58.0	57.4	53.7	49.4	44.5	43.9	48.72
7 „	41.8	42.0	42.6	47.7	53.3	57.5	60.5	59.8	55.0	49.7	44.5	43.9	49.66
8 „	41.9	42.6	44.1	49.9	55.2	59.3	62.7	61.2	57.2	51.2	44.9	44.0	51.27
9 „	42.5	43.7	46.2	52.1	57.5	61.2	64.7	64.3	59.8	53.5	46.1	44.6	53.03
10 „	43.7	45.3	48.1	53.3	59.0	62.6	66.1	66.1	61.6	55.0	47.7	45.8	54.55
11 „	44.8	46.9	49.6	54.9	60.1	63.6	67.2	67.4	63.2	56.7	49.0	47.0	55.87
Noon	45.9	48.2	50.7	55.7	61.1	64.8	68.3	68.7	64.2	57.8	49.9	47.8	56.93
1h. p.m.	46.5	48.9	51.2	56.2	61.9	65.0	69.1	69.2	64.6	58.1	50.1	48.2	57.41
2 „	46.6	49.1	51.6	56.8	62.1	64.9	69.4	69.5	64.6	58.0	50.3	48.4	57.62
3 „	46.2	48.8	51.3	56.6	62.2	64.7	69.2	69.3	64.1	57.2	49.6	47.8	57.25
4 „	45.4	48.0	50.6	55.9	61.2	64.0	68.8	68.1	61.9	54.8	48.4	47.0	56.36
5 „	44.5	46.8	49.4	54.4	60.9	63.1	67.6	66.7	61.2	54.5	47.3	46.5	55.16
6 „	43.9	45.7	47.7	53.0	58.0	61.6	65.8	64.9	59.4	54.3	46.7	46.1	53.85
7 „	43.4	44.9	46.4	51.1	55.8	60.0	63.6	62.6	57.8	52.5	46.3	43.8	52.52
8 „	43.1	44.6	45.3	49.9	53.4	57.9	61.5	60.7	56.7	51.9	45.9	45.8	51.39
9 „	43.0	44.1	44.6	48.9	51.7	56.2	59.8	59.3	55.9	51.3	45.6	45.6	50.49
10 „	42.9	43.8	44.2	48.3	50.5	55.3	58.9	58.3	55.5	50.9	45.3	45.3	49.93
11 „	42.7	43.6	43.8	47.8	50.0	54.5	58.3	57.7	54.9	50.7	45.2	45.3	49.54
Means	43.4	44.6	46.0	50.6	54.9	58.7	62.4	62.2	58.1	52.7	46.4	45.5	52.12
Number of Days employed }	194	147	114	90	115	148	157	200	151	149	128	183	..

TABLE XCV.—Monthly Mean Temperature of the Air at every Hour of the Day, through the Range of Years 1849 to 1868, during prevalence of West Wind.

Hour, Greenwich Mean Solar Time (Civil reckoning).	January.	February.	March.	April.	May.	June.	July.	August.	September.	October.	November.	December.	Yearly Means.
Midnight	40.3	42.1	43.2	46.0	49.3	53.7	56.0	56.9	53.1	49.1	43.0	41.4	47.84
1 a.m.	40.2	41.9	42.9	45.4	48.7	53.1	55.3	56.3	52.6	48.9	42.7	41.4	47.43
2 ,,	40.2	41.6	42.6	45.0	48.4	52.3	54.7	55.9	52.3	48.3	42.4	41.4	47.00
3 ,,	40.1	41.4	42.4	44.6	48.5	51.0	54.3	55.5	52.2	47.9	41.9	41.2	46.82
4 ,,	39.8	40.9	42.1	44.1	48.3	51.8	54.0	55.1	52.0	47.5	41.5	41.2	46.53
5 ,,	39.3	40.6	41.7	44.1	48.9	52.3	54.3	55.0	52.0	47.2	41.0	41.1	46.47
6 ,,	38.9	40.2	41.4	44.8	50.4	54.6	56.2	55.7	52.2	47.2	40.8	41.1	46.96
7 ,,	38.4	40.0	41.8	46.6	52.2	57.4	58.9	57.9	53.6	47.5	40.6	41.2	48.01
8 ,,	38.2	40.3	43.1	48.5	53.2	60.0	61.5	60.2	56.1	49.1	41.1	41.2	49.41
9 ,,	38.6	41.6	45.1	50.0	54.6	62.4	63.5	62.6	58.9	51.6	42.4	41.7	51.15
10 ,,	39.6	43.8	47.0	51.9	56.7	63.7	65.4	64.5	60.9	53.7	44.3	42.7	52.85
11 ,,	40.8	45.5	48.3	53.5	58.3	64.7	67.4	65.6	62.5	55.8	46.1	43.6	54.34
Noon	41.9	46.7	49.3	54.9	60.9	66.0	69.0	67.2	63.9	56.7	47.1	44.6	55.68
1 p.m.	42.6	47.4	50.2	55.6	62.2	66.8	69.8	67.8	64.3	57.0	47.6	45.2	56.38
2 ,,	42.6	47.6	50.7	55.9	63.1	66.8	70.0	68.3	64.8	56.9	47.8	45.3	56.65
3 ,,	42.3	47.1	50.5	56.4	62.9	66.8	69.9	68.4	64.5	55.9	46.8	44.7	56.35
4 ,,	41.7	46.4	49.4	55.9	61.6	65.8	68.3	67.2	63.5	54.7	45.4	43.9	55.40
5 ,,	40.7	45.3	48.1	54.4	60.6	64.9	68.2	65.8	61.5	52.9	44.1	43.4	54.16
6 ,,	39.9	44.2	46.6	52.8	59.5	63.9	66.0	64.2	59.6	51.2	43.1	43.0	52.83
7 ,,	39.6	43.4	44.8	50.5	57.2	61.6	64.0	61.7	57.5	50.2	42.3	42.8	51.30
8 ,,	39.3	42.0	43.8	48.5	54.5	59.4	61.7	59.9	55.9	49.4	41.8	42.6	49.07
9 ,,	39.0	42.3	43.8	47.1	52.6	57.5	59.8	58.3	54.9	48.5	41.2	42.3	48.86
10 ,,	38.9	42.0	42.1	46.1	51.4	56.2	58.5	57.3	54.0	47.8	40.7	42.1	48.09
11 ,,	38.7	41.4	41.8	45.0	50.6	55.0	57.4	56.1	53.2	47.4	40.3	41.8	47.39
Means	40.1	43.2	45.1	49.5	54.8	59.5	61.9	61.0	57.3	50.9	43.2	42.5	50.75
Number of Days employed	32	38	34	25	15	33	51	51	38	26	15	43	..

TABLE XCVI.—Monthly Mean Temperature of the Air at every Hour of the Day, through the Range of Years 1849 to 1868, during prevalence of North-West Wind.

Hour, Greenwich Mean Solar Time (Civil reckoning).	January.	February.	March.	April.	May.	June.	July.	August.	September.	October.	November.	December.	Yearly Means.
Midnight	39.2	38.3	39.6	41.5	44.6	54.2	53.3	56.2	52.3	48.9	39.7	39.7	45.62
1 a.m.	39.1	37.8	39.2	40.6	44.3	54.3	51.5	55.8	51.8	48.7	39.6	39.4	45.18
2 ,,	39.0	37.1	38.9	39.7	43.5	52.9	52.0	55.1	51.0	48.5	39.5	39.3	44.71
3 ,,	38.7	36.9	38.2	38.7	42.9	51.8	51.8	54.8	50.4	48.4	39.3	39.3	44.33
4 ,,	38.5	36.4	38.0	37.7	42.5	52.2	51.6	54.6	50.0	48.5	39.0	38.8	43.99
5 ,,	38.5	36.1	38.0	37.2	42.6	52.3	51.8	54.1	49.9	48.1	38.9	38.6	43.86
6 ,,	38.4	33.5	37.9	38.0	44.3	53.6	53.7	54.7	49.8	48.0	38.5	38.4	44.23
7 ,,	38.1	35.4	38.4	40.6	49.0	55.9	56.0	56.6	50.6	48.0	38.4	37.9	45.15
8 ,,	37.8	35.7	39.7	42.7	48.0	57.0	57.9	58.7	52.6	49.1	38.4	37.9	46.29
9 ,,	38.2	36.8	41.4	44.4	49.4	58.0	59.4	60.6	55.9	50.6	39.5	37.8	47.74
10 ,,	38.8	38.1	42.9	46.0	50.4	60.3	61.2	61.5	57.9	52.4	41.3	38.4	49.10
11 ,,	39.8	39.5	44.5	47.3	51.4	61.8	62.3	62.9	60.0	53.6	42.4	39.2	50.47
Noon	40.8	40.5	45.6	48.6	54.8	63.2	62.9	64.7	60.5	54.9	43.7	40.0	51.47
1 p.m.	41.1	41.2	46.7	48.8	54.8	63.6	63.7	65.7	61.7	55.2	44.4	40.1	52.25
2 ,,	43.2	41.0	47.2	50.0	54.3	62.9	64.1	66.2	62.1	55.3	44.6	40.2	52.51
3 ,,	41.0	41.0	47.3	50.3	55.0	64.0	64.7	66.6	61.1	54.4	43.7	39.6	52.39
4 ,,	40.3	40.0	46.5	49.0	53.6	63.5	64.2	66.1	60.5	53.1	42.9	38.9	51.58
5 ,,	39.3	38.3	45.6	47.4	53.6	62.6	63.7	64.6	58.7	52.1	41.9	38.3	50.51
6 ,,	38.9	37.4	44.1	46.2	52.2	61.4	62.1	63.1	56.7	51.0	40.9	37.9	49.33
7 ,,	38.2	36.4	42.9	44.3	50.5	59.7	61.0	60.9	55.0	50.3	40.2	37.4	48.07
8 ,,	37.4	35.7	42.3	43.8	51.5	58.6	58.9	59.9	53.6	49.6	39.6	37.2	47.79
9 ,,	36.8	33.0	41.5	41.0	47.4	56.1	56.9	59.2	52.5	49.1	39.1	36.7	45.78
10 ,,	36.5	34.6	40.8	40.3	46.3	54.8	55.3	56.5	51.6	48.5	38.8	36.3	45.04
11 ,,	36.3	34.1	40.1	39.9	45.3	54.1	54.0	55.3	50.6	47.8	38.5	35.9	44.32
Means	38.8	37.5	42.0	43.4	48.6	57.9	58.1	59.6	54.9	50.6	40.5	38.5	47.53
Number of Days employed	12	14	30	13	12	18	21	27	11	18	27	32	..

TABLE XCVII.—MONTHLY MEAN TEMPERATURE of EVAPORATION at every HOUR of the DAY, through the RANGE of YEARS 1849 to 1868, during prevalence of NORTH WIND.

Hour, Greenwich Mean Solar Time (civil reckoning).	January.	February.	March.	April.	May.	June.	July.	August.	September.	October.	November.	December.	Yearly Means.
Midnight 1h. a.m.	32.5	30.7	34.3	36.9	43.4	50.2	54.3	53.8	59.1	44.9	37.3	34.2	41.80
2 „	32.7	30.6	34.1	36.7	42.0	49.9	54.0	53.5	59.1	44.7	37.1	34.0	41.61
3 „	32.8	30.4	33.8	36.5	42.5	49.5	53.8	53.4	59.0	44.6	36.9	33.9	41.43
4 „	32.8	30.4	33.9	36.3	42.1	49.3	53.6	53.1	59.0	44.3	36.7	33.7	41.27
5 „	32.9	30.1	33.8	36.2	41.9	49.3	53.3	52.7	48.9	44.3	36.4	33.5	41.11
6 „	32.7	30.1	33.6	36.3	41.9	49.7	53.4	52.3	48.8	43.9	36.4	33.4	41.04
7 „	32.7	29.9	33.5	36.6	42.5	50.6	53.9	52.5	49.0	43.7	36.3	33.3	41.21
8 „	32.7	29.9	33.7	37.5	43.6	51.9	54.9	53.4	49.8	43.8	36.1	33.1	41.70
9 „	32.8	30.1	34.4	38.9	44.6	53.1	55.9	54.1	51.0	44.4	36.4	33.0	42.39
10 „	32.9	31.0	35.7	40.1	45.6	54.1	56.9	55.1	52.4	46.0	37.2	33.3	43.36
11 „	33.5	32.1	36.5	41.2	46.3	54.9	57.9	56.0	53.1	47.3	38.2	33.8	44.22
Noon	34.0	33.1	37.3	42.3	47.1	55.8	58.5	56.8	53.7	48.1	39.1	34.5	45.03
1h. p.m.	34.4	34.0	37.8	43.1	47.7	56.7	59.2	57.6	54.0	48.2	39.9	35.5	45.66
2 „	34.3	34.4	38.3	43.5	48.0	56.8	59.7	57.8	54.3	48.2	40.3	35.7	45.96
3 „	34.5	34.5	38.1	43.8	48.4	56.8	59.9	58.0	54.5	48.2	40.3	35.7	46.06
4 „	34.3	34.5	37.9	44.0	48.4	56.4	59.7	58.2	54.3	47.7	39.8	35.4	45.88
5 „	33.8	34.0	37.7	43.4	48.1	56.1	59.4	57.9	53.9	47.1	39.1	35.0	45.44
6 „	33.3	33.2	37.0	42.6	47.5	55.6	59.0	57.2	53.2	46.3	38.5	34.6	44.83
7 „	32.9	32.5	36.2	41.7	46.7	54.6	58.4	56.6	52.1	45.7	38.1	34.4	44.16
8 „	32.5	32.0	35.5	40.7	45.6	53.7	57.3	55.5	51.0	45.3	37.6	34.1	43.58
9 „	32.2	31.5	34.7	39.6	44.7	52.5	55.8	54.3	50.6	44.6	37.3	33.7	42.62
10 „	31.8	31.1	34.2	38.6	44.1	51.3	54.9	53.5	49.9	44.1	36.9	33.5	41.99
11 „	31.6	30.4	33.8	37.7	43.8	50.5	54.2	52.9	49.4	43.6	36.5	33.2	41.47
—	31.4	30.0	33.4	37.4	43.4	49.9	53.9	52.1	49.4	43.2	36.2	32.8	41.09
Means	33.0	31.7	35.4	39.7	45.0	52.9	56.3	54.9	51.2	45.5	37.7	34.0	43.11
Number of Days employed	15	32	37	27	42	32	25	24	26	22	40	29	..

TABLE XCVIII.—MONTHLY MEAN TEMPERATURE of EVAPORATION at every HOUR of the DAY, through the RANGE of YEARS 1849 to 1868, during prevalence of NORTH-EAST WIND.

Hour, Greenwich Mean Solar Time (civil reckoning).	January.	February.	March.	April.	May.	June.	July.	August.	September.	October.	November.	December.	Yearly Means.
Midnight 1h. a.m.	31.1	30.6	33.4	39.2	42.8	51.2	54.4	55.1	52.1	46.6	39.5	34.3	42.52
2 „	31.0	30.4	33.2	38.8	42.4	50.8	54.0	55.0	51.7	46.3	39.2	34.2	42.25
3 „	30.9	30.4	33.0	38.5	42.1	50.4	53.7	54.7	51.3	46.2	39.2	34.0	42.05
4 „	30.9	30.2	31.8	38.3	41.8	50.0	53.7	54.6	51.1	45.9	39.0	33.9	41.85
5 „	30.8	30.3	31.8	38.3	41.8	49.9	53.7	54.4	50.7	45.9	38.8	33.9	41.87
6 „	30.7	30.2	32.8	38.8	43.4	51.7	55.1	54.8	50.9	45.7	38.7	33.7	42.21
7 „	30.7	30.1	33.2	40.0	45.6	54.6	56.0	56.0	52.2	45.8	38.7	33.5	42.94
8 „	30.8	30.4	34.0	41.4	46.6	54.6	58.1	57.1	53.8	46.7	39.2	33.4	43.85
9 „	31.0	31.3	35.1	42.7	48.0	56.8	58.6	58.6	55.8	48.1	40.0	33.5	44.96
10 „	31.5	32.2	36.1	43.8	48.9	56.8	60.5	59.4	57.1	49.5	41.2	33.9	45.91
11 „	32.0	32.9	37.0	44.9	49.6	57.6	61.3	60.2	57.8	50.1	41.9	34.7	46.67
Noon	32.5	33.7	37.6	45.6	50.2	58.2	62.1	61.0	58.4	50.6	42.4	34.9	47.27
1h. p.m.	32.7	33.8	37.7	46.3	50.5	58.5	62.7	61.4	58.5	50.8	42.5	35.1	47.51
2 „	32.7	33.8	38.0	46.3	50.5	58.5	63.1	61.6	58.3	50.8	42.2	35.3	47.58
3 „	32.5	33.4	37.9	46.1	50.4	58.3	62.2	61.2	58.0	50.5	41.7	34.8	47.33
4 „	32.0	33.1	37.1	45.4	49.8	58.2	62.5	60.9	57.2	49.5	40.3	34.0	46.76
5 „	31.5	31.9	36.3	44.6	48.9	57.4	61.5	60.1	56.1	48.5	40.3	34.0	45.92
6 „	31.2	31.3	35.2	43.3	47.8	56.5	60.3	59.2	54.7	47.8	39.8	33.8	45.08
7 „	30.9	30.9	34.3	41.8	46.5	55.0	59.1	58.1	53.6	47.1	39.5	33.5	44.19
8 „	30.8	30.5	33.8	40.6	45.3	54.0	57.8	56.9	52.9	46.5	39.2	33.3	43.35
9 „	30.7	30.3	33.3	39.6	44.1	52.7	56.5	56.0	52.1	46.1	38.9	33.3	42.80
10 „	30.4	29.9	32.8	38.6	44.1	52.7	55.5	55.5	51.7	45.9	38.6	33.2	42.35
11 „	30.1	29.7	32.7	38.5	42.7	51.1	55.1	55.0	51.2	45.7	38.3	33.1	41.93
Means	31.3	31.3	34.7	41.7	46.0	54.3	58.1	57.6	54.1	47.6	39.9	34.0	44.21
Number of Days employed	57	58	74	77	97	49	43	37	66	53	71	31	..

TABLE XCIX.—MONTHLY MEAN TEMPERATURE of EVAPORATION at every HOUR of the DAY, through the RANGE of YEARS 1849 to 1868, during prevalence of EAST WIND.

Hour, Greenwich Mean Solar Time (Civil reckoning).	January.	February.	March.	April.	May.	June.	July.	August.	September.	October.	November.	December.	Yearly Means.
Midnight	29.5	33.7	32.9	40.2	45.4	52.7	53.6	56.2	51.8	47.3	36.8	33.8	42.83
1 a.m.	29.6	33.6	33.0	39.8	44.0	52.2	53.3	56.0	51.6	47.0	36.5	33.2	42.56
2 ,,	29.8	33.3	32.8	39.5	44.6	51.9	52.9	56.0	51.0	47.0	36.1	32.8	42.31
3 ,,	30.1	32.9	32.5	39.2	44.2	51.6	52.6	55.9	50.9	47.1	36.1	32.6	42.14
4 ,,	30.3	32.7	32.3	38.9	44.0	51.4	51.8	55.6	51.2	47.1	35.8	32.4	42.00
5 ,,	30.3	32.6	32.1	38.7	44.4	52.1	53.2	55.6	51.2	46.8	35.9	32.4	42.12
6 ,,	30.1	32.5	32.1	39.5	46.0	54.3	54.6	57.0	51.3	47.0	36.0	32.4	42.75
7 ,,	30.0	32.3	32.6	41.2	48.2	57.3	56.2	59.6	52.7	47.4	36.1	32.2	43.82
8 ,,	29.6	32.6	33.8	43.1	50.0	59.3	58.4	61.5	55.0	48.6	36.5	32.2	45.05
9 ,,	29.5	33.6	35.1	44.9	51.4	60.7	59.7	63.1	57.3	50.4	37.5	32.6	46.32
10 ,,	30.1	34.3	36.3	46.2	52.3	61.5	60.8	64.1	58.9	51.9	39.4	33.4	47.43
11 ,,	30.7	34.9	37.2	47.3	52.8	62.2	61.8	64.6	59.8	52.9	41.1	34.2	48.29
Noon	31.3	35.7	38.0	47.7	53.4	62.4	62.8	64.8	60.3	53.5	41.9	34.9	48.89
1 p.m.	31.5	35.9	38.3	48.1	53.8	62.6	63.1	64.6	60.4	53.9	42.1	34.9	49.06
2 ,,	31.4	36.0	38.4	47.9	53.1	62.1	63.1	64.6	60.6	53.9	41.6	34.8	48.96
3 ,,	30.7	35.9	38.3	47.4	52.7	61.7	62.9	64.2	60.1	53.4	40.9	34.3	48.54
4 ,,	30.1	35.7	37.6	46.7	52.2	61.2	62.1	63.9	59.1	52.4	39.9	33.8	47.89
5 ,,	29.6	34.8	36.6	45.6	51.4	60.0	61.3	62.8	57.6	51.8	39.0	33.5	47.00
6 ,,	29.2	34.4	35.5	44.3	50.2	58.7	59.9	61.9	56.2	51.1	38.4	33.3	46.10
7 ,,	28.6	34.3	34.6	42.7	49.0	58.0	58.3	60.8	55.4	50.7	38.0	33.1	45.29
8 ,,	28.2	34.2	34.3	41.6	47.7	56.4	57.1	59.6	54.7	50.3	37.7	33.1	44.57
9 ,,	27.5	34.1	33.9	41.0	46.9	55.1	55.8	59.1	54.1	49.9	37.4	32.8	43.97
10 ,,	27.1	34.0	33.6	40.6	46.3	54.4	55.1	58.7	53.6	49.5	37.0	32.7	43.63
11 ,,	27.1	33.8	33.4	40.3	46.0	53.9	54.6	58.2	53.1	49.1	36.7	32.5	43.23
Means -	29.7	34.1	34.8	43.0	48.8	57.2	57.7	60.4	55.3	50.0	38.1	33.2	45.19
Number of Days employed }	6	20	35	51	26	22	9	13	21	32	31	17	..

TABLE C.—MONTHLY MEAN TEMPERATURE of EVAPORATION at every HOUR of the DAY, through the RANGE of YEARS 1849 to 1868, during prevalence of SOUTH-EAST WIND.

Hour, Greenwich Mean Solar Time (Civil reckoning).	January.	February.	March.	April.	May.	June.	July.	August.	September.	October.	November.	December.	Yearly Means.
Midnight	34.0	34.1	35.5	40.7	43.9	49.7	57.2	59.8	50.1	50.4	40.7	35.4	44.29
1 a.m.	34.0	33.7	35.3	40.4	43.5	49.3	56.6	59.2	49.7	50.4	40.7	35.2	44.00
2 ,,	33.8	33.6	35.1	40.3	43.4	49.1	56.1	58.8	49.6	50.1	41.0	35.0	43.83
3 ,,	33.9	33.7	35.0	40.3	43.1	48.8	55.8	58.4	49.2	50.1	41.0	34.7	43.67
4 ,,	33.8	33.8	34.8	40.2	42.9	48.7	55.5	58.2	48.9	49.9	40.9	34.9	43.54
5 ,,	33.7	33.7	34.9	40.2	43.4	49.6	56.2	58.2	48.3	49.8	40.9	34.9	43.57
6 ,,	33.6	33.5	34.7	41.0	43.8	50.6	58.6	59.4	48.3	49.8	40.9	34.7	44.37
7 ,,	33.5	33.5	35.2	42.3	48.0	54.4	60.5	61.3	49.8	50.5	41.1	34.8	45.49
8 ,,	33.6	33.6	36.8	45.7	49.9	55.8	63.6	63.3	52.8	51.8	41.5	35.0	46.91
9 ,,	33.9	34.3	39.2	47.7	51.2	57.1	64.7	65.0	56.0	53.6	42.6	35.6	48.42
10 ,,	34.5	36.2	41.1	48.7	52.1	57.9	65.6	65.6	57.3	54.7	43.5	36.7	49.41
11 ,,	35.4	36.2	42.1	49.1	52.5	58.6	65.7	66.2	58.1	55.8	44.0	37.9	50.13
Noon	36.1	37.4	43.0	49.9	52.5	58.8	66.0	66.9	58.6	56.6	44.6	38.9	50.86
1 p.m.	36.6	37.9	43.1	50.3	53.6	60.4	66.3	67.1	58.9	56.7	45.2	39.2	51.18
2 ,,	36.5	37.8	43.2	49.9	52.5	59.9	66.4	66.6	58.6	56.1	44.6	38.8	50.89
3 ,,	36.0	37.5	42.5	49.4	51.9	59.2	65.9	66.0	57.6	55.2	43.7	37.9	50.23
4 ,,	35.6	36.7	41.6	48.5	51.1	58.4	65.0	65.7	56.4	54.0	43.0	37.3	49.44
5 ,,	35.8	36.0	40.4	47.4	50.4	57.6	64.1	65.0	55.2	53.1	42.7	36.9	48.69
6 ,,	35.6	35.7	39.3	46.0	49.0	56.7	62.8	63.9	54.0	52.6	42.3	36.7	47.88
7 ,,	35.6	35.3	38.6	45.1	47.8	55.3	61.3	62.8	53.3	52.1	42.1	36.7	47.15
8 ,,	35.3	34.9	38.0	44.4	47.2	54.4	60.0	62.3	52.8	52.1	42.1	36.8	46.68
9 ,,	35.6	34.9	38.0	44.4	47.2	54.2	60.0	61.5	52.8	52.1	41.1	36.3	46.68
10 ,,	35.8	34.5	37.6	43.9	46.7	52.3	58.9	61.5	52.6	51.9	41.9	36.2	45.92
11 ,,	35.9	34.4	37.3	43.8	46.5	51.6	57.6	60.9	52.2	51.7	43.0	36.2	45.92
Means -	35.0	35.2	38.6	45.3	48.4	55.0	61.5	62.9	53.6	52.7	42.4	36.4	47.25
Number of Days employed }	30	23	27	27	12	14	5	12	22	31	30	33	..

TABLE CI.—MONTHLY MEAN TEMPERATURE of EVAPORATION at every HOUR of the DAY, through the RANGE of YEARS 1849 to 1868, during prevalence of SOUTH WIND.

Hour, Greenwich Mean Solar Time (Civil reckoning).	January.	February.	March.	April.	May.	June.	July.	August.	September.	October.	November.	December.	Yearly Means.
Midnight	39·6	38·8	37·6	42·8	45·1	51·0	53·4	54·9	53·5	48·3	44·1	41·9	46·08
1ʰ a.m.	39·4	39·0	37·6	42·8	44·5	50·7	55·3	54·9	53·2	48·5	44·0	42·0	45·97
2 ,,	39·3	38·8	37·4	42·9	44·1	50·6	55·1	54·5	53·1	48·3	44·0	42·0	45·84
3 ,,	39·4	38·9	37·4	42·7	43·7	50·5	55·3	53·9	53·2	48·0	44·3	42·3	45·80
4 ,,	39·4	38·7	37·4	43·1	43·3	50·5	55·6	53·6	53·2	48·1	44·4	42·5	45·82
5 ,,	39·4	38·7	37·4	43·3	43·9	50·9	55·9	53·5	53·0	47·0	44·5	42·7	45·93
6 ,,	39·4	38·6	37·7	43·9	46·3	52·1	56·9	54·6	53·3	47·8	44·6	42·9	46·31
7 ,,	39·4	38·8	38·1	45·5	48·7	53·5	58·6	56·7	54·4	48·5	44·9	43·1	47·50
8 ,,	39·5	39·1	39·7	47·2	50·5	54·6	60·0	58·2	56·1	49·8	45·3	43·2	48·58
9 ,,	40·3	40·3	41·7	48·7	51·8	55·7	61·1	59·2	57·4	51·0	46·4	43·6	49·85
10 ,,	41·5	41·5	43·6	49·2	52·9	56·3	62·1	59·6	57·9	53·2	47·2	44·1	50·76
11 ,,	42·4	42·8	44·4	49·8	53·5	56·5	62·9	60·3	58·4	54·0	48·3	45·1	51·53
Noon	43·2	44·0	44·8	50·2	53·8	57·2	64·0	60·5	59·5	54·6	49·1	45·6	52·21
1ʰ p.m.	43·4	44·4	44·8	50·0	54·1	57·4	63·7	60·7	59·4	54·5	49·4	45·7	52·29
2 ,,	43·6	44·9	44·5	49·8	54·1	57·5	63·5	60·4	59·4	54·2	49·3	45·6	52·23
3 ,,	43·5	44·7	44·2	49·8	54·1	56·7	63·3	60·7	59·0	54·0	48·8	45·2	52·00
4 ,,	43·0	44·2	43·8	49·0	53·9	55·9	63·3	60·0	58·9	53·3	48·1	44·7	51·52
5 ,,	42·5	43·4	43·3	48·9	53·2	55·4	62·9	59·9	57·9	52·6	47·3	44·4	50·98
6 ,,	42·1	42·5	42·4	48·4	52·4	54·8	62·4	60·0	56·9	52·0	46·9	44·1	50·41
7 ,,	41·9	42·0	41·8	47·2	51·4	54·0	62·3	59·2	56·1	51·4	46·7	44·0	49·83
8 ,,	41·7	41·6	41·5	45·9	49·8	52·6	61·2	58·6	55·5	51·1	46·6	43·7	49·15
9 ,,	41·6	41·5	40·5	45·1	48·5	51·7	60·0	58·1	55·0	50·9	46·3	43·7	48·56
10 ,,	41·5	40·9	40·0	44·6	47·9	50·9	59·1	57·7	54·6	50·6	46·1	43·5	48·12
11 ,,	41·4	40·7	39·5	44·0	47·3	50·9	58·4	57·3	54·1	50·6	46·1	43·1	47·78
Means	41·2	41·2	40·9	46·4	49·5	53·7	59·9	57·8	56·0	51·0	46·4	43·7	48·97
Number of Days employed	32	19	15	15	15	14	8	11	17	22	19	31	..

TABLE CII.—MONTHLY MEAN TEMPERATURE of EVAPORATION at every HOUR of the DAY, through the RANGE of YEARS 1849 to 1868, during prevalence of SOUTH-WEST WIND.

Hour, Greenwich Mean Solar Time (Civil reckoning).	January.	February.	March.	April.	May.	June.	July.	August.	September.	October.	November.	December.	Yearly Means.
Midnight	40·5	40·7	40·9	44·8	48·1	51·7	55·2	55·8	55·1	48·3	43·1	42·6	47·07
1ʰ a.m.	40·5	40·6	41·0	44·8	47·8	51·3	54·8	55·6	52·9	48·2	43·0	42·6	46·95
2 ,,	40·4	40·5	40·9	44·4	47·5	51·0	54·4	55·3	52·7	48·2	43·1	42·6	46·75
3 ,,	40·4	40·5	40·9	44·4	47·4	50·9	54·3	55·2	52·6	48·1	43·1	42·5	46·68
4 ,,	40·4	40·3	40·8	44·2	47·3	50·9	54·2	55·0	52·7	48·0	43·1	42·5	46·63
5 ,,	40·3	40·5	40·7	44·1	47·7	51·5	55·1	55·6	52·6	48·0	43·0	42·5	46·72
6 ,,	40·3	40·5	40·8	44·4	49·0	52·8	55·8	55·8	52·7	48·0	43·1	42·5	47·14
7 ,,	40·4	40·7	42·2	45·6	50·6	54·2	57·2	57·4	53·5	48·3	43·2	42·6	47·91
8 ,,	40·5	41·2	42·3	47·1	51·7	55·3	58·3	58·5	55·1	49·4	43·4	42·7	48·79
9 ,,	41·0	42·2	43·9	48·5	53·0	56·2	59·5	59·7	56·4	51·0	44·3	43·2	48·98
10 ,,	41·8	43·4	45·1	49·3	53·7	56·9	60·7	60·3	57·3	51·9	45·4	44·0	50·73
11 ,,	42·7	43·5	46·0	49·9	54·3	57·5	60·2	60·7	57·9	52·9	46·3	44·9	51·47
Noon	43·4	45·2	46·6	50·4	54·8	58·0	60·7	61·4	58·3	53·5	46·9	45·5	52·06
1ʰ p.m.	43·8	45·5	46·9	50·7	55·0	58·2	61·1	61·7	58·4	53·5	47·1	45·7	52·30
2 ,,	43·9	45·6	47·0	50·5	55·2	58·1	61·2	61·6	58·5	53·4	47·1	45·9	52·38
3 ,,	43·6	45·4	46·8	51·0	55·2	58·1	61·2	61·5	58·3	53·0	46·7	45·6	52·20
4 ,,	43·1	45·0	46·4	50·7	54·9	57·7	61·2	61·1	57·8	52·3	45·9	45·1	51·77
5 ,,	42·5	44·2	45·7	49·7	54·1	57·2	60·6	60·4	56·9	51·6	45·2	44·7	51·07
6 ,,	42·1	43·6	44·9	48·7	53·3	56·3	59·7	59·4	56·0	50·9	44·8	44·5	50·34
7 ,,	41·7	43·1	44·0	48·1	51·5	55·5	58·7	58·4	55·2	50·4	44·5	44·2	49·61
8 ,,	41·5	42·8	43·4	47·3	50·1	54·3	57·6	57·4	54·6	50·0	44·3	44·2	48·96
9 ,,	41·4	42·3	43·9	46·7	49·2	53·5	56·8	56·7	54·1	49·7	44·1	44·0	48·47
10 ,,	41·4	42·3	43·4	46·4	48·6	53·0	56·3	56·3	53·7	49·4	43·9	43·9	48·13
11 ,,	41·2	42·1	42·3	46·0	48·3	52·6	56·0	56·0	53·5	49·3	43·7	43·8	47·90
Means	41·6	42·6	43·5	47·4	51·2	54·7	57·9	58·2	55·2	50·3	44·5	43·8	49·24
Number of Days employed	194	147	114	90	115	146	150	200	151	149	128	183	..

TABLE CIII.—MONTHLY MEAN TEMPERATURE of EVAPORATION at every HOUR of the DAY, through the RANGE of YEARS 1849 to 1868, during prevalence of WEST WIND.

Hour, Greenwich Mean Solar Time (Civil reckoning).	January.	February.	March.	April.	May.	June.	July.	August.	September.	October.	November.	December.	Yearly Means.
Midnight	38·8	40·3	41·8	43·8	47·3	51·7	54·3	55·3	51·1	47·7	41·4	40·2	46·16
1ʰ. a.m.	38·7	40·3	41·6	43·5	47·1	51·3	54·0	54·9	51·0	47·5	41·2	40·1	45·03
2 „	38·6	40·0	41·3	43·0	46·9	50·8	53·5	54·5	50·7	47·0	41·1	39·9	45·61
3 „	38·5	39·8	41·2	42·6	46·9	50·4	53·2	54·2	50·6	46·6	40·6	39·9	45·38
4 „	38·1	39·4	40·9	42·3	46·8	50·4	53·1	54·0	50·6	46·5	40·0	39·9	45·17
5 „	37·8	39·0	40·7	42·3	46·6	50·9	53·2	53·7	50·5	46·2	39·7	39·9	45·04
6 „	37·4	38·7	40·4	42·7	47·7	52·4	54·3	54·1	50·7	46·1	39·6	39·8	45·32
7 „	36·8	38·5	40·6	44·0	48·9	54·1	55·0	55·4	51·7	46·4	39·3	39·8	45·95
8 „	36·6	38·7	41·2	45·2	49·6	55·4	57·3	56·4	53·0	47·4	39·7	39·8	46·69
9 „	36·7	39·6	42·6	46·3	50·6	56·3	58·4	57·6	54·6	49·2	40·7	40·2	47·73
10 „	37·4	40·8	43·7	47·2	51·6	56·8	59·3	58·3	55·6	50·3	41·8	40·9	48·64
11 „	38·1	42·0	44·3	48·2	52·7	57·3	60·2	58·8	56·1	51·2	43·1	41·7	49·43
Noon	39·0	42·7	44·8	48·8	54·4	58·2	61·0	59·5	56·5	51·6	43·6	42·3	50·20
1ʰ. p.m.	39·3	43·0	45·4	49·3	54·0	58·6	61·4	59·7	56·6	51·9	43·9	42·6	50·58
2 „	39·6	43·1	45·5	49·4	55·3	58·9	61·4	60·1	56·8	51·5	44·0	42·6	50·68
3 „	39·5	42·9	45·5	49·3	55·2	59·0	61·3	60·1	56·9	51·0	43·4	42·4	50·54
4 „	39·0	42·5	44·9	49·0	54·6	58·6	60·9	59·7	56·4	50·3	42·7	41·8	50·03
5 „	38·3	42·0	44·2	48·1	53·9	58·2	60·6	59·0	55·6	49·3	41·8	41·6	49·38
6 „	37·7	41·3	43·3	47·1	53·1	57·5	59·8	58·1	54·7	48·4	41·0	41·3	48·61
7 „	37·5	40·8	42·4	46·2	51·8	56·3	58·7	57·1	53·7	47·9	40·4	41·1	47·84
8 „	37·4	40·5	41·6	45·1	50·4	55·6	57·8	56·3	53·0	47·4	39·9	40·0	47·16
9 „	37·2	40·1	40·9	44·2	49·3	54·4	56·8	55·5	52·3	46·8	39·5	40·8	46·48
10 „	37·2	40·0	40·4	43·3	48·5	53·5	56·1	55·0	51·9	46·4	39·0	40·6	46·05
11 „	37·2	39·8	40·2	42·9	48·0	52·9	55·5	54·1	51·4	46·1	38·7	40·4	45·63
Means	38·0	40·7	42·5	45·6	50·3	55·0	57·4	56·7	53·4	48·4	41·1	40·9	47·51
Number of Days employed	32	38	34	25	15	33	48	50	37	26	15	43	..

TABLE CIV.—MONTHLY MEAN TEMPERATURE of EVAPORATION at every HOUR of the DAY, through the RANGE of YEARS 1849 to 1868, during prevalence of NORTH-WEST WIND.

Hour, Greenwich Mean Solar Time (Civil reckoning.)	January.	February.	March.	April.	May.	June.	July.	August.	September.	October.	November.	December.	Yearly Means.
Midnight	37·1	35·9	37·5	39·2	42·3	51·3	50·6	53·8	50·7	47·3	38·3	38·2	43·55
1ʰ. a.m.	37·1	35·9	37·3	38·5	42·2	51·1	50·0	53·5	50·3	47·3	38·2	38·0	43·28
2 „	37·0	35·3	37·0	37·9	41·5	50·8	49·6	53·1	49·7	47·1	38·2	37·9	42·91
3 „	36·7	35·0	36·6	37·9	40·8	50·1	49·3	52·9	49·2	46·8	37·8	37·9	42·53
4 „	36·7	34·5	36·4	36·3	40·2	49·9	49·5	52·7	48·8	46·9	37·8	37·7	42·28
5 „	36·7	34·1	36·1	36·0	40·4	49·8	49·8	52·5	48·7	46·5	37·6	37·4	42·16
6 „	36·7	33·7	36·3	36·5	41·4	50·6	50·9	53·9	48·8	46·4	36·9	36·0	42·36
7 „	36·7	33·4	36·8	37·8	43·8	51·8	51·3	53·9	49·3	46·4	36·9	36·6	42·96
8 „	36·3	33·5	37·4	39·2	43·9	51·4	53·3	54·9	50·7	47·2	36·9	36·3	43·50
9 „	36·6	34·0	38·6	40·8	44·8	53·1	53·9	55·8	51·0	48·3	37·7	36·0	44·55
10 „	37·0	34·8	39·3	41·6	46·6	54·2	54·5	56·2	51·6	49·5	36·0	36·2	45·07
11 „	37·8	35·8	40·2	42·0	46·4	54·7	54·9	56·8	55·6	50·4	39·8	36·6	45·75
Noon	38·0	36·1	40·7	42·3	46·5	55·1	57·6	55·8	51·1	40·5	37·1	46·18
1ʰ. p.m.	38·2	36·6	41·2	41·9	47·7	55·6	55·5	57·8	54·2	51·3	40·9	37·3	46·58
2 „	38·2	36·2	41·7	43·4	48·2	55·5	55·6	57·9	54·3	51·5	41·1	37·2	46·73
3 „	38·0	36·3	41·9	43·6	48·2	55·5	55·9	58·2	54·1	50·7	40·6	37·0	46·67
4 „	37·5	35·8	41·4	42·1	47·8	55·4	55·8	57·7	53·7	49·9	40·0	36·4	46·21
5 „	37·0	35·1	41·2	42·2	47·4	55·0	55·9	57·0	52·8	49·3	39·4	36·1	45·70
6 „	36·4	34·4	40·4	41·3	46·7	54·6	55·0	56·2	52·2	48·5	38·7	35·7	45·03
7 „	36·0	33·9	39·8	40·4	46·1	53·8	54·4	55·4	51·3	48·4	38·3	35·2	44·42
8 „	35·4	33·1	39·5	39·4	45·1	52·7	53·0	54·5	50·5	47·8	37·8	35·2	43·67
9 „	34·9	32·6	38·9	38·5	44·3	51·8	52·3	53·7	50·1	47·6	37·5	34·8	43·08
10 „	34·8	32·4	38·3	38·2	43·8	51·3	51·3	53·8	49·7	47·2	37·3	34·6	42·70
11 „	34·7	32·2	38·0	37·7	43·1	50·8	50·8	52·8	49·0	46·4	37·0	34·2	42·23
Means	36·7	34·6	38·9	39·8	44·5	52·8	52·9	55·1	51·3	48·3	38·5	36·5	44·16
Number of Days employed	12	14	30	15	11	18	20	27	11	18	27	32	..

TABLE CV.—MEAN TEMPERATURE of the Air at every Hour of the Day, during prevalence of WINDS referred to EIGHT Points of Azimuth, through the RANGE of YEARS 1849 to 1868.

Hour, Greenwich Mean Solar Time (Civil reckoning).	N.	N.E.	E.	S.E.	S.	S.W.	W.	N.W.
Midnight	43·4	43·8	44·0	45·6	47·8	48·6	47·8	45·6
1ʰ. a.m.	43·1	43·4	43·6	45·1	47·6	48·4	47·4	45·2
2 „	42·9	43·1	43·3	44·9	47·3	48·2	47·1	44·7
3 „	42·6	42·9	43·1	44·7	47·3	48·0	46·8	44·3
4 „	42·4	42·8	42·9	44·5	47·2	47·9	46·5	44·0
5 „	42·4	42·9	43·1	44·6	47·4	48·1	46·5	43·9
6 „	42·7	43·4	44·0	45·5	48·2	48·7	47·0	44·2
7 „	43·5	44·3	45·7	47·3	49·6	49·9	48·0	45·1
8 „	44·6	46·0	47·7	49·3	51·3	51·3	49·4	46·3
9 „	46·1	47·7	49·9	51·8	53·3	53·0	51·1	47·7
10 „	47·6	49·4	51·9	53·8	54·9	54·6	52·8	49·1
11 „	49·1	50·8	53·3	55·3	56·1	55·9	54·3	50·3
Noon	50·2	52·0	54·7	56·7	57·2	56·9	55·7	51·5
1ʰ. p.m.	50·8	52·6	55·2	57·2	57·5	57·4	56·4	52·3
2 „	51·0	52·7	55·2	57·4	57·5	57·6	56·7	52·5
3 „	50·6	52·3	54·5	56·9	57·1	57·2	56·4	52·4
4 „	50·0	51·4	53·4	55·7	56·3	56·4	55·4	51·6
5 „	48·9	50·1	51·9	54·2	55·2	55·2	54·2	50·5
6 „	47·7	48·6	50·0	52·7	54·0	53·8	52·8	49·3
7 „	46·3	47·1	48·4	50·9	52·8	52·5	51·3	48·1
8 „	45·1	45·8	46·0	49·5	51·6	51·4	50·0	46·8
9 „	44·1	44·7	45·9	48·5	50·8	50·5	48·9	45·8
10 „	43·3	44·1	45·2	47·9	50·1	50·0	48·1	45·0
11 „	42·7	43·5	44·6	47·3	49·7	49·5	47·4	44·3
Means	45·9	46·9	48·3	50·3	52·0	52·1	50·7	47·5

TABLE CVI.—MEAN DIURNAL INEQUALITY of the TEMPERATURE of the Air for each WIND, referred to EIGHT Points of AZIMUTH, through the RANGE of YEARS 1849 to 1868.

Hour, Greenwich Mean Solar Time (Civil reckoning).	N.	N.E.	E.	S.E.	S.	S.W.	W.	N.W.
Midnight	− 2·5	− 3·1	− 4·3	− 4·7	− 4·2	− 3·5	− 2·9	− 1·9
1ʰ. a.m.	− 2·8	− 3·5	− 4·7	− 5·2	− 4·4	− 3·7	− 3·3	− 2·3
2 „	− 3·0	− 3·8	− 5·0	− 5·4	− 4·7	− 3·9	− 3·6	− 2·8
3 „	− 3·3	− 4·0	− 5·2	− 5·6	− 4·7	− 4·1	− 3·9	− 3·2
4 „	− 3·5	− 4·1	− 5·4	− 5·8	− 4·8	− 4·2	− 4·2	− 3·5
5 „	− 3·5	− 4·0	− 5·2	− 5·7	− 4·6	− 4·0	− 4·2	− 3·6
6 „	− 3·2	− 3·5	− 4·3	− 4·8	− 3·8	− 3·4	− 3·7	− 3·5
7 „	− 2·4	− 2·4	− 2·6	− 3·0	− 2·4	− 2·2	− 2·7	− 2·4
8 „	− 1·3	− 0·9	− 0·6	− 1·0	− 0·7	− 0·8	− 1·3	− 1·2
9 „	+ 0·2	+ 0·8	+ 1·6	+ 1·5	+ 1·3	+ 0·9	+ 0·4	+ 0·2
10 „	+ 1·7	+ 2·5	+ 3·6	+ 3·5	+ 1·9	+ 2·5	+ 2·1	+ 1·6
11 „	+ 3·2	+ 3·0	+ 5·2	+ 5·0	+ 4·1	+ 3·8	+ 3·6	+ 3·0
Noon	+ 4·3	+ 5·1	+ 6·4	+ 6·4	+ 5·2	+ 4·8	+ 5·0	+ 4·0
1ʰ. p.m.	+ 4·9	+ 5·7	+ 6·9	+ 6·9	+ 5·5	+ 5·3	+ 5·7	+ 4·8
2 „	+ 5·1	+ 5·8	+ 6·9	+ 7·1	+ 5·5	+ 5·5	+ 6·0	+ 5·0
3 „	+ 4·7	+ 5·4	+ 6·2	+ 6·6	+ 5·1	+ 5·1	+ 5·7	+ 4·9
4 „	+ 4·1	+ 4·5	+ 5·1	+ 5·4	+ 4·3	+ 4·3	+ 4·7	+ 4·1
5 „	+ 3·0	+ 3·2	+ 3·6	+ 3·9	+ 3·2	+ 3·1	+ 3·5	+ 3·0
6 „	+ 1·8	+ 1·7	+ 1·7	+ 2·4	+ 2·0	+ 1·7	+ 2·1	+ 1·8
7 „	+ 0·4	+ 0·2	+ 0·1	+ 0·6	+ 0·8	+ 0·4	+ 0·6	+ 0·6
8 „	− 0·8	− 1·1	− 1·4	− 0·8	− 0·4	− 0·7	− 0·7	− 0·7
9 „	− 1·8	− 2·3	− 2·4	− 1·8	− 1·2	− 1·6	− 1·8	− 1·7
10 „	− 2·6	− 2·8	− 3·1	− 2·1	− 1·9	− 2·1	− 2·6	− 2·5
11 „	− 3·2	− 3·4	− 3·7	− 3·0	− 2·3	− 2·6	− 3·3	− 3·2

TABLE CVII.—MEAN TEMPERATURE of EVAPORATION at every HOUR of the DAY, during prevalence of WINDS referred to EIGHT Points of AZIMUTH, through the RANGE of YEARS 1849 to 1868.

Hour, Greenwich Mean Solar Time (Civil reckoning).	N.	N.E.	E.	S.E.	S.	S.W.	W.	N.W.
	°	°	°	°	°	°	°	°
Midnight	41·8	42·5	42·8	44·3	46·1	47·1	46·2	43·5
1 a.m.	41·6	42·2	42·6	44·0	46·0	46·9	45·9	43·5
2 ,,	41·4	42·0	42·3	43·8	45·8	46·8	45·6	42·9
3 ,,	41·3	41·9	42·1	43·7	45·8	46·7	45·4	42·5
4 ,,	41·1	41·8	42·0	43·5	45·8	46·6	45·2	42·3
5 ,,	41·0	41·9	42·1	43·7	45·9	46·7	45·0	42·2
6 ,,	41·2	42·2	42·8	44·4	46·5	47·1	45·3	42·4
7 ,,	41·7	42·9	43·8	45·5	47·5	47·9	45·9	42·9
8 ,,	42·4	43·9	45·0	46·9	48·6	48·8	46·7	43·5
9 ,,	43·4	45·0	46·3	48·4	49·8	49·9	47·7	43·3
10 ,,	44·2	45·9	47·4	49·4	50·8	50·7	48·6	43·1
11 ,,	45·0	46·7	48·3	50·1	51·5	51·5	49·5	45·7
Noon	45·7	47·3	48·9	50·9	52·2	52·1	50·2	46·2
1 p.m.	46·0	47·5	49·1	51·2	52·3	52·3	50·6	46·6
2 ,,	46·1	47·6	49·0	51·2	52·2	52·4	50·7	46·7
3 ,,	45·9	47·3	48·5	50·9	52·0	52·2	50·5	46·7
4 ,,	45·4	46·8	47·9	50·2	51·5	51·8	50·0	46·1
5 ,,	44·8	45·9	47·0	49·4	51·0	51·1	49·4	45·7
6 ,,	44·2	45·1	46·1	48·7	50·4	50·3	48·6	45·0
7 ,,	43·4	44·2	45·3	47·9	49·8	49·6	47·8	44·4
8 ,,	42·6	43·5	44·6	47·2	49·2	49·0	47·2	43·7
9 ,,	42·0	42·8	44·0	46·7	48·6	48·5	46·5	43·1
10 ,,	41·5	42·3	43·6	46·3	48·1	48·1	46·0	42·7
11 ,,	41·1	41·9	43·2	45·9	47·8	47·9	45·6	42·2
Means	43·1	44·2	45·2	47·3	49·0	49·2	47·5	44·2

Comparing the Means with the corresponding Temperatures of the Air given in Table CIV., the DEW POINT TEMPERATURES are found to be—

	N.	N.E.	E.	S.E.	S.	S.W.	W.	N.W.
	39·9	41·2	41·8	44·1	45·9	46·2	44·1	40·5

TABLE CVIII.—MEAN DIURNAL INEQUALITY of the TEMPERATURE of EVAPORATION for each WIND, referred to EIGHT Points of AZIMUTH, through the RANGE of YEARS 1849 to 1868.

Hour, Greenwich Mean Solar Time (Civil reckoning).	N.	N.E.	E.	S.E.	S.	S.W.	W.	N.W.
	°	°	°	°	°	°	°	°
Midnight	− 1·5	− 1·7	− 2·4	− 3·0	− 2·9	− 2·1	− 1·3	− 0·7
1 a.m.	− 1·5	− 2·0	− 2·6	− 3·3	− 3·0	− 2·3	− 1·6	− 0·9
2 ,,	− 1·7	− 2·2	− 2·9	− 3·5	− 3·2	− 2·4	− 1·9	− 1·3
3 ,,	− 1·8	− 2·3	− 3·1	− 3·6	− 3·2	− 2·3	− 2·1	− 1·7
4 ,,	− 2·0	− 2·4	− 3·2	− 3·8	− 3·2	− 2·6	− 2·3	− 1·9
5 ,,	− 2·1	− 2·3	− 3·1	− 3·6	− 3·1	− 2·5	− 2·5	− 2·0
6 ,,	− 1·9	− 2·0	− 2·4	− 2·9	− 2·5	− 2·1	− 2·2	− 1·8
7 ,,	− 1·4	− 1·3	− 1·4	− 1·8	− 1·5	− 1·3	− 1·6	− 1·3
8 ,,	− 0·7	− 0·3	− 0·2	− 0·4	− 0·4	− 0·4	− 0·8	− 0·7
9 ,,	+ 0·3	+ 0·8	+ 1·1	+ 1·1	+ 0·8	+ 0·7	+ 0·2	+ 0·1
10 ,,	+ 1·1	+ 1·7	+ 2·2	+ 2·1	+ 1·8	+ 1·5	+ 1·1	+ 0·9
11 ,,	+ 1·9	+ 2·5	+ 3·1	+ 2·8	+ 2·5	+ 2·3	+ 2·0	+ 1·5
Noon	+ 2·6	+ 3·1	+ 3·7	+ 3·6	+ 3·2	+ 2·9	+ 2·7	+ 2·0
1 p.m.	+ 2·9	+ 3·3	+ 3·9	+ 3·9	+ 3·3	+ 3·1	+ 3·1	+ 2·4
2 ,,	+ 3·0	+ 3·4	+ 3·8	+ 3·9	+ 3·2	+ 3·2	+ 3·2	+ 2·5
3 ,,	+ 2·8	+ 3·1	+ 3·3	+ 3·6	+ 3·0	+ 3·0	+ 3·0	+ 2·5
4 ,,	+ 2·3	+ 2·6	+ 2·7	+ 2·9	+ 2·5	+ 2·6	+ 2·5	+ 2·0
5 ,,	+ 1·7	+ 1·7	+ 1·8	+ 2·1	+ 2·0	+ 1·9	+ 1·9	+ 1·5
6 ,,	+ 1·1	+ 0·9	+ 0·9	+ 1·4	+ 1·4	+ 1·1	+ 1·1	+ 0·8
7 ,,	+ 0·3	0·0	+ 0·1	+ 0·6	+ 0·8	+ 0·4	+ 0·3	+ 0·2
8 ,,	− 0·5	− 0·7	− 0·6	− 0·1	+ 0·2	− 0·2	− 0·3	− 0·5
9 ,,	− 1·1	− 1·4	− 1·2	− 0·6	− 0·4	− 0·7	− 1·0	− 1·1
10 ,,	− 1·6	− 1·9	− 1·6	− 1·0	− 0·9	− 1·1	− 1·1	− 1·5
11 ,,	− 2·0	− 2·3	− 2·0	− 1·4	− 1·2	− 1·3	− 1·9	− 2·0

TABLE CIX.—List of Cloudless or nearly Cloudless Days during the Period 1849-1868.

Days in this Table marked * have been omitted in the formation of Tables CXI. and CXIII., and those marked ‡ in the formation of Table CXIII.

Year	January	February	March	April	May	June	July	August	September	October	November	December
1849	2*	11, 12, 17	17	30	4	24	7*, 8*, 11		6, 25	18	17	6*, 28, 30
1850	5, 6	10, 13	10, 12, 13, 29	31	1, 2, 3, 4, 23, 24, 25			7, 16	14, 28, 29	20		
1851	9, 22, 24	15, 16, 17, 23		29	1, 27, 28, 29, 30	5	19	9, 10, 12, 13, 14		20, 25		
1852	18, 23	12, 20	4, 5, 6, 7, 10	10, 14, 20, 26	16		4*, 6*, 7*, 11*, 23	1	2, 25	12, 18, 19		
1853	31	19	12, 29*, 30*		1, 5, 14, 18, 22, 23			11, 18, 19		18, 19, 21	2, 25, 29	
1854		26	1, 2, 3, 12, 13, 31	1, 4, 5, 6, 8, 9, 14, 18, 19	17		21, 22, 23, 24, 25	30	2, 3, 4, 6, 11, 12, 26, 27, 28, 29, 30	2, 12, 27	1, 6	7, 10, 12, 28
1855				16, 17, 18, 19, 20, 22	2	11	8	16, 26	8, 12, 20, 21, 22, 26		19, 20	
1856	13, 14		30, 31	1		11, 29	31	1, 2, 3*, 4, 5, 6				
1857		16		14*, 17*, 18, 31	13, 14, 15, 23	12	23, 26, 27, 30	13, 17, 18, 29	1	14		5

Year	January	February	March	April	May	June	July	August	September	October	November	December
1857 *cont.*									23, 24, 26, 27			
1858	27, 28	8*, 17, 18, 19, 20, 22, 25*	11*, 21, 22, 23, 24, 29	11, 18, 19, 21, 23*				15, 25		12, 13	16	11
1859	9	28	10		6, 13, 25*	12, 13, 17	20, 24	5	4*	24	18	
1860					1*, 2*, 21		5			22	2, 3	
1861	8*, 9*, 29				10, 11, 16		13, 14, 17	12	1*, 11*	19	24	3, 4, 24, 25*, 26*
1862					29, 30	25	26, 27, 25	1, 19, 23	10	12*, 13*, 17, 23	12, 14	
1863		13, 15, 16, 17	3	2	1‡	2	6, 10, 12, 15*				12	14
1864	6	16, 18, 19, 20, 24	13, 14, 19, 20, 21	14, 16, 17, 18, 19			27, 28	5, 7			10	10
1865			20	9, 10, 11, 12, 21, 22, 23, 24, 25, 26	20, 25, 26	8, 9, 13, 20, 21, 22	15, 26	27	3, 7, 8, 14, 15, 17, 19, 20, 25, 26, 27	4, 5, 6, 7	4, 10, 12, 13	30
1866		18		22, 23, 24	19, 20, 21	24, 26		21		15, 16	17, 28, 30	8

TABLE CIX.—LIST OF CLOUDLESS OR NEARLY CLOUDLESS DAYS—concluded.

Year.	January.	February.	March.	April.	May.	June.	July.	August.	September.	October.	November.	December.	Year.	January.	February.	March.	April.	May.	June.	July.	August.	September.	October.	November.	December.
1866 cont.			25	22 23									1868	16	30 31	4 5 15	2 4 7 18 28	13 14 17 18 19 26	20 24 23 27	1 2	1 2 3 4 5 6 7 10	11 12			
1867	13 14			4 5 6 11 23 26 27	1 10	10 12 13 22 23			1	7 8															

TABLE CX.—LIST OF COMPLETELY OVERCAST DAYS during the Period 1849-1868.

Days in this Table marked * have been omitted in the formation of Tables CXV. and CXVII., and those marked ‡ in the formation of Table CXVII.

Year.	January.	February.	March.	April.	May.	June.	July.	August.	September.	October.	November.	December.	Year.	January.	February.	March.	April.	May.	June.	July.	August.	September.	October.	November.	December.
1849	4* 5 7 8 11 13 16 21 24 30	2 3 4 5 6 7 19* 24 25 28	3 5 11 13 14 15 16 18 19 21 23 26 27 28	9 10 13 19* 22* 16 23 24 25 20 28	1 2 9 10 17 18 19	6 15 18 21 30	17 18 20 21 23* 16	3 10 12 14 15 6 7 13 20	1* 8 1 3 4 7 9 19 20 21 22 13	3 2 4 7 8 11 12 13 14 15 16 18	2* 3* 5* 7 8 10* 11 12 13 14 15 16		1851 cont.	20 29	18 19 17 18 19 22 23 24 25	15 17 21 26 25 27	15 21 13 14 15	25 12 13 14 15	11 12 25 26 27	13 24 27 29 31 28 31	26	19 20 21 22 23 24 25 26 28	16 17 18 20 21 22 28 29 31
1850	2 3 9 10 11 12 14 15 16 17 18 19 20 21 22 24 28 29 31	1 2 5 15 19 23 24 25 16 24 19	3 5 7 6 8 14 19 20 22 14 16 19 23	1* 3 4 6 8 16 17 27	12 14	3 6 7 18 19 20 25 26 28 31	1 2 13 16 17 19 21 26	8 9 15 8 17 19 20 24 25 30	3 4 13 14 18 20 21 23 24 25 30	7 10 17 18 21 26 23 30	1 2 3 4 8 9 10 11 15	5* 6* 7 8 9 13 19 22 23 24		1852	1 12 14 14 15 20 21 24 31	2 3 4 16 16 17	11 14 8 30 31	6 17 18 19 30	13 7 21 13 25	3 7 9 12 13	17 26 20	3 11 12	6 7 19 27* 16	6 8 15 16 24	1 7 10 11* 11 15 17 28 29	4 5* 6* 13 19 22 23 24
1851	1 2 3 11 12 13	3 5 7 10 13 14	3 7 8 10 12 14	2 9 11 21 23	5 6 7 17 19 20	8 6 13 19 20	1 8 9 21 13 30 16	4 10 13 30 15 18	9* 23 26 15 28	8 6 9 14 15 14			1853	10* 24 25 27 28 29 30 24 26	3 4 5 6 10 13 14 22	1 2* 5* 16* 7* 17 19* 21 24	3* 6* 13 16* 18* 28 11 22	6 21 22 27 27 28	1 14 16 23 26 27 28	10 13 16 23 26 29 30	14 15 16 28 29	1 2 7 11 12 15 16 23 28	5 6 8 13 20 21 22 23
1854	4 5 7 9	1 6 15	8 19 25	22 27 28		2 7 8	1 10 11 12	3 5 8	13 14 15 18	6 14 19	14 20* 22 24

TABLE CX.—LIST of COMPLETELY OVERCAST DAYS—*continued.*

Year.	January.	February.	March.	April.	May.	June.	July.	August.	September.	October.	November.	December.
1854 cont.	10 11 12 15 16 17 18 24 31		26	29 30		9 11* 15 16	14			25	19 20 21 25 27 28	25 30 31
1855	1 2 3 4 6 7 8 12 20 25 26 30 31	3 4 6 7 8 9 23 25 26 27	17 21 22 23 24 28	8 9 30	12 13 14 15* 21 28 31	1 14 17	2 11 26	6*	2 16 17 18 29	3 12 23 25 18 29 30 31	2* 3* 10 12 13 17 19 20 21 29	4 10 12 13 15 16 17 21 22 26 28 29 30* 31*
1856	5 6 9 11 16 18 21 22	1 2 6 7 8 10 11 13 18 19 20 21 22 26 27 28	1 2 4 9 15 17 18 21 24 25	3 8 9 22 29 30 31	7 8 9 19 20 21*	1 7 8 12 20	7 8 13 19 25		4 6 7 8 9 14 15 16	8 21 22 23		18 20 21 22
1857	4 6 7 8 9 11 13 18 20 25 26	3* 5* 6 7 19	2 3 10 11 19 25 29 31	4 5 6 13 22 26 27	22 29	1 4 5 7	7 8 11 20	2 3 8 9 11	3 4 8 9* 15 18 21 22	2 3* 4 5 6 7 8 13		7 12 13 24
1858	2 5* 30	2* 3* 11 12 13 14 15	1 2 3 31	6 7 9	12 17 24*			4 7 10 20 28	18 19 24 27	14 16 19 24 27	4 6 8 9 10 11 12 13 14	

Year.	January.	February.	March.	April.	May.	June.	July.	August.	September.	October.	November.	December.
1858 cont.												16 17 23 31
1859	1 3 4 6 18 21	9 20 13	12 13 14 24	27 28 30	17 18	19 20 28	23	9 10	26 27	11 13		4* 11 12 25 26 31*
1860	5 10 14 15 10	18		24	10* 17* 18* 25* 31	9 17 19 27	3 10 16* 24	2 16* 18 19	9 17 18 22 23 18 29	1	6 10 11 13 14 17 26 28 29 30* 31*	4 12 13 15 16 21 22 27
1861	1 13* 17 18 19* 20* 21 22 23 30	5 8 9 20 23 24 25	23	13 14‡ 15 20 28	8 11	3 6 8 9	18‡ 19‡ 20‡		22* 28	6* 16	12 13 22 26 29	12 13 15 16 17 21 22 23 28 29 30 31
1862	1 6 9* 14 15 20 21 30 31	1* 3* 4 11* 13 14 25 26 27 28	6 11* 15 17 20 21* 29 30	2 4 5 6 7 8 11* 19	15 27 28 30 31‡	12 19 20 21 22	7 9 11	11 16 17 21	21* 24* 28 29*	2 4 19* 28	1 2 4 7 21 26 30	4 6 7 24
1863	6 10 16 17	2 6 19 24 26	30	11 19		25*		15	2 19 20	4 3 5 8 14 15 17	11
1864	13 14 15 17 20 22 23	11 12 13 26 27	3 5* 8 9 22 26	6 3 16 4 30 8	2	3		7 14 16	13 17 26	4 13 16 22 23 24 25 26 29

M

TABLE CX.—LIST of COMPLETELY OVERCAST DAYS—concluded.

Year.	January.	February.	March.	April.	May.	June.	July.	August.	September.	October.	November.	December.
1865	3 10 11 24 25 26 27	4 5 6 7 8 14 21 26	6 11 12 13 14 15 29	18	10 11	2 3 30	13	15		18 22 23 31	25 29	6 7 8 9 10 12 13 14
1866	18 27	16	20 31	7 9	1 31	12 15 18	24 27 28	6 15 29	8 26 30	1 2 4 5 18 20		4 5 6 24

Year.	January.	February.	March.	April.	May.	June.	July.	August.	September.	October.	November.	December.
1867	10 17 21 22 23 24 25 26 27	1 13* 18 22 25	9 10 11 12 13	16 25	12 14 13 16	5 19 20 21	13 26 27	1	11	22 30 31	4 17 18 20 25 26	1 8 13 15 25 26 28 30
1868	4 5 8 9 10 11 18 22 28	19 27	14	17 24				4 29	16 17 19 20	3	11 13 17 18 27 28 30	1 6

TABLE CXI.—MONTHLY MEAN TEMPERATURE of the Air at every Hour of the Day, through the Range of Years 1849 to 1868, during CLOUDLESS PERIODS.

Hour, Greenwich Mean Solar Time (Civil reckoning).	January.	February.	March.	April.	May.	June.	July.	August.	September.	October.	November.	December.	Yearly Means.
Midnight	31.9	33.2	35.6	43.1	47.8	54.7	57.8	58.3	53.3	46.4	37.0	34.8	44.49
1 a.m.	31.8	32.7	35.2	42.3	46.9	53.7	56.7	57.4	52.4	45.8	36.7	34.5	43.84
2 ,,	31.4	31.9	34.8	41.5	46.1	52.9	55.7	56.8	51.6	45.4	36.1	34.2	43.20
3 ,,	31.0	31.5	34.0	40.9	45.6	51.4	55.1	55.9	51.0	44.7	35.9	33.7	42.64
4 ,,	30.3	31.0	33.4	40.4	45.1	52.1	54.7	55.3	50.5	44.3	35.3	33.1	42.13
5 ,,	29.7	30.4	33.0	40.1	45.9	53.2	55.4	55.0	50.0	43.7	35.0	32.7	42.01
6 ,,	29.5	30.2	32.6	41.1	46.0	57.3	58.4	56.6	50.0	43.5	34.7	32.3	42.93
7 ,,	29.4	29.8	33.4	44.5	53.9	62.6	62.9	60.8	51.8	44.4	34.2	31.9	44.97
8 ,,	29.3	30.6	36.7	48.8	57.8	63.6	66.7	63.3	56.3	46.4	34.4	31.8	47.48
9 ,,	30.1	33.3	41.8	53.2	61.6	69.2	70.5	69.5	62.1	50.7	36.1	32.5	50.88
10 ,,	32.4	36.6	45.6	56.9	64.2	72.0	73.6	72.6	66.7	54.5	39.1	34.6	54.07
11 ,,	35.5	39.4	48.8	59.5	65.7	73.8	75.4	74.8	70.0	57.4	42.1	37.1	56.63
Noon	37.5	42.1	51.8	61.8	67.2	75.5	77.7	77.4	72.5	60.1	44.4	38.6	58.88
1 p.m.	39.3	43.6	53.1	63.0	67.7	76.1	78.9	78.3	73.6	61.1	43.7	39.5	59.99
2 ,,	39.8	44.4	53.8	63.3	67.7	76.4	79.2	79.0	74.0	61.0	45.9	39.8	60.36
3 ,,	38.9	44.0	53.4	63.1	67.4	76.0	79.2	78.8	73.5	60.0	44.1	38.1	59.71
4 ,,	36.7	42.5	52.1	61.7	67.2	75.3	78.3	77.5	71.4	57.6	41.6	36.0	58.11
5 ,,	34.8	39.5	49.4	59.7	64.5	74.1	76.8	75.1	68.2	54.5	39.6	34.7	55.92
6 ,,	33.7	37.5	46.0	57.2	61.7	70.6	73.5	72.2	64.4	52.2	38.1	33.8	53.41
7 ,,	32.4	36.1	43.1	52.4	58.2	67.5	69.9	68.1	61.1	50.8	37.0	33.0	50.80
8 ,,	31.8	35.0	41.2	49.4	54.6	62.9	66.0	64.8	58.7	49.7	36.1	32.6	48.57
9 ,,	31.0	34.4	39.8	47.4	52.3	59.9	63.0	62.5	56.7	48.0	35.5	32.0	46.95
10 ,,	30.6	34.0	38.5	45.9	50.7	57.8	61.3	60.8	55.3	48.5	34.8	31.8	45.83
11 ,,	30.3	33.6	37.9	44.5	49.7	56.4	60.1	59.6	54.3	47.9	34.3	31.6	45.02
Means	32.9	35.7	41.9	50.9	56.6	64.5	66.9	66.3	60.4	50.8	38.1	34.4	49.95
Number of Days employed	17	27	54	56	42	48	29	27	57	27	29	24	..

TABLE CXII.—MONTHLY MEAN DIURNAL INEQUALITY of the Temperature of the Air, through the Range of Years 1849 to 1868, during CLOUDLESS PERIODS.

Hour, Greenwich Mean Solar Time (Civil reckoning).	January.	February.	March.	April.	May.	June.	July.	August.	September.	October.	November.	December.	Yearly Means.
Midnight	− 1.0	− 2.5	− 6.3	− 7.8	− 8.8	− 9.8	− 9.1	− 8.0	− 7.1	− 4.1	− 0.1	+ 0.4	− 5.46
1 a.m.	− 1.1	− 3.0	− 6.7	− 8.6	− 9.7	− 10.8	− 10.2	− 8.9	− 8.0	− 5.0	− 1.4	+ 0.1	− 6.11
2 ,,	− 1.5	− 3.8	− 7.1	− 9.4	− 10.3	− 11.6	− 11.2	− 9.8	− 8.8	− 5.4	− 2.0	− 0.2	− 6.75
3 ,,	− 1.9	− 4.2	− 7.9	− 10.0	− 11.0	− 12.1	− 11.8	− 10.4	− 9.4	− 6.1	− 2.2	− 0.7	− 7.31
4 ,,	− 2.6	− 4.7	− 8.5	− 10.5	− 10.5	− 12.4	− 11.2	− 11.0	− 9.9	− 6.5	− 2.8	− 1.3	− 7.82
5 ,,	− 3.2	− 5.3	− 8.9	− 10.8	− 10.7	− 11.3	− 11.5	− 11.3	− 10.4	− 7.1	− 3.1	− 1.7	− 7.94
6 ,,	− 3.4	− 5.5	− 9.3	− 9.8	− 7.6	− 7.2	− 8.5	− 9.7	− 10.4	− 7.3	− 3.4	− 2.1	− 7.02
7 ,,	− 3.5	− 5.9	− 8.5	− 6.4	− 2.7	− 1.9	− 4.0	− 5.5	− 8.6	− 6.4	− 3.9	− 2.5	− 4.98
8 ,,	− 3.6	− 5.1	− 5.2	− 2.1	+ 1.2	+ 1.1	− 0.2	− 1.0	− 4.1	− 4.4	− 3.7	− 2.6	− 2.47
9 ,,	− 2.8	− 2.4	− 0.1	+ 2.3	+ 5.0	+ 4.7	+ 3.6	+ 3.2	+ 1.7	− 0.1	− 2.0	− 1.9	+ 0.93
10 ,,	− 0.5	+ 0.9	+ 3.7	+ 6.0	+ 7.6	+ 7.5	+ 6.7	+ 6.3	+ 6.3	+ 3.7	+ 1.0	+ 0.2	+ 4.12
11 ,,	+ 0.6	+ 3.7	+ 6.9	+ 8.6	+ 9.1	+ 9.3	+ 8.5	+ 8.5	+ 9.6	+ 6.6	+ 4.0	+ 2.7	+ 6.68
Noon	+ 4.6	+ 6.9	+ 9.9	+ 10.9	+ 10.6	+ 11.0	+ 10.8	+ 11.1	+ 12.1	+ 9.3	+ 6.3	+ 4.2	+ 8.93
1 p.m.	+ 6.4	+ 7.9	+ 11.2	+ 12.1	+ 11.1	+ 11.6	+ 12.0	+ 12.0	+ 13.2	+ 10.3	+ 6.7	+ 5.1	+ 10.04
2 ,,	+ 6.9	+ 8.7	+ 11.9	+ 12.4	+ 11.1	+ 11.9	+ 12.3	+ 12.7	+ 13.6	+ 10.2	+ 7.8	+ 5.4	+ 10.41
3 ,,	+ 6.0	+ 8.3	+ 11.5	+ 12.2	+ 10.8	+ 11.5	+ 11.5	+ 11.5	+ 13.1	+ 9.2	+ 6.0	+ 3.7	+ 9.76
4 ,,	+ 3.8	+ 6.8	+ 10.3	+ 10.8	+ 9.9	+ 10.8	+ 11.4	+ 11.2	+ 11.0	+ 6.8	+ 3.5	+ 1.6	+ 8.16
5 ,,	+ 1.9	+ 3.8	+ 7.5	+ 8.8	+ 8.1	+ 9.6	+ 9.9	+ 8.8	+ 7.8	+ 4.7	+ 3.1	+ 0.3	+ 5.97
6 ,,	+ 0.8	+ 1.8	+ 4.1	+ 6.3	+ 5.1	+ 6.1	+ 6.6	+ 5.9	+ 4.0	+ 1.4	0.0	− 0.6	+ 3.46
7 ,,	− 0.5	+ 0.4	+ 1.2	+ 1.5	+ 1.6	+ 3.0	+ 3.0	+ 3.6	+ 0.7	0.0	− 1.1	− 1.4	+ 0.85
8 ,,	− 1.1	− 0.7	− 0.7	− 1.5	− 2.0	− 1.6	− 0.9	− 1.5	− 1.7	− 1.1	− 2.0	− 1.8	− 1.38
9 ,,	− 1.9	− 1.3	− 2.1	− 3.5	− 4.3	− 4.6	− 3.9	− 3.8	− 3.7	− 1.9	− 2.0	− 2.4	− 3.00
10 ,,	− 2.3	− 1.7	− 3.4	− 5.0	− 5.9	− 6.7	− 5.6	− 5.5	− 5.1	− 2.3	− 3.3	− 2.6	− 4.12
11 ,,	− 2.6	− 2.1	− 4.0	− 6.4	− 6.9	− 8.1	− 6.8	− 6.7	− 6.1	− 2.9	− 3.8	− 2.8	− 4.93

TABLE CXIII.—MONTHLY MEAN TEMPERATURE of EVAPORATION at every HOUR of the DAY, through the RANGE of YEARS 1849 to 1868, during CLOUDLESS PERIODS.

Hour, Greenwich Mean Solar Time (Civil reckoning).	January.	February.	March.	April.	May.	June.	July.	August.	September.	October.	November.	December.	Yearly Means.
Midnight	30·7	32·0	34·3	41·1	46·3	52·9	55·7	56·6	52·3	45·3	36·1	33·9	43·12
1ʰ. a.m.	30·4	31·5	34·1	40·5	45·6	52·3	54·9	56·2	51·9	44·7	35·8	33·5	42·62
2 „	30·0	31·1	33·7	40·1	45·3	51·7	54·2	55·7	51·2	44·3	35·3	33·2	42·15
3 „	29·9	30·6	33·2	39·5	44·8	51·4	53·7	55·1	50·7	43·7	35·0	32·8	41·70
4 „	29·3	30·0	32·7	39·2	44·4	50·9	53·2	54·6	50·2	43·3	34·6	32·3	41·24
5 „	28·7	29·7	32·4	38·9	45·0	51·8	53·6	54·3	49·8	43·1	34·3	31·9	41·14
6 „	28·5	29·3	32·1	39·8	47·1	54·1	55·3	55·5	49·8	42·9	33·9	31·4	41·66
7 „	28·4	29·1	32·6	42·2	50·4	56·9	58·1	58·3	51·3	43·6	33·5	31·0	42·97
8 „	28·4	29·8	35·1	45·3	52·9	59·0	60·4	60·8	54·6	45·1	33·6	30·9	44·66
9 „	29·1	31·9	38·5	48·1	55·1	61·0	61·2	63·1	58·2	48·3	35·1	31·4	46·83
10 „	30·8	34·0	41·2	49·9	56·2	62·0	63·4	64·3	60·4	50·7	37·5	32·8	48·60
11 „	33·3	36·3	42·9	51·2	56·8	62·7	64·0	65·0	61·6	52·3	39·9	34·6	50·07
Noon	34·9	38·1	44·3	52·3	57·4	63·4	64·6	65·8	62·3	53·8	41·1	35·8	51·17
1ʰ. p.m.	35·9	38·9	44·8	52·6	57·3	63·5	65·0	65·9	62·5	54·1	41·5	36·4	51·55
2 „	36·3	39·4	44·9	52·9	57·3	63·4	65·0	66·1	62·6	53·8	41·4	36·4	51·63
3 „	35·9	39·2	45·0	52·8	56·9	63·1	65·1	66·1	62·6	53·2	40·5	35·5	51·31
4 „	34·5	38·7	44·0	51·8	56·3	62·7	64·7	66·0	61·5	51·9	38·7	34·1	50·41
5 „	33·1	36·9	42·6	50·6	55·4	61·7	64·2	65·0	60·0	50·5	37·3	33·2	49·23
6 „	32·5	35·4	40·8	49·0	54·0	60·1	62·9	63·7	58·4	49·3	36·3	32·5	47·92
7 „	31·2	34·5	39·1	46·9	52·5	59·2	61·5	62·3	56·8	48·3	35·7	32·0	46·61
8 „	30·5	33·7	38·0	45·0	50·5	57·3	60·0	60·5	55·8	47·6	35·1	31·5	45·46
9 „	29·8	33·1	37·2	43·7	49·3	55·3	58·5	59·4	54·6	47·1	34·6	31·1	44·51
10 „	29·5	32·8	36·4	43·0	48·2	54·5	57·9	58·6	53·9	46·8	34·1	31·1	43·90
11 „	29·2	32·5	35·9	42·4	47·7	53·9	57·2	57·9	53·2	46·3	33·7	31·0	43·41
Means	31·3	33·7	38·2	45·8	51·4	57·7	59·8	60·7	56·1	47·9	36·4	32·9	46·00
Number of Days employed	17	27	34	36	41	48	29	27	57	27	29	24	..

TABLE CXIV.—MONTHLY MEAN DIURNAL INEQUALITY of the TEMPERATURE of EVAPORATION, through the RANGE of YEARS 1849 to 1868, during CLOUDLESS PERIODS.

Hour, Greenwich Mean Solar Time (Civil reckoning).	January.	February.	March.	April.	May.	June.	July.	August.	September.	October.	November.	December.	Yearly Means.
Midnight	− 0·6	− 1·7	− 3·9	− 4·7	− 5·1	− 4·8	− 4·1	− 4·1	− 3·6	− 2·6	− 0·3	+ 1·0	− 2·88
1ʰ. a.m.	− 0·9	− 2·2	− 4·1	− 5·3	− 5·8	− 5·4	− 4·9	− 4·5	− 4·2	− 3·2	− 0·6	+ 0·6	− 3·38
2 „	− 1·3	− 2·6	− 4·5	− 5·7	− 6·1	− 6·0	− 5·6	− 5·0	− 4·9	− 3·6	− 1·1	+ 0·3	− 3·85
3 „	− 1·4	− 3·1	− 5·0	− 6·3	− 6·6	− 6·3	− 6·1	− 5·6	− 5·4	− 4·2	− 1·4	− 0·1	− 4·30
4 „	− 2·0	− 3·7	− 5·5	− 6·6	− 7·0	− 6·8	− 6·5	− 6·1	− 5·9	− 4·4	− 1·8	− 0·6	− 4·76
5 „	− 2·6	− 4·0	− 5·8	− 6·9	− 6·4	− 5·9	− 6·2	− 6·2	− 6·3	− 4·8	− 2·1	− 1·0	− 4·86
6 „	− 2·8	− 4·4	− 6·1	− 6·0	− 4·3	− 3·6	− 4·3	− 5·2	− 6·3	− 5·0	− 2·5	− 1·5	− 4·34
7 „	− 2·9	− 4·6	− 5·6	− 3·6	− 1·0	− 0·8	− 1·7	− 2·4	− 4·6	− 4·3	− 2·9	− 1·9	− 3·03
8 „	− 2·9	− 3·9	− 3·1	− 0·5	+ 1·5	+ 1·3	+ 0·6	+ 0·1	− 1·5	− 2·8	− 2·0	− 1·0	− 1·34
9 „	− 2·2	− 1·8	+ 0·3	+ 2·3	+ 3·7	+ 3·3	+ 2·4	+ 2·4	+ 2·1	+ 0·4	− 1·3	− 1·5	+ 0·83
10 „	− 0·5	+ 0·3	+ 3·0	+ 4·1	+ 4·8	+ 4·3	+ 3·6	+ 3·6	+ 4·3	+ 2·8	+ 1·1	− 0·1	+ 2·60
11 „	+ 2·0	+ 2·6	+ 4·7	+ 5·4	+ 5·4	+ 5·0	+ 4·2	+ 4·3	+ 5·5	+ 4·6	+ 3·5	+ 1·7	+ 4·07
Noon	+ 3·6	+ 4·4	+ 6·1	+ 6·5	+ 6·0	+ 5·7	+ 4·8	+ 5·1	+ 6·2	+ 5·9	+ 4·7	+ 1·9	+ 5·17
1ʰ. p.m.	+ 4·6	+ 5·2	+ 6·6	+ 6·8	+ 6·1	+ 5·8	+ 5·2	+ 5·2	+ 6·4	+ 6·2	+ 5·1	+ 3·5	+ 5·55
2 „	+ 5·0	+ 5·7	+ 6·7	+ 7·1	+ 5·9	+ 5·7	+ 5·2	+ 5·4	+ 6·5	+ 5·9	+ 5·0	+ 3·5	+ 5·62
3 „	+ 4·6	+ 5·5	+ 6·8	+ 7·0	+ 5·5	+ 5·4	+ 5·3	+ 5·4	+ 6·5	+ 5·3	+ 3·9	+ 2·6	+ 5·31
4 „	+ 3·2	+ 5·0	+ 5·8	+ 6·0	+ 4·9	+ 5·0	+ 4·9	+ 5·3	+ 5·4	+ 4·0	+ 2·3	+ 1·2	+ 4·41
5 „	+ 1·8	+ 3·2	+ 4·4	+ 4·8	+ 4·0	+ 4·0	+ 4·4	+ 4·3	+ 3·9	+ 2·6	+ 1·1	+ 0·3	+ 3·23
6 „	+ 1·0	+ 1·7	+ 2·6	+ 3·2	+ 2·6	+ 2·3	+ 3·1	+ 3·0	+ 2·3	+ 1·4	+ 0·1	− 0·4	+ 1·92
7 „	− 0·1	+ 0·8	+ 0·9	+ 1·1	+ 1·1	+ 1·5	+ 1·7	+ 1·6	+ 0·7	+ 0·4	− 0·7	− 0·9	+ 0·67
8 „	− 0·8	0·0	− 0·2	− 0·8	− 0·9	− 0·4	+ 0·2	− 0·2	− 0·3	− 0·3	− 1·3	− 1·4	− 0·54
9 „	− 1·5	− 0·6	− 1·0	− 2·1	− 2·1	− 2·0	− 1·3	− 1·5	− 0·8	− 1·8	− 1·8	− 1·0	− 1·49
10 „	− 1·8	− 0·9	− 1·8	− 2·8	− 3·2	− 3·2	− 1·9	− 2·1	− 2·2	− 1·1	− 2·3	− 1·8	− 2·10
11 „	− 2·1	− 1·2	− 2·3	− 3·4	− 3·7	− 3·8	− 2·6	− 2·8	− 2·9	− 1·6	− 2·7	− 1·9	− 2·59

TABLE CXV.—MONTHLY MEAN TEMPERATURE of the Air at every Hour of the Day, through the RANGE of YEARS 1849 to 1868, during OVERCAST PERIODS.

Hour, Greenwich Mean Solar Time (Civil reckoning).	January.	February.	March.	April.	May.	June.	July.	August.	September.	October.	November.	December.	Yearly Means.
Midnight	38·4	39·9	39·4	44·5	47·7	53·1	56·8	57·5	55·1	50·3	43·3	39·7	47·14
1h. a.m.	38·2	39·0	39·2	44·0	47·4	52·7	56·4	57·1	55·0	50·1	43·3	39·7	46·92
2 „	38·1	39·8	39·2	43·8	47·0	52·3	56·1	56·8	54·9	50·0	43·2	39·7	46·74
3 „	38·1	39·7	39·1	43·6	46·8	52·2	55·8	56·8	55·0	49·8	43·2	39·8	46·66
4 „	38·1	39·6	39·0	43·6	46·7	52·2	55·6	56·6	55·0	50·1	43·1	39·7	46·61
5 „	38·1	39·5	38·9	43·5	46·9	52·6	55·9	56·5	55·0	50·0	43·0	39·8	46·64
6 „	38·1	39·5	38·9	43·9	47·7	53·6	57·0	57·0	55·1	50·1	43·0	39·9	46·98
7 „	38·1	39·6	39·2	44·9	48·6	55·0	58·3	58·3	56·0	50·3	43·1	40·0	47·62
8 „	38·3	40·0	39·9	45·9	49·8	55·9	59·4	59·8	57·4	51·0	43·4	40·1	48·41
9 „	38·6	40·6	40·9	47·1	50·8	57·1	60·9	61·1	58·8	52·0	44·0	40·4	49·36
10 „	39·2	41·5	41·9	48·1	51·7	58·0	62·0	62·0	60·0	53·0	44·7	41·0	50·26
11 „	39·5	42·2	42·8	49·1	52·6	58·9	63·9	62·7	60·8	53·7	45·3	41·5	51·02
Noon	40·1	42·8	43·5	49·6	53·4	59·7	63·5	63·6	61·2	54·2	46·1	41·9	51·63
1h. p.m.	40·3	43·0	43·8	49·9	53·7	60·0	63·5	64·0	61·4	54·6	46·4	42·2	51·90
2 „	40·3	43·2	43·9	50·1	53·8	59·9	63·7	63·4	61·4	54·8	46·5	42·2	52·02
3 „	40·3	43·1	43·8	49·9	53·8	59·5	63·8	63·8	61·1	54·4	46·1	42·1	51·81
4 „	40·0	42·8	43·6	49·4	53·5	59·1	63·5	63·3	60·5	53·8	45·7	41·8	51·42
5 „	39·6	42·0	43·9	48·5	52·9	58·7	62·5	62·6	59·4	53·0	45·2	41·6	50·74
6 „	39·5	41·6	42·1	47·6	52·1	57·8	61·4	61·4	58·1	52·2	45·0	41·5	50·02
7 „	39·5	41·2	41·5	46·6	51·0	56·3	60·3	60·3	57·0	51·8	44·7	41·2	49·30
8 „	39·4	41·0	41·0	45·9	50·1	55·4	59·0	59·4	56·5	51·5	44·5	41·2	48·74
9 „	39·4	40·8	40·5	45·3	49·4	54·5	58·1	58·7	55·9	51·1	44·4	41·1	48·27
10 „	39·3	40·6	40·1	44·9	48·8	54·0	57·5	58·2	55·6	50·9	44·2	40·9	47·92
11 „	39·3	40·4	39·8	44·4	48·2	53·5	56·9	57·7	55·3	50·6	43·9	40·7	47·56
Means	39·1	41·0	41·0	46·4	50·2	55·9	59·6	60·0	57·6	51·8	44·4	40·8	48·99
Number of Days employed	162	125	118	86	84	77	72	67	71	110	133	149	..

TABLE CXVI.—MONTHLY MEAN DIURNAL INEQUALITY of the TEMPERATURE of the Air, through the RANGE of YEARS 1849 to 1868, during OVERCAST PERIODS.

Hour, Greenwich Mean Solar Time (Civil reckoning).	January.	February.	March.	April.	May.	June.	July.	August.	September.	October.	November.	December.	Yearly Means.
Midnight	− 0·7	1·1	− 1·6	− 1·9	− 2·5	− 2·8	− 2·8	− 2·5	− 2·5	− 1·5	− 1·1	− 1·1	− 1·85
1h. a.m.	− 0·9	1·1	− 1·8	− 2·4	− 2·8	− 3·2	− 3·2	− 2·9	− 2·6	− 1·7	− 1·1	− 1·1	− 2·07
2 „	− 1·0	1·2	− 1·8	− 2·6	− 3·2	− 3·6	− 3·5	− 3·2	− 2·7	− 1·8	− 1·1	− 1·1	− 2·25
3 „	− 1·0	1·3	− 1·9	− 2·8	− 3·4	− 3·7	− 3·8	− 3·2	− 2·6	− 2·0	− 1·2	− 1·0	− 2·33
4 „	− 1·0	1·4	− 2·0	− 2·8	− 3·5	− 3·7	− 4·0	− 3·4	− 2·6	− 1·7	− 1·3	− 1·1	− 2·38
5 „	− 1·0	1·5	− 2·1	− 2·9	− 3·3	− 3·3	− 3·7	− 3·5	− 2·6	− 1·8	− 1·4	− 1·0	− 2·35
6 „	− 1·0	1·5	− 2·1	− 2·5	− 2·5	− 2·3	− 2·6	− 3·0	− 2·5	− 1·7	− 1·4	− 0·9	− 2·01
7 „	− 0·8	1·0	− 1·1	− 1·3	− 1·6	− 0·9	− 1·3	− 1·7	− 1·6	− 1·5	− 1·3	− 0·8	− 1·37
8 „	− 0·5	0·4	− 0·1	+ 0·7	+ 0·6	+ 1·2	+ 1·3	+ 1·1	+ 1·2	+ 0·2	− 0·4	− 0·4	+ 0·37
9 „	+ 0·1	0·5	+ 0·9	+ 1·7	+ 1·5	+ 2·1	+ 2·4	+ 2·0	+ 2·4	+ 1·2	+ 0·3	+ 0·2	+ 1·27
10 „	+ 0·4	1·2	+ 1·8	+ 2·7	+ 2·4	+ 3·0	+ 3·3	+ 2·7	+ 3·2	+ 1·9	+ 0·7	+ 0·7	+ 2·13
Noon	+ 1·0	1·8	+ 2·5	+ 3·2	+ 3·2	+ 3·8	+ 3·9	+ 3·6	+ 3·6	+ 2·4	+ 1·7	+ 1·1	+ 2·64
1h. p.m.	+ 1·2	2·0	+ 2·8	+ 3·5	+ 3·5	+ 4·1	+ 3·9	+ 4·0	+ 3·8	+ 2·8	+ 2·0	+ 1·4	+ 2·91
2 „	+ 1·2	2·2	+ 2·9	+ 3·7	+ 3·6	+ 4·0	+ 4·1	+ 4·4	+ 3·8	+ 3·0	+ 2·1	+ 1·4	+ 3·03
3 „	+ 1·2	2·1	+ 2·8	+ 3·5	+ 3·6	+ 3·6	+ 4·2	+ 3·8	+ 3·6	+ 2·6	+ 1·7	+ 1·3	+ 2·82
4 „	+ 0·9	1·8	+ 2·6	+ 3·0	+ 3·3	+ 3·2	+ 3·9	+ 3·3	+ 2·9	+ 2·0	+ 1·3	+ 1·0	+ 2·43
5 „	+ 0·5	1·0	+ 1·9	+ 2·1	+ 2·7	+ 2·8	+ 2·9	+ 2·6	+ 1·8	+ 1·2	+ 0·8	+ 0·8	+ 1·75
6 „	+ 0·4	0·6	+ 1·1	+ 1·2	+ 1·9	+ 1·9	+ 1·8	+ 1·4	+ 0·5	+ 0·4	+ 0·6	+ 0·7	+ 1·03
7 „	+ 0·4	0·2	+ 0·5	+ 0·2	+ 0·8	+ 0·7	+ 0·3	− 0·6	0·0	+ 0·1	+ 0·4	+ 0·31
8 „	+ 0·3	0·0	0·0	− 0·5	− 0·1	− 0·5	− 0·6	− 0·6	− 1·1	− 0·3	+ 0·1	+ 0·4	− 0·15
9 „	+ 0·3	− 0·2	− 0·5	− 1·1	− 0·8	− 1·4	− 1·5	− 1·3	− 1·7	− 0·7	− 0·2	− 0·72
10 „	+ 0·2	− 0·4	− 0·9	− 1·5	− 1·4	− 1·9	− 2·1	− 1·8	− 2·0	− 0·9	− 0·2	+ 0·1	− 1·07
11 „	+ 0·2	− 0·6	− 1·2	− 1·0	− 2·0	− 2·4	− 2·7	− 2·3	− 2·3	− 1·2	− 0·3	− 0·1	− 1·43

TABLE CXVII.—MONTHLY MEAN TEMPERATURE of EVAPORATION at every HOUR of the DAY, through the RANGE of YEARS 1849 to 1868, during OVERCAST PERIODS.

Hour, Greenwich Mean Solar Time (Civil reckoning).	January.	February.	March.	April.	May.	June.	July.	August.	September.	October.	November.	December.	Yearly Means.
Midnight 1ʰ. a.m.	37.2	38.8	38.0	43.0	46.1	51.3	51.8	56.0	53.7	49.2	42.2	38.7	45.75
1 ,,	37.2	38.0	37.9	42.7	45.0	51.1	54.6	55.7	53.8	49.1	42.2	38.6	45.64
2 ,,	37.0	38.8	37.9	42.6	45.7	50.8	54.3	55.6	53.7	48.9	42.2	38.6	45.50
3 ,,	37.1	38.9	37.9	42.3	45.5	50.5	54.1	55.5	53.7	48.9	42.2	38.6	45.43
4 ,,	37.1	38.9	37.8	42.3	45.4	50.6	54.0	55.5	53.8	49.0	42.1	38.6	45.43
5 ,,	37.1	38.8	37.8	42.2	45.6	51.0	54.2	55.5	53.7	48.9	42.0	38.7	45.44
6 ,,	37.1	38.9	37.8	42.6	46.2	51.6	55.0	55.7	53.8	48.9	42.1	38.8	45.71
7 ,,	37.2	39.1	38.0	43.4	46.9	52.4	55.7	56.5	54.5	49.2	42.1	38.9	46.16
8 ,,	37.3	39.3	38.6	44.1	47.7	53.0	56.4	57.4	55.3	49.7	42.3	39.0	46.68
9 ,,	37.5	39.9	39.3	45.0	48.4	53.8	57.2	58.1	56.1	50.5	42.8	39.3	47.33
10 ,,	37.9	40.3	39.8	45.6	49.0	54.4	57.8	58.5	56.7	51.1	43.4	39.7	47.85
11 ,,	38.3	40.7	40.3	46.3	49.6	55.0	58.2	59.0	56.8	51.6	43.9	40.1	48.32
Noon	38.7	40.9	40.8	46.7	50.0	55.4	58.8	59.5	57.2	52.0	44.3	40.4	48.73
1ʰ. p.m.	38.8	41.0	41.0	47.0	50.3	55.7	59.0	59.7	57.4	52.3	44.5	40.6	48.94
2 ,,	38.8	41.2	41.2	47.0	50.5	55.7	59.1	59.8	57.5	52.4	44.5	40.7	49.03
3 ,,	38.9	41.0	41.1	47.0	50.4	55.4	59.1	59.6	57.2	52.1	44.4	40.6	48.90
4 ,,	38.7	40.7	41.0	46.7	50.2	55.2	58.8	59.3	57.0	51.8	44.1	40.5	48.67
5 ,,	38.5	40.4	40.5	46.0	49.7	54.9	58.2	58.8	56.5	51.2	43.8	40.2	48.23
6 ,,	38.4	40.1	40.0	45.4	49.3	54.4	57.7	58.3	55.8	50.8	44.6	40.1	47.83
7 ,,	38.4	39.7	39.3	44.7	48.6	53.8	57.2	57.7	55.3	50.6	43.3	39.9	47.37
8 ,,	38.3	39.6	39.3	44.1	48.1	53.1	56.4	57.3	54.8	50.3	43.2	39.8	47.02
9 ,,	38.3	39.5	38.8	43.7	47.6	52.6	55.9	56.9	54.3	50.0	43.2	39.8	46.72
10 ,,	38.3	39.4	38.5	43.3	47.2	52.1	55.5	56.6	54.0	49.9	42.9	39.6	46.44
11 ,,	38.2	39.2	38.3	43.0	46.8	51.9	55.0	56.2	53.8	49.6	42.7	39.4	46.18
Means	37.9	39.8	39.2	44.4	47.9	53.2	56.5	57.4	55.3	50.3	43.1	39.6	47.05
Number of Days employed	162	125	118	85	83	77	69	67	71	110	133	149	..

TABLE CXVIII.—MONTHLY MEAN DIURNAL INEQUALITY of the TEMPERATURE of EVAPORATION, through the RANGE of YEARS 1849 to 1868, during OVERCAST PERIODS.

Hour, Greenwich Mean Solar Time (Civil reckoning).	January.	February.	March.	April.	May.	June.	July.	August.	September.	October.	November.	December.	Yearly Means.
Midnight 1ʰ. a.m.	− 0.7	− 1.0	− 1.2	− 1.4	− 1.8	− 1.9	− 1.7	− 1.4	− 1.6	− 1.1	− 0.0	− 0.9	− 1.30
1 ,,	− 0.7	− 0.9	− 1.3	− 1.7	− 2.0	− 2.1	− 1.9	− 1.7	− 1.5	− 1.2	− 0.9	− 1.0	− 1.41
2 ,,	− 0.9	− 1.0	− 1.3	− 1.9	− 2.2	− 2.4	− 2.2	− 1.8	− 1.6	− 1.4	− 0.9	− 1.0	− 1.55
3 ,,	− 0.8	− 0.9	− 1.3	− 2.1	− 2.4	− 2.7	− 2.4	− 1.9	− 1.6	− 1.4	− 0.9	− 1.0	− 1.62
4 ,,	− 0.8	− 0.9	− 1.4	− 2.1	− 2.5	− 2.6	− 2.5	− 1.9	− 1.5	− 1.3	− 1.0	− 1.0	− 1.62
5 ,,	− 0.8	− 1.0	− 1.4	− 2.2	− 2.3	− 2.2	− 2.3	− 2.1	− 1.6	− 1.4	− 1.1	− 0.9	− 1.61
6 ,,	− 0.8	− 0.9	− 1.4	− 1.8	− 1.7	− 1.6	− 1.5	− 1.7	− 1.7	− 1.4	− 1.0	− 0.8	− 1.34
7 ,,	− 0.7	− 0.7	− 1.2	− 1.0	− 1.0	− 0.8	− 0.8	− 0.9	− 0.8	− 1.1	− 1.0	− 0.7	− 0.89
8 ,,	− 0.6	− 0.5	− 0.6	− 0.3	− 0.2	− 0.2	− 0.1	0.0	0.0	− 0.6	− 0.8	− 0.6	− 0.37
9 ,,	− 0.4	+ 0.1	+ 0.1	+ 0.6	+ 0.5	+ 0.6	+ 0.7	+ 0.7	+ 0.8	+ 0.2	− 0.3	− 0.3	− 0.28
10 ,,	0.0	+ 0.5	+ 0.6	+ 1.2	+ 1.1	+ 1.2	+ 1.3	+ 1.1	+ 1.4	+ 0.8	+ 0.3	+ 0.1	+ 0.80
11 ,,	+ 0.4	+ 0.9	+ 1.1	+ 1.9	+ 1.7	+ 1.8	+ 1.7	+ 1.6	+ 1.5	+ 1.3	+ 0.8	+ 0.5	+ 1.27
Noon	+ 0.8	+ 1.1	+ 1.6	+ 2.3	+ 2.1	+ 2.2	+ 2.3	+ 2.1	+ 1.9	+ 1.7	+ 1.2	+ 0.8	+ 1.68
1ʰ. p.m.	+ 0.9	+ 1.1	+ 1.8	+ 2.6	+ 2.4	+ 2.5	+ 2.5	+ 2.3	+ 2.0	+ 1.8	+ 1.0	+ 1.0	+ 1.89
2 ,,	+ 0.9	+ 1.4	+ 2.0	+ 2.6	+ 2.6	+ 2.5	+ 2.6	+ 2.4	+ 2.2	+ 2.1	+ 1.4	+ 1.1	+ 1.98
3 ,,	+ 1.0	+ 1.2	+ 1.9	+ 2.6	+ 2.5	+ 2.2	+ 2.6	+ 2.2	+ 1.9	+ 1.8	+ 1.3	+ 1.0	+ 1.85
4 ,,	+ 0.8	+ 0.9	+ 1.8	+ 2.3	+ 2.3	+ 2.0	+ 2.3	+ 1.9	+ 1.7	+ 1.5	+ 1.0	+ 0.9	+ 1.62
5 ,,	+ 0.6	+ 0.6	+ 1.3	+ 1.6	+ 1.6	+ 1.7	+ 1.7	+ 1.4	+ 1.2	+ 1.0	+ 0.7	+ 0.6	+ 1.18
6 ,,	+ 0.5	+ 0.3	+ 0.8	+ 1.0	+ 1.4	+ 1.2	+ 1.2	+ 0.9	+ 0.5	+ 0.5	+ 0.5	+ 0.5	+ 0.78
7 ,,	+ 0.5	− 0.1	+ 0.3	+ 0.3	+ 0.7	+ 0.6	+ 0.7	+ 0.3	− 0.2	+ 0.3	+ 0.3	+ 0.3	+ 0.31
8 ,,	+ 0.4	− 0.2	+ 0.1	− 0.3	+ 0.2	− 0.1	− 0.1	− 0.1	− 0.5	0.0	+ 0.1	+ 0.2	− 0.03
9 ,,	+ 0.4	− 0.3	− 0.4	− 0.7	− 0.3	− 0.6	− 0.6	− 0.5	− 1.0	− 0.1	+ 0.1	+ 0.2	− 0.33
10 ,,	+ 0.4	− 0.4	− 0.7	− 1.1	− 0.7	− 1.1	− 1.0	− 0.8	− 1.3	− 0.4	− 0.2	0.0	− 0.61
11 ,,	+ 0.3	− 0.6	− 0.9	− 1.4	− 1.1	− 1.3	− 1.3	− 1.2	− 1.5	− 0.7	− 0.4	− 0.2	− 0.87

TABLE CXIX.—MEAN TEMPERATURE of the Air in each MONTH, through the RANGE of YEARS 1849 to 1868, under DIFFERENT ATMOSPHERIC CIRCUMSTANCES.

Special Atmospheric Condition.	January.	February.	March.	April.	May.	June.	July.	August.	September.	October.	November.	December.	Yearly Means.
Under all Atmospheric Circumstances	38·9	39·7	41·5	47·2	52·7	59·7	62·5	61·9	57·5	50·9	42·8	40·8	49·7
Direction of Wind.													
N.	34·5	33·4	38·5	42·9	48·2	57·6	60·7	58·2	54·7	47·4	39·5	33·3	43·9
N.E.	32·4	32·8	36·8	44·6	40·5	58·4	65·1	60·9	57·9	49·5	41·5	35·3	46·9
E.	31·4	33·4	37·1	46·1	53·0	61·3	61·3	66·1	59·0	52·3	39·7	34·6	48·3
S.E.	36·2	36·7	41·5	49·0	51·6	60·5	67·0	67·4	58·9	54·6	43·9	37·4	50·3
S.	42·7	42·7	43·8	50·6	54·0	58·3	64·5	61·8	59·0	53·1	48·1	45·3	52·0
S.W.	43·4	44·6	46·0	50·6	54·9	58·7	62·4	62·2	58·1	52·7	46·4	43·5	52·1
W.	40·1	43·2	45·1	49·5	54·8	59·5	61·9	61·0	57·3	50·9	43·2	42·5	50·8
N.W.	38·8	37·5	42·0	43·4	48·6	57·9	58·1	59·6	54·9	50·6	40·5	38·5	47·5
State of Sky.													
Cloudless	32·9	35·7	41·9	50·9	56·6	64·5	66·9	66·3	60·4	50·8	38·1	34·4	50·0
Overcast	39·1	41·0	41·0	46·4	50·2	53·9	59·6	60·0	57·6	51·8	44·4	40·8	49·0

TABLE CXX.—EXCESS of MEAN TEMPERATURE of the Air in each MONTH, under DIFFERENT ATMOSPHERIC CIRCUMSTANCES, through the RANGE of YEARS 1849 to 1868, above the MEAN for the MONTH under all ATMOSPHERIC CIRCUMSTANCES.

Special Atmospheric Condition.	January.	February.	March.	April.	May.	June.	July.	August.	September.	October.	November.	December.	Yearly Excess.
Direction of Wind.													
N.	− 4·4	− 6·3	− 3·2	− 4·3	− 4·5	− 2·1	− 1·8	− 3·7	− 2·8	− 3·5	− 3·5	− 5·5	− 3·8
N.E.	− 6·5	− 6·9	− 4·7	− 2·6	− 3·2	− 1·3	+ 0·6	− 1·0	+ 0·4	− 1·4	− 1·3	− 5·5	− 2·8
E.	− 7·5	− 4·3	− 4·4	− 1·1	+ 0·3	+ 2·6	− 0·2	+ 4·2	+ 1·3	+ 1·4	− 3·1	− 6·2	− 1·4
S.E.	− 2·7	− 3·0	0·0	+ 1·8	− 0·1	+ 0·8	+ 4·5	+ 5·5	− 0·6	+ 3·7	+ 1·1	− 3·4	+ 0·6
S.	+ 3·8	+ 3·0	+ 2·3	+ 3·4	+ 1·5	− 1·4	+ 2·0	− 0·1	+ 1·5	+ 2·2	+ 5·3	+ 4·5	+ 2·3
S.W.	+ 4·5	+ 4·9	+ 4·5	+ 3·4	+ 2·2	− 1·0	− 0·1	+ 0·3	+ 0·6	+ 1·8	+ 3·6	+ 4·7	+ 2·4
W.	+ 1·2	+ 3·5	+ 3·6	+ 2·3	+ 2·1	− 0·2	− 0·6	− 0·9	− 0·2	0·0	+ 0·4	+ 1·7	+ 1·1
N.W.	− 0·1	− 2·2	+ 0·5	− 3·8	− 4·1	− 1·8	− 4·4	− 2·3	− 2·6	− 0·3	− 2·3	− 2·3	− 2·2
State of Sky.													
Cloudless	− 6·0	− 4·0	+ 0·4	+ 3·7	+ 3·9	+ 4·8	+ 4·4	+ 4·4	+ 2·9	− 0·1	− 4·7	− 6·4	+ 0·3
Overcast	+ 0·2	+ 1·3	− 0·3	− 0·8	− 2·5	− 3·8	− 2·9	− 1·9	+ 0·1	+ 0·9	+ 1·6	0·0	− 0·7

TABLE CXXI.—EXTREMES of the TEMPERATURES which are obtained by taking separately for each MONTH the MEANS of TEMPERATURES at the same separate HOUR of the DAY, through all the YEARS of the entire Period 1849 to 1868.

Month.	Temperature of the Air.		Temperature of Evaporation.	
	Lowest, and Hour of Day.	Highest, and Hour of Day.	Lowest, and Hour of Day.	Highest, and Hour of Day.
January	37·4 7ᵇ. a.m.	42·0 2ᵇ. p.m.	36·3 7ᵇ. a.m.	39·5 2ᵇ. p.m.
February	37·1 7 a.m.	44·1 2 p.m.	36·0 7 a.m.	40·7 2 p.m.
March	37·4 6 a.m.	47·1 2 p.m.	36·3 6 a.m.	42·5 2 p.m.
April	41·3 5 a.m.	54·3 2 p.m.	40·1 5 a.m.	48·2 2 p.m.
May	45·7 4 a.m.	60·2 2 p.m.	44·6 4 a.m.	53·2 2 p.m.
June	52·3 4 a.m.	67·4 2 p.m.	51·0 4 a.m.	59·1 2 p.m.
July	55·1 4 a.m.	70·4 2 p.m.	53·7 4 a.m.	61·5 2 p.m.
August	55·5 5 a.m.	69·7 2 p.m.	54·4 5 a.m.	61·5 2 p.m.
September	52·1 5 a.m.	63·1 2 p.m.	51·2 5 a.m.	58·1 2 p.m.
October	47·6 5 & 6 a.m.	56·5 2 p.m.	46·7 6 a.m.	52·3 2 p.m.
November	40·7 6 a.m.	46·9 2 p.m.	39·6 6 a.m.	44·0 1 p.m.
December	39·4 7 a.m.	43·4 2 p.m.	38·2 7 a.m.	41·2 1 p.m.

TABLE CXXII.—EXTREMES of the TEMPERATURES which are obtained by taking separately for each MONTH in each separate YEAR the MEANS of TEMPERATURES through all the HOURS of the DAY.

Month.	Temperature of the Air.				Temperature of Evaporation.			
	Lowest, and Year.		Highest, and Year.		Lowest, and Year.		Highest, and Year.	
January	34·1	1850	43·1	1866	32·9	1850	41·4	1851
February	29·2	1855	44·7	1867	28·3	1855	42·7	1867
March	36·6	1853	46·8	1859	34·6	1853	44·0	1859
April	42·9	1860	52·9	1865	39·9	1860	48·3	1865
May	47·9	1855	58·4	1868	44·3	1855	53·9	1868
June	53·8	1860	64·8	1858	32·7	1852	58·7	1858
July	58·1	1860	68·9	1859	54·9	1860	62·9	1850
August	58·3	1860	65·7	1857	53·9	1864	61·8	1857
September	53·6	1860	63·8	1865	50·7	1863	59·7	1865
October	46·7	1830	54·2	1861	44·4	1850	52·1	1861
November	37·7	1851	49·0	1852	35·3	1851	46·4	1852
December	34·3	1853	47·4	1852	33·6	1853	44·8	1852

TABLE CXXIII.—EXTREMES of the DEW POINTS, inferred from the combination of the MEAN AIR and EVAPORATION TEMPERATURES at the same separate HOUR of the DAY, obtained separately for each MONTH, through the entire Period 1849 to 1868.

Month.	Lowest, and Hour of Day.		Highest, and Hour of Day.		Month.	Lowest, and Hour of Day.		Highest, and Hour of Day.	
January	34·7	8ʰ a.m.	36·4	0ʰ, 2ʰ, 3ʰ. p.m.	July	52·3	3ʰ & 4ʰ a.m.	54·8	0ʰ p.m.
February	34·5	6 & 7 a.m.	36·9	1 p.m.	August	53·4	4 & 5 a.m.	55·4	0 a.m.
March	34·8	6 a.m.	37·4	3 p.m.	September	50·3	5 & 6 a.m.	52·8	11 a.m.
April	38·5	4 a.m.	42·3	2 p.m.	October	45·7	4, 5, 6, 7 a.m.	48·4	0 & 1 p.m.
May	43·2	4 a.m.	47·2	1 p.m.	November	38·5 {	5, 6, 7 a.m. ; 11 p.m.	40·8	1 p.m.
June	49·7	3 & 4 a.m.	52·6 {	11 a.m. ; 0, 1 p.m.	December	36·7	2, 4, 6, 7, 8 a.m.	38·6	1 p.m.

TABLE CXXIV.—EXTREMES of HOURLY TEMPERATURES in the MEANS of the AGGREGATES of GROUPS defined by PHYSICAL CIRCUMSTANCES, through the entire Period 1849 to 1868.

Grouping.	Temperature of the Air.				Temperature of Evaporation.			
	Lowest, and Hour of Day.		Highest, and Hour of Day.		Lowest, and Hour of Day.		Highest, and Hour of Day.	

(*a*.) Waves of Temperature.

Grouping.								
High	48·5	4ʰ a.m.	60·0	2ʰ p.m.	47·3	4ʰ a.m.	53·8	2ʰ p.m.
Low	41·8	4 & 5 a.m.	51·4	2 p.m.	40·6	5 a.m.	46·4	2 p.m.

(*b*.) Waves of Atmospheric Pressure.

Grouping.								
High	44·4	4ʰ a.m.	56·1	2ʰ p.m.	43·3	4ʰ a.m.	50·2	2ʰ p.m.
Low	45·9	4 a.m.	54·4	2 p.m.	44·6	4 a.m.	49·7	1 p.m.

(*c*.) Days defined by the Direction of the Wind.

Direction.								
N.	42·4	5ʰ. a.m.	51·0	2ʰ. p.m.	41·0	5ʰ. a.m.	46·1	2ʰ. p.m.
N.E.	42·8	4 a.m.	52·7	2 p.m.	41·8	4 a.m.	47·6	2 p.m.
E.	42·9	4 a.m.	53·2	1 p.m.	42·0	4 a.m.	49·1	1 p.m.
S.E.	44·5	4 a.m.	57·4	2 p.m.	43·5	4 a.m.	51·2	1 & 2 p.m.
S.	47·2	4 a.m.	57·5	1 p.m.	45·8	3 a.m.	52·3	1 p.m.
S.W.	47·9	4 a.m.	57·6	2 p.m.	46·6	4 a.m.	52·4	2 p.m.
W.	46·5	5 a.m.	56·7	2 p.m.	45·0	5 a.m.	50·7	2 p.m.
N.W.	43·9	5 a.m.	52·5	2 p.m.	42·2	5 a.m.	46·7	2 p.m.

TABLE CXXIV.—Extremes of Temperature in the Means of the Aggregates of Groups—concluded.

Month.	Temperature of the Air.		Temperature of Evaporation.	
	Lowest, and Hour of Day.	Highest, and Hour of Day.	Lowest, and Hour of Day.	Highest, and Hour of Day.
(d.) Cloudless Days.				
January	29·3 — 8ʰ. a.m.	59·8 — 2ʰ. p.m.	28·4 — 7ʰ. & 8ʰ. a.m.	36·3 — 2ʰ. p.m.
February	29·8 — 7 a.m.	44·4 — 2 p.m.	29·1 — 7 a.m.	39·4 — 2 p.m.
March	32·6 — 6 a.m.	53·8 — 2 p.m.	32·1 — 6 a.m.	45·0 — 3 p.m.
April	40·1 — 5 a.m.	63·5 — 2 p.m.	38·9 — 5 a.m.	52·9 — 2 p.m.
May	45·1 — 4 a.m.	67·7 — 1 & 2 p.m.	44·4 — 4 a.m.	57·5 — 1 p.m.
June	52·1 — 4 a.m.	76·4 — 2 p.m.	50·9 — 4 a.m.	63·5 — 1 p.m.
July	54·7 — 4 a.m.	79·2 — 2 & 3 p.m.	53·2 — 4 a.m.	65·1 — 3 p.m.
August	55·0 — 5 a.m.	79·0 — 2 p.m.	54·5 — 5 a.m.	66·1 — 2 & 3 p.m.
September	50·0 — 5 & 6 a.m.	74·0 — 2 p.m.	49·8 — 5 & 6 a.m.	62·6 — 2 & 3 p.m.
October	43·5 — 6 a.m.	61·1 — 1 p.m.	42·9 — 6 a.m.	54·1 — 1 p.m.
November	34·2 — 7 a.m.	45·9 — 2 p.m.	33·5 — 7 a.m.	41·5 — 1 p.m.
December	31·6 — 11 p.m.	39·8 — 2 p.m.	30·9 — 8 a.m.	36·4 — 1 & 2 p.m.
(e.) Overcast Days.				
January	38·1 — 2ʰ,3ʰ,4ʰ,5ʰ,6ʰ,7ʰ. a.m.	40·3 — 1ʰ, 2ʰ, 3ʰ. p.m.	37·0 — 2ʰ. a.m.	38·9 — 3ʰ. p.m.
February	39·5 — 5 & 6 a.m.	43·2 — 2 p.m.	38·8 — 0, 2, 5 a.m.	41·2 — 2 p.m.
March	38·9 — 5 & 6 a.m.	43·9 — 2 p.m.	37·8 — 4, 5, 6 a.m.	41·2 — 2 p.m.
April	43·5 — 5 a.m.	50·1 — 2 p.m.	42·2 — 5 a.m.	47·0 — 1, 2, 3 p.m.
May	46·7 — 4 a.m.	53·8 — 2 & 3 p.m.	45·4 — 4 a.m.	50·5 — 2 p.m.
June	52·2 — 3 & 4 a.m.	60·0 — 1 p.m.	50·5 — 3 a.m.	55·7 — 1 & 2 p.m.
July	55·6 — 4 a.m.	63·8 — 3 p.m.	54·0 — 4 a.m.	59·1 — 2 & 3 p.m.
August	56·5 — 5 a.m.	64·4 — 2 p.m.	55·3 — 5 a.m.	59·8 — 2 p.m.
September	54·9 — 2 a.m.	61·4 — 1 & 2 p.m.	53·7 — 0, 2, 3, 5 a.m.	57·5 — 1 p.m.
October	49·8 — 3 a.m.	54·8 — 2 p.m.	48·9 — 2, 3, 5, 6 a.m.	52·4 — 2 p.m.
November	43·0 — 5 & 6 a.m.	46·5 — 2 p.m.	42·0 — 5 a.m.	44·5 — 1 & 2 p.m.
December	39·7 — 0, 1, 2, 4 a.m.	42·2 — 1 & 2 p.m.	38·6 — 1, 2, 3, 4 a.m.	40·7 — 2 p.m.

N

ROYAL OBSERVATORY, GREENWICH.

RESULTS

OF THE

OBSERVATIONS OF THE TEMPERATURE OF THE EARTH AT DIFFERENT DEPTHS,

1847 TO 1873.

TABLE CXXV.—MEAN TEMPERATURE of the AIR for each MONTH, and for each QUARTER of the YEAR, deduced from EYE-OBSERVATIONS of the STANDARD DRY-BULB THERMOMETER for YEARS 1847–1873.

Year.	January.	February.	March.	April.	May.	June.	July.	August.	September.	October.	November.	December.	January, February, March.	April, May, June.	July, August, September.	October, November, December.	Yearly Means, reduced and compared with January.	Yearly Means, reduced and compared with the preceding.
	°	°	°	°	°	°	°	°	°	°	°	°	°	°	°	°	°	°
1846										50·3	46·0	32·9				43·1		
1847	35·6	35·3	41·4	45·3	56·4	58·0	65·4	62·1	54·4	52·9	46·9	42·7	37·3	53·2	60·6	47·5	46·72	48·63
1848	34·6	43·4	43·8	47·6	59·7	58·5	62·3	58·9	56·7	51·6	43·8	44·0	40·6	53·3	59·3	46·3	50·41	50·67
1849	40·1	43·2	43·3	34·2	34·4	62·1	62·9	58·8	51·1	44·1	39·1	41·9	32·0	62·3	61·3	44·8	49·08	50·41
1850	33·7	44·7	39·0	46·3	51·3	60·8	63·2	60·2	56·4	47·0	46·3	40·6	39·4	53·5	59·6	44·7	49·32	49·33
1851	42·9	40·1	42·6	44·7	50·9	58·9	60·1	62·3	56·9	52·6	37·9	40·4	41·9	51·5	59·8	43·6	49·19	49·46
1852	42·0	40·8	41·3	45·9	51·5	56·1	66·6	62·1	56·8	47·9	48·9	47·6	41·4	51·2	61·8	48·1	50·63	49·50
1853	42·4	33·3	38·5	43·2	52·0	58·2	60·3	60·0	55·3	50·9	42·1	34·0	38·1	51·8	58·5	42·3	47·68	49·13
1854	39·0	39·2	43·5	48·4	50·9	55·7	60·3	60·9	58·1	49·4	40·3	41·3	40·6	51·7	59·8	43·7	48·63	48·58
1855	34·8	29·1	37·9	45·9	58·0	62·2	61·4	57·2	51·2	41·3	35·6	33·9	31·0	60·6	42·7	47·03	47·31
1856	36·3	42·0	38·9	46·8	49·3	58·8	61·1	63·6	55·2	51·7	40·7	40·2	40·1	51·7	60·0	44·2	48·98	48·61
1857	36·6	39·2	41·8	45·7	54·0	61·8	64·5	63·4	59·7	52·9	43·8	45·1	39·2	53·8	63·2	47·9	51·04	50·11
1858	37·5	34·6	41·4	46·2	51·7	64·9	60·7	62·0	60·3	50·8	39·6	41·0	37·8	54·3	61·0	43·8	49·22	50·26
1859	40·4	43·1	46·4	46·6	53·1	61·4	68·1	63·3	56·7	50·9	41·9	36·8	43·3	53·7	62·8	45·2	50·74	50·89
1860	39·7	33·7	41·1	42·9	53·8	54·8	57·7	53·4	50·6	40·8	36·3	38·8	50·5	56·2	42·6	47·03	47·19
1861	33·8	42·1	43·8	44·3	51·9	59·1	60·9	63·2	57·1	54·9	40·8	41·0	36·9	51·8	60·4	45·6	49·41	48·66
1862	39·0	41·1	43·1	48·4	55·1	56·3	59·1	59·3	57·7	51·8	39·8	43·6	41·1	53·4	58·8	45·1	49·57	49·69
1863	41·8	42·1	43·9	49·1	52·0	58·1	60·8	61·9	53·7	51·6	45·7	43·2	42·6	53·1	58·8	46·8	50·33	49·88
1864	36·5	36·0	41·3	48·2	53·8	57·4	61·8	59·6	56·9	50·3	42·0	38·3	37·9	53·1	59·4	43·7	48·54	49·33
1865	36·3	36·6	36·6	52·3	56·1	60·2	63·8	59·9	63·9	50·9	44·8	42·7	36·5	56·2	61·0	45·2	50·54	49·72
1866	42·6	40·5	40·3	47·9	50·1	60·9	61·0	59·4	56·4	51·3	44·3	42·9	41·2	53·0	58·9	46·2	49·81	49·81
1867	34·2	44·7	37·7	49·0	53·4	58·1	59·4	62·0	57·6	48·7	41·4	37·8	38·9	53·5	59·7	42·3	48·64	49·33
1868	37·2	43·0	44·0	48·1	57·3	62·0	67·5	63·6	60·3	47·9	41·3	46·0	41·4	55·8	63·9	47·1	51·55	50·90
1869	41·1	46·3	37·3	50·3	50·5	55·3	64·5	60·8	59·0	48·9	43·9	37·9	41·3	52·0	61·4	43·3	49·51	49·98
1870	38·3	36·2	39·6	48·9	53·4	60·9	63·4	61·1	53·7	49·8	41·3	33·6	38·0	54·4	60·7	41·6	48·70	49·11
1871	33·2	42·4	44·9	47·7	51·9	54·8	61·7	64·8	57·4	49·4	37·6	38·3	40·2	51·5	61·3	41·8	48·67	48·64
1872	41·3	44·8	44·0	48·3	50·9	59·2	63·0	60·9	57·4	47·8	45·3	42·9	43·6	52·8	61·1	45·3	50·70	49·81
1873	42·1	34·3	41·9	45·9	50·6	58·9	63·4	62·7	54·7	47·8	44·2	40·6	39·4	51·8	60·3	44·2	48·93	49·31
Means 1847-1873	38·37	39·74	41·50	47·09	52·79	58·72	62·51	61·61	57·18	50·47	42·69	40·50	39·87	52·87	60·43	44·53	49·43	49·42

TABLE CXXVI.—MONTHLY MEANS of READINGS, made at NOON, of a THERMOMETER within the CASE covering the DEEP-SUNK THERMOMETERS, whose BULB is placed on a level with their SCALES, for each YEAR 1847–1873.

Year.	January.	February.	March.	April.	May.	June.	July.	August.	September.	October.	November.	December.	Yearly Means.
	°	°	°	°	°	°	°	°	°	°	°	°	°
1847	37·1	38·3	46·3	50·5	62·4	64·3	72·0	68·2	59·3	57·1	49·5	44·3	54·17
1848	36·3	45·8	46·2	52·1	68·0	63·9	68·7	63·0	63·3	55·3	46·7	46·3	54·65
1849	41·9	45·8	46·8	49·1	60·6	68·3	68·8	69·4	65·3	55·8	47·3	40·6	53·01
1850	35·9	47·3	45·0	54·0	56·3	69·7	68·7	67·0	63·4	52·2	49·5	42·5	54·20
1851	43·5	44·3	46·8	51·5	59·1	69·1	67·8	70·6	64·7	57·3	41·6	41·7	54·93
1852	44·1	44·1	47·3	55·5	59·1	62·4	77·4	68·5	63·3	52·5	51·6	49·0	56·23
1853	44·8	37·1	43·7	50·3	61·4	66·9	67·5	68·7	62·1	55·9	45·6	36·4	53·37
1854	41·7	44·4	50·1	59·4	58·0	65·3	65·8	69·1	68·0	56·7	43·9	43·1	55·63
1855	38·4	34·0	43·7	54·6	56·3	66·3	69·1	70·6	65·2	57·1	44·3	37·8	53·12
1856	41·8	45·1	43·1	53·3	58·9	66·3	69·0	71·4	63·3	57·2	43·7	42·3	54·67
1857	38·6	44·6	47·3	51·3	63·7	72·6	75·3	73·5	66·7	58·4	49·1	48·0	57·26
1858	41·0	39·4	46·6	55·6	60·0	76·4	68·3	73·5	67·6	56·9	43·0	42·7	55·92
1859	43·9	47·2	51·0	53·9	62·4	70·3	77·6	74·2	63·0	56·3	46·5	38·8	57·27
1860	41·3	38·8	45·0	49·1	61·8	61·8	64·8	63·6	61·4	55·6	45·3	39·0	52·37
1861	36·5	45·7	48·2	55·2	60·9	68·3	68·4	71·7	65·0	62·1	45·8	43·6	55·78
1862	41·9	44·1	48·0	54·7	62·6	63·7	67·3	68·5	65·4	57·0	42·7	43·1	55·08

TABLE CXXVI.—MONTHLY MEANS of READINGS, made at NOON, of a THERMOMETER within the CASE covering the DEEP-SUNK THERMOMETERS—*concluded*.

Year.	January.	February.	March.	April.	May.	June.	July.	August.	September.	October.	November.	December.	Yearly Means.
1863	44·0	45·0	49·5	56·4	60·5	65·4	70·2	68·7	60·7	56·6	49·5	46·2	55·21
1864	39·1	39·5	46·1	56·3	62·0	65·9	69·8	67·8	63·5	57·8	46·8	41·0	54·62
1865	39·2	40·1	42·2	61·8	64·9	70·9	72·6	66·9	74·2	58·2	48·8	44·8	57·15
1866	45·0	44·3	45·2	56·2	58·8	69·6	69·5	65·5	62·6	56·5	48·1	45·6	55·58
1867	37·2	47·8	41·6	54·4	61·9	66·9	67·4	69·5	64·2	55·7	46·1	38·8	54·29
1868	39·5	47·7	49·8	55·8	67·2	71·4	76·9	71·3	69·2	54·2	45·2	48·0	58·02
1869	43·2	48·6	41·9	57·5	57·6	63·9	71·6	69·1	65·6	55·0	46·6	40·6	55·10
1870	40·1	38·8	44·2	57·4	63·3	70·3	73·1	68·4	63·9	55·6	45·1	36·2	54·70
1871	35·4	45·1	49·7	54·2	60·4	62·1	68·7	73·3	64·1	55·8	41·8	40·6	54·27
1872	43·8	48·3	49·6	54·8	58·7	67·7	73·0	69·3	64·6	53·6	40·2	43·8	56·37
1873	44·3	36·7	46·6	53·8	58·4	66·8	72·1	70·4	62·1	54·2	47·9	43·8	54·76
Means 1847–1873.	40·85	43·29	46·35	54·43	60·87	67·27	70·46	69·32	64·54	56·18	46·35	42·67	55·21

From observations of this thermometer made every two hours between 1846, June, and 1847, December, it appeared that the excess of the mean reading at noon above the mean from all the observations was—in January, 1°·0 ; February, 1°·9 ; March, 4°·31 ; April, 4°·5 ; May, 5°·0 ; June, 5°·6 ; July, 5°·1 ; August, 4°·5 ; September, 4°·8 ; October, 3°·3 ; November, 1°·9 ; December, 1°·5.

TABLE CXXVII.—MONTHLY and QUARTERLY MEANS of READINGS, made at NOON, of a THERMOMETER whose BULB is sunk to the Depth of 1 Inch below the SURFACE of the SOIL, for each YEAR 1847–1873.

Year.	January.	February.	March.	April.	May.	June.	July.	August.	September.	October.	November.	December.	January, February, March.	April, May, June.	July, August, September.	October, November, December.	Yearly Means, commencing with January.	Yearly Means, commencing with October preceding.
1846										55·0	47·9	36·4						45·8
1847	37·8	38·0	42·9	47·2	58·0	61·1	67·4	64·7	56·9	54·5	48·7	44·5	39·6	55·4	63·0	49·2	51·81	50·94
1848	37·4	44·1	44·6	49·5	61·6	61·7	65·0	60·8	58·8	53·5	45·5	42·0	42·0	57·6	61·5	48·2	51·33	52·47
1849	41·5	43·6	44·3	46·3	56·5	63·5	65·0	65·2	61·8	55·0	46·5	41·1	43·1	55·4	64·0	46·9	51·54	52·67
1850	36·7	44·4	41·9	50·4	55·0	64·1	65·2	63·0	58·7	49·5	48·7	42·7	41·0	55·8	62·3	47·0	51·52	51·50
1851	44·2	42·7	41·0	48·5	54·8	62·2	63·8	65·5	60·0	54·7	41·2	42·2	42·6	53·6	63·1	46·0	51·98	52·22
1852	42·8	42·0	43·0	49·9	55·1	59·4	71·0	65·2	61·1	50·2	50·4	48·0	42·6	54·8	65·8	49·5	53·18	52·50
1853	44·3	37·0	43·8	47·4	55·7	62·3	63·2	64·1	60·3	55·1	44·9	38·0	41·0	55·1	62·5	46·0	51·18	52·06
1854	40·6	41·6	43·3	51·7	54·2	59·8	64·2	64·6	61·6	52·9	46·1	42·0	42·5	55·6	63·5	46·6	52·06	51·90
1855	38·4	33·4	41·9	50·4	51·9	61·3	65·6	66·6	60·9	54·7	44·3	38·3	37·6	54·4	64·2	45·8	50·47	50·69
1856	41·5	43·5	41·7	50·4	51·6	63·0	64·8	66·7	59·0	54·5	43·9	41·0	42·2	55·5	65·5	46·8	51·04	51·69
1857	38·9	40·7	43·7	48·3	57·6	65·6	67·0	67·0	62·5	55·2	45·8	46·6	41·1	57·2	65·8	50·2	53·57	52·71
1858	39·6	37·8	42·1	49·6	54·5	68·6	64·5	66·0	62·7	54·2	42·2	42·4	39·9	57·5	64·4	46·3	52·01	52·99
1859	42·4	43·5	47·3	49·3	55·8	64·4	70·7	66·7	59·7	54·4	44·3	39·3	44·4	56·5	65·7	46·0	53·15	53·22
1860	40·9	37·4	42·1	45·2	56·7	58·2	61·3	60·4	57·0	51·4	44·0	39·9	40·1	55·4	56·6	45·4	49·62	49·77
1861	35·5	42·6	44·6	47·7	54·9	63·2	64·6	66·2	60·3	57·5	43·9	42·8	40·9	55·3	63·7	48·0	51·97	51·32
1862	40·7	42·9	45·6	50·6	57·8	60·0	62·6	63·5	60·6	54·3	42·7	44·0	43·1	56·1	62·2	47·0	52·11	52·36
1863	43·2	45·2	45·0	51·1	54·3	60·5	64·0	63·9	57·6	54·3	48·0	45·6	43·8	55·5	61·8	49·3	52·56	51·98
1864	39·6	39·0	43·2	50·0	56·0	65·0	63·2	62·2	59·5	53·3	41·6	41·6	40·7	57·0	61·7	45·5	51·81	51·92
1865	38·8	38·9	39·5	53·3	57·8	64·4	66·1	61·5	65·6	54·7	47·5	45·1	39·0	58·5	64·7	49·1	52·85	52·51
1866	44·1	43·1	41·0	50·3	52·8	63·5	65·0	61·7	59·0	52·6	45·2	39·9	41·7	55·7	62·4	45·9	51·43	52·23
1867	38·3	46·1	40·7	49·9	55·9	61·4	62·6	64·1	60·5	52·6	45·2	39·9	41·7	55·7	62·4	45·9	51·43	52·23
1868	39·4	44·5	45·9	50·5	59·8	64·3	69·9	66·7	63·0	52·2	45·0	47·0	43·3	58·4	66·5	48·1	52·02	52·48
1869	43·0	46·8	40·8	51·5	54·3	58·6	66·2	63·2	60·9	52·4	45·8	40·5	43·5	54·8	63·4	46·2	52·02	52·46
1870	40·1	38·1	41·5	50·0	56·1	61·2	67·1	63·8	60·9	52·4	41·7	38·1	39·8	55·8	63·2	47·1	51·32	51·60
1871	36·2	42·0	45·0	49·6	54·2	58·4	63·7	66·6	60·7	52·0	41·2	39·2	41·1	54·1	63·7	44·1	50·73	50·97
1872	41·6	42·0	45·0	49·8	53·4	61·6	66·0	63·0	60·6	50·8	47·1	43·0	43·7	43·0	63·8	47·0	52·36	51·65
1873	42·8	36·4	42·4	48·5	53·3	61·2	66·0	65·2	57·7	51·4	45·7	42·7	40·5	54·3	63·0	46·6	51·11	51·20
Means 1847–1872.	40·38	41·40	43·25	49·50	55·54	62·08	65·44	64·46	60·21	53·45	45·43	42·50	41·67	55·71	65·36	47·13	51·97	51·66

From observations of this thermometer made every two hours between 1846, June, and 1847, December, it appeared that the excess of the mean reading at noon above the mean from all the observations was—in January and February, 0°·0 ; March, 0°·6 ; April, 0°·8 ; May, 1°·3 ; June, 1°·6 ; July, 1°·1 ; August and September, 1°·0 ; October, 0°·8 ; November and December, 0°·3.

TABLE CXXVIII.—MONTHLY MEANS of READINGS, made at NOON, of a THERMOMETER whose BULB is sunk to the Depth of 3·2 Feet (3 French Feet) below the SURFACE of the SOIL, for each YEAR 1847 to 1873.

Year.	January.	February.	March.	April.	May.	June.	July.	August.	September.	October.	November.	December.	Yearly Means.
1847	39·42	39·64	41·20	44·51	51·24	57·34	61·65	62·44	57·90	54·78	50·66	46·47	50·60
1848	41·28	42·00	43·30	47·72	54·54	58·36	61·21	60·15	58·45	54·75	47·53	45·88	51·25
1849	42·55	43·28	43·56	44·86	51·15	58·36	61·69	61·44	60·11	54·42	49·75	44·08	51·27
1850	39·13	41·87	42·44	46·04	49·50	57·84	60·75	61·26	57·97	52·61	48·85	44·21	50·20
1851	43·62	41·80	42·26	45·84	49·97	56·63	60·75	61·76	59·52	55·32	46·63	43·39	50·71
1852	42·17	42·21	41·49	46·33	51·24	55·07	63·70	63·41	60·60	52·84	50·59	47·55	51·43
1853	45·16	40·50	40·35	44·59	50·16	56·59	60·10	61·51	58·49	53·94	48·14	41·92	50·12
1854	39·25	41·15	42·61	48·09	51·08	55·52	59·90	61·63	61·17	54·51	47·48	43·38	50·48
1855	41·48	36·94	39·05	44·64	49·25	55·12	61·43	62·03	60·05	53·66	47·97	41·52	49·60
1856	41·39	41·66	42·22	46·20	49·57	56·85	61·01	63·90	59·32	55·37	48·72	44·13	50·83
1857	41·33	40·22	42·67	46·23	51·19	59·16	62·82	64·76	61·76	56·43	51·46	47·21	52·11
1858	42·23	39·84	40·42*	46·29	51·03	61·65	62·73	63·82	61·28	56·52	47·37	44·57	51·48
1859	42·76	43·53	45·69	47·12	51·89	60·07	65·72	63·32	60·28	56·80	47·74	42·24	52·44
1860	42·33	39·53*	40·93	44·42	51·44	55·34	58·86	58·52	57·28	52·85	47·47	43·80	49·42
1861	38·20*	41·15	43·18	46·26	50·39	58·17	61·43	63·28	60·24	57·08	47·33	44·54	50·94
1862	41·13	42·73	43·29	47·41	53·71	57·39	59·37	61·51	59·89	55·87	47·32	44·60	51·19
1863	45·23	43·29	43·67	47·94	51·42	56·44	60·54	61·64	57·83	54·72	50·92	46·75	51·53
1864	42·14	41·03	42·15	46·17	52·26	56·16	59·43	61·12	58·26	54·75	48·55	44·41	50·54
1865	41·04*	39·74*	40·11*	46·98	53·37	59·50	67·31	61·75	63·21	57·42	49·72	47·18	51·87
1866	41·93	44·04	41·86	47·34	50·85	57·62	62·00	60·48	58·77	56·16	50·30	46·29	51·70
1867	41·59	44·55	42·53	46·82	52·34	57·22	60·35	61·12	60·55	54·18	49·24	43·76	51·17
1868	41·11	42·72	44·85	47·48	54·38	59·83	64·71	65·12	62·36	55·35	48·62	47·30	52·82
1869	44·55	45·63	42·78	47·30	52·50	53·68	61·70	61·63	60·49	53·88	48·52	43·66	51·68
1870	42·24	39·65	41·86	46·31	51·69	59·31	62·85	63·22	58·55	54·87	48·09	43·29	50·99
1871	39·06	41·19	44·85	47·65	52·04	56·64	61·32	64·62	62·37	54·96	47·78	42·69	51·26
1872	43·02	44·86	45·94	48·38	51·81	57·93	63·56	63·78	61·79	54·41	49·87	46·04	51·62
1873	43·63	40·76	42·80	47·65	51·37	57·36	62·77	64·45	59·83	55·53	48·54	46·21	51·93
Means 1847–1873	41·92	41·69	42·51	46·55	51·51	57·33	61·65	62·48	59·94	55·11	48·69	44·71	51·19

* In those months the values are wholly or in part estimated, in consequence of the fluid having gone out of range. From observations of this thermometer made every two hours between 1846, April, and 1847, December, it appeared that the excess of the mean reading at noon above the mean from all the observations was—from January to March, 0°·03; in April and May, 0°·07; from June to September, 0°·11; in October and November, 0°·04; and in December, 0°·03.

TABLE CXXIX.—MONTHLY MEANS of READINGS, made at NOON, of a THERMOMETER whose BULB is sunk to the Depth of 6·4 Feet (6 French Feet) below the SURFACE of the SOIL, for each YEAR 1847 to 1873.

Year.	January.	February.	March.	April.	May.	June.	July.	August.	September.	October.	November.	December.	Yearly Means, commencing with January.	Yearly Means, commencing with February.
1847	43·99	44·86	43·28	45·14	48·68	54·00	57·11	58·91	57·90	55·39	52·78	49·48	50·79	50·94
1848	45·80	44·26	44·93	47·45	51·09	53·28	57·99	58·87	57·78	55·78	51·07	48·73	51·59	51·59
1849	45·88	43·67	45·48	46·00	49·14	54·50	57·67	58·31	58·06	55·75	51·64	48·15	51·45	51·31
1850	44·22	43·06	44·70	45·83	48·54	53·61	57·06	58·02	57·57	54·69	51·16	48·08	50·70	50·88
1851	46·27	44·79	44·33	46·19	48·86	53·22	57·14	58·87	58·48	56·08	51·35	47·10	51·06	50·99
1852	45·43	44·97	43·98	46·30	49·53	51·73	57·72	59·29	59·17	55·14	52·26	49·98	51·38	51·62
1853	48·21	45·21	43·53	45·18	48·43	53·46	57·11	58·86	58·00	55·1	51·78	46·79	50·97	50·57
1854	43·50	43·96	44·22	47·13	49·80	52·91	56·12	58·91	58·65	56·2	51·29	47·31	50·82	51·00
1855	45·46	42·17	41·79	44·47	48·07	51·98	56·86	58·83	58·31	56·42	51·57	46·81	50·53	50·14
1856	44·38	44·22	44·42	46·12	48·60	53·29	57·05	58·84	58·61	56·00	51·88	47·79	50·94	51·00
1857	45·08	43·15	44·14	46·14	49·00	54·82	58·95	61·27	60·94	57·86	54·42	50·76	52·11	52·07
1858	47·47	44·46	43·85*	46·22	49·76	55·88	59·32	60·69	60·03	57·65	52·24	48·38	52·16	52·07
1859	46·39	45·91	46·86	48·06	50·42	55·82	60·43	62·38	60·25	58·04	52·17	47·49	52·59	52·80
1860	45·72	44·00*	43·80*	45·47	49·14	53·06	57·73	59·32	58·75	53·71	52·00	48·20	51·25	51·48
1861	42·80*	43·75*	44·69	46·54	48·65	54·10	57·73	60·73	59·32	57·21	52·00	48·05	51·25	51·48
1862	43·48	45·06	45·20	47·38	51·39	54·74	56·49	58·84	58·73	56·88	51·81	48·05	51·67	51·75

* In these months the values are wholly or in part estimated, in consequence of the fluid having gone out of range.

TABLE CXXIX.—MONTHLY MEANS of READINGS, made at NOON, of a THERMOMETER whose BULB is sunk to the Depth of 6·4 Feet (6 French Feet) below the SURFACE of the Soil.—*concluded.*

Year.	January.	February.	March.	April.	May.	June.	July.	August.	September.	October.	November.	December.	Yearly Means, commencing with January.	Yearly Means, commencing with February.
1863	46·40	45·91	45·68	47·64	50·58	53·72	57·52	59·18	58·28	55·82	52·71	50·04	51·96	51·06
1864	46·46	44·93	44·40	46·19	50·36	53·83	56·56	58·09	58·18	56·04	52·20	48·61	51·40	51·32
1865	45·57	44·10*	43·60*	45·90*	51·01	55·65	58·82	59·88	60·81	58·79	53·35	50·73	52·35	52·57
1866	48·16	47·19	45·13	47·47	50·16	54·40	58·51	59·09	58·61	57·02	53·58	49·83	52·43	52·27
1867	46·24	46·20	45·66	47·02	50·98	54·38	57·71	58·89	59·75	56·23	52·89	48·40	52·03	51·96
1868	45·41	45·24	46·42	47·84	51·83	56·27	60·24	62·30*	61·26	57·81	52·65	50·14	53·12	53·34
1869	48·10	47·59	46·38	47·29	51·51	54·01	57·70	59·65	59·71	57·58	52·44	48·37	52·54	52·38
1870	46·21	44·20*	44·24*	46·22	50·08	53·27	59·16	60·68	58·88	56·55	52·11	48·06	51·82	51·66
1871	44·27	43·90*	46·00	47·86	50·66	54·20	57·64	60·82	61·16	57·13	52·53	47·51	51·97	52·15
1872	46·38	46·81	47·66	48·53	51·05	54·58	59·18	61·10	60·00	56·81	53·04	49·69	52·98	53·17
1873	48·67	45·45	45·10	47·75	50·37	54·24	58·55	61·18	59·82	57·21	52·22	49·83	52·53	52·45
1874	47·68	..	..	..	..	..	..	..	..	..	..	..	..	..
Means 1847-1873	45·84	44·81	44·80	46·65	46·93	54·22	57·87	59·65	59·11	56·50	52·27	48·59	51·69	51·70

* In those months the values are wholly or in part estimated, in consequence of the fluid having gone out of range. From observations of this thermometer made every two hours between 1846, April, and 1847, December, it appeared that the excess of the mean reading at noon above the mean from all the observations was—from January to March, o°·01; in April and May, o°·03; from June to September, o·05; in October, o°·03; and in November and December, o°·01.

TABLE CXXX.—MONTHLY MEANS of READINGS, made at NOON, of a THERMOMETER whose BULB is sunk to the Depth of 12·8 Feet (12 French Feet) below the SURFACE of the Soil, for each YEAR 1847 to 1873.

Year.	January.	February.	March.	April.	May.	June.	July.	August.	September.	October.	November.	December.	Yearly Means, commencing with January.	Yearly Means, commencing with March.
1847	48·98	46·75	45·79	45·82	46·82	49·52	51·94	54·25	56·15	54·60	53·63	51·82	50·42	50·53
1848	49·64	47·39	46·57	46·93	48·28	50·90	53·01	54·70	55·28	55·07	53·43	51·19	50·93	50·84
1849	49·20	47·89	47·11	46·91	47·46	49·92	52·63	54·51	55·50	55·20	53·73	51·52	50·97	50·84
1850	48·80	46·68	46·37	46·17	47·19	49·26	51·96	54·06	54·88	54·38	53·67	53·46	50·87	50·77
1851	48·84	47·50	46·35	46·29	47·29	49·24	51·88	54·02	55·30	54·98	53·46	50·55	50·48	50·42
1852	48·43	47·21	46·23	46·15	47·34	49·52	51·85	54·90	56·07	55·33	53·48	51·90	50·69	50·98
1853	50·40	48·68	46·65	45·99	46·84	49·20	51·97	53·97	55·00	54·57	53·23	50·36	50·59	50·15
1854	47·56	46·24	45·59	46·07	47·06	48·04	50·91	51·43	53·71	55·11	53·22	50·61	50·13	50·22
1855	48·53	46·44	44·41	44·50	46·06	48·04	51·64	53·23	54·75	54·78	53·26	50·63	49·66	49·50
1856	47·69	46·39	45·87	45·76	46·89	48·87	51·64	54·11	53·53	54·89	53·49	50·87	50·15	50·25
1857	48·50	46·49	45·62	45·82	46·46	49·46	52·58	55·08	56·44	55·88	54·98	52·80	50·90	51·22
1858	50·62	48·22	46·18	46·00	47·41	49·91	53·29	55·22	56·21	56·03	54·24	51·35	51·22	51·08
1859	49·27	47·87	47·43	46·93	48·43	50·67	53·69	56·35	57·07	55·61	54·66	51·48	51·76	51·66
1860	48·77	47·18	45·67	45·60	46·62	49·11	51·26	53·01	53·91	53·59	52·25	50·13	49·75	49·4
1861	47·31	45·57	45·24	45·66	46·71	48·89	51·81	54·04	55·33	53·33	53·74	50·86	50·01	50·20
1862	48·67	47·04	46·37	46·56	48·05	50·28	53·90	54·98	55·06	53·53	53·74	50·72	50·60	50·64
1863	48·68	47·49	46·79	46·79	47·33	48·75	51·41	54·24	56·29	57·00	56·35	54·83	52·35	50·94
1864	49·47	47·52	46·13	45·94	47·42	49·77	51·98	54·16	55·18	54·03	53·51	51·14	50·60	50·46
1865	48·69	46·65	45·38	45·11	47·45	50·38	53·13	55·25	56·41	56·87	55·03	52·71	51·10	51·47
1866	50·62	49·17	47·80	47·31	48·51	50·42	53·17	55·19	55·82	55·66	54·48	52·25	51·70	51·53
1867	49·84	47·89	47·50	46·98	48·09	50·30	52·95	54·75	56·08	55·74	54·08	51·39	51·36	51·25
1868	48·91	47·32	46·99	47·33	48·75	51·41	54·24	56·29*	57·00*	56·55*	54·83	52·35	51·83	52·12
1869	50·58	49·16	48·41	47·55	49·04	50·86	52·98	55·34	56·36	56·24	54·50	51·71	51·50	51·67
1870	49·54	47·61	46·25	46·20	47·77	50·35	53·32	55·69	56·47	55·83	54·12	51·36	51·19	51·03
1871	48·58	46·63	46·65	46·50	47·13	48·42	51·49	53·25	55·06	57·11	56·55	54·53	51·39	51·41
1872	49·06	48·07	48·02	48·11	49·18	50·75	53·35	55·66	56·75	56·53	54·33	52·29	51·03	51·12
1873	50·47	48·92	47·26	47·32	48·54	50·37	53·03	53·63	56·75	56·20	54·27	52·04	51·73	51·68
1874	50·08	48·71	..	..	..	..	..	..	..	..	..	..	..	..
Means 1847-1873	49·09	47·40	46·47	46·43	47·69	49·89	52·50	54·71	55·77	55·47	53·86	51·42	50·89	50·90

* In these months the values are wholly or in part estimated, in consequence of the fluid having gone out of range. From observations of this thermometer made every two hours between 1846, April, and 1847, December, it appeared that the excess of the mean reading at noon above the mean from all the observations was—from January to May, o°·01; from June to October, o°·03; and in November and December, o°·01.

TABLE CXXXI.—MONTHLY MEANS of READINGS, made at NOON, of a THERMOMETER whose BULB is sunk to the Depth of 25·6 Feet (24 French Feet) below the SURFACE of the SOIL, for each YEAR 1847 to 1873.

Year.	January.	February.	March.	April.	May.	June.	July.	August.	September.	October.	November.	December.	Yearly Means, commencing with January.	Yearly Means, commencing with May.
1847	52·05	51·18	50·22	49·35	48·83	48·70	49·10	49·81	50·65	51·35	51·72	51·30	50·40	50·32
1848	51·47	50·02	50·08	49·39	49·07	49·15	49·68	50·41	51·19	51·81	52·16	51·04	50·61	50·64
1849	51·54	50·87	50·15	49·37	49·15	49·01	49·42	50·22	50·97	51·67	52·04	52·03	50·55	50·51
1850	51·57	50·83	49·99	49·32	48·87	48·79	49·10	49·81	50·65	51·29	51·63	51·54	50·28	50·20
1851	51·16	50·55	49·86	49·18	48·76	48·73	49·07	49·78	50·60	51·34	51·72	51·71	50·21	50·19
1852	51·16	50·46	49·79	49·15	48·71	48·69	49·04	49·77	50·77	51·68	52·20	52·09	50·29	50·48
1853	51·66	51·11	50·46	49·62	48·94	48·78	49·12	49·88	50·73	51·48	51·83	51·70	50·44	50·16
1854	51·09	50·22	49·38	48·74	48·42	48·48	48·88	49·57	50·40	51·16	51·61	51·57	49·96	49·95
1855	51·02	50·32	49·48	48·53	47·95	47·85	48·21	49·01	49·93	50·77	51·40	51·38	49·65	49·57
1856	50·75	49·93	49·13	48·53	48·10	48·08	48·53	49·32	50·32	51·15	51·58	51·60	49·75	49·83
1857	51·05	50·26	49·37	48·65	48·24	48·23	48·72	49·64	50·68	51·69	52·29	52·34	50·10	50·43
1858	51·97	51·36	50·50	49·54	48·92	48·85	49·30	50·22	51·12	51·91	52·27	52·23	50·68	50·63
1859	51·71	51·02	50·29	49·71	49·43	49·41	49·83	50·71	51·70	52·31	52·94	52·76	51·00	50·98
1860	52·0·	51·11	50·12	49·21	48·67	48·51	48·90	49·63	50·40	51·01	51·31	51·21	50·18	49·77
1861	50·66	49·84	48·91	48·20	47·89	47·93	48·43	49·33	50·27	51·08	51·56	51·61	49·64	49·86
1862	51·12	50·41	49·67	48·96	48·61	48·71	49·21	49·88	50·61	51·28	51·70	51·68	50·15	50·18
1863	51·10	50·40	49·75	49·18	48·86	48·66	49·04	49·35	50·08	50·91	51·62	51·94	51·87	50·33
1864	51·48	50·83	50·02	49·18	48·66	48·64	49·11	49·86	50·76	51·57	51·92	51·86	50·33	50·25
1865	51·37	50·61	49·71	48·95	48·45	48·59	49·28	50·28	51·32	52·13	52·75	52·78	50·52	50·90
1866	52·33	51·65	50·97	50·28	49·78	49·74	50·11	50·88	51·68	52·31	52·66	52·65	51·25	51·17
1867	52·17	51·46	50·64	50·01	49·54	49·57	50·01	50·79	51·58	52·28	52·63	52·63	51·10	51·01
1868	51·90	51·15	50·33	49·75	49·49	49·61	50·23	51·12	52·15	52·86*	53·23*	53·14*	51·25	51·52
1869	52·58	51·95	51·23	50·64	50·14	50·12	50·49	51·11	51·94	52·64	53·05	52·95	51·57	51·39
1870	52·34	51·51	50·64	49·81	49·31	49·31	49·83	50·71	51·73	52·50	52·84	52·71	51·10	51·01
1871	52·09	51·22	50·28	49·63	49·35	49·43	49·87	50·63	51·59	52·48	52·93	52·84	51·03	51·12
1872	52·18	51·33	50·63	50·13	49·82	49·93	50·28	51·08	51·99	52·75	53·15	53·03	51·36	51·48
1873	52·30	51·82	51·08	50·31	49·84	49·78	50·12	50·86	51·78	52·57	52·98	52·84	51·37	51·33
1874	52·32	51·65	50·95	50·31	..	..	..	..	..	..	..	..	..	..
Means 1847 1873	51·64	50·90	50·10	49·39	48·96	48·95	49·38	50·16	51·05	51·81	52·22	52·17	50·56	50·67

* In these months the values are wholly or in part estimated, in consequence of the fluid having gone out of range.

From observations of this thermometer made every two hours between 1846, April, and 1847, December, it appeared that the excess of the mean reading at noon above the mean from all the observations was 0°·01 throughout the year.

TABLE CXXXII.—MONTHLY MEANS of the TEMPERATURE of the AIR, and MONTHLY MEANS of the TEMPERATURE at NOON within the CASE covering the DEEP SUNK THERMOMETERS, and at Depths of 1 Inch, 3·2 Feet, 6·4 Feet, 12·8 Feet, and 25·6 Feet respectively below the SURFACE of the SOIL, through the RANGE of YEARS 1847 to 1873.

Position of Thermometer, or Depth of Thermometer Bulb.	January.	February.	March.	April.	May.	June.	July.	August.	September.	October.	November.	December.	Yearly Means.
In the Air	38·37	39·74	41·50	47·09	52·79	58·72	62·51	61·61	57·18	50·47	42·69	40·50	49·43
Within Case 1 inch	40·85	43·29	46·35	51·43	60·87	67·27	70·46	69·32	64·54	56·18	46·35	42·67	55·21
1 inch	40·38	41·40	43·25	49·50	55·54	62·08	65·44	64·46	60·21	55·43	45·43	41·50	51·97
3·2 feet	41·92	41·69	42·51	46·55	51·51	55·53	61·65	62·48	59·94	55·11	48·69	44·71	51·19
6·4 „	45·84	44·81	44·80	46·65	49·93	54·22	57·87	59·65	59·11	56·50	52·27	48·59	51·48
12·8 „	49·09	47·40	46·47	46·43	47·69	49·89	52·50	54·71	55·77	55·47	53·86	51·42	50·89
25·6 „	51·64	50·90	50·10	49·39	48·96	48·95	49·38	50·16	51·03	51·81	52·22	52·17	50·56

TABLE CXXXIII.—ANNUAL MEANS of the READINGS of the DEEP SUNK THERMOMETERS and related THERMOMETERS.

YEAR.	Means of Temperature of the Air.	Means of Temperature at Noon of the Interior of the Case covering the Thermometer-Scales.	Means of Temperature at Noon at the Depth of 1 Inch.	Means of Temperature at Noon at the Depth of 3·2 Feet.	Means of Temperature at Noon at the Depth of 6·4 Feet, from February to January of the following Year.	Means of Temperature at Noon at the Depth of 12·8 Feet, from March to February of the following Year.	Means of Temperature at Noon at the Depth of 25·6 Feet, from May to April of the following Year.
1847 - -	49.72	54.17	51.81	50.60	50.94	50.53	50.32
1848 - -	50.41	54.63	52.33	51.25	51.59	51.04	50.64
1849 - -	49.98	55.01	52.34	51.27	51.31	50.83	50.52
1850 - -	49.32	54.29	51.52	50.20	50.88	50.35	50.20
1851 - -	49.19	54.93	51.98	50.71	50.99	50.42	50.19
1852 - -	50.63	56.23	53.18	51.43	51.62	50.98	50.48
1853 - -	47.68	53.37	51.18	50.12	50.57	50.15	50.16
1854 - -	48.93	55.63	52.06	50.48	51.00	50.22	49.95
1855 - -	47.05	53.12	50.47	49.60	50.14	49.59	49.57
1856 - -	48.98	54.67	51.94	50.83	51.00	50.23	49.83
1857 - -	51.04	57.26	53.57	52.11	52.41	51.22	50.43
1858 - -	49.22	55.92	52.01	51.48	52.07	51.08	50.63
1859 - -	50.74	57.27	53.15	52.44	52.80	51.66	50.98
1860 - -	47.03	52.37	49.62	49.42	50.13	49.49	49.77
1861 - -	49.41	55.78	51.97	50.94	51.48	50.26	49.86
1862 - -	49.57	55.08	52.11	51.19	51.75	50.64	50.18
1863 - -	50.33	56.21	52.56	51.53	51.96	50.94	50.42
1864 - -	48.54	54.62	51.17	50.54	51.32	50.46	50.25
1865 - -	50.34	57.13	52.83	51.87	52.37	51.47	50.90
1866 - -	49.82	55.58	52.38	51.70	52.27	51.53	51.17
1867 - -	48.64	54.29	51.43	51.17	51.96	51.23	51.01
1868 - -	51.55	58.02	54.02	52.82	53.34	52.12	51.52
1869 - -	49.51	55.10	52.00	51.68	52.38	51.67	51.39
1870 - -	48.70	54.70	51.32	50.99	51.66	51.05	51.01
1871 - -	48.67	54.27	50.73	51.26	52.15	51.41	51.12
1872 - -	50.70	56.37	52.36	52.62	53.17	52.12	51.48
1873 - -	48.93	54.76	51.11	51.93	52.45	51.68	51.33
Means -	49.43	55.21	51.97	51.19	51.70	50.90	50.37

TABLE CXXXIV.—EXCESS of each ANNUAL MEAN of the READINGS of each DEEP-SUNK THERMOMETER and related THERMOMETER above the GENERAL MEAN for that THERMOMETER.

YEAR.	Annual Excess for Temperature of the Air.	Annual Excess for Temperature of the Interior of the Case covering the Thermometer-Scales.	Annual Excess for the Temperature at the Depth of 1 Inch.	Annual Excess for the Temperature at the Depth of 3·2 Feet.	Annual Excess from February to January of the following Year for the Temperature at the Depth of 6·4 Feet.	Annual Excess from March to February of the following Year for the Temperature at the Depth of 12·8 Feet.	Annual Excess from May to April of the following Year for the Temperature at the Depth of 25·6 Feet.
1847 - -	+ 0.29	− 1.04	− 0.16	− 0.59	− 0.76	− 0.37	− 0.25
1848 - -	+ 0.98	− 0.56	+ 0.36	+ 0.06	− 0.11	+ 0.14	+ 0.07
1849 - -	+ 0.55	− 0.20	+ 0.37	+ 0.08	− 0.39	− 0.07	− 0.05
1850 - -	− 0.11	− 0.92	− 0.45	− 0.99	− 0.82	− 0.55	− 0.57
1851 - -	− 0.24	− 0.28	+ 0.01	− 0.48	− 0.71	− 0.48	− 0.38
1852 - -	+ 1.20	+ 1.02	+ 1.21	+ 0.24	− 0.08	+ 0.08	− 0.09
1853 - -	− 1.75	− 1.84	− 0.79	− 1.07	− 1.13	− 0.75	− 0.41
1854 - -	− 0.50	+ 0.42	+ 0.09	− 0.71	− 0.70	− 0.68	− 0.62
1855 - -	− 2.38	− 2.09	− 1.50	− 1.59	− 1.56	− 1.31	− 1.00
1856 - -	− 0.45	− 0.54	− 0.03	− 0.36	− 0.70	− 0.67	− 0.74
1857 - -	+ 1.61	+ 2.05	+ 1.60	+ 0.92	+ 0.71	+ 0.32	− 0.14
1858 - -	− 0.21	+ 0.71	+ 0.04	+ 0.29	+ 0.37	+ 0.18	+ 0.06
1859 - -	+ 1.31	+ 2.06	+ 1.18	+ 1.25	+ 1.10	+ 0.76	+ 0.41
1860 - -	− 2.40	− 2.84	− 2.35	− 1.77	− 1.57	− 1.41	− 0.60
1861 - -	− 0.02	+ 0.57	0.00	− 0.25	− 0.22	− 0.64	− 0.71
1862 - -	+ 0.14	− 0.13	+ 0.14	0.00	+ 0.05	− 0.26	− 0.39
1863 - -	+ 0.90	+ 1.00	+ 0.59	+ 0.34	+ 0.26	+ 0.04	− 0.15
1864 - -	− 0.89	− 0.59	− 0.80	− 0.65	− 0.38	− 0.44	− 0.32
1865 - -	+ 0.91	+ 1.92	+ 0.86	+ 0.68	+ 0.87	+ 0.57	+ 0.33
1866 - -	+ 0.39	+ 0.37	+ 0.41	+ 0.51	+ 0.57	+ 0.63	+ 0.60
1867 - -	− 0.79	− 0.92	− 0.54	− 0.02	+ 0.26	+ 0.33	+ 0.44
1868 - -	+ 2.12	+ 2.81	+ 2.05	+ 1.63	+ 1.64	+ 1.22	+ 0.95
1869 - -	+ 0.08	− 0.11	+ 0.03	+ 0.49	+ 0.68	+ 0.77	+ 0.82
1870 - -	− 0.73	− 0.51	− 0.65	− 0.20	− 0.04	+ 0.15	+ 0.44
1871 - -	− 0.76	− 0.94	− 1.24	+ 0.07	+ 0.45	+ 0.51	+ 0.35
1872 - -	+ 1.27	+ 1.16	+ 0.39	+ 1.43	+ 1.47	+ 1.22	+ 0.91
1873 - -	− 0.50	− 0.45	− 0.86	+ 0.74	+ 0.75	+ 0.78	+ 0.76

TABLE CXXXV.—EXTREMES of MONTHLY MEAN TEMPERATURES of the Air in each YEAR.†

Year.	Lowest Monthly Mean, and Month.	Highest Monthly Mean, and Month.	Year.	Lowest Monthly Mean, and Month.	Highest Monthly Mean, and Month.
1847	52·9 December*	63·4 July	1861	33·8 January	63·2 August
1848	34·6 January	62·3 July	1862	39·0 January	59·3 August
1849	40·1 January	62·9 August	1863	39·8 November*	61·9 August
1850	35·7 January	62·2 July	1864	36·0 February	61·8 July
1851	40·1 February	62·8 August	1865	36·3 January	63·9 September
1852	37·9 November*	66·6 July	1866	40·3 Feb. & Mar.	61·0 July
1853	33·3 February	60·3 July	1867	34·2 January	62·0 August
1854	34·0 December*	60·9 August	1868	37·2 January	67·5 July
1855	29·1 February	61·4 August	1869	37·3 March	64·5 July
1856	35·6 December*	63·6 August	1870	36·2 February	65·4 July
1857	36·6 January	65·4 August	1871	33·2 January	64·8 August
1858	34·6 February	64·9 June	1872	37·6 November*	65·0 July
1859	39·6 November*	68·1 July	1873	34·3 February	63·4 July
1860	35·7 February	57·7 August			

† In Tables CXXXV., CXXXVI., CXXXVII., and CXXXVIII. the entries under "Lowest, and Month" refer exclusively to the winter terminating the preceding year and commencing the year opposite which the entry appears. Value taken from the preceding year are indicated by an asterisk. Thus 52·9 opposite 1847, in Table CXXXV., refers to December of the year 1846.

TABLE CXXXVI.—EXTREMES of MONTHLY MEANS of READINGS at NOON of a THERMOMETER within the CASE covering the SCALES of the DEEP-SUNK THERMOMETERS.

Year.	Lowest Monthly Mean, and Month.	Highest Monthly Mean, and Month.	Year.	Lowest Monthly Mean, and Month.	Highest Monthly Mean, and Month.
1847	34·7 December*	72·0 July	1861	36·5 January	71·7 August
1848	36·3 January	68·7 July	1862	41·9 January	68·3 August
1849	41·9 January	69·4 August	1863	42·7 November*	70·2 July
1850	35·9 January	69·7 June	1864	39·1 January	69·8 July
1851	42·5 December*	70·6 August	1865	39·2 January	74·2 September
1852	41·6 November*	77·4 July	1866	44·3 February	69·6 June
1853	37·1 February	68·7 August	1867	37·2 January	66·3 August
1854	36·4 December*	69·1 August	1868	38·8 December*	76·9 July
1855	34·0 February	70·6 August	1869	41·0 March	71·6 July
1856	37·8 December*	71·4 August	1870	38·8 February	73·1 July
1857	38·6 January	73·3 August	1871	35·3 January	73·3 August
1858	39·4 February	76·4 June	1872	40·6 December*	73·0 July
1859	42·7 December*	77·6 July	1873	36·7 February	72·1 July
1860	38·8 February	64·8 July			

TABLE CXXXVII.—EXTREMES of MONTHLY MEANS of READINGS at NOON of a THERMOMETER whose BULB is 1 Inch below the SURFACE of the SOIL.

Year.	Lowest Monthly Mean, and Month.	Highest Monthly Mean, and Month.	Year.	Lowest Monthly Mean, and Month.	Highest Monthly Mean, and Month.
1847	36·4 December*	67·4 July	1861	35·5 January	66·2 August
1848	37·4 January	65·0 July	1862	40·7 January	63·5 August
1849	41·5 January	63·2 August	1863	42·7 November*	64·0 July
1850	36·7 January	65·2 July	1864	30·0 February	63·3 July
1851	42·7 Dec.* & Feb.	65·5 August	1865	38·8 January	66·1 July
1852	41·2 November*	71·0 July	1866	42·0 March	65·0 July
1853	37·0 February	64·1 August	1867	38·3 January	64·1 August
1854	38·0 December*	64·6 August	1868	39·4 January	69·9 July
1855	33·4 February	66·0 August	1869	40·8 March	66·2 July
1856	38·5 December*	66·7 August	1870	38·1 February	67·1 July
1857	38·0 January	67·0 August	1871	36·2 January	66·6 August
1858	37·8 February	68·6 June	1872	39·2 December*	66·9 July
1859	42·2 November*	70·7 July	1873	36·4 February	66·0 July
1860	37·4 February	61·3 July			

TABLE CXXXVIII.—EXTREMES of MONTHLY MEANS of READINGS at NOON of a THERMOMETER whose BULB is 3·2 Feet below the SURFACE of the SOIL.

Year.	Lowest Monthly Mean, and Month.		Highest Monthly Mean, and Month.		Year.	Lowest Monthly Mean, and Month.		Highest Monthly Mean, and Month.	
1847	39·42	January	62·44	August	1861	38·20	January	63·28	August
1848	41·28	January	61·21	July	1862	41·13	January	61·51	August
1849	42·55	January	61·69	July	1863	43·23	January	61·64	August
1850	39·13	January	61·26	August	1864	41·03	February	61·12	August
1851	41·80	February	62·76	August	1865	39·74	February	63·21	September
1852	42·17	January	63·70	July	1866	41·86	March	62·00	July
1853	40·35	March	61·51	August	1867	41·59	January	61·12	August
1854	39·25	January	61·63	August	1868	41·11	January	65·12	August
1855	36·94	February	62·03	August	1869	42·78	March	61·70	July
1856	41·39	January	63·90	August	1870	39·65	February	63·22	August
1857	40·22	February	64·76	August	1871	39·06	January	64·62	August
1858	39·84	February	63·82	August	1872	42·69	December*	63·78	August
1859	43·76	January	63·72	July	1873	40·76	February	64·45	August
1860	39·53	February	58·86	July					

TABLE CXXXIX.—EXTREMES of MONTHLY MEANS of READINGS at NOON of a THERMOMETER whose BULB is 6·4 Feet below the SURFACE of the SOIL.

Year.	Lowest Monthly Mean, and Month.		Highest Monthly Mean, and Month.		Year.	Lowest Monthly Mean, and Month.		Highest Monthly Mean, and Month.	
1847	42·86	February	58·91	August	1861	42·80	January	59·73	August
1848	44·26	February	58·87	August	1862	45·06	February	58·84	August
1849	45·48	March	58·31	August	1863	45·68	March	59·18	August
1850	43·96	February	58·92	August	1864	44·40	March	58·99	August
1851	44·33	March	58·87	August	1865	43·60	March	60·81	September
1852	43·98	March	59·29	August	1866	45·13	March	59·09	August
1853	43·53	March	58·86	August	1867	45·66	March	59·73	September
1854	43·30	January	58·91	August	1868	45·24	February	62·30	August
1855	41·79	March	58·83	August	1869	46·38	March	59·71	September
1856	44·22	February	58·84	August	1870	44·20	February	60·88	August
1857	43·15	February	61·27	August	1871	43·90	February	61·16	September
1858	43·85	March	60·69	August	1872	46·38	January	61·10	August
1859	45·91	February	61·38	August	1873	45·10	March	61·18	August
1860	45·80	March	57·07	August					

TABLE CXL.—EXTREMES of MONTHLY MEANS of READINGS at NOON of a THERMOMETER whose BULB is 12·8 Feet below the SURFACE of the SOIL.

Year.	Lowest Monthly Mean, and Month.		Highest Monthly Mean, and Month.		Year.	Lowest Monthly Mean, and Month.		Highest Monthly Mean, and Month.	
1847	45·79	March	55·15	September	1861	45·24	March	55·33	September
1848	46·57	March	55·28	September	1862	46·37	March	55·06	October
1849	46·92	April	55·50	September	1863	46·79	Mar. & Apr.	55·45	September
1850	46·17	April	54·88	September	1864	45·94	April	55·18	September
1851	46·29	April	55·30	September	1865	45·12	April	56·87	October
1852	46·15	April	56·07	September	1866	47·32	April	55·82	September
1853	45·99	April	55·00	September	1867	46·94	April	56·08	September
1854	45·59	March	55·11	September	1868	46·90	March	57·00	September
1855	44·50	April	54·78	October	1869	47·53	April	56·56	September
1856	45·76	April	55·33	September	1870	46·20	April	56·47	September
1857	45·62	March	56·44	September	1871	46·51	March	56·07	September
1858	46·00	April	56·21	September	1872	48·02	March	57·11	September
1859	47·43	March	57·07	September	1873	47·26	March	55·73	September
1860	45·60	April	55·91	September					

TABLE CXLI.—EXTREMES of MONTHLY MEANS of READINGS at NOON of a THERMOMETER whose BULB is 25·6 Feet below the Surface of the Soil.

Year.	Lowest Monthly Mean, and Month.		Highest Monthly Mean, and Month.		Year.	Lowest Monthly Mean, and Month.		Highest Monthly Mean, and Month.	
1847	48·70	June	51·80	December	1861	47·89	May	51·61	December
1848	49·07	May	52·16	November	1862	48·61	May	51·70	November
1849	49·01	June	52·04	November	1863	48·86	May	51·94	November
1850	48·79	June	51·63	November	1864	48·64	June	51·92	November
1851	48·73	June	51·72	November	1865	48·45	May	52·78	December
1852	48·69	June	52·20	November	1866	49·74	June	52·66	November
1853	48·78	June	51·83	November	1867	49·34	May	52·63	November
1854	48·42	May	51·61	November	1868	49·49	May	53·23	November
1855	47·85	June	51·40	November	1869	50·12	June	53·05	November
1856	48·08	June	51·60	December	1870	49·31	May & June	52·84	November
1857	48·13	June	52·34	December	1871	49·35	May	52·93	November
1858	48·85	June	52·27	November	1872	49·82	May	53·15	November
1859	49·41	June	52·94	November	1873	49·78	June	52·98	November
1860	48·51	June	51·31	November					

ERRATA.

Page 29. Sub-headings of Tables XXXIV. and XXXV. Dele the words "Hour, Greenwich Mean Solar Time (Civil reckoning)."

Page 66. Line 3 of heading of Table. Dele " reductions, and those marked ‡ in the reductions referring to the Temperature of Evaporation only." and insert " formation of Tables LXXXIX. to CIV., and those marked ‡ in the formation of Tables XCVII. to CIV."

Plate III. Value of Zero for September. For 29^{in}·789, read 29^{in}·791.

Plate I.

ROYAL OBSERVATORY, GREENWICH.

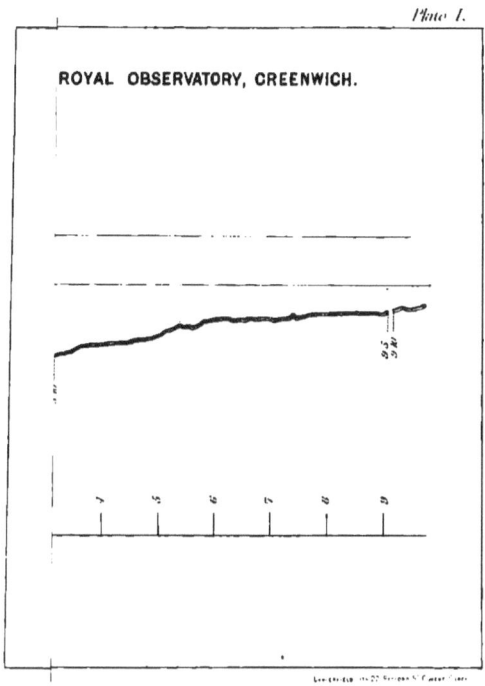

Plate II.

ΉETER AND DRY BULB THERMOMETER

ℍ TO AUGUST 2.1ℍ

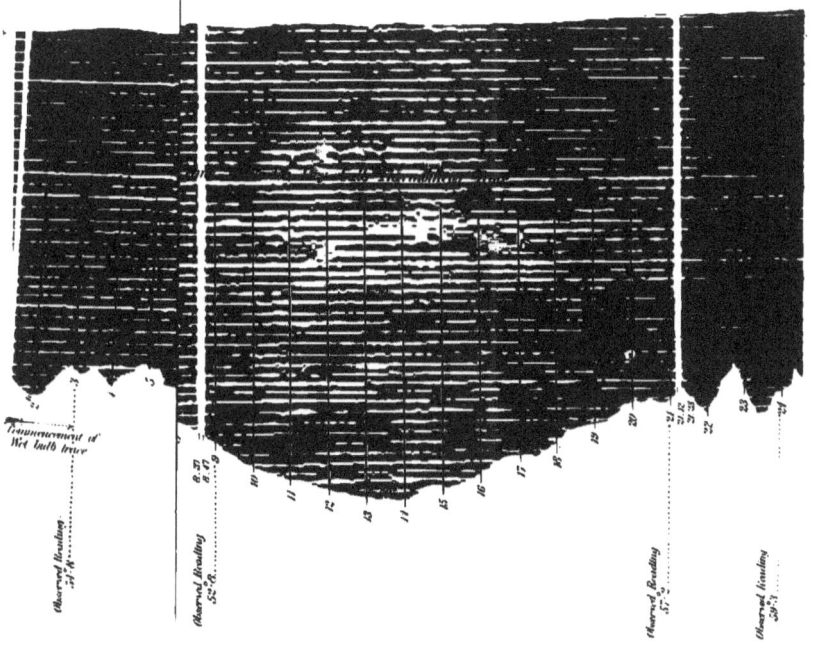

Plate III.

ROYAL OBSERVATORY, GREENWICH.

Curves representing the Diurnal Changes of the Barometer in each Month, and also for the Year, from the Mean of Observations 1854 to 1873.

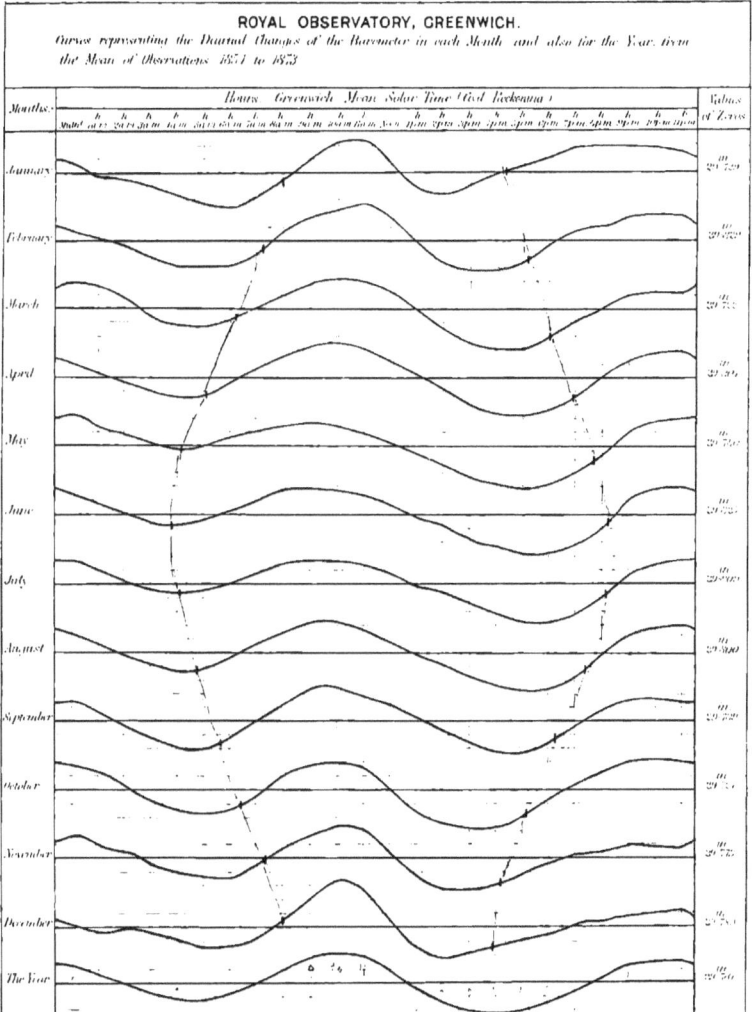

Each vertical space corresponds to 0·005 inch of barometer reading.
The points upon the curves correspond to the times of sunrise and sunset at Greenwich.

Plate IV.

ROYAL OBSERVATORY, GREENWICH.

Curves representing the Diurnal Changes of the Barometer under the influence of different Winds, referred to eight points of Azimuth, from the Mean of Observations 1841 to 1845.

Winds.	Hours. Greenwich Mean Solar Time (Civil Reckoning.)	Values of Zeros
Mid.t		

North

North East

East

South East

South

South West

West

North West

Each Vertical Space corresponds to 0.003 inch of Barometer reading.

Plate V.

ROYAL OBSERVATORY, GREENWICH.

Curves representing the Diurnal changes of the Mean Temperature of the Air, of Evaporation, and of the Dew Point; of the Mean Temperature of the Air in Waves of High and Low Mean Temperature; and of the Mean Temperature of the Air in Waves of High and Low Mean Atmospheric Pressure. from the mean of Observations 1849 to 1868.

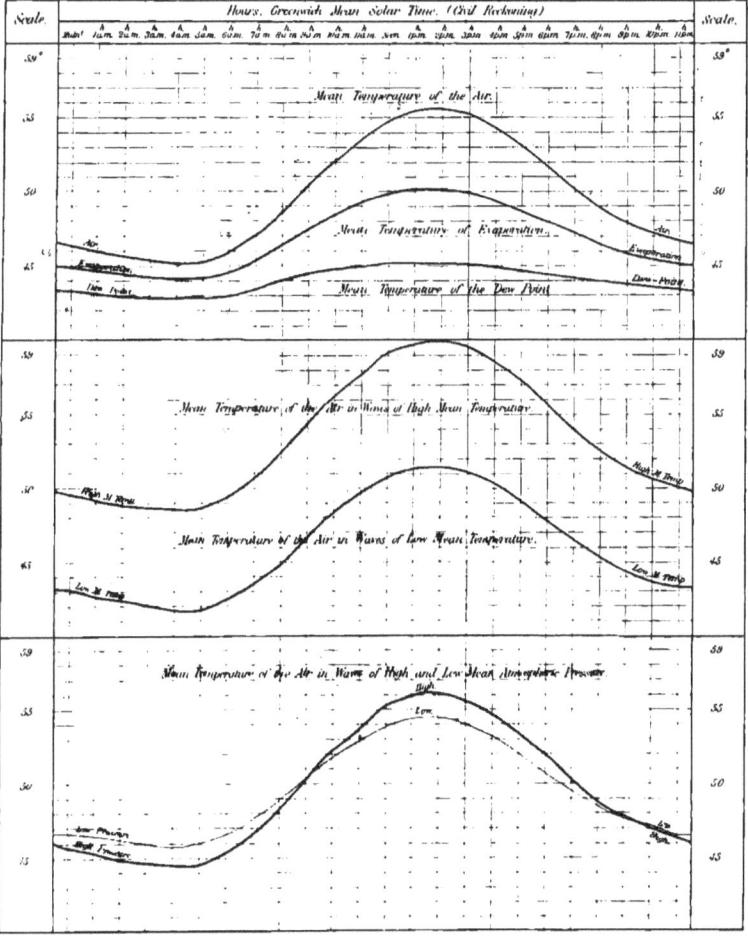

Plate VI.

ROYAL OBSERVATORY, GREENWICH.

Curves representing the Diurnal changes of the Mean Temperature of the Air, of Mean Temperature of Evaporation, and of Mean Temperature of the Dew Point: in Quarterly Periods, from the Mean of Observations 1849 to 1868.

Hours. Greenwich Mean Solar Time (Civil Reckoning.)

Means of Months. January, February, and March.

Means of Months. April, May, and June.

Means of Months. July, August, and September.

Means of Months. October, November, and December.

Plate VII.

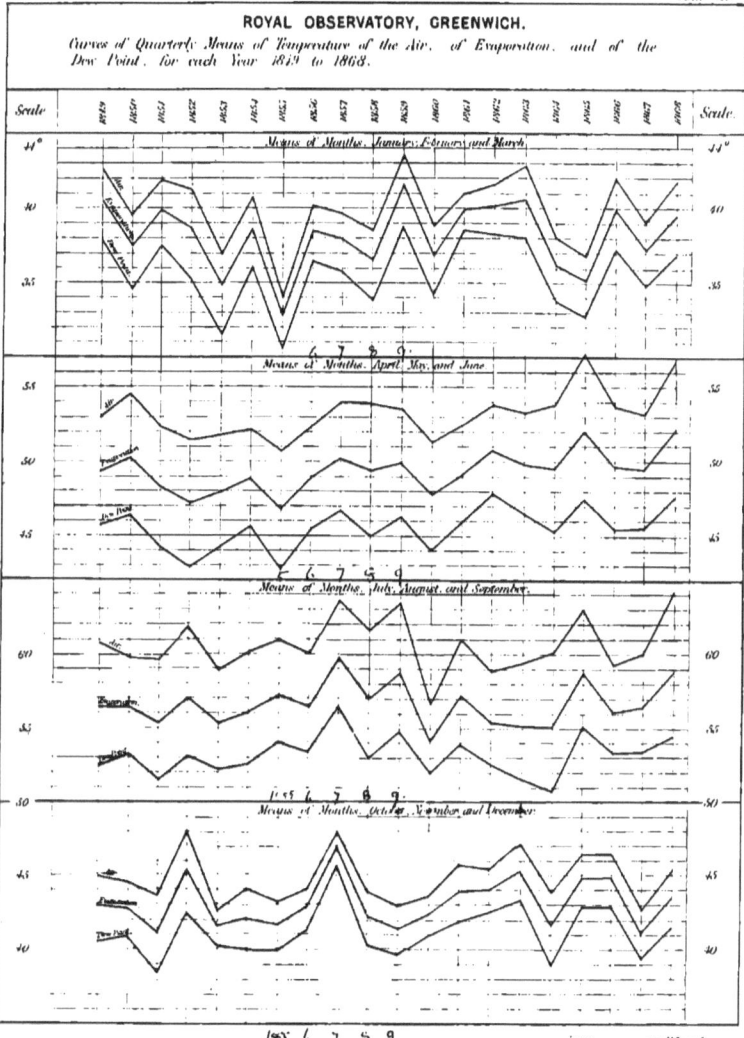

ROYAL OBSERVATORY, GREENWICH.

Curves of Quarterly Means of Temperature of the Air, of Evaporation, and of the
Dew Point, for each Year 1849 to 1868.

Plate VIII.

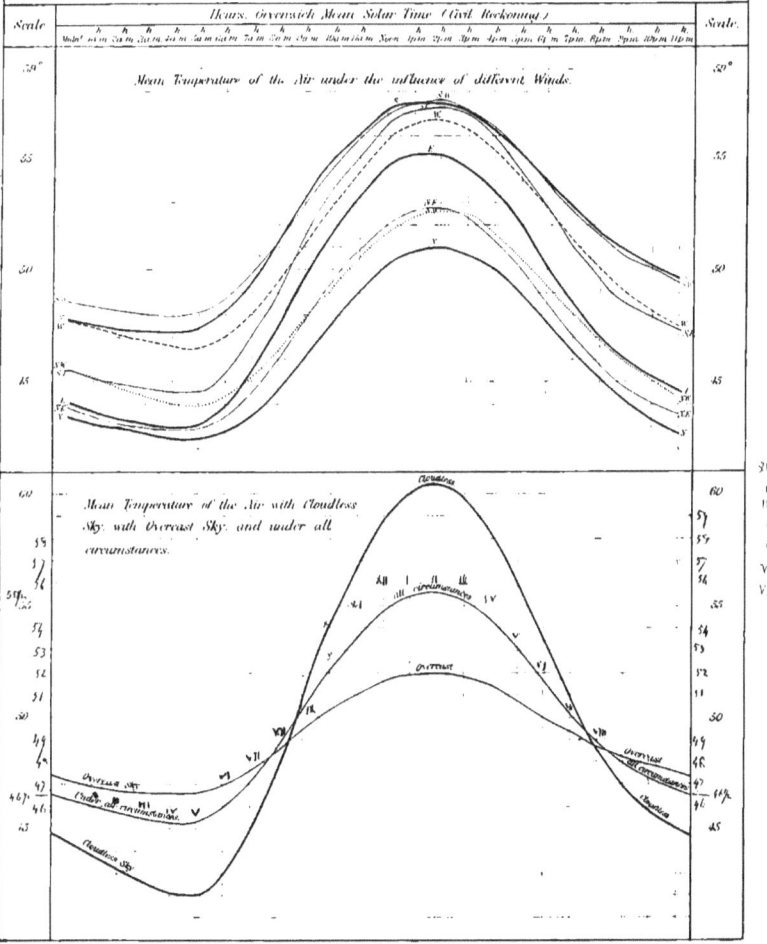

ROYAL OBSERVATORY, GREENWICH.

Curves representing the Diurnal Changes of the Mean Temperature of the Air under the influence of different Winds referred to eight points of Azimuth; also the Mean Temperature of the Air with a Cloudless Sky, with Overcast Sky, and under all circumstances, from the Mean of Observations 1849 to 1868.

Plate LV.

ROYAL OBSERVATORY, GREENWICH.

Changes through the Year of the Mean Temperature of the Air and of the Temperature at different depths below the surface of the soil, from the mean of observations 1847 to 1873. The Mean Temperature of the Air is derived from observations at all hours; the other Temperatures from readings at noon only.

Temperature — December · January · February · March · April · May · June · July · August · September · October · November · December · January — Temperature

70°   70°

65   65

60   60

55   55

50   50

45   45

40   40

Within Glass

1 inch deep

Mean Temperature of the Air

3½ feet deep

6.4 feet deep

12.6 feet deep

25.6 feet deep

12.6 feet deep

6 feet deep

3½ feet deep

1 inch deep

Of the Air

25.6 feet

12.6 feet

6 feet

3½ feet

1 inch

Of the Air

Plate X.

ROYAL OBSERVATORY, GREENWICH.

Mean Annual Temperature of the Air, and Temperatures at different depths below the surface of the soil, for each year 1847 to 1873, the years being supposed to commence for the depths 6·4 feet, 12·8 feet, 25·6 feet, with February, March, and May respectively.

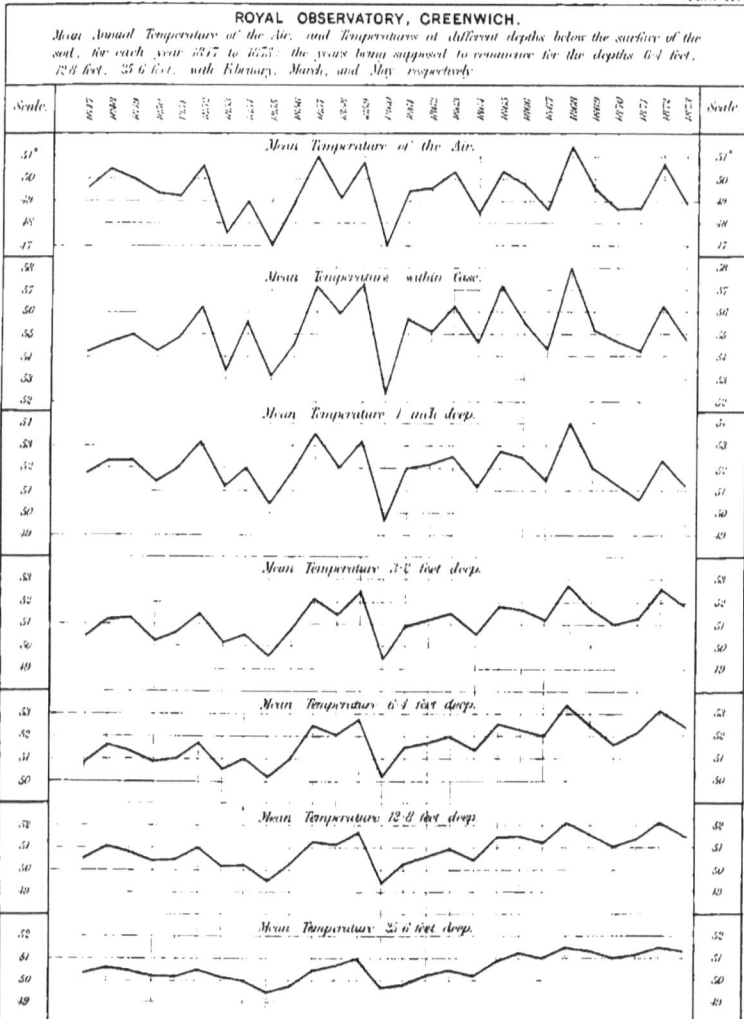

The Mean Temperature of the Air is derived from observations at all hours, the other Temperatures from readings at noon only.